Coming Home

By David Lewis

Sanctuary (with Beverly Lewis)
Coming Home

DAVID LEWIS

Coming Home

BETHANYHOUSE
MINNEAPOLIS, MINNESOTA

Coming Home
Copyright © 2004
David Lewis

Cover design by Lookout Design Group, Inc.

Published by Bethany House Publishers
11400 Hampshire Avenue South
Bloomington, Minnesota 55438
www.bethanyhouse.com

Bethany House Publishers is a Division of
Baker Book House Company, Grand Rapids, Michigan.

Printed in the United States of America

ISBN 0-7642-2677-0 (Trade Paper)
ISBN 0-7642-2680-0 (Hardcover)
ISBN 0-7642-2678-9 (Large Print)
ISBN 0-7642-2679-7 (Audio)

Library of Congress Cataloging-in-Publication Data

Lewis, David, date
    Coming home / by David Lewis.
        p.   cm.
    ISBN 0-7642-2680-0 (alk. paper) —ISBN 0-7642-2677-0 (pbk.)
    1. Young women—Fiction.   2. First loves—Fiction.   I. Title.
    PS3612.E8484C66   2004
    813'.6—dc22   2003023582

Dedication

For Bev,

for always.

Prologue

THE GRANDEUR OF THE OCEAN took her breath away. Like a wide-eyed child, she sat smack dab in the middle of the beach, staring in wonder, a single rose in her lap. Surrounded by shell seekers, she soaked up every detail—the brilliant sun, the salty wind, the endless blue horizon—feeling more alive than she had ever felt in her life.

Then gradually, as if in tandem with the setting sun, the wonder faded and she was left alone, hugging herself against the descending Oregon temperatures. She'd spent a lifetime getting here. A lifetime of planning and preparation. But now that she had finally arrived . . . *what?* The ancient philosophers were right. The journey was better than the arrival; the fantasy greater than the reality.

Maybe I expected too much, she thought. Was it the endless grains of sand that made her feel so empty? The never-ending reach of rolling water? Or was it beauty itself—the melding of cerulean and turquoise—that reminded her of something she had once lost?

She smiled wistfully. Perhaps it was much simpler than that. Even now, she couldn't stop thinking of him—his playful blue eyes, the warmth of his smile, the way he'd made her laugh so effortlessly . . . and how much she missed him.

She struggled to her feet, brushing sand from her gray sweats. The beach was now deserted. The rocks beyond seemed cold and unforgiving, and the sea birds chirped mournfully.

Stepping gingerly across the beach in her sandals, making her way to the ocean's edge, Jessie became annoyed at the clingy granules of sand between her toes. She chuckled suddenly at a memory of one of her father's favorite shows, *Star Trek,* and the segment in which interstellar hippies hijacked the *Enterprise* for a trip to paradise, only to find it unfit for habitation. Not only unfit, in fact, but deadly. The apples were poisonous and the grass melted the soles of their feet.

As a child, Jessie had never understood her father's fascination with Captain Kirk and, especially, with Mr. Pointy-Ears. Even then, she suspected her father had a lot more in common with the emotionally distant Vulcan than with his own daughter. Her mother once said, "When I get well, your father will get well, too." But Mom never got well . . . so neither did he.

Jessie gazed beyond the crashing waves and kept herself from surrendering to her disappointment. The rose she carried was a fitting reminder of how her journey had begun—with an entire bouquet of roses, their blooms unopened, full of promise.

Carefully avoiding the thorns, she breathed in the aroma of her rose, her senses filled with the fragrance of hope. *A rose is worth its thorns,* she reminded herself, smiling at her own inclination to ponder the unfathomable, realizing that most people accept life at face value and seem much happier for it.

When she was ready, she stood at the edge of the moss-covered rocks, struggling against the windy roar of eternity, and tossed the rose into the ocean.

Ashes to ashes, dust to dust . . .

The rose floated, rolling with the waves. Jessie watched, allowing herself to wonder, for a moment, what might have been. Then the rose began to sink, merging with the ocean foam, until only the memory of its scent remained. . . .

Chapter One

IN THE MORNING, his bouquet of roses had seemed little more than a consolation prize. The stubbornly unopened petals, once a glorious promise of their unfolding future, now appeared to be a harbinger of their demise.

Jessica Lehman held the flowers to her face, breathing in the fresh apple-sweet fragrance, but the lingering aromatic sensation was more in line with the foul-smelling weeds in the field behind their apartment building. At least weeds never made false promises.

The night before they were to leave together for Oregon, a simple dinner conversation had turned into a train wreck, and now the entire evening played over and over in her mind, like the hopeless melody of a maudlin country song.

Over salmon and chicken, she'd been prattling on about tomorrow's trip, places to visit on the way, suggesting a quick side trip to Lincoln City once they'd settled in Corvallis, all the while oblivious to Brandon's growing preoccupation.

To anyone else, his sudden question would have seemed innocent—"How did your parents die?"—but she had to gather herself momentarily, glancing out the window to buy herself time. The brilliant sunset was casting purple hues across the horizon, a peaceful contrast to her sudden internal storm.

"It's a simple question, Jess."

She'd brought her napkin to her mouth, dabbing it slowly—her mind racing. In her experience, one question was never enough. They always led to another, and then another, and *none* of them were simple. She must have made some kind of deferring remark, but she couldn't recall exactly. She might have said, "It was a sad time," without answering his question at all.

Brandon removed his own napkin from his lap, placing it on the table. "We've been dating for how long now?"

"Uh . . . let's see," she said, glancing at the date on her watch as a humorous gesture. "Six months?"

Brandon wasn't amused. "It might as well be a week."

She pursed her lips.

"It's not just your parents, Jess. Or your past. It's *everything*. I know you want to live in Oregon, but do you have any *other* dreams? Anything substantial?"

You don't want to know about my dreams, she thought, waiting for him to finish. He ended with the typical cliché, the one that is rarely spoken with honesty, "Maybe it's just me, Jess. Maybe I just need more than you can give."

Brandon bowed his head slightly as if defeated or acquiescing to something bigger than himself. She felt her eyes fill with moisture and while stung by his criticism, she didn't want to lose him. She wanted to make this relationship work. After all, the whole thing was her fault. She opened her mouth and willed the words to come. "My mother died when I was twelve. . . ."

Even now, after all these years, the words sounded empty on her lips. Impossible to believe. Brandon looked up, meeting her eyes, and for a moment it seemed hopeful.

"She was sick for a long time." Jessie paused and added a lie. "I thought I told you."

Her stomach clenched as Brandon's frown transitioned into an expression of disbelief. He shook his head, his shoulders rising slightly as if to say, So what? And she felt a sudden mixture of emotions—mainly anger, but a little stupidity, too. Anger with Brandon for making her say it, and stupidity for how difficult this was. Normal people adapt to loss and death. How many times over the last twelve years had she told herself that?

She forced another smile, still hoping what she saw in his eyes wasn't true.

"Jess . . ."

"Brandon, can we talk about something else? I'm getting another headache, and we need to leave early tomorrow. Have you gotten any munchies for the trip, because I'll be stopping by the store to get a few personals. I could pick up a *Sports Illustrated*. Do you have the latest? You know, the one with—"

She was about to say, *Chiefs on the cover,* but stopped because Brandon was shaking his head again. "I thought I could do this, Jess."

"Do what?"

"I'm not going."

She stared back at him for the longest time, watching as an expression of stone now masked his usually soft handsome features. He leaned back appraising her, shaking his head softly but deliberately. "This isn't working."

She reached over and covered his hand, but he pulled away. She felt embarrassed, wondering if anyone had noticed, and she lowered her voice to a whisper. "Brandon, you're making too much of this."

"You don't get it, do you?"

She glanced furtively about the restaurant. "Can't we work through this in private?"

"What do we have to work through? Tell me. I don't even know. Do you?"

She didn't answer.

"You have issues, Jess." He turned from her as if dismissing her. When he looked back at her, his eyes were cruel. "What happened to you?"

"Brandon—"

"How did you get this way?"

She blinked, and the first tear slipped down her cheek.

"Have you considered getting help?"

"Brandon, please . . ."

"I'm serious, Jess. Psychiatric counseling. Therapy . . . drugs . . . the full meal deal."

Jessie rose slowly from her seat, her legs weak. "Please . . . I need to go. . . ."

Jessie lifted the roses to her face one last time, then raised the lid of the Dumpster and idly dropped them in. She paused at the back fence, looking out over the campus. *What a way to end my college years.* Yet she couldn't help thinking their breakup was a fitting punctuation to the four years that had seen more failure than success. If romance had been a class—Romantic Love 101—Danielle Steele would have given Miss Jessica Lehman a big fat D minus.

She noticed a couple of early birds tossing a baseball in the distance and thought of Brandon's passion for baseball statistics. At this point, taking into account all the boys with whom she had contemplated marriage, she was batting oh for nine.

She smiled bitterly. *High school doesn't count. Oh for four, then.* Four serious boyfriends in the space of four years. In the end, with a few minor variations here and there, they'd all said the same thing: *Who are you?*

"You okay?" Her roommate, Darlene, leaned against the doorframe of the apartment building entrance, still in her nightshirt and sweat pants, a bandana over her tight black curls.

"Never liked yellow roses anyway," Jessie replied.

"Me neither," Darlene said.

Jessie picked up her suitcase and carried it down the driveway to her Honda hatchback. A week earlier, the two had graduated from Wichita State University, Darlene with a degree in social work,

Jessie's in finance. Having been accepted at Oregon State University at Corvallis as a tutor for summer students, Jessie had two weeks of free time before her summer job began. In the fall, she would begin her MBA program. Originally, she and Brandon had planned to attend together.

Darlene shuffled down the walk in her sheepskin slippers. "What's the rush?" She glanced at her watch. "It's not even eight yet."

Jessie shrugged and made a face.

"He's not worth it, Jess."

Jessie sighed. "This isn't about him."

Darlene gave her a knowing squint. Of all Darlene's mannerisms, this was Jessie's least favorite. "I'll miss you, roomie. I was thinking we'd have a few more days to hang out. Drown our sorrows in chocolate sundaes and French fries."

Wistfully, Jessie looked past her apartment building, seeing the spires and rooftops of the university buildings beyond. Four years of memories. There was plenty of opportunity to wax nostalgic, and not even that was tempting. She was itching to get on the road. Eager to end this chapter of her life.

This morning she'd modified the plans originally made with Brandon. She would drive to Lincoln City first, a small town on the Oregon coast, and sleep on the beach if accommodations weren't available. It occurred to her that she might simply pitch the whole postgraduation plan. Get a job somewhere. College was starting to feel too much like limbo anyway.

"If I don't go now, I might *never* go," Jessie replied, rearranging the luggage. It was a silly excuse. No matter how long she waited, nobody, nothing, was going to keep her from this trip. She'd been planning it since her sixteenth birthday. Time to pull the trigger. Finally. Boyfriend or not.

Darlene crossed her arms, looking intently at Jessie. Their eyes met, and Jessie felt a sting of regret. Now that they were saying good-bye, it seemed as if their friendship had hardly begun. She wondered if Darlene felt the same way.

She reached for Darlene and they hugged tightly. "Take care of Cubby," she whispered. Cubby was Darlene's Labrador mutt, whose misshapen features bore some resemblance to a bear cub, and who had an insatiable appetite for ear rubs, not to mention an inexhaustible upbeat temperament. Cubby seemed happy whatever happened—empty dish, full dish, it didn't matter. "*Be* the bear!" Darlene had once exclaimed when Jessie had been depressed over a test score in statistics. They'd both laughed until their faces hurt.

Darlene's expression was a mixture of worry and hope. Jessica slammed the hatch shut. Darlene crossed her arms again, and her eyes were glossy, reflecting the late-morning sun.

"I'm going to lose it if *you* do," Jessie said, forcing a smile, which must have looked like a grimace.

Darlene wiped her eyes. "I'll be praying for you, Jess."

Jessie smiled again. It had almost become a private joke between them. The first time Darlene had ever said she'd pray for her, Jessie had been annoyed enough to retort, *"Like that ever helped anyone."* Darlene had shot back, *"I knew there was a reason we were roommates."* But Jessie never let Darlene get started, nipping every religious discussion in the bud the moment things got too personal.

"You can't stop me from praying for you," Darlene had replied once in frustration when Jessie had drawn a determined line in the sand.

Ironically, in the two years they'd been roomies, Jessie had never dared to reveal that she and Darlene had a lot more in common than she was willing to admit. In fact, Jessie had been raised in a Christian home herself, complete with weekly trips to church and Sunday school, with two weeks in the summer spent in Vacation Bible School. But an admission of that magnitude would have opened the floodgates.

"Will you call me when you get there?"

"I'll be fine, Darlene."

"Will you . . ." Darlene's tone was tentative. "Will you be seeing your grandmother on the way? I guess I forgot where she lived. Was it . . . Grand Junction . . . or . . . ?"

"Colorado Springs," Jessie replied absently, remembering her grandmother's call about a year ago while Jessie had been out shopping. Darlene had answered the phone, and they must have spent a good half hour in conversation. When Jessie returned, Darlene filled her in and commented on the pleasant chat. *"Your grandmother wants you to call her when you get in. You never said she lived in Colorado. I guess her number has changed, 'cause she wanted you to have it. . . ."*

Jessie was reluctant to explain, so she didn't. After a few days, however, Darlene was still pressing. "Have you called her yet?"

"I don't talk to my grandmother," Jessie finally admitted.

"Why not?" Darlene asked, which only led to another argument, another painful truce, and yet another line drawn in the sand.

Now Darlene appeared to consider Jessie's reply. "So it's . . . what? An hour, hour and a half out of your way?"

"Too far south."

"Oh . . . yeah. Sure."

They hugged again and minutes later she was on the road, heading for her glorious ocean.

Chapter Two

SHE DROVE NORTH from Wichita on I-135 and tried not to think. She planned to take I-70 all the way to Denver, then travel north on I-25 to I-80 going west and then I-84 to Oregon. She listened to a country station for most of the morning, and then she slipped in a Dixie Chicks CD and clicked to number two, her favorite. Natalie crooned: "She needs wide open spaces, room to make a big mistake. . . ."

Can't get any wider than the ocean, Jessie thought wistfully.

She remembered the first time she'd driven this road, heading in the opposite direction. That had been four years ago, and this stretch of road reminded her that at the end of things, it was always the beginning that loomed so large. Just as thinking about last night's breakup reminded her of the first time Brandon had winked at her across the room, the promise of his smile melting her heart.

Why did I ever think this time would be different? she wondered now.

Bits and pieces of last night's conversation continued to play over and over in her mind. But none more than *"You need help,"* and she felt a renewed sting of regret. Yet deep down hadn't she sometimes wondered this herself?

"No," Jessie whispered. "He's wrong."

Thinking of Oregon in general and men in particular, she wondered how she'd ever start over again: The first shared smile. The first date. The first flowers—maybe roses, maybe carnations. The first "our song." (How many "our songs" did she have?) The first kiss—and that was the most painful to imagine.

I'm a good person, she argued to herself. *Worth dating. I'm a lot of fun. I have a sense of humor. I'm supportive. I'm generous. I'm . . .*

It sounded like a personal ad. She turned the rearview mirror so she could see herself and cringed at the sight of her swollen eyelids. *On a good day, I'm passably cute.*

"You need help," he'd said. *"Psychiatric counseling. The full meal deal . . . therapy . . . drugs."* He might as well have added *"shock treatment and a tight-fitting straitjacket. And don't forget the padded walls."*

She gritted her teeth. "I'm a good person," she said aloud. She repeated it until the tears came again, and it occurred to her that beginning again was pointless. Hadn't she learned her lesson? Some things just didn't work out.

I'm done, she thought, trying it on for size, and it seemed to fit. But Darlene would have said, *"Yeah, right."*

The interior car temperature was stifling under the noontime June sun. The air-conditioner struggled to keep up, but she barely noticed. At about two o'clock, she reached Limon, Colorado, and saw the sign for Highway 24 leading to Colorado Springs.

"Will you be seeing your grandmother?" Darlene had asked.

Jessie's grandmother lived in the Springs, but Jessie had grown up about a half hour to the north in the small town of Palmer Lake. She pulled onto the shoulder and gripped the wheel, taunted with indecision. *This is ridiculous,* she thought. *I'm not going back. . . .*

She took a look around. Limon appeared to be the capital of fast foods. She hadn't eaten anything since breakfast. What would it hurt?

Inside a burger joint, she sat at a warped Formica table and ate a chicken sandwich while she gazed through the smudged window. From where she sat, she could see busy I-70 as well as the exit sign for Colorado Springs. She smiled wryly—*the road less traveled.*

Back in the car, she twisted the key in the ignition. The music came alive again and an old memory surfaced. Brandon had told her he would never have pegged her as a country music fan. She'd asked him why, and he'd shrugged. *"It's so hokey."*

When she'd later related the conversation to Darlene, her room-mate was quick to fill in the blanks. *"Hokey is just the first rung, honey. Climb a little higher and you get sappy, silly, annoying . . . shall I continue?"*

"It's a-wink-and-a-nod music," Jessie had argued. *"Like an inside joke. . . ."*

"It's awfully optimistic," Darlene had replied finally, and what she'd really meant was: It's awfully optimistic . . . for you.

Jessie's ruby-red-slipper key chain clicked with the motion of the idling car, and for a few sways at least, it matched the rhythm of the beat. The sound triggered a sudden mysterious dread within her, like the rapidly fading echo of a door clicking shut and opening again, or maybe a door locking and then unlocking . . . and she had a clear sense that some decisions alter the course of your life and others don't, and perhaps right now she had one of those life-changing decisions to make.

A scattering of faint images came to her, seemingly out of nowhere. Tall pine trees, towering over her . . . a little boy standing at the grave site beside her . . . a lifetime ago. What was his name? And why was she even thinking about *him?*

She glanced at the now motionless keys. Turning off the engine, she stared at the ruby-red-slipper key ring closely, as if trying to remember something long forgotten. Yet knowing instinctively that pondering this further would be like recklessly pulling the thread in an expensive Berber carpet only to witness the entire floor come undone.

In her smoldering, claustrophobic Honda, locked in with a

relentless barrage of torturous thoughts, four years of empty memories and friendships barely begun, the past became painfully clear. She leaned back in her seat and closed her eyes, whispering the obvious truth, the truth she conveniently ignored most of the time: *The past is your future, kiddo. Have you noticed yet?*

Suddenly she became aware that she'd been pressing the heel of her hand against the steering wheel, and her wrist flared painfully. She released the wheel and sat there for another minute.

Right to Denver. Left to Colorado Springs.

She picked up her cell phone from the passenger seat and dialed her old number. She had to concentrate, the number already fading from her memory. Darlene answered on the first ring and sounded surprised. "Jessie?"

"I just wanted to . . . uh . . . I forgot to tell you that, uh . . ." she struggled. "I'll let you know when I get there." She must have sounded absurd.

"Oh, Jessie. I've been—" Darlene paused long enough for Jessie to feel another pang of regret—"I've been worried."

"Would you consider visiting the West Coast in the fall?" Jessie asked, closing her eyes, wincing again. Surely by now Darlene would have washed her hands of this unsatisfying friendship.

"I'd love to, Jessie. So we'll keep in touch, then?"

"Let's" was all Jessie could manage before saying good-bye again.

She tossed the cell phone over to the passenger seat and felt weak and vulnerable. Starting the engine, she pulled out of the parking lot, continuing north on I-70. She set her jaw and pursed her lips with new resolve.

But five miles later she reconsidered again. *I've been running my whole life. I'll never be this close to home again—*

"It's not home," she corrected herself. "Going back won't solve anything."

Brandon's cruel words echoed again: *"What happened to you, Jess? How did you get this way?"*

At the next turnoff she gritted her teeth again and switched directions, heading south. By now her hands were shaking. Her stomach hurt, churning an indigestible sandwich. She knew once she reached the outskirts of Colorado Springs, she would take Highway 105 directly to Palmer Lake. The thought nearly unnerved her.

Eventually she regathered her composure, wiping her eyes clumsily with her shirt sleeve. *Fine then. I'll face the boogeyman, and the boogeyman will disappear. I'll look under the bed with a flashlight and discover only dust bunnies, because monsters don't exist.*

Then I'll drive to paradise. . . .

Chapter Three

TRAVELING SOUTHWEST, the mountains loomed before her, rising slowly from the horizon, and a sense of dread rose within her, as well. When she reached the outskirts of the city, she saw the turnoff for 105 and headed directly west. The road was poorly marked, difficult to follow, but soon enough she found her way, finally crossing Highway 83.

After another few minutes she reached Monument, a reformed truck stop, now obviously inundated by the northern expansion of Colorado Springs, twenty minutes to the south. Jessie took a breath. Palmer Lake was just two miles away to the northwest—situated in the foothills.

I'll just drive through, she thought. Minutes later, she was surprised by the sign that appeared a mile before what she had always considered to be Palmer Lake proper. To her, home had been the little hamlet built on a gradual incline, like a miniature Swiss village. Instead, she now realized the place called Palmer Lake encompassed the whole range of sparsely populated land along the Front Range. Not so sparse anymore.

According to her late father, only two kinds of people had lived here: artists and antigovernment militants. Even as a child, she suspected her father of having a tendency to reduce life to stark shades of black and white. According to Mrs. Robinette, the village locals were a furiously loyal bunch who relished their private haven, living in the shadow of western bluffs, facing Elephant Rock toward the east. The magnificent rock formation—the final culmination of an east/west-running mountain ridge—overlooked the lake from the east side. The surrounding hills seemed to cradle the small community.

She drove past the Welcome to Historic Palmer Lake sign—the second sign—past the ballpark and the gas station, then slowed in front of the Rock House Ice Cream Shoppe.

She stared at the place . . . almost stunned. *It really exists,* she thought. But the more she stared, the less she felt—not even bittersweet nostalgia, as if somewhere down the line she'd placed an unconscious filter across her brain, blocking every emotion, good or bad.

Was Mrs. Robinette there? she wondered.

She continued on her way, another half block, until she reached Finders Keepers and pulled into the tiny gravel parking lot. Sitting there, it suddenly struck her: she'd done it. She'd arrived and was, for all practical purposes, scratch free. She stared at the shop and again felt nothing. Only a fuzzy mental Novocain feeling. A pervading numbness.

Why was I so worried?

The gift shop was perched on the edge of a sagging sidewalk. Painted in unimaginative shades of brown topped with splintered cedar shingles, it resembled an oversized storage shed with bay windows.

The gray weathered park bench beneath the display windows held an elderly man who seemed as worn out as the seat he occupied. Jessica's eyes flitted across his somewhat familiar face several times, but she couldn't place him. Nor did she see any hint of recognition in his return glances. Relieved, she looked away to the ubiquitous candles and holders artfully arranged in the window. She sat there for the longest time staring at the Open sign, nervously tapping the steering wheel. The shop would close in thirty minutes—rather early for a summer day. She pushed a strand of tawny hair behind her ear and kept staring, tapping. Considering. Reconsidering.

Moments later, a thirty-something woman with a blond ponytail peered out from behind the display, then smiled curiously at Jessica through the glass.

This is getting ridiculous, she thought.

Taking a deep breath, she twisted the rearview mirror one more time to examine her face, mentally comparing eyes, nose, chin to that childhood image of herself. Sighing, she reached into her purse for the oval amber-tinted sunglasses. She could almost hear Darlene's voice: *"Face it, honey. You're a drama queen."*

She put on the glasses but felt silly. No one could possibly remember her anyway. Stepping out of the car, she glanced once more at the old man, who appeared to be asleep. She closed the car door quietly so as not to awaken him and took a step toward the gift shop. A flash of color at her feet caught her eye, and she was startled to see a gossamer-winged butterfly fluttering in panicked desperation against the cement.

Jessie paused for a moment—another wave of indecision. Another tug, as if something were pulling at her from the inside.

The buzzing sound of the dying butterfly filled her ears, and then the entire community seemed to come alive with the wispy chatter of aspen leaves, the drone of a distant mower, the almost undetectable sound of laughing children, and the annoying persistence of a barking dog. The sounds threatened to break through, but she resisted, maintaining her composure. The old man had opened his eyes and seemed to be watching her out of the corner of his eye, his expression one of amusement. *You ain't from around here, are ya?*

At last she knelt, watching the butterfly beat helplessly in a futile attempt to fly. It was rare to see a butterfly die in a public place. Normally, they died in secret. She recalled her year as a fourth-grader at the elementary school just up the street. For Mrs. Fletcher's science unit, Jessie's project had been Colorado butterflies—identifying the various kinds and studying the mysterious transformation from cocoon to a thing of grace and beauty. But in the end she'd received only a C for her efforts. Completing the assignment meant mounting all the butterfly varieties she'd gathered, and she'd flat out refused to kill even one.

She rose and brushed at her knees, staring at the dying butterfly. That long-ago fourth-grader would have shed a tear over its fate. That overly sensitive child would have cradled the poor creature in her hands in a gallantly naïve effort to save it. *A butterfly only lives a few weeks anyway,* she told herself now. And butterflies were merely one more reminder of life's futility. The most beautiful of earthly creatures, it was doomed from birth, destined to blaze brilliantly for a tiny measure of time, then arrive at a pointless death at the hands of a ruthless predator.

Welcome to planet earth, pretty one. Jessie sighed at how easily her mind could veer to the lowest common denominator. And then, as if on cue, the butterfly ceased its struggle and lay on its side, wings folded. Jessie bent to pick up the tiny carcass, placing the creature beneath the bordering aspen tree, its leaves flickering in the slight breeze.

Her entrance into the gift shop was greeted with a *ching-ching* and an almost overwhelming aroma of potpourri, scented soaps, and candles. The rather small space was comfortably filled with displays of home and garden décor—spun-glass figurines, porcelain collectibles, dolls, gift baskets, and birdhouses of all shapes and sizes. The walls from floor to ceiling displayed framed prints and tapestries.

It seemed so safe. She relaxed slightly, and suddenly her mind swirled with a mixture of happy memories. Of spending hours in this very place, delighting in its visual and aromatic splendor.

She whirled to the left, then breathed out slowly when she saw the entire wall-shelf unit devoted to Dorothy's Wizard of Oz. Cups, plates, and water globes with tiny Emerald City scenes lined the top shelves. The middle shelves were filled with pewter, porcelain, and nutcracker variations of Dorothy and her friends—the heartless Tin Man, the cowardly Lion, and the madcap Scarecrow. Jessie nearly giggled aloud, putting her hand to her mouth.

Then she spotted the Wicked Witch and, with an almost morbid fascination, picked up the Ruth Hamilton likeness, remembering the first time she'd seen the figurine at age ten or so and thinking immediately of her grandmother. The resemblance was striking. *"Of course, Grandma isn't as mean as the Wicked Witch of the West,"* she'd once told her father.

"Oh really?" he'd replied, his tone skeptical.

"No," she had said adamantly. *"That wouldn't be fair to the witch."*

Jessie smiled at the memory—one of the few times her father had actually chuckled. Also one of the few things they had in common—a mutual disregard for Doris Crenshaw, her mother's mother.

Jessie replaced the figurine, turning to her left. Prominently displayed on a special table was a meticulously hand-painted rendition of Dorothy in those ruby red slippers with dog Toto and the angelic-looking Witch of the East waving a magic wand over her head. Less prominent was its $250 price tag. A tent-shaped sign in front of the music box invited the browser to "Wind me up and enjoy the ageless melody of Somewhere Over the Rainbow."

"Those are very popular." A cheerful voice interrupted Jessie's reverie. She turned to face the clerk who wore a flowered chintz smock and blue slacks. "They're handcrafted, and they come with certification. We can't keep them in stock. They don't make too many."

"Very nice," Jessie replied, her eyes glued to the display. Bracing herself for disappointment, she asked, "Do you still—do you have those key chains?"

"Sure," the woman said without missing a beat, apparently

eager to make any sale, large or small. She pulled out the partly opened drawer of a small wooden chest and removed a key chain. Miniature ruby red slippers dangled below her fingers. "This is the most popular. Aren't they cute?" She carefully passed them to Jessie and began her sales pitch. "Just look at the detail. They're made of . . ."

". . . real tempered glass with tiny inlaid pearls," Mrs. Peterson, the shopkeeper, had sternly told eleven-year-old Andy as his friend Jessie had peered over his shoulder.

"Cool," he said with boyish aplomb, reaching for the key chain.

With thinly concealed distrust, the woman allowed Andy to hold it, warning that it was expensive.

"It's so beautiful," Jessie breathed in awe, touching it with one finger.

"You break it, you buy it, young man," Mrs. Peterson said.

"I'll take it," Andy declared.

"Andy, what're you doing?" Jessie gasped.

"Don't you like it?"

"Of course, but—"

"Well, then," he said, as if the matter were settled. He turned to the clerk as he dug in his pocket.

"We don't accept returns," the woman told him, but she did accept the twenty he held out to her.

"Andy!" Jessie exclaimed, frustrated with Andy's impulsiveness, yet her heart was bursting with excitement. . . .

Jessica handed the ruby-red-slipper key chain back to the clerk. "Do you have the Toto key chain?" she asked.

The woman frowned thoughtfully. "I think so—at least we did last week." She leaned down and pulled the drawer nearly out of its rails, catching it on her knee, searching through the collection. "Oh dear, I think I sold the last one.. I can order it, though."

"That's all right," Jessie said evenly, surprised at her own disappointment. She backed toward the door. "I need to get on the road anyway."

"No trouble," the clerk persisted. "It only takes a few days."

I won't be back, she almost said. "I'm from . . . out of town. Thank you, though." She forced a smile and hurried toward the door, nearly toppling a floor display of wooden figurines. Just as her hand reached for the doorknob, her eye caught a photo hanging on the wall beside the door. Two gray-haired women stood beside a park gazebo, smiling above the caption: "Mrs. Browning, Palmer Lake's own award-winning gardener, and Mrs. Robinette, local photographer, historian, and merchant." Surrounding the personal snapshot were several framed photos of flowers, each including a printed bit of colloquial wisdom.

"Mrs. Browning is our local gardening magician," the clerk offered from behind Jessica. "Her roses are the talk of the county. Mrs. Robinette owns the Rock House Ice Cream Shoppe down the street. She took all these pictures and framed them. We've been selling 'em for years now."

"They're good," Jessica murmured. *Betty Robinette is still alive. . . .*

"Real camera buff," the woman continued. "She's been here forever. Most of her photos are displayed in the town hall, but she has some different flowers and more photos on her shop wall if you want to see a bigger selection."

Jessica's mind drifted away from the chatty voice beside her, remembering the time when her own picture had been displayed on Mrs. Robinette's wall. She swallowed before offering an appreciative thank-you, and opened the door.

Back in her car, she noticed that the park bench was now empty. Reaching into her purse, she pulled out her own key chain and studied it—still good as new after all these years. As she started the engine the tiny red slippers clicked softly together again.

She'd been totally absorbed in the gift shop. What was she thinking? Looking for a key chain, of all things. Would she really have mailed it to him if the shopkeeper had found it? *You won't remember me, but I was that little blond girl next door, and I forgot to give this to you for your twelfth birthday. . . .*

She swung her head to look over her shoulder and shoved the car into reverse. If she hurried, she could be in Denver in half an hour.

Suddenly the door of Finders Keepers flew open and the pony-tailed clerk burst out the door, cupping a tiny white box in her hands.

Jessica slowly rolled down the car window.

"I was afraid you'd left!" the woman called exuberantly. "Look what I found."

With dramatic flair, the shopkeeper opened the box, peeled back the tissue paper, and proudly revealed a golden key chain dangling from the neck of a miniature hand-painted Toto, his eyes sparkling in the sunlight.

Chapter Four

JESSIE RECOGNIZED THE STREET that led to her old house, three or four blocks away. She peeked at her watch, then tapped the steering wheel. *Get it over with,* she finally decided.

Before shifting into gear, she noticed a young mother wearing a red-striped maternity tunic pushing a stroller. Holding a balloon in her hands, her blond daughter couldn't have been more than two. Jessie cherished the scene for a moment and was reminded of Brandon's pointed remark.

I do have other dreams, Jessie thought, pulling away from the curb.

Past the brand-new post office, she turned onto High Street and headed west up the gradually ascending hill. As she drove she steeled herself, expecting the worst—an empty lot or maybe even an entirely new home built upon the ashes.

The trees were taller, bushier, than she remembered; the sidewalks were worn from age and use. Some homes had obviously declined in appearance. When the two-story Victorian house appeared on the left, she parked across the street and stared, strangely relieved. The house was well kept. The white clapboard siding was freshly painted and the lawn neatly mowed.

On the other hand, Andy's old house, right next door, looked worn and badly in need of paint, not at all as pristine as when Mrs. McCormick was running the roost.

You're here, she reminded herself. *There it is. The house really exists.* As rampant as her imagination could be at times, she had never imagined how it would feel to return, and it was difficult to think of the old house as anything other than the home of her childhood. And truly, looking at it now, she felt as if she could walk right in that door, climb the stairs, and . . . *what?*

Step back into my past?

The thread was beginning to unravel. The foundation beneath her feet was coming undone. A mixture of emotions began circling like vultures—old memories fighting for dominance. She searched out the Russian olive tree, remembering the chalky sweet scent, and in spite of the competing thoughts, one memory broke through . . . and she remembered . . .

. . . walking home after an evening school event . . . clutching a photo frame, careful not to drop it. It was her favorite picture of her mother, dressed in her nurse's uniform. To Jessie, her mother looked like an actress dressed for a starring role, and not because she was so beautiful—which she was—but because she looked so real. Her mother had a spunky confident look, as if there weren't a thing she couldn't handle. Not a pushy sort of confidence, like Mrs. Roberts, her fifth-grade teacher. It was more like: *We can get through anything together. Just take my hand and hold on, sweetie.*

The night air chilled her, and the lampposts looked like frozen statues, glowing with frosty halos. She felt stupid for having gone to the school party and leaving her mom alone. She was in a hurry to get home.

A block away something spooked Mrs. Finch's dog, Goober, who barked at the tall pine tree at the edge of the yard. Normally Goober's barking didn't bother her, but tonight his constant *rowp-rowp* was annoying.

The windows were dark in their two-story Victorian house—the oldest house in Palmer Lake. In the shadows it looked like something out of a Halloween movie, the kind her mother never allowed her to see.

Jessie stood shivering in the front yard when suddenly Goober stopped barking and the neighborhood fell quiet again, except for the crickets, who were having a party.

She opened the front door, which prompted another hissy fit from Goober, and propped her foot in the widening gap to prevent Mr. Whiskers from getting out. Mr. Whiskers meowed his displeasure but wasn't able to slip around Jessie's stubborn foot. Jessie closed the front door behind her and reached down to console the disappointed mouse catcher, who was now mewing angrily.

"There are cat catchers out there," Jessie said, referring to the never-ending supply of red foxes in the area.

She made her way through the dark living room and replaced her mother's framed photo on the wall, careful to get it perfectly straight, then headed up the squeaky stairs to the second floor, where her mother would be sleeping. These days, Mom rarely stayed awake past eight o'clock.

Softly, Jessie pushed against the door. It whispered open, thanks to her latest administration of WD-40. She held her breath as if that would help matters. The room was dark, but she recognized the still form propped against the pillows, the pale white arms gently folded, the wheelchair leaning against the wall. The arms flinched and the shadowy figure leaned up. Her mother's recently washed hair glimmered in the dim hallway light.

"Jessie?"

"Did I wake you?"

"No . . . I was dozing. How did it go tonight?"

"It was boring."

Her mother extended her hand. "Come, sit by me."

Jessie crossed the room. Her mother's once smooth and soft hand had acquired a pasty, sweaty texture, but Jessie gripped it tightly anyway, unafraid of what it meant, refusing the repulsion.

Jessie sat on the edge of the bed. Slowly her eyes grew accustomed to the dim room, and she recognized the dark circles around her mother's eyes. Each morning, Jessie applied cover-up for her mother, but by evening, most of the makeup was worn off.

"They had cookies and punch."

"Were they *good* cookies?"

Her mom knew her well. Jessie was very picky when it came to cookies. "Raisin oatmeal. Can you believe it? Of all the cookies in the world."

Wrinkling her nose in agreement, Mom said, "Too bad they didn't have chocolate chip. What were they thinking?"

Mom's eyes sparkled when she smiled. In spite of everything, nothing could change that smile. No matter how ill, there was power behind Mom's smile. But the cheerful expression faded, and Mom's eyes turned shiny like lip gloss. She sniffled slightly, quickly, as if trying to disguise the pain, smiling hard at the end of each sniff.

Jessie was on to her. "I'm glad you didn't go, Mom. You didn't miss anything. I should have stayed home, too. We could have finished *Beauty and the Beast*."

Mom nodded, but a cautious look crept onto her face. "Your father told me about the missing picture."

"Well . . . some of the other kids haven't met you yet. And the picture looks just like you."

"Did you find one of your dad?" Mom asked graciously.

Jessie bit her lip and thought about that. "Everyone knows Dad from the gas station."

Nodding again, Mom gently stroked Jessie's arm. "He loves us very much, honey. . . ."

Jessie shrugged, letting her gaze drift to the pink bedspread and sheets. Since this was her mother's favorite color, Jessie made sure the pink sheets were always freshly laundered.

"Dad works very hard to make up for the loss of my income. He's under a lot of stress and doesn't talk things out like we do because he never learned how. We have to be patient with him. When I'm better, he'll get better, too."

"No, he won't, Mom. He won't change."

"We have to believe in him, too, sweetie," her mother said, smiling wistfully. "There's a whole other side to your dad you don't remember, but I know it well."

Jessie sighed, feeling guilty. "I'll try better, Mom."

"That's all I can ask for, sweetie."

They hugged tightly, and Jessie felt her own tears struggle to the surface, beginning in her throat and moving up to her face. Mom whispered a giggle. It sounded so strange that Jessie broke free to catch her mother's expression. "What?"

"We're quite the pathetic pair, you know."

Jessie smiled, wiping her face, the sudden tension fading from her shoulders and face. "I'm proud of our . . . pathetic . . . ness."

Mom's face broke into a grin, the dark circles melting into the tight gray flesh surrounding her eyes. They fell into each other's arms again, this time laughing without restraint. For a moment things were normal again.

Jessie broke away and locked eyes with Mom as hard as she could, as if she could heal her by her will and desire alone. They were looking into each other's souls, and a sense of knowing passed between them, as it often did, a sense of connection, as if no secrets separated them, as if they were one person. It was the weirdest feeling and yet the happiest feeling in the world—this sense of closeness with someone who knew you best and yet loved you totally. Jessie actually pitied other kids who had normal moms.

She also pitied herself, because another part of her wished her mother *were* normal. Like Michelle's mom, who yelled a lot and had a sarcastic sense of humor. Or Andy's mom, who looked at Jessie with unforgiving eyes, as if something were wrong with her because her mother was sick. Or Cindy's mom, who practically lived at the country club and was always late picking Cindy up. Sometimes Jessie wouldn't have minded having a mom who wasn't so cool, just to have a mom who wasn't so sick.

Then it happened again, as it often did. Mom's eyes twitched, not on the outside but from the inside. And then, like the flicking off of a light switch, they turned vacant. She closed them momentarily, then opened them again and frowned, as if confused and scared.

"Mom?"

"Jessie?"

"Mom?"

"You're home?"

Jessie shuddered, her heart sinking, but she sucked it up. "I went to school tonight," she said, forcing a painful smile and swallowing the lump in her throat.

Mom smiled back sleepily. "Oh yes . . . tell me about it."

"Sure," Jessie said. "They had cookies. . . ."

A small panic trickled through her veins, and Jessie placed both hands on the steering wheel, steadying herself. She remembered once as a little girl holding a cracked glass in the palm of her hand and feeling the water seep out the bottom. The sensation had frightened her. The glass was ruined, wasn't it? Just throw it away. But no, she couldn't. She'd become obsessed with the leak. She tried masking tape, glue, duct tape, clay, but nothing worked. The more she tried, the more determined she became. In the end, the water dissipated, leaving an empty container, and Jessie wept. *It's just a glass!* she told herself.

Now the old feelings were back as if they had been floating in the air somehow. The thread was unraveling at an alarming rate. She removed her hands from the wheel of temptation. *Just drive away, Jess!* She hugged herself, but the whirlpool continued to spin. . . .

"I'm floundering here . . ." she whispered, her voice a barely audible squeak.

What's the matter with me? she thought for the thousandth time.

Kids lose their parents. You cherish the good times. You move on. You grow up.

But here she was, little Jessie, still refusing to grow up. Her body was racked by such emotional heaves she wondered if she were becoming physically ill. Tossing her sunglasses to the passenger seat, she clutched her stomach. It was like riding a roller coaster. Up, down, twisting this way and that . . .

Twenty minutes later she was still sitting there, eyes closed. She knew her eyelids were swollen as if stung by invisible bees. She took long, deep breaths, exhaling slowly. The inside of the car was stuffy with her body heat.

"Mom . . ." she whispered again, the panic as thick as a rock in the pit of her stomach. "I'll get through this and I will make you proud. I promise."

Just when it seemed as if she were descending again, Jessie was granted a reprieve. The old "knowing" washed over her, as it had so many times, like a physical touch, and in spite of its familiarity, shivers sparked up and down her spine. She jerked to look behind her, but no one was there. As quickly as the feeling came, it passed. Jessie felt a shudder of emptiness. She sighed, appraising the house again, a place that had once given her a sense of complete and utter security.

Surely some brave soul lived there now. Surely the circumstances of her father's death couldn't haunt the place. Perhaps she might summon the courage to visit with the new owners, whoever had carefully painted the siding and religiously mowed the lawn.

Jessie inhaled deeply. After checking up and down the street, she pushed the car door open and headed for the house, trying to appear as nonchalant as possible. She suddenly remembered Mrs. Graybill from across the street, whose nose had been pasted to her front window and who seemed to know everything about everyone on their block. As a child Jessie had been constantly aware of being watched by her nosy neighbor, who probably didn't mean any harm, but whose observation made Jessie feel as if her life were lived in a fishbowl.

Even Mom would humorously caution her, *"Dress warm, sweetie. Or Mrs. Graybill will wonder what kind of mother you have."*

Halfway up the sidewalk she paused at the cement step her dad had replaced. She remembered watching him mix the cement and pour it into a form made out of wood from the garage. Afterward he'd invited her to press her tiny fingers into the moist and gritty cement, leaving her mark for future generations to ponder. Instead, here she was coming back and pondering it herself. Oblivious to curious onlookers, Jessie knelt on one knee, studying the edge of the step—recognizing her faint imprint.

Jessie rose and once again appraised the front door, aware of a gathering conflict between curiosity and fear. Heart thudding in her ears, she climbed the porch steps, and before she could change her mind, knocked on the screen door, the same one she'd peeked back through when Andy would beg her to ride bikes—nearly every day. But that was nothing compared to a deeper realization. She turned to the street, and her mind did a weird *click* and *whirr* . . .

It was as if she'd never left. She was still the same little girl, coming home every day to make sure her mother was alive, believing that everything was going to be okay. The old hopes . . . the old beliefs were in the air . . . floating around, unfinished somehow as if the power of her twelve-year-old determination had been so intense that she'd actually made a physical impression upon this place. She could feel it infusing her again, like putting on an old coat, warm to the touch, soothing to her soul. Hope wasn't dead. Not yet. *My mother is still alive.* . . .

Jessie slumped to the porch step and with both hands clasped her neck, leaning her head into her elbows, rocking back and forth— nearly curling into a ball right there in her old neighborhood, and for a moment she didn't care who saw it. She was losing it again.

It's over! Jessie repeated to herself, over and over again. *She's gone! They're both gone! Dead and buried!*

But the most startling thought occurred to her, strange enough to snap her out of her morbid self-pity: *Your mother was never buried . . . remember?*

It came to her so suddenly she had to ponder it a second before dismissing it as one of her imaginative ramblings.

Chapter Five

ANDY McCORMICK sucked in a deep breath, reached up, and grasped the bar. Shifting his shoulders, he exhaled and for a moment questioned his sanity. Two-seventy was twenty pounds more than his normal routine.

"Ready?" Chris asked, leaning over him.

"Ready as I'll ever be."

Andy pushed up, then allowed the bar to sink within an inch of his chest, and for a split second saw the headlines: *Denver Man Bites Off More Than He Can Chew . . . Freak Accident Beheads Him.*

Andy pushed up again, stopping short of locking his elbows. Then again, and again, five times in a row. Fortunately, with Chris spotting him, Andy was protected from his overeager aspirations.

"Enough?" Chris asked, grasping the bar.

Andy grunted, and with Chris's help, guided the bar back to the holder. Sitting up to catch his breath, he wiped his face with the back of his leather-gloved hand.

"My turn," Chris asserted, tacking on another twenty pounds to each side.

Andy completed his Saturday morning routine with leg squats and crunches. Chris curled his seventeen-inch biceps, ending with dips and presses. Afterward they cooled down with several laps around the track that circled the pool, satisfied their macho "wild-at-heart" routine was complete. *We're men again,* Andy thought as he smiled, exhausted. *Hear us . . . whimper.*

He sat on the tiled edge of the pool while Chris completed several more laps. Eight o'clock. They'd been at the gym for nearly two hours.

"Still on for breakfast?" Chris asked, towel drying his brown hair in the locker room. He was already losing his hair on the crown, an occupational hazard, it seemed, for the testosterone-saturated gym rat.

"Starving," Andy replied. "You pick."

"Debbie's meeting us," Chris announced, almost too casually.

"Don't you two want to be alone?" Andy asked, pulling on his jeans.

Chris stood up and slipped on his white shirt. "I've been holding out on you, buddy."

"You two are secretly married?"

Chris laughed. "No. Marilyn's coming, too."

"Oh."

"They went to that women's retreat together; you know, the one in Estes Park. Shared a room. Inseparable ever since."

"I can see it," Andy said, wondering how awkward it would be for Marilyn. Maybe he should decline.

Chris placed his foot on the bench and proceeded to tie his shoelaces. "It's a setup, Andy, pure and simple." His tone had turned apologetic.

Andy put two and two together. The whole thing must have been Debbie's idea. "Should I run?"

"Backward maybe." Chris winked and grabbed his bag from the locker. "Did Marilyn ever tell you she once almost won a beauty contest?" He said it with an undisguised reverential tone. In many ways, he and Chris were a lot alike—both had careers in sales for one thing—but they differed in their evaluation of women.

Andy began buttoning his shirt. "No, but I heard. Second runner-up. Oklahoma, was it?"

"Tennessee."

"Got the southern part."

Chris sighed again. "I'm supposed to find out if you've gone blind or something."

"We had a wonderful time," Andy replied, shrugging, remembering his first and last date with Marilyn, nearly a month ago. They'd gone to a fancy steak place on Colorado Avenue. She'd worn a flowery skirt and blue blouse. Talking had seemed almost effortless. She'd joked about being a brunette instead of a blonde. "They called me Monroe in school," she'd laughed. "Accused me of dying my hair brown."

By the end of the meal Andy had determined she was the real deal, a genuinely sweet girl, not to mention a committed Christian.

Chris frowned. "But . . ."

"No *but*," Andy replied firmly.

Chris went to the mirror, pulled a comb across his scalp, and continued to parrot Debbie's instructions. "I'm supposed to tell you she's been waiting by the phone."

Andy was chagrined. They'd had a good time, but he didn't think he'd made that big of an impression. "I didn't lead her on," he insisted, combing his own hair, aware of how defensive he sounded.

"I know, but girls are like flypaper sometimes," Chris said casually.

Andy flinched. "Good thing Debbie's not here. She'd burn you alive."

Chris grabbed his bag from the locker. "Okay. I'm done. 'Nough said. Feel like I'm in high school again."

"You did well. Did you practice?"

"I was winging it the whole time," Chris said.

"I'm only mildly annoyed."

* * * * *

They drove Andy's gray Toyota sedan to the Denver suburb of Littleton. Debbie was standing by the curb in front of Denny's. She looked at her watch as Andy pulled up.

"Are we late?" he asked Chris, who shrugged. "I don't know, maybe five minutes."

Debbie leaned in the window frame and kissed her boyfriend on the cheek. She smiled at Andy. "Did Chris tell you?"

"Pretty sneaky."

Debbie narrowed her eyes. "Marilyn's holding our table. She thinks she did something wrong."

Chris turned to him. "Girls are always thinking, as if—"

Debbie slugged him playfully in the arm.

"Ow!"

She turned her attention back to Andy. "She's going to ask you to the church picnic. And you, my friend, need to say yes." She gave him a humorous take-no-prisoners look.

Chris turned to Andy. "You've got your marching orders. Hut, hut, hut . . . ."

"Are you going to slug me, too?" Andy asked, smiling.

"Depends," Debbie laughed. "So . . . are we set?"

Andy paused. "Debbie . . ."

"Don't even start with me, Andrew. One date is not enough." She pushed away from the car. "I'll see you both inside."

Andy parked behind the restaurant and set the brake. "I think your girlfriend's a bit strong willed."

Chris shrugged. "You think?"

"She's pretty, though."

"My only consolation."

◆　◆　◆　◆　◆

Marilyn and Debbie were waiting at a table by the window, the morning sun beating down on their backs. Debbie acted as if nothing had been said in the parking lot. Marilyn looked a bit sheepish, but just as he remembered, her eyes were soft blue, her face silky smooth, her brunette hair delicious but conservatively styled. She was wearing a flowery blue blouse, pleated skirt, and sandals . . . and her beauty was intimidating. She'd been robbed of that Tennessee title. Marilyn lifted her eyes to Andy and smiled demurely. "Hi."

Chris looked at her, then back at Andy. Chris's expression clearly said, *Are you blind?*

Breakfast progressed effortlessly. They discussed church, sports, and national politics and laughed at Debbie's humorous puns. Marilyn was rather quiet, yet when she did speak, she had a simple, confident, expressive charm. Andy found himself watching her out of the corner of his eye and the more drawn he was, the more depressed he felt. Soon, he was counting the minutes till the end of the meal.

Eventually, Debbie grabbed Chris for some "important" conversation by the rest rooms, leaving Marilyn and Andy alone.

"Debbie's a bit obvious," Marilyn offered apologetically.

Andy shrugged, embarrassed for Marilyn. "She's a great gal. Chris is lucky."

"Good friend, too," Marilyn added, and just as Debbie had foretold, she asked Andy to accompany her to the church picnic. Andy hesitated and felt like an absolute jerk.

"I wanted to give it another try," she offered. "I'm interested, but if you're not, that's fine. I respect that."

Andy sighed softly. "I'm sorry, Marilyn."

"I'm a big girl, Andy."

He wanted to say more, but Debbie and Chris were already returning. Debbie raised her eyebrows at Marilyn, who gave a subtle smile and a slight shake of the head. Debbie looked incredulous, glaring back at Andy, who pretended he hadn't seen the nonverbal exchange. When they said their good-byes on the curbside, Debbie didn't speak or make eye contact with him.

"So . . ." Chris replied when they'd gotten in his car. "That went reasonably terrible."

"Are you in trouble?" Andy asked.

"Why? Because my best friend turns down my girlfriend's best friend? Are you kidding? Debbie and I . . . we're solid."

Andy slipped the car into reverse. "You are, aren't you?"

"Big. Big. Trouble," Chris replied, sighing. "Will you come to my funeral?"

"I'll even *sing* at your funeral."

Chris frowned. "But you can't sing."

"I'm willing to make that sacrifice. For you."

"I'm thinking I want someone who can sing on key."

"Very picky you are," Andy commented. "There's always karaoke."

"Fake sing at my funeral?"

"Kind of fitting, eh?" Andy looked over his shoulder and began backing out of the parking place.

"I like it," Chris said as he seemed to reflect. "What would you sing?"

Andy twisted the steering wheel and headed for the parking lot exit. "I'm thinking, 'What Kind of Fool Am I?'"

"Hmm . . . I was thinking 'How Can I Live Without You?' might be more like it. . . ."

◆ ◆ ◆ ◆ ◆ ◆

Andy dropped Chris off at the health club, where he'd left his car, then drove north to the Hamden exit before turning toward the mountains, a rugged shadow of blue-gray against the horizon. He had moved out of his parents' home two years ago, renting an apartment in Castle Rock, about fifteen miles south of Denver. Having spent the first twelve years of his life in blink-and-miss-it Palmer Lake, he'd never acquired a taste for the big city, relishing instead the rustic small-town feel of Castle Rock. After a hard day at the office, he could feel the gentle decompression from big-city stress as he drove home.

On Saturdays he spent part of the day visiting his parents. Thirteen years ago his father had transferred his medical practice from Monument to Denver, more specifically, the southern suburb of Englewood. Due to his father's compassionate nature, his general practice had exploded after the move, making him a reluctantly rich man. At first his father had tried commuting, but the travel eventually grew tiresome. His mother, who'd grown up in Hartford, Connecticut, was bored with rugged small-town living anyway. So they moved.

Andy turned into a curved driveway leading to a Spanish stucco home. Entering through the double wooden doors, Andy heard the sound of professional baseball filtering from beyond the open hallway.

"That you, Andy?" His father's voice echoed from the family room, which, if combined with the separate dining room, was larger than their entire last home had been. A cathedral ceiling hung high over the rooms, and a giant wall of windows faced the mountain range. Expensive hardwood flooring accentuated the slate stone fireplace, and there was a big-screen TV on the opposite wall.

"Who's winning?"

"Who do you think?" his dad came back with a disgusted tone. He was lounging in the beige sectional sofa, wearing his comfortable gray chino slacks.

"Maybe they'll pull it out."

His father snorted. "Staying for lunch?"

"And dinner," Andy replied, grinning.

"Given any thought to the trip?" his father asked, referring to a medical missions trip to India. He had invited Andy to tag along.

"I'd like to, Dad, but you know—job and everything."

"Say no more."

"Andy, come give me a hand," his mother called from the kitchen.

Dad winked at him. "Your mother's got a list a mile long. Wouldn't think of asking me."

Andy headed for the kitchen. "Everyone knows you have two left thumbs, Dad."

"You should move back, Andy. Fix this place up."

Andy gave a respectful but dismissive wave. They'd had this discussion before. He entered the stainless-steel kitchen with hardwood flooring and white cupboards and kissed his mother on the cheek. She was wearing a pink apron over blue slacks, stirring her mixing bowl. Her brown hair was pulled back and pinned in a simple knot.

"So how's the best-looking unmarried man in Denver?"

"Content."

"Impossible." Susan McCormick pointed to the light fixture hanging from the ceiling. One bulb had died on the vine.

"Hmm. We might need to hire this out," Andy mused.

"Don't get smart, young man."

"Where's the stepladder?"

"Wherever your dad lost it last."

"Garage?"

"I can't guarantee your safety out there."

"Just needs a little organization."

"Nothing a giant fire can't fix. We could start over."

Andy smiled. If his mom had her way, they'd move to a new house every couple of years. She had a restless spirit and loved interior decorating.

"A man is required to keep a messy garage, Mom. It's an unwritten code."

She gave him the *look*. The same look that petrified him as boy. Now it seemed comical. "Still going to that church of yours?" she asked, her lips pursed as if dreading the answer, daring him to tell the truth.

"Yep." He didn't say he hadn't attended in a few weeks.

"Is it an all-male church?"

"Nope. Last I heard, they let women in."

His mother raised her eyebrows. "*Single* women?"

"Sure," Andy said, smiling. "But mostly single women over fifty-five. I'm dating a sweet widow lady—sixty-four, wonderful grandchildren, a little older than me, but hey, love is ageless. Did I forget to tell you about her?"

Mom gave him another look and began to wrap potatoes in tin foil.

After replacing the light, Andy went out to organize the garage, starting with the tools. He wondered why his father even bothered to purchase them. Five minutes later, his dad peeked his head out the door. "Need some help?"

"Sure."

"I'll see if I can find someone."

Andy chuckled. A few minutes later his father returned in his grubbies.

"You're really making me look bad, son." He grabbed a pail of rusty nails.

"That's why I visit, Dad."

"I suspected."

Two hours later they emerged, greasy and ruffled, their weekly father-son bonding ritual complete. After washing up in the laundry room, the trio ate turkey sandwiches on the deck overlooking distant Mount Evans. By now Andy was old enough to cherish these times as much as his folks did. After lunch they moved to the lower level and worked on a puzzle, the scene of two peaks in the Rockies called Maroon Bells, they'd begun two weeks earlier.

"That blue is the sky, not the water," his mother complained, looking at Andy's gathering pile.

"How can you tell?"

"Oh, for mercy's sake," Mom replied.

As a child, assembling puzzles always seemed like a monumental waste of time to him until he understood the true function they served—the same reason some men assembled to play poker.

"Remember when we went to Maroon Bells?" Dad asked, pressing a small piece into the corner.

Maroon Bells was just a few miles from the richest small town in America—the only place where the billionaires were pushing out the millionaires. His parents weren't the Aspen types, though, and it took one visit to shake the dust of that heathen place from the soles of their feet.

"I remember," Andy said.

"We took that little girl along, didn't we?" His mother appeared distracted, plugging another blue piece into her sky. Each of them had their preferred approach to puzzle assembly. Andy had always wondered what that said about them. Mom always did the sky first. Dad was fixated with constructing the border. Andy merely liked to group similar colors and patterns together.

"That's right," Dad said in his let's-not-go-there tone of voice. His resistance only fanned her flame.

"What's the matter?" Mom asked.

"Nothing, dear."

She leaned toward Andy as if to confide in him. "Your father hates to lose."

Oh boy, Andy thought, *That'll do it. . . .*

And it did. His father pushed himself right in the middle of the topic, just as his mother had intended. "Losing has nothing to do with medicine, dear."

"You take these things personally, as if sickness were the opposite team in a football game."

"That little girl's mother wasn't even my patient."

"But her father was."

"I think we tried to rescue her for a weekend," Andy said, trying to deflect the conversation back to its origins. They looked at him curiously.

"You know . . . Jessie."

"What do you think ever happened to her?" his mother asked, frowning at her puzzle pieces.

"I don't know."

"Boy, oh boy," his mother said after a few moments of silence as she popped in another puzzle piece. "I used to worry about you two."

"Why?"

"She followed you around like a lost puppy."

His father glanced over at Andy and chuckled.

"How did we start talking about this? That was eons ago. I was barely out of the cradle."

His father nodded toward the puzzle and smiled as if to say, *You're on your own.* . . .

Andy sighed. "C'mon, Mom, she was just a pudgy little tomboy who lived next door."

"Methinks—" his mother said, beginning her favorite quote from Shakespeare. This, of course, signaled a return to her favorite topic—Andy's marital prospects.

"You sound like an Italian movie, Mom. Men don't get married anymore until they're in their thirties."

"Nice try," she said, as if that were an argument of monumental proportions.

Another humorous glance from his dad. They spent the better part of the day dissecting every woman Andy had ever dated, starting in junior high school and working up to college, with his parents weighing in on their favorites. He was surprised to discover that his mother liked *any* of his old girlfriends and not surprised that his father liked most of them. But they didn't touch Elizabeth. *She* was off limits. His mother's all-time favorite daughter-in-law prospect. A major sore point for all of them.

Andy briefly wondered how a girl like Marilyn might fit in with his folks. Almost certainly they would adore her from the first meeting, admiring her quiet yet fervent faith. His mother would be giving him the winks and the nudges, just as she had done with

Elizabeth five years earlier. Eventually Marilyn would bond with his mom, appreciating the directness that accompanied her demonstrative love. *To know my mother is to love her,* Andy thought, varying the old cliché. Marilyn would especially admire his dad, a man who proclaimed his faith in every medical or personal deed of his life, as long as it didn't involve repairing or remodeling.

No, he would be a fool to mention Marilyn's invitation. Mom would be demanding the poor girl's phone number so she could call and apologize for her son's rude behavior. Then she'd invite her over for a Saturday night meal and surprise her unsuspecting son.

Andy cringed. He couldn't allow that to happen. He saw the end from the beginning. If Marilyn knew the truth about him, she'd be thankful—*very* thankful—that he'd declined her invitation.

"So . . . what was so bad about Jessie?" Andy finally asked, playfully taunting his mother.

His mother bristled. "Oh, honey. That little girl was so messed up after her parents died. She ran away, you know. They never found her."

Andy broke into a grin. "C'mon, Mom, you're exaggerating. Of course they found her."

"Her poor grandmother, what was her name? Doris Crenshaw. What she went through!"

"Did you ever *meet* her grandmother?" he asked.

"Nothing wrong with that woman."

His dad weighed in. "She was a bit high strung, dear."

"She was from the *East,* you know. I understand her."

Andy met his father's gaze and they both roared. "Of course!" Andy exclaimed, and his father echoed, "The East! You and she are practically sisters."

"New England's a small place," she argued, squinting her eyes at the puzzle, which only got them going again.

"Laugh it up, big boys, but you know as well as I do that Jessica Lehman will spend the rest of her life trying to recover, and that's it in a nutshell. I hate to think of what's become of her. The Lord bless her."

With that, a whisper of silence fell over them. Andy nodded and so did his dad. His mother seemed more than a little relieved when their conversation took a more benign turn, the question of "Whatever became of little Jessie?" forgotten.

Chapter Six

JESSIE KNOCKED AGAIN. When no one answered she gave up and headed for the car. She was crossing the lawn when she heard the slam of a screen door to her right. Startled, she turned toward "Andy's" house, and for a split second she thought she saw him running across the yard, *"Hey, Jess! Let's ride bikes!"*

Instead, she saw a big dog—larger than a German shepherd—come flying off the front steps, barking so furiously that saliva splattered from its mouth.

Oh boy, she thought.

A brown-haired girl bolted out the door after it. "Molly! Molly, come here!"

Oh girl, Jessie corrected herself.

Jessie froze as Molly the dog tore up the ground between devourer and devouree. Prepared to cover her throat at the last moment, she braced for impact. Molly came to an abrupt halt within five feet of Jessie, continuing to bark furiously. More saliva scattered. Jessie was still frozen solid when the young girl ran up behind Molly and grabbed the collar. "Down, Molly! Stop it!"

Wearing denim overalls, a light blue T-shirt, and dirty white tennis shoes, the stranger almost fell over her giant pet. It took all her weight to restrain the dog, leaning backward until Molly whined loudly. Finally the dog gave in and shuffled back, growling from the back of her throat. The girl nearly collapsed with exhaustion.

"She's too big for me," she complained, leaning over to catch her breath. "I need a poodle instead."

"Is it safe for me to leave?" Jessie asked, smiling through the fear.

The girl shook her head. "Maybe not. She might start barking again. Let me carry her home first."

Carry her?

Molly's growl had shifted to a low vibration. The girl tugged at Molly's collar again, but the dog was fixed like cement. "C'mon, girl. Quit terrorizing the neighborhood."

Jessie crouched down, her eyes meeting Molly's. The dog sniffed and growled, looking away.

"Careful," the girl cautioned. "I think she's upset because you're hanging out at her house."

"*Her* house?"

"Yeah, she's claimed it."

"Claimed it?"

"You know how a dog—"

"I get the idea," Jessie said, smiling. Molly took a couple of hesitant steps toward Jessie, sniffing warily.

"Molly, stop it!"

Jessie opened her palms and extended her hand.

"Careful, lady, she doesn't like . . ."

Molly began licking Jessie's hand. She placed a gentle finger under Molly's chin and began scratching. In the wink of an eye, Molly was a changed dog.

The girl looked astonished. "How did you do that?"

Jessie smiled. "Tell me your name and I'll tell you my secret."

"Laura," she said after a slight hesitation. "My mom got her to, you know, protect us at night. We picked her out at the pound. Mom thought a mean dog would be best, but we didn't realize how mean Molly was. My mom can barely go near her." Laura raised her eyebrows. It looked cute and inquisitive. "So . . . your turn."

"Simple," Jessie replied, now rubbing Molly's ears. "Molly knows me."

Laura looked confused. "Huh?"

Jessie nodded toward the house. "I used to live there."

"In the haunted house?"

"Why do you call it haunted?"

Laura shrugged. "Because it looks lived in, but it's not. 'Least not by anyone you can see."

Jessie looked back at the house, and the vaguely disturbing details clicked. Not what she saw—the painted siding and mani-cured lawn—but what she *didn't* see. No toys in the yard, no cars, no bicycles, no flowers . . .

By this time Molly had dropped to the ground and was offering her underside to Jessie for a tummy rub. She obliged.

"Unbelievable," Laura said again, hands on her hips, shaking her head. "You're Batwoman."

"I was friends with every dog in this town," Jessie explained. "Has anyone ever lived there?" she asked, gesturing toward her house.

"Not since we've been here," Laura replied.

The wind had picked up considerably, and a soft clanging sound broke through the Sunday afternoon stillness. Another memory flickered at the edge of her mind.

"What's wrong with your eyes?" Laura asked suddenly.

Jessie shrugged. "They puff up sometimes."

"Cool."

"Oh . . . yeah," Jessie murmured wryly.

Laura shrugged. "When did you live there?"

"Twelve years ago."

"Wow. I'm only ten!"

"I was best friends with the boy who lived in *your* house," Jessie said, pulling Molly's ears down, sending him to doggy heaven.

"You probably have his room, you know, the one on the second floor. . . ." Jessie pointed toward Andy's window.

Laura's eyes grew wide. "No way!"

"Way," Jessie rebutted, laughing.

"Are you . . . it can't be . . . are you Jessie?"

"How'd you know?"

Laura giggled. "This is so cool. I always wondered who Jessie was and here you are, you just show up! That's *so* cool!"

Jessie laughed with her, but her curiosity was bursting at the seams.

"It's in my room," Laura explained. "My closet. It's carved in the wood, you know, behind the door."

"What is?"

"Your name."

Jessie had forgotten how she and Andy had secretly carved their names with his pocketknife. Mrs. McCormick had not been pleased, mostly because Jessie had been in Andy's room. And then she heard the flagpole clanging.

"Was he your boyfriend or something?"

"No." Again, the ringing of the flagpole. "We were only twelve or so."

"Well . . . I'm only ten," Laura said again, as if twelve were plenty old.

"Don't you hear that?" Jessie asked.

"Sure, that's the flagpole at my school. Noisy, isn't it?"

Jessie nodded. "That's where I used to wait for him. Then we'd walk home after school together."

Laura smiled slyly, "You liked him, didn't you?"

"How old are you again?"

"I told you already," Laura said, kneeling to help rub Molly. "I like Robby," she whispered.

"Robby, huh? Does he like you back?"

"I don't know," Laura said, shrugging. "Sometimes, he acts weird around me, like yesterday when he stole my chocolate chip cookie and I had to chase him around the lunchroom to get it back."

"Annoying, huh?"

"He can be *so* annoying," Laura said.

"He likes you," Jessie announced with a grin.

Laura brightened. "You think?"

"*I know.*" She paused. "But you're way too young to have a boyfriend. You need to wait . . . twenty years or so."

Laura made a face. "Twenty years? I'll be . . ." She concentrated hard. "I'll be . . ."

"You'll be old enough to pick out a really nice boy who won't break your heart."

"All the cute ones'll be taken by then."

"Good point."

"I like ghost stories," Laura admitted suddenly, as if explaining her fascination with the house.

"Maybe you shouldn't read so many of them, sweetie."

"Maybe *you're* a ghost!" Laura exclaimed. "I mean, for all I know, you died and you've come back to haunt your old house."

Jessie winced. "So I'm dead now?"

"And you wouldn't even know it," Laura replied matter-of-factly, as if offering common knowledge. "And maybe that's why Molly likes you, because dogs can see ghosts, you know. And ghosts come back to their favorite places. Maybe next time I'll see you at the flagpole."

"Why?"

"Because you said you waited there a lot. Maybe that's why you *really* came back. You know, to keep waiting there . . . for Andy. That's what a ghost does; it keeps doing the things it used to do when it was alive."

"Sweetie . . ." Jessie began. Laura had taken this ghost idea way too far.

"I know, I know," Laura said, shrugging. "Mom says I'm mental."

Jessie reached out and touched Laura's shoulder gently, putting as much comfort as she could into the small gesture. "Does that feel like a ghost?"

Laura met Jessie's eyes, and her own eyes glistened for a moment. She shook her head. "No . . ."

Jessie heard the sound of Andy's screen door, and then a woman's voice. Even Molly flinched.

"Laura, get over here—now!"

Jessie removed her hand, and Laura looked terrified. She studied Jessie and then lowered her voice to a whisper. "Mom doesn't like me talking to strangers."

She pulled at Molly's collar, and the dog scrambled reluctantly to her feet. When Laura got to her concrete steps, she turned and waved. Jessie stood to her feet and smiled reassuringly, but Laura's mother only glared back.

"Molly got out," Laura explained, climbing the steps.

Her mother swatted her backside. "You didn't finish the kitchen. Get in there, young lady. How many times have I—"

"Aw, Mom—"

"—told you, Laura—"

The screen door slammed behind them, but suddenly Laura popped out again.

"Laura!" her mother yelled from within the house.

Laura squinted as if Jessie might have suddenly disappeared. Then she brightened and waved again. Jessie waved back, trying to appear very solid. The little girl's smile increased and then an arm, like a hook in a melodramatic vaudeville stage show, yanked her back into the house.

Jessie sighed and returned to her car. She stared back at the house, the home of her childhood, apparently just as solid but un-inhabited. It made no sense. But she was happy with her renewed sense of perspective, and meeting Laura had snapped her out of her self-pity.

She started the ignition, the car keys swinging. A strange notion occurred to her. She reached down and grasped the keys. *No way,* she thought, then smiled. She turned off the ignition and pondered the possibility.

Twelve years ago she'd placed the only key she owned on the key ring Andy had given her for her birthday. It was impossible to imagine, but she flipped through the keys anyway, one by one—her apartment key, car key, trunk key, storage key . . . and another key she hadn't used for years.

She stared at it, unbelieving. What else could it be? *Yeah, but it's a little freaky,* she thought. *Even for you.* She looked back at the vacant house. It had acquired an almost sinister appearance.

What's the point? Jessie decided.

Checking her watch, she saw that the time had slipped away. Four o'clock. Too late to get back on the road. If she drove north now, she wouldn't make it as far as Cheyenne, and she didn't like the idea of staying in small-town hotels. Denver was her best choice, which gave her time for a quick visit with her old friend. Just now, the idea didn't seem nearly as daunting as it had an hour ago.

Chapter Seven

THE ROCK HOUSE Ice Cream Shoppe had been constructed from red cement and small boulders—like giant peanuts in raspberry ice cream. Attached to the back of the shop was a small addition, displaying antiques and knickknacks. According to the signs, customers could feast on two scoops of delicious ice cream in the shop up front, then peruse an assortment of antique plates, bottles, glasses, and silverware in back. They might even purchase a rustic turn-of-the-century ice-cream maker.

Entering the busy shop, Jessie automatically placed her open hand behind her back, catching the screen door. Instead of banging against the frame, it *twapped* against her hand. Old habits never die.

The aroma of vanilla and cinnamon filled her senses. The black-and-white floor tile, yellowed and scuffed with age, felt hard beneath her white sandals. Directly in front of her, beyond the line of parents and children, a glass-enclosed display offered an assortment of ice-cream flavors. Several high school girls were taking customer orders and ringing up their totals. Behind them was the menu board, advertising chili dogs and hamburgers, apple pie and cinnamon buns, and beyond that the food kitchen. Little had changed.

Jessie nervously swept her gaze past the short hallway leading to the antique room—then to the wall on the right. Dominated from top to bottom by a collage of photos, it was a mosaic of faces. There were pictures of happy families, giggling children, and cranky old gentlemen eating ice cream, fishing by the lake, sitting at picnic benches. All posed for the trusty camera of the town historian, Betty Robinette. Photos of flowers, framed and priced, were intermixed with the other photos.

A thin woman who looked to be about eighty emerged from a back room, wiping her hands on a towel. She wore a green apron tied tightly over a white T-shirt, her white hair confined by a thin mesh netting. She had a tiny nose and chin, and her heart-shaped face seemed shrunken with deep wrinkles. Her pinkish lips were stark against her pale white skin, but her eyes were kind and gentle with a hint of no-nonsense scrutiny. She wore glasses around her neck for close viewing, just as Jessie had remembered.

Betty Robinette delivered a plate of chili and hot dogs to a waiting family, then retreated to the back again. When Jessie's turn at the counter finally came, one of the young girls in matching green aprons took her order. Jessie asked for a single dip of pistachio, then wandered over to the wall of photos, licking her cone.

She recognized many of the faces—neighbors from long ago and classmates who had grown up but apparently never left the sleepy town. After a bit, it occurred to her that she was looking at friendships she might have nurtured, memories she might have made, a past that might have been.

Eventually people began to leave, and just a trickle of customers remained. Jessie was still standing at the wall, lost in the pictures, when she was startled by a familiar voice behind her. "Like my artwork?"

Jessie turned to see Betty Robinette, only a few feet away, her right hand gripping a cane. The woman stood there motionless, looking proud, and then her eyes flickered. She frowned, scrutinizing Jessie's face.

Jessie opened her mouth to introduce herself but stopped. Betty was already smiling broadly. "Well, I'll be. Is that you, Jessie?"

Jessie broke into a smile. "I didn't think—"

"That I'd remember you? Oh, for pete's sake. Stop talking and give me a hug."

Jessie melted into her arms. Her old friend smelled the same but felt much smaller. The Mrs. Robinette she remembered was a towering woman. *People seem bigger when you're a kid,* Jessie realized.

"How's Mr. Robinette?"

"Oh, he got to go a few years back."

"I'm sorry," Jessie whispered.

"Weak heart, you know," she said. "He didn't suffer, thank the Lord."

She held Jessie by the arms, examining her face. "You look wonderful, Jessie. Look at you, all grown up. It's so good to see you. I've been hoping you'd come back."

Jessie suppressed a smile. In spite of her kind manner, Betty was never one for mincing words.

"I'm just passing through," Jessie hedged. "I'm on my way out to Oregon for grad school. Just thought I'd stop by."

"I've been so worried about you. I've called your grandmother for years, but . . ." She hesitated.

Jessie shrugged, knowing that if Betty had kept in touch with her grandmother, she would be aware of the estrangement. It was an awkward moment. Betty glanced away, nodding thoughtfully. She pointed at her wall. "Did you find yourself?"

"You mean I'm still up there?"

Studying the photos near the middle of the wall, Betty placed her glasses on the end of her tiny nose. She crooked her head back, peering downward through the lenses, then tapped a photo of a brown-haired boy and a blond girl straddling bikes. The two held up ice-cream cones like trophies, smiling at the camera.

It really happened, Jessie thought again, feeling terribly honored. *Twelve years later, I'm still there. . . .*

"Remember how you kids used to come by after school?"

Jessie nodded, lost in the picture. It was like a trigger sparking more long-forgotten memories. Or a line of dominoes, each memory falling into the next.

"You loved bubble-gum ice cream. Can't give the stuff away now, but you practically lived on it."

Jessie laughed. "We did get sick of it."

Betty pointed to the round wooden table by the window. "You two would sit right over there and do your homework together. Your hair was so blond, I called you my little cherub."

Jessie gave Betty a humorous frown. "I disliked that name intensely."

Betty chuckled. "As I recall, Andy disliked math. But he was a dimple-cheeked charmer, wasn't he? Got Bs instead of Ds 'cause of you."

Jessie shrugged, giving a subtle nod. "I was glad to help."

"We used to joke about you two. The whole town did, you know."

"The whole town?"

Betty laughed again, her eyes dancing. "You and Andy were practically joined at the hip. Drove his mother crazy! Bless her heart."

"She wasn't very fond of me, was she?"

"Well . . . she was a real proper sort, you know. In her book, little boys and girls didn't play together. In the end, it didn't matter what she thought. We all knew you'd get married someday." Betty paused, shaking her head. "Can't even remember what day it is half the time. But some things you just never forget." She sighed, appraising her again.

"I'm so glad to see you," Jessie said suddenly.

Betty beamed. "You look good, sweetie."

"I drove by the house, too," Jessie said. "It seems well kept, but the girl next door says no one lives there now."

"No one has *ever* lived there."

"But why?"

Betty just looked at her as if Jessie should know the answer.

Jessie frowned. "Who owns it?"

"Well . . . honey . . ." She pursed her lips as if trying to find the words.

"My grandmother?"

Betty nodded slightly.

Jessie felt a shudder of anger. "Why would she do that?"

"I think maybe you should ask her that yourself," Betty said with a shrug.

Their eyes met and Jessie forced her features into a pleasant expression, but her anger was boiling. Betty seemed tentative, careful. "I know she's a tough cookie, Jessie. You don't have to tell me that, but—" she stopped and her eyes lingered on Jessie's face— "people change. Sometimes they do anyway."

Jessie bit her lip and changed the subject. "How long did Andy stay?"

Betty frowned. "I think they moved to Denver the following summer." She tapped her cane against the tile. "He came back, though. My word, he's tall now. Gave me a big hug. Nearly crushed my feeble bones." Betty's eyes twinkled and she sighed. She opened her mouth and then hesitated. There was more to the story.

Jessie nodded. "It's okay."

Betty's eyes dimmed, her sense of loyalty showing through. "Had a girl with him—a TV preacher's daughter . . . something like that. Elizabeth something. Engaged to be married. My word, he graduated with a degree in business. Now that I think of it, I can't imagine him handling the math without you, but I guess he did."

Jessie felt a sinking feeling in her stomach, and for the moment it overshadowed the growing rage. Betty appeared apologetic again, unsure of what to say. She paused and then her voice became distant, as if she were conjuring memories from a rarely visited mental storehouse. "He asked about you."

Andy remembered me?

"I told him you were away at college somewhere. That's all I knew."

"I'm sorry to be so—"

"Don't you dare be sorry," Betty interrupted. "We all worried for you, sweetie . . . and . . ." Her voice trailed off and she glanced at the wall, seemingly overcome with emotion.

Jessie felt guilty, remembering that Betty had always carried more than her share of others' burdens.

"Everything's okay now," Jessie whispered, more to sound reassuring than truthful. She put her hand on her dear friend's arm. Why had she waited so long to make contact? Even a simple phone call would have sufficed. "I missed you," Jessie whispered, about to say she was sorry again, but catching herself.

Betty nodded confident reassurance, her eyes closing as she did so, and she crept closer to Jessie, embracing her in another hug.

They sat and talked for another hour, trading history and current life. Jessie kept staring at the dear woman, now old and feeble, who had practically rescued her family during her mother's illness. She had delivered groceries and covered dishes. She had mended their clothes. And she never let Jessie pay for her own ice cream.

Jessie smiled and reminded her dear friend of the memory. Betty put her hand on her chest and clucked.

"You took *Andy's* money!" Jessie kidded. "It used to make me so mad!" She reached over and covered Betty's hand. "But thank you . . . twelve years too late."

Betty merely waved it off. But their eyes met and the old rapport passed between them. "So where are you headed next?"

Good question, Jessie thought, taking a deep breath. Her blood boiled as she thought of her grandmother again, and in the space of a moment, her plans had changed. Time to do what she should have done years ago.

Chapter Eight

DORIS CRENSHAW . . .

Jessie should have known. Who else could afford to buy the house and then display it like a trophy—or the spoils of a victory? Who else wanted to own everything that had once belonged to her father? And her mother? And to her? None other than the woman who'd kidnapped her mother. And caused her father's death. The woman Jessie swore she would never see again.

People don't change, Jessie thought, remembering Betty's comment. Betty was still her old sweet self—Pollyanna, to be sure, but that was forgivable, and frankly refreshing. But no less naïve.

No, Jessie thought again. *People don't change. They only become exaggerated versions of their younger selves. They finish the journey they began. If they were insensitive and tactless in youth, they become mean and twisted in old age.*

She could only imagine what had become of her grandmother. Even now, at twenty-four, her childhood imagination flew away with her, landing squarely on the image of none other than the wicked witch. Jessie squeezed the steering wheel. It wasn't her grandmother's house. It was *their* house. Her father had restored it, and her mother had painstakingly made it a home. Jessie had seen the before-and-after pictures. Sure, it wasn't a castle. And it wasn't the Broadmoor, obviously. But it was theirs. Well, theirs *and* the bank's. Jessie's parents had had little money and owed the bank a great deal for both the house and the gas station. Jessie had always assumed that after her parents' deaths, the house had surely been sold and any profits used to pay off debts. But she had never imagined her grandmother as the buyer. Doris Crenshaw didn't even *like* the house. Jessie couldn't remember but a handful of visits by her grandmother. How dare she take the house! Wasn't taking her mother away enough?

Jessie's rage only deepened. As much as she despised her grandmother, she had questions and she wanted answers.

Barge right in there, eh? Begin a machine-gun fire of insinuations and accusations? Hi, Grandma, haven't seen you in years. Thought I would drop by and yell a bit. Ratta-tat-tat!

No. She would start slowly. Give her grandmother a chance to answer. Then she'd start firing away.

Jessie settled into the drive south, having nearly convinced herself of her reasons, ignoring the underlying feeling that her motives were more complicated.

Before she'd left the ice-cream shop, she had made a promise for dinner the following night, which pushed her trip west back another day or two. As they were saying good-bye, Betty had pointed to a yellowed photo a couple of photos above the one of Jessie and Andy. Jessie had been aware of crossing her arms, as if defending herself.

A smiling blond woman leaned against the Russian olive near Jessie's bedroom window. Mom was wearing a light blue sweater and a navy blue skirt. Her skin was milky smooth, her eyes soft, compassionate and playful. Seeing the picture only fueled Jessie's sense of loss . . . and her anger toward the person responsible for it.

Eyes focused now on the road, she felt her throat close again. She blinked furiously.

. . . "She was so pretty," Betty had said as she and Jessie examined that particular photo on the wall. "She and your dad used to take walks around the lake. They'd stop by the shop, holding hands, Frank's face just beaming! Olivia would be holding you in her arms, back when you were a tiny thing. Frank absolutely adored your mother."

Pain emanated from Betty's eyes. She seemed to study Jessie and then smiled proudly. "You look *just* like her, you know."

"Thank you," Jessie replied, struggling to maintain her composure.

Unexpectedly, Betty said the strangest thing, "Looking so much like her, it must feel as if she's always with you somehow. . . ."

Now Jessie pondered the comment again as she drove. What a weird thing to say. Couldn't anyone say that about one's parents? But as far as resembling her mother, her appearance was where it ended. Her mother was a saint and everyone knew it. Jessie, however, had her father's temperament. *"Thank heavens she looks like her mother,"* she'd once heard a cousin remark during a family gathering when he didn't think Jessie was within earshot. He finished with, *"Because she sulks just like her father,"* and then laughed at his little joke. She was ten or so at the time but old enough to get it. She'd stormed off, effectively proving his point.

Jessie passed the Air Force Academy to the west of I-25, noting the expansive growth of neighborhoods on the opposite side. She glanced at her cell phone on the passenger seat, haunted by the once-recurring habit of Brandon's daily call, reminding herself again that they weren't going to Oregon together.

"It'll take a while to sink in," Darlene had told her.

I'm a pro at this stuff, Jessie thought.

She wished she could phone her mother. No matter the triumph or tragedy throughout her life, that was always the first thought. After dinner with Brandon she would have cried on her mom's shoulder and Mom would have understood, just as she always did.

Every turning point in life was another reminder that her mom was gone.

As a teenager she'd had persistent dreams of Mom tucking her in . . . walking along the beach . . . swinging at the park. While they were the happiest dreams, they were also the most painful upon awakening. For years it seemed as if Mom had never died. Jessie often awakened breathless, panicked, her grief renewed again.

To think she'd run away from her grandmother's house five times, each time fighting "extradition" back to her grandmother's care. She was finally made a ward of the state for her own well-being. She spent the remainder of her adolescent years in one foster home after another, all with predictable results.

Sometimes her foster parents were only interested in the monthly paycheck, which suited Jessie fine because they were the types who would leave her alone. Other times, her guardians seemed interested in getting to know her, and it didn't take Jessie long to disabuse them of that foolish notion. And the idea of getting too attached to her foster parents' "real" children was out of the question. She would go to school, then come home and hide in her room, doing her homework or reading a novel.

When not in school or in her room, she spent time at some therapist's office, court-ordered to "assist her in emotional healing." They'd all insisted on dredging up her childhood, as if by remembering the details she might finally forget. *What a strange idea,* she'd thought at the time. Rarely did she care to divulge personal details of her life with her mother, which would have been a betrayal. What they had together was so sacred, so wonderful, that she refused to submit her memories to their impersonal dissection.

On paper she must have appeared to be a conundrum. Even the therapists contradicted one another, some declaring her of sound mind, albeit a little rattled, others pronouncing her scarred and damaged for life. By the time Jessie was sixteen and pursuing legal emancipation, her grandmother was still calling the shots from afar. Eventually she summoned the big guns as a last-ditch effort.

. . . Michael Roeske, a Harvard-educated Freudian, was a large man with a full gray-flecked beard, slicked-back brown hair, and the obligatory gold-rimmed spectacles. He had reminded her of Orson Welles as she'd once seen him on a movie poster advertising the old classic *Citizen Kane,* and she'd told him so. He seemed delighted with the comparison.

His office was lavishly furnished with dark wood, and the carpet reminded her of a giant argyle sock. The walls were covered with something resembling crushed straw, as if made flat by extensive ironing. The windows were semiopaque with a lacy winter frost, and the trees just outside, where people walked freely in the parking lot, were glazed with melting ice, the sun reflecting off a sparkling world of post-Christmas white.

In spite of his austere appearance, he was a kind man. Friendly and engaging. She actually enjoyed the visits, which seemed more like conspiratorial meetings against her grandmother than counseling sessions. In later years, she realized the brilliance of his technique.

"I'm impressed with your unique sense of self-equilibrium," he'd once told her. "Your relationship with your mother was simply marvelous; I wish I could have met her."

True to his Freudian roots, he was particularly interested in her dreams.

"They're not *bad* dreams," Jessie told him.

"But your mother comes to you. No?"

"She tucks me in at night, takes me to the park, that sort of thing."

"Very natural," he stated. "They'll fade in time."

I hope not, she thought.

"Do you hate your grandmother?"

"Have you *met* my grandmother?"

"Yes," he replied. "And she does seem . . . a difficult woman."

Jessie was surprised he would admit this.

"She wants to have a relationship with you," he said somewhat tentatively.

"I can't."

"Perhaps one day?"

Jessie only shrugged.

"She may not have had bad motives for what she did," Dr. Roeske said, referring to the lawsuit that had led to the unexpected court order consigning her mother to a mental institution, instead of a care center, as her grandmother had insisted. Essentially, Olivia became a ward of the state.

"Doesn't matter," she said. "As far as I'm concerned she stole my mother."

Roeske set down his ever-present dark blue and gold-scripted coffee cup. "But hating your grandmother won't bring your mother back."

"I don't hate her," she said. "I just can't stand to be around her."

"Your memories are like a festering wound," he told her. "Inflamed and infected. You can't just put on a Band-Aid and expect it to heal. Now that you're older, you can deal with all this. . . ."

She wasn't interested. Fortunately, a few months after her seventeenth birthday, her emancipation was complete and she was free to conduct her life as she wished. In spite of mixed feelings, she canceled her therapy sessions, got a part-time job, made arrangements to rent a room in a school friend's house, and finished high school. Things settled down after that and her grandmother finally let go.

It was during her junior year in college that Jessie read of Roeske's death. He'd died of a heart attack on a Sunday morning in the middle of winter while retrieving his Sunday paper. Jessie had wept for him. Until that moment she hadn't realized her affection for this dear grandfatherly man. Unlike her foster parents, Roeske had broken through, becoming almost a surrogate parent. In fact, her counseling sessions with him had made such a profound impression she nearly changed her career decision.

To fulfill a class requirement, her roommate, Darlene, had signed up to answer calls for a suicide hotline. Every Tuesday and Thursday evening Darlene was on call, her phone linked to the local suicide prevention agency. It was a Tuesday in January when Darlene begged Jessie to take her place. She had mistakenly agreed to a midweek date, forgetting the previous obligation.

"Are you kidding?" Jessie exclaimed. "I wouldn't know what to say."

"It's easy," Darlene said, explaining the basic procedure for talking someone out of suicide. Then she left Jessie alone sweating in her dorm room, hoping no one would find this Tuesday a particularly depressing day.

Sure enough, when Jessie received a call from a despairing woman named Brenda, she surprised herself and rose to the occasion. Years of her own therapy had given her the right phrases to articulate. By the time she hung up, she had managed to pull Brenda out of her deep turmoil.

Several weeks later, Jessie scheduled an appointment with her adviser.

. . . "How do I get a master's in counseling?" Jessie had asked.

The college counselor had smiled curiously as if to say, *That's a good one, Jess.*

"I'm serious."

Another hesitation. "We don't offer it. But somewhere else? Maybe another year of undergraduate studies. Two years of postgraduate. Give or take. Come to think of it, since you're interested in Oregon, I'm sure the University of Portland offers something comparable—perhaps psychology?"

But her adviser's initial reaction continued to bother her. *It's obvious to everyone except me,* she finally realized, and Brandon probably would have told her, *"Work out your own problems first before you destroy someone else's life."*

Jessie dropped the idea. Besides, wasn't she more at home in the world of business anyway, with its cold, hard facts and solid statistics? . . .

Sighing again, she rolled down the window. Her evening headache was putting in an early appearance. Although she'd packed some aspirin in her overnight case, it was buried beneath a box of books.

She glanced at the cell phone again and considered calling first. Her grandmother had never been one for impromptu visits. Jessie was sure her life was planned to the minute, as if living by a schedule etched in stone. Just showing up on the doorstep was bound to infuriate her, and it would virtually guarantee an unproductive visit.

I'm not pussyfooting around her anymore, Jessie thought, leaving the cell on the passenger seat.

Chapter Nine

THE PANELED WALLS were in dark mahogany. The oversized desk, also mahogany, dominated the small room. The carpet, a tightly woven beige, had been installed in 1965. Located toward the back of her colonial home, her deceased husband's office looked out to the backyard, which was surrounded by tall privacy fences, with grass the greenest plush possible in arid Colorado. And flowers *everywhere*—marigolds, petunias, fuchsia—along the fence, lining the house, surrounding the gazebo.

From the hidden speakers—one of handyman Bill's miracle projects—an orchestral version of Grieg's *Holberg Suite* resonated throughout the house. For years she'd taught her students the suite from Liszt's piano transcription, but nothing could compare to the original orchestral score—an amazing piece, both triumphal and heartbreaking.

Just outside, her handyman was putting the finishing touches on a white paint job to the gazebo, centered in the middle of her generous yard.

. . . "As Victorian as they come," he'd observed skeptically the day he'd shown her the plans.

"Wonderful," she replied.

"Doris, I may be out of order but—"

"Never stopped you before."

"Frankly, you don't seem the gazebo type."

"Oh, Bill. Just exactly what *is* the gazebo type?"

He paused. "The type of person who sits and *thinks*."

She nearly came uncorked. "Sometimes you're like a porcupine in a balloon shop. So now you're calling me stupid?"

"I'm calling you *busy*."

"Build it, Bill."

"Yes, ma'am." . . .

Doris watched the hunched-over cowboy, and he seemed to sense her eyes on his back. He turned and smiled, waving his white paintbrush, then thumbed proudly toward his work and made a humorous grimace.

She shook her head, recalling Bill's argument against painting the gazebo. *"Aw, Dory, why would you want to hide that natural wood?"*

"Paint it white and don't call me Dory."

"How 'bout I stain it redwood and see what you think?"

"White."

"How 'bout I just seal it, leave the wood natural, and you see what you think?"

"No."

"How 'bout a white stain?"

"No."

"Yes, ma'am."

And then she added, *"While you're at it, put a swing in it."*

"Oh boy," he said to himself as he started walking away. *"Maybe the squirrels will like it."*

"Oh, and Bill?"

He turned, his features pained. *"Yes, Dory."*

"Paint the swing white, too."

Bill appeared at the doorway, leaning against the threshold and crossing one leg over the other. She finished licking an envelope. "Gazebo looks good."

"Whadd'ya say we take it for a spin?"

"I'm too busy."

He smiled. "The paint is dry inside, the weather is cool, and the swing is dying for affirmation. It told me so."

"How 'bout later?"

He chuckled, whispering under his breath, "How 'bout never," and headed for the kitchen so Doris could answer the ringing phone in privacy.

It was Betty Robinette. "It's sixty-seven degrees up here, Doris."

Although they rarely conversed more than two or three times a year, it had become a ritual to compare Colorado Springs weather with Palmer Lake temps, twenty miles to the north.

"Bill?" Doris called across the family room. "What's the temperature?"

"Seventy-five," Bill called from the kitchen, where he was throwing something together for dinner. Years ago, he'd hung a thermometer just outside the window.

"Isn't that something? Betty voiced. "Nearly ten degrees different."

"How's the garden?" Doris asked, referring not to Betty's but to Mrs. Browning's.

"It's still the seventh wonder of Colorado."

"I need to send Bill up. He could learn a thing or two from that woman."

"I heard that," Bill called in a matter-of-fact voice from across the house.

"You know how hard it is to get good help, Betty."

Betty chuckled.

"Just as hard as it is to get good employment," he yelled back.

They made more small talk until Betty seemed to hesitate and the call began to take a different turn. "I debated whether to call you, Dory. . . ."

Another moment of silence as Doris began putting it all together. She had suspected this wasn't just a social call. It had something to do with the house in Palmer Lake . . . or . . . a stray thought nudged her: something about Jessica. Doris just assumed that her granddaughter would never call her, but she'd hoped that perhaps one day Jessica might contact Betty. Doris felt her spirits sink. More than a decade had passed since Jessica had lived with Doris, and only one foster family had taken the time to forward pictures. The most recent ones she had were of Jessie at age fourteen, and Doris still carried the pictures in her purse.

She ventured into the dark, navigating by nervous intuition. "How is she, Betty?"

Betty sighed audibly, and Doris felt sorry for placing her friend in such a position.

"She seems fine," Betty replied, but the undertow in her voice told Doris more than the words themselves. Doris opened her mouth but didn't know what to ask or say next. She waited instead. Betty filled the silence. "She looks just like Olivia. She's a beautiful young woman."

Doris felt a mixture of pride and regret.

"Carries herself so well. Polite. Smart as a whip. You'd be proud."

Doris ventured again—afraid to ask but afraid not to. "Did she say anything?"

"No, but I encouraged her to call you. We're going to have dinner tomorrow."

So she's still around, Doris thought.

"I have her cell number, but—"

"No, you mustn't," Doris interrupted. "No point in her being angry with both of us."

Another uncomfortable silence. "I *will* tell her I spoke with you," Betty offered. "Is there something that—"

"Don't even tell her that," Doris insisted. "Perhaps you two can stay in touch if you leave my name out of it."

Bill was already back, leaning against the doorway. When Doris hung up, he gave her one of his annoying how-can-I-help-you looks. "What was that all about?"

"Is any part of my life private anymore?"

He cleared his throat, casting his eyes downward, but she could see right through his wounded-puppy act.

"Jessie's in the area," she finally relayed.

He brightened. "Shall I put on the dog?"

"Oh, for pete's sake, Bill. She won't be visiting us."

"Give her a call, then. Invite her."

"Don't have her number."

"Call Information or something. Call that roommate gal of hers."

"Bill, stop it."

He glanced at his watch. "I'm gonna check the guest room. Make sure the toilet's working—"

"Don't bother—"

"Make sure Maria changed the sheets, maybe give it a little mopping while I'm at it, maybe even rip those pompous photos off the wall—"

"Do you ever pay attention?"

He smiled a toothy grin. "Didn't you ever see that baseball film?"

"Bill, please."

He seemed lost in thought. "If you build it, they'll come? *Field of Dreams*, that's it—"

"Oh, for pete's sake."

His eyes twinkled. "If we fix it up, who knows what might happen?"

Doris shook her head to an empty room. Bill was already gone.

◆　◆　◆　◆　◆

Jessie parked her car at the curb and turned off the radio. Bordered by a wrought-iron fence and fronted by a circular driveway, her grandmother's large colonial home appeared to be a fortress. When she was six or seven, she'd asked her father why her grandmother lived in a mansion. He'd frowned and assured her that although the house was very big, it wasn't a mansion.

Maybe not, Jessie thought presently. But it sure looked like one, complete with dormers, white pillars, black shutters, and a maroon multipaneled front door. She still saw the house through the eyes of her youth—the young girl who'd kept running away until the authorities gave her what she wanted—and it looked as cold and austere as the day she'd slipped away for the final time. Unapproachable. Designed to dishearten and defray warmth. Or *impress,* depending on your social status.

She spotted the second-story window, which seemed rather high from this distance. Perhaps not so high if you're desperate—as she had been. She checked the time. Nearly seven. The sun was already disappearing behind the mountains, creating an early twilight. She flicked on the radio again, determined to lighten her darkening mood, and she realized she was slowly losing a grip on her angry resolve.

◆ ◆ ◆ ◆ ◆

Andy's cell phone twittered.

It was Chris. "Where were you?"

"Say what?"

"I thought you'd be at your folks'."

"Missed me by minutes."

"I accidentally grabbed your weight-lifting gloves at the gym."

"It can wait till—" Andy paused—"next week sometime."

Chris seemed disappointed. "Skipping church?"

"I don't know, maybe."

"Well . . . I just wanted to warn you."

Warn me? Andy shuddered. *Warn me about what?* His mind instantly jumped to his mother. *Oh no. What did Chris say to Mom?*

"Still there?" Chris asked.

Andy groaned inwardly. What could be so bad? Maybe Chris told Mom that Andy hadn't attended church in a while. That *would* be bad. Wait a minute. Debbie was probably with him. His mother would have invited them in. *I'm so sorry; Andy just left, but would you two like some pumpkin pie?* Andy cringed. Debbie had entered into the inner sanctum of his parents' house. His mother's kitchen. The den of inquisition.

Andy broke the silence. "Is this what I think it is?"

"I tried to stop her. Honest I did." Chris's voice had taken on a melodramatic tone. "You know how your mother is always—"

"Complaining about my lack of marital prospects. Yeah, I know."

Chris continued, "Well . . . one thing led to another. Debbie mentioned Marilyn's name. Your mother said, 'Who's Marilyn?' Debbie said, 'You mean you don't know?' and the whole thing suddenly leapt out my control. Like a raging fire, I'm telling you, and it was ugly. . . ."

"How much control did you have to begin with?"

"Very little."

"I'm thinking zero."

Someone was beeping through. Andy checked the ID and smiled. He said good-bye to Chris, thanked him for nothing, and took the call.

"Honey . . ."

"Yes, Mom."

"Who's Marilyn?"

Andy swallowed and prepared to speak in a measured tone. "Marilyn? Oh . . . well, she's just a friend from church. Why do you ask?"

"For just a friend, she seems very nice."

Seems nice?

"Mom, you didn't—"

"Didn't what?"

"Call her."

"Oh . . . my." Her voice dripped of innocence. "Was that wrong?"

◆ ◆ ◆ ◆ ◆

Andy's townhouse in Castle Rock was tiny, but it suited him fine. His porch offered a view of the Front Range, but only if you held your head just right and peered through the narrow space between the apartment buildings across the street.

At least life was a bit calmer here. Quieter. Less frenetic. Unfortunately, Castle Rock was growing rapidly. In a matter of years, it would be little more than a suburb of Denver. No matter. He was renting. Perhaps in six months, when his lease expired, he might consider options closer to the mountains, perhaps farther south— Perry Park or Larkspur—something closer to Palmer Lake. Maybe even Palmer Lake itself.

He tossed his keys onto the counter, went to turn on the stereo, then slumped into the couch, replaying the conversation with his mother. He'd come within inches of telling her the full truth. The time to come clean was nearing if not here already, but he wouldn't do that over the phone. Yet he couldn't imagine sitting his parents down and 'fessing up:

"What's wrong, Andy?" his mother would ask with a worried tone.

"Mom. Dad. There's something you don't know about me."

"What is it, son?"

"I'm not really a Christian anymore."

Mom would break into tears, and Dad would attempt damage control. "All Christians struggle with their faith now and then. Even the disciples had difficulty trusting Jesus."

Andy would try to explain himself further. "You don't understand, Dad. . . ."

And no matter what he might say, they *wouldn't* understand. Raised in a conservative home, he'd been taught the Christian way of life at a very young age. Breezing through junior high and high school with his principles intact, he had made an unabashed stand for Christ, yet remained one of the popular kids. Good looks, a confident demeanor, athletic talent—all had undoubtedly greased his social wheels. Struggle was almost unknown to him.

As a freshman in college he'd met the beautiful daughter of a prominent Denver TV evangelist, and they'd dated for several years. When they became engaged, his soon-to-be father-in-law offered him a future job with the ministry.

Andy's downfall probably originated with a certain naïveté and the sense that his faith was invulnerable. As a young man fascinated with apologetics, he had devoured the works of C. S. Lewis, Peter Kreeft, Alvin Plantinga, and William Craig, among others. For the second semester of his junior year, he signed up for what he thought would be a benign history course: The Historical Origins of Christianity. When he discovered the extreme liberal nature of the professor, Andy decided to stay and duke it out, counter fallacy with fact, lies with truth. *I can take him,* Andy had thought.

The professor ate him alive. Dr. Neal raised hundreds of questions in the name of biblical criticism and historical accuracy, questions Andy had never considered before. In spite of digging through his apologetics books for endless hours, looking for answers, his faith began to slowly disintegrate.

"The Bible is a myth," his teacher stated. "A beautiful myth, sure, but a myth all the same. . . . I'll show you the true origins of the Christian faith. . . . Let's discuss the strange differences between the Synoptic Gospels and the Gospel of John. . . . Where did Paul's mentality come from? Well, I'll tell you. . . ."

It was like being attacked with intellectual bombs, each one tearing out another piece of his house of faith. By the end of the semester, Andy was despairing, the historical roots for his faith having been all but destroyed.

Of course, Elizabeth couldn't help but sense his struggle. Finally in a fit of despair, he told her the truth, fearful of her response. As he expected, she was horrified. "Just believe. It's about faith, not about evidence."

But his struggles continued. After a difficult few months, Elizabeth finally broke the engagement. "My father is an evangelist, Andy! He needs a son-in-law to stand by his side without wavering!"

His parents never knew the true reason for the breakup, despite his mother's persistent quizzing over the following months, finding ever new ways to inquire of the romantic demise.

Andy's life floundered in every way but professionally. He graduated from college, found a good job, made good money, and kept up the appearance of going to church. He found his own church, in fact—a decision that disappointed his parents but isolated him from his mother's prying eyes.

But lately, keeping up appearances had begun to wear on him. While he enjoyed the social nature of church attendance, making Christian friends, living a lie was exhausting. Something had to give, especially now that he'd begun to seriously entertain the notion of getting married.

What kind of young woman did he want to marry? No question: an upstanding Christian woman. Thus the dilemma deepened. His overall integrity, in spite of a blazing corner of deceit, prevented him from bringing a sincere Christian woman into his life, and yet he couldn't—not in his wildest imagination—envision himself marrying a nonbeliever.

He'd basically lied to his mother tonight, telling her that Marilyn was not his type.

. . . "What type is that?" she'd asked.

"It's a personality thing," he'd replied.

"You two don't click?" she asked incredulously.

"I can't explain it."

"Maybe Debbie is right. Give her another chance," his mom insisted. She paused. "Andy, we know the truth, you know. You can't hide it from us."

His stomach lurched. "Sorry?"

"Dad and I. We know that you still grieve over Elizabeth. She was a wonderful girl. But you have to move on. Get back into the game. There are more Elizabeths out there."

Andy exhaled deeply. "Mom, I'm over Elizabeth."

"Oh good! Can I invite Marilyn for dinner?"

"No."

"Maybe if you saw her in a family setting, you'd think differently."

"No."

"Andy—"

"No."

On and on for another five minutes or so. He could not imagine any other mother on the planet as relentlessly determined to marry off her only son. Finally their conversation petered out. "May I, at the very least, take a look for myself?" she asked in a final fit of desperation.

What? Invite Marilyn over for tea and crumpets? Devise a strategy together?

"No, Mom."

She chuckled. "You're a stubborn man, Andrew McCormick."

"Perhaps I inherited it?"

"From your father, maybe," Mom clucked. "Everyone knows I'm a pushover."

Chapter Ten

THE FEW MINUTES in front of her grandmother's house was enough to bring Jessie to her senses. She was about to shift into drive, intending to forget the whole thing, when she heard a voice.

"Well, looky here!"

Startled, she noticed an elderly man in a cowboy hat push through the gate, carrying a giant wrench-type thing in his left hand. Had her grandmother sold her *own* house?

The tall, lanky man strolled across the street with a bright smile. Jessie registered the shiny belt buckle, plaid shirt, cowboy shoes, and faded jeans but was still trying to digest his greeting.

She smiled stiffly at the man, her mind racing with stories of malevolent strangers. "I'm sorry. I was just leaving." She shifted into drive, but just before she depressed the accelerator, she paused. The man puzzled her. When he reached the car, his smile broadened. Silvery hair peeked out from beneath his hat and deep lines surrounded his cheery eyes. Looking like an extra in a cowboy western, he stuck out his free hand almost like a dare.

After eyeing it skeptically—*we're in a public place*, she reminded herself—she shifted quietly back into park. She reached up through the window and shook it. His hand felt like coarse sandpaper, but strong and firm. Her own hand nearly disappeared into the cavern of his burly mitts.

"Pleased to meetcha. Name's Bill. I'm your grandmother's whatchamacallit."

She was taken aback. *My grandmother?* How could this man have recognized her from across the street? No. There was some mistake. A freaky coincidence. He was looking for someone else.

"We've been expecting ya."

"Listen, there's been some—"

"You're Jessica, right?"

"Oh . . ." Jessie said, confused again. Then suddenly, she put it all together. Betty must have called. "I'm sorry . . . who are you?"

"I work for your grandmother—gardener, handyman, chauffeur, tree trimmer, cook, and bottle washer. Actually, I don't do much bottle washing, but I suppose I would if she asked me."

Jessie smiled nervously.

"You plan on coming in?"

"I was just . . . passing by."

"Why don'tcha see what it looks like on the inside? Dip your toe in, check the temp. Frankly, water runs hot or cold most of the time—wouldn't mind something in between on occasion—but I guess I've gotten used to it!" Bill laughed and then his face turned oddly crimson.

Jessie resisted the urge to frown, but her mouth must have dropped open. What was he talking about? She glanced at the giant wrench. *The plumbing?* "I think I should go. . . ."

Bill, the whatchamacallit, crouched, setting the tool on the ground, and removed his hat. He suddenly seemed sober. "Listen, Jessie—if I may call you that—I meander when I'm nervous. And I can say the darnedest things when I'm trying to . . . uh . . . it's just that . . . well, I'd—we'd—be delighted if you might see fit to actually come inside."

He put the hat back on, nodded, and looked away, seemingly embarrassed. She stared at him for a moment. In spite of his touching little speech, going inside was out of the question, but she could only imagine what her grandmother might say to this Bill person later: *"Are you kidding? She just left?"*

"I can't," she said, feeling stupid. "I thought I could."

Bill shifted his weight, his eyes betraying disappointment. "Would you like me to tell her you was here?"

Jessie shook her head. "Please don't."

Another quick nod. "Then I won't." He stood up and began backing away. "It was my pleasure indeed to have met you. Short as it was. From what your grandmother has said, I consider it an honor." He smiled again, dipped his hat, and headed back toward the gate.

She watched him walk away, his gait steady and confident. What did he mean? *"What your grandmother has said."* She heard the scrape of iron as he opened the gate, then saw him turn back and wave at her. Her own emotions were an enigma to her. Was she scared? Still angry? Curious? They all coalesced into an in-determinate lump of indecision.

"Bill?" she whispered, worried that he might actually hear her and surprised when he did.

Her next question was as nonsensical as driving by and then leaving. As foolish as meeting her grandmother's handyman and practically pouring out her heart. But it just came out. "Do you like George Strait?"

Jessie cringed, squeezing her eyes shut for a moment. *What a stupid question.*

Bill was like a dog wagging his tail. He approached the car again, all smiles. "Well, as far as I'm concerned, he's the king of our day, Miss Jessie. Never did fancy this newcomer, what's-his-name . . ."

She thought a moment. "Garth Brooks?"

Bill laughed. "Hit the nail on the head. A little fancy for my blood."

Jessie forced a smile. She glanced from Bill to the house again. *What about this picture doesn't fit?*

"But we know the real king, don't we," he said, winking. It felt like a secret handshake.

"The man in black."

Bill smiled reverently, almost proudly, and gave another curt nod. He thumbed toward the house. "And I'm sure that place must look like the ring of fire itself."

Jessie broke into a grin in spite of herself, and a strange sense of relief fell over her. She hadn't come for a social visit. She'd come to confront her grandmother. But now that she was here, something else tugged at her.

Another moment passed. Bill's mouth was working in a nervous fashion, but his eyes seemed sincere. "Between you and me, Jessie girl, nothing's going to happen to you, okay? I know what you're thinking, and I don't blame you one teeny-weeny bit. You go in there with me and the moment she steps out of line, she's going to have me to contend with, okay? I can roar like a lion if I need to, but I really think you'll want to stay once you try it on for size. Like I said, the water runs hot or cold most of the time, but once you get in, the swimming ain't so bad."

Jessie nodded and pushed the car door partly open. "May I park it here?"

He looked ecstatic. "You can park it anywhere you want. Do you have a suitcase?"

"Oh, Bill—"

He raised his hands in a mock defense. "Say no more. We'll take it slow. You decide later."

Jessie closed the door and for the first time wondered about her appearance, strangely worried about making a good impression. *Why?*

Bill made small talk as they walked, pointing out the various flowers he'd planted, talking as if they'd known each other a lifetime.

When they arrived at the door he rang the bell and winked at her. "She'll want to show you everything the moment you set foot inside. She's got an order to her madness, or should I say, a little madness to her order. Either way, I may have to catch her fall when she sees you."

A few moments passed, long enough for Jessie to wonder if she was crazy. A thin elderly woman in a brown wool skirt and a light tan blouse answered the door. Her immaculately styled gray-blond hair contrasted with her light brown penetrating eyes. Her pleasant expression disappeared, and her eyes widened.

She turned to Bill, and he nodded proudly. "Spittin' image."

"Jessica?" Doris seemed to recover and held out her arms, and for a brief moment, Jessie wasn't sure what to do. The two hugged quickly and uncomfortably. Her grandmother smelled of the kind of perfume that costs a fortune. Jessie's mind flipped through images of the past, trying to reconcile the reality of the woman who stood before her. Like Betty Robinette, her grandmother seemed much smaller than Jessie had imagined. The word *frail* crossed her mind.

Doris held on to Jessie's arms and studied her face. She shook her head, as if amazed, or was it chagrined? "You're so thin," she finally said.

Jessie forced a smile. "I'm not a chubby little cubby anymore."

"No, I should say not."

Bill broke in. "Thin is *power*. Just look at all those paper-clip-thin New Yahk models."

Doris gave him a disapproving glance. "Bill, most of those emaciated girls are on drugs." She poked a thumb toward him. "Don't you mind Bill. He's still finding his way off the ranch. Hope he didn't frighten you out there. I bet he threatened to lasso you."

Jessie chuckled nervously. *Close.* They stepped through the portico, beneath a narrow second-story balcony, and in through the double doors. Immediately, Jessie was reminded of the movie *Gone With the Wind* and Clark Gable's famous utterance: *"Frankly, my dear . . ."* She also remembered feeling rather witty one night when at the age of seven she'd asked her grandmother if Rhett Butler might be persuaded to make an entrance. Her grandmother had tartly replied, *"Honey, you're thinking of a* southern *colonial home. World of difference, you know."*

"Oh yeah, of course," little Jessie had said.

The entryway was ridiculously spacious but smaller than she'd remembered. The vast mahogany floor greeted spindled double staircases, one on each side of the large room. In a magnificent sweep they curved upward, joining at the second-floor balcony, overlooking both the entryway and the grand room below.

This is crazy, she thought again. *Why did I come here?*

"Have you eaten?" Grandmother asked.

The memories were like dominoes again. She was eleven. Her grandmother had stopped by the Rock House Ice Cream Shoppe, for some reason Jessie couldn't remember now. Jessie and Andy were slurping on bubble-gum ice cream. Grandmother gave a fierce look of disapproval. *"Oh my, Jess. If you want your mother's figure, you can't eat Mrs. Robinette's ice cream."* Already self-conscious about her weight, she'd nearly died of embarrassment.

Jessie glanced at Bill. His eyes twinkled and he nodded again.

They were staring at her. Waiting. The question registered. "Oh no. I haven't eaten yet. But please don't—"

"Join us," Bill interjected. "We're gonna dine out with the common folk tonight."

"Bill, for pete's sake."

Jessie stammered. "Oh, I didn't mean to impose. . . ." *Sure you did, Jessie. You intended to be quite the imposition, as a matter of fact.*

She could barely catch her breath. Only a minute ago she was waiting in the car across the street and now . . . "We'll see the house later," her grandmother explained while Bill retrieved the car—a Lincoln Town Car, it turned out, complete with "bells and whistles and a few party kazoos," he said before leaving, and Jessie noticed the warning smile he gave her grandmother. "Behave, now. I'll be right back." Grandmother had clearly bristled at his remark.

As they waited for him to pull out of the garage, the moment was as awkward as any Jessie had ever experienced. Her grandmother made pointless small talk.

Once they were situated inside the plush interior with leather seats, they headed down Lake Avenue, the wide and grand street Jessie had traveled on the way to the house. Sitting in the backseat, she felt safer, removed from her grandmother's direct observation.

Her grandmother handled the conversation as if they'd never lost touch. She talked about growing fuchsia in the garden and her failed effort at blue hydrangeas, an apparent attempt to mimic the oceanfront beauty of her vacation home in Groton, Connecticut.

Jessie tried to pay attention, but her mind was spinning. She felt overwhelmed, unable to sort things out on the fly. *I'm making this up as I go,* she consoled herself.

Bill chimed in. "I was misting those bushes three times a day."

"And I'm up for trying again."

"I'll build you a greenhouse."

"I don't *want* a greenhouse."

In the course of the next few minutes, Jessie discovered that her grandmother spent two months out of every year in New England, daring the humid weather to play havoc with her arthritis. Eventually, the climate won out again, forcing her to yield to Colorado long before she was ready. She kept in close touch with a dozen friends in southeastern Connecticut, friendships made thirty years back, because, as she put it, "Friends from the East are friends for life."

The memories came back to Jessie like a thousand pinpricks. She felt like she was sinking as she continued wrestling with a mixture of emotions. She kicked herself again and again, wishing she had reconsidered. *"Sorry, Bill, thanks for the invite, but I have to be going. . . ."*

Bill motioned toward his left and playfully taunted Doris. "They got mountains like that in Connecticut?"

Jessie looked out the window. The mountains seemed to loom over them, closer now than when she'd traveled down I-25—almost menacing.

"The mountains are overrated, Bill," her grandmother replied with a tone of finality.

"Well . . . maybe that's why everyone's moving *here*," Bill said, chuckling. Jessie held her breath, expecting a sharp-tongued retort, but her grandmother was silent.

They stopped at an all-you-can-eat buffet just off I-25. Bill dropped them off in front of the restaurant and went to park the car. Grandmother prattled on with trivial matters as they waited alone for the second time. Once again, Bill's return was a welcome rescue.

Later, after they were settled by a corner window in the safety of a noisy restaurant, Grandmother accompanied Jessie to the salad bar. More small talk followed. Bill ordered a rare steak, and when it arrived, it was so bloody Jessie had to avoid looking so as not to lose the remainder of her tiny appetite.

"Comes from living on a Montana ranch," her grandmother offered, as if reading Jessie's mind. "Bill could eat the flesh off a living bull."

"But I wouldn't," Bill said, digging in with fork and knife. "They bite back."

Her grandmother leaned over, whispering conspiratorially, but within Bill's hearing, "He's come a long way, but you can't tell from here."

At that comment, Bill dropped his utensils and pulled up his pant leg. Doris winced. "Oh, Bill . . ."

"What do ya see there?" he asked.

"A cowboy boot?" Jessie ventured, grinning.

"The day I give these up is the day I die. I plan to be buried in 'em. You can take me off the ranch, little girl, but you can't take the ranch outta me." He finished with a curt nod.

Jessie smiled as an old Hank Williams Jr. song began playing through her mind: *"You can do anything . . . but oh, don't you step on my cowboy boots." Too many tumbles off the wild bull,* she thought, but Bill's eyes twinkled as if he'd caught his own joke.

"Bill, you're a walking cliché," her grandmother said with a look of embarrassed disgust.

"I'm proud of you, Bill," Jessie said. "Stick to yer guns. Yee ha!" In the next breath, she was surprised at her own behavior and with how easy it had been to develop a solidarity with her grandmother's handyman.

Bill laughed. "I had to give my guns up." He took another bite of rare meat. "They got laws in these civilized parts, you know."

The same pattern unfolded over and over again throughout the meal—Bill's humorous bantering, her grandmother's dismayed responses. Jessie felt as if she'd stepped into the twilight zone.

Chapter Eleven

THEY FINISHED SUPPER a little after nine. By then, Jessie's grandmother had hushed Bill into sociable behavior. A few times, Jessie was tempted to ask, *Why did you buy my parents' house?* but she realized that she would be poking merely at the tip of a very angry iceberg. Besides, the question itself sounded petty and immature.

Mostly, Jessie wondered if she could trust herself to maintain her composure. She imagined her grandmother answering flippantly, *"Well, I own everything else; thought I'd snap that up, too."* In the end, Jessie bit her tongue.

On the way back to the house in the Broadmoor, the elite section of town, Doris launched off on "the problem of city congestion," lamenting the California migration. "They've turned our midsized town into a mini–Los Angeles," she complained. She dropped the mayor's name more than once, implying a few "private discussions."

By now the mountains were variegated purple silhouettes against the backdrop of a star-speckled sky. When conversation died down, Jessie found herself wondering again how it was that she'd left Kansas for Oregon just this morning and ended up here.

When they returned to the stately house, Bill pulled up to the front steps and jumped out, hurrying to open the doors for Jessie and her grandmother. "I don't understand this stucco craze," Grandmother was saying, getting out of the car before Bill could work his way around to assist her. "If I wanted to live in Santa Fe, I'd move there."

Bill closed Jessie's door and whispered, "Calls it Adobe World."

"I've never been," Jessie said absently, already planning her getaway. She looked longingly at her car across the street.

Doris was moving up the sidewalk when she turned back to them. "Telling secrets out of school, are we, Bill?"

He brightened. "Just saying how much you enjoy New Mexico."

Doris made a dismissive grimace and shook her head. "What I need is a *serious* handyman."

"Where do you live, Bill?" Jessie asked, assuming he might be leaving soon for home.

Her grandmother broke in. "I rent him the bonus room on the second floor. You may remember that's where Maria once stayed but we—I—only need her twice a week now."

Bill winked. "Did I forget to tell you I'm also half maid?"

Doris looked like she might swat him with her purse. "I didn't have the patience for him to drive halfway across town. My garden would be brown and wrinkled by the time he arrived."

"I only lived three miles away," Bill said.

"Still . . ."

"You still employ Maria?" Jessie asked, remembering the sweet Hispanic woman who once told enchanting stories of her childhood in Mexico.

Doris nodded. "No point retraining these people. I pay her well. She raised a family on my salary alone. You'll see her tomorrow."

Jessie cringed. *These people* . . . Like a slap in the face, it all came back to her, as if she hadn't heard enough already. In her grandmother's world, not only was it important to travel in the right circles, talk to the right people, and wear the right clothes, but by all means, you never made friends below your class. And those who helped you maintain your appearances were referred to as *these people*. Her mind whirled so fast she almost didn't register the word *tomorrow*.

Bill touched her elbow and winked. "Wanna see the house? Won't take long."

Jessie nodded, still distracted. Her grandmother led them into the family area straight ahead, the kitchen off to the left, the alcove overlooking the backyard. She pointed to various knickknacks and paintings, describing in detail her reasons for each purchase, adding a plethora of insignificant details. It was almost eerie the way Grandmother could carry on so superficially, as if only the surface of life seemed to matter. Jessie wondered how her own mother had emerged from this world unscathed.

As a child Jessie had once watched a *Munsters* rerun, a popular wacky comedy from the sixties. The pretty blond daughter, who'd been saddled with an unusual family, had reminded Jessie of her own mother. In fact, Jessie had once gone so far as to ask her mother if she'd been adopted.

Mom had burst out laughing. *"I don't think so, honey. And I have the birth certificate to prove it. Besides, you're the spitting image of your grandmother."*

Jessie must have looked aghast with the pain of it all, because her mom had pulled her into a comforting and laugh-filled hug. *"Honey, I'm just kidding. I'm so sorry. I didn't think it would scare you so."*

Truth was, Mom seemed oblivious to Doris Crenshaw's faults. Jessie still remembered her mother's patient words to her dad after numerous conflicts: *"She doesn't mean any harm, Frank. We must be patient with her. Just humor her, if you can."*

That was never enough for her father. Nor for her. Yes, it was unbelievable that Mom had grown up within the walls of this house. A true miracle. It all came back in frightening clarity.

They were now back in the foyer. What followed next was more like a military briefing than a tour. Apparently, her grandmother expected her to spend the night. She provided a point-by-point explanation of all the amenities, obviously a speech she had recited many times before. Her heels clicked against the wood floor as she explained the breakfast routine, the maid schedule, the locations of the various rooms.

Bill fidgeted while Grandmother prattled on. "Doris . . ."

The woman continued, seeming not to hear.

"Doris . . ."

"Bill, what?"

"Jessie has not been properly invited to stay."

"Oh . . . well. But you are staying, aren't you?" She looked from Jessie over to Bill again, her manner suddenly hesitant and perplexed.

"Do you think she *assumed* she could stay?" Bill said rather meekly.

"Oh, well . . . no . . ."

Bill turned to Jessie, his eyes twinkling again. "Ms. Lehman, we'd love to have the pleasure of your company. However, we would understand fully if you have a schedule that may prohibit . . ."

"Is that you in there, Bill?" Jessie replied, smiling but embarrassed with his courtesy. After all, according to etiquette, *she* was the one in the wrong for showing up unannounced.

He grinned back. "What do you say? I make a mean omelet. I even *cook* the bacon for guests. But there's only one way I can introduce you to a true Montana breakfast. You have to be here to eat it."

Grandmother seemed terribly ill at ease. An impossible thought crossed Jessie's mind. In spite of the whirlwind feelings—anger, confusion, frustration, even curiosity—she felt a strange inner pull, detached from everything else. While she still could scarcely look at her grandmother without feeling a surge of anger, she couldn't say no, either. At least not for Bill's sake.

"I can stay . . . the night," she replied, acutely aware of how rude it must have sounded.

"Fine, then," Grandmother said, tossing Bill a crusty look. "And you're welcome to attend church with me tomorrow. I certainly hope you won't rush off." Doris eyed Bill again. "Bill does his own thing on Sunday mornings, but . . . I would . . . appreciate your company."

He placed his hand gently on Jessie's shoulder, aligning himself with her again. "She'll decide about church tomorrow, Doris. She may be tired after a long drive."

"Yes, of course," Grandmother nodded quickly.

They said good-night and Grandmother darted down a narrow hallway toward the master bedroom. The moment of her leaving was punctuated by a sense of relief.

Bill asked Jessie for her car keys and brought in her overnight bag. Together, they started up the wooden steps. Midway, Bill stopped. "Notice the squeaks?"

Jessie took another step, testing her weight, listening. "What squeaks?"

"Exactly," he said, looking pleased. "Couple years ago, I redid these steps. There's a special technique for it. It's all in how you place the wood."

"You must be a genius."

Bill chuckled, apparently embarrassed. When they reached the balcony overlook, Jessie leaned hard, taking several deep breaths. She felt light-headed just from ascending the stairs.

"We're a mile above the ocean," he reminded her. "Take it slow."

Bill wasn't kidding.

"You okay? I can get some water."

She shook her head. "I'm fine, just . . . out of breath."

Standing straight again, she placed her hands on her waist, taking another deep breath. Out of the corner of her eye, she noticed her mother's childhood room, only ten paces down the hall, and felt a knot in the pit of her stomach. She met Bill's worried gaze. "I'm fine," she assured him.

He gestured toward his room in the opposite direction. "If there's anything I can do, just call. I'm only a few footsteps away." The softness in his eyes glistened with a natural moistness.

"It's good of you to stay, Jessie," he said. "It means a lot to her, you know." With an air of uneasiness, he looked away, as if he'd said too much. A rather striking contrast to his country-bumpkin demeanor.

Jessie smiled tentatively, unsure of herself.

Bill led her to the end of the hall toward her old room, opposite her mother's former room. She looked away, unable to deal with the strange emotions connected with the room.

Along the hallway wall was a collection of framed photos of her mother.

"That's just a few," Bill supplied, as if reading her mind. "Most of 'em are down in the grand room."

Jessie had seen them all before: her mother's elementary school years, a high-school graduation photo, the nursing photo that had been her personal favorite, several wedding pictures—without the groom, naturally, and one of her mother in a wheelchair, apparently taken in a park setting, with the fragment of a white building off to the right side. Pine trees provided a shadowy cover, lending an artistic contrast to her mother's face.

"She was a beautiful woman," he said after a moment. "I'm sorry I never met her."

"You would have liked her," Jessie said, realizing she had crossed her arms again.

"I'm sure of that," he agreed.

He cracked the door open for her and bid her good-night before retreating to the opposite end of the hallway.

◆ ◆ ◆ ◆ ◆

Taking two steps into the room, she locked her gaze on the window with its white jail-like crossbar panes and wondered if she still had the limberness to negotiate the steep asphalt roof and climb down between the shuttered windows. She was almost tempted, in spite of remembering her earlier assessment of the second-story height from the street.

The room had a quaint feel with its hardwood floor and assortment of antiques. A dark wood dresser stood against one wall, and linen-covered nightstands flanked the canopy bed. She'd forgotten about the window seat overlooking the front yard. Since her final getaway, the room had apparently become a place to board overnight guests. From tonight's conversation, Jessie had learned—actually, she was reminded—that her grandmother enjoyed entertaining important people in the classical music world.

Apparently, her music teachers' group didn't have the budget to fly in the big-name workshop conductors, thus leaving her grandmother to spring for the expenses, something she obviously didn't mind. She was also the person of choice to entertain traveling violinists, singers, and guest conductors when they preferred a more personal touch. Grandmother didn't neglect to mention her personal connection with the symphony personnel, most notably, the conductor and his wife.

All evening, Grandmother had dropped names with abandon, which seemed pointless because Jessie wasn't familiar with half of them, but it did explain the photos here in the guest room. Two walls were filled with garish snapshots of her grandmother with nearly every important classical musical figure in the world. It was blatant and embarrassing, and Jessie wondered if her guests didn't see right through it.

Front and center, the largest photo showed her grandmother, in much younger days, with an affectionate arm around Vladimir Horowitz himself. Standing on the other side, his wife, Wanda Horowitz, the daughter of the famed conductor Toscanini, looked less than pleased. She scowled defensively at the camera as if worried the camera might steal her husband's world-renowned pianistic soul. All this made Jessie wonder again how Bill, the aw-shucks handyman, fit in with Grandmother's world.

The hardwood floor began to feel harsh beneath her feet. She sat on the white-laced bed, removed her shoes, and searched for the appropriate location for them. She thought of Darlene and the misguided promise to call her upon arrival. She wouldn't arrive in Oregon anytime soon.

Suddenly feeling exhausted, Jessie quickly disrobed and slipped into her striped pajamas—*"antiromantic apparel,"* Darlene had called them. *"When you get married, I'd trade those in,"* she'd said and the irony of it hit her between the eyes. *I won't be getting married anytime soon, either.*

She lay back on the bed, closing her eyes as the events of the entire day swirled in her mind: visiting the old gift shop, weeping like a baby in front of the old house, eating ice cream at the Rock House, visiting with Mrs. Robinette, who couldn't stop talking about Andy, who was, by now, a happily married man. *"My word, he's tall now. . . ."*

Jessie smiled wistfully. *Life goes on without me.*

Then there was Laura, the ghost-obsessed girl. She pondered Laura's perky behavior and felt a closeness to the youngster. *"Molly knows me,"* Jessie remembered telling her. Laura had said, *"Maybe you're a ghost! They keep doing the things they did when they were alive."*

Pretty much fits me, Jessie thought.

As a desperate girl of twelve, she would never have imagined she'd finally return here of her own free will. The surreal sensation was even more pervasive now. She felt her mother's presence everywhere she turned in this old house.

Jessie pulled herself up slowly and went to the window. She placed her hand against the wall to steady herself, almost too weary to stand, and spotted her car across the street. She felt a wave of claustrophobia when she realized that Bill had locked the gate with her car outside of the fortress. *I can still get out,* she consoled herself.

"Nobody locks anything in the Broadmoor, but you know how your grandmother is," Bill had said.

Yes, I sure do, she'd thought. And with her car parked outside the protection of her grandmother's wrought-iron estate, it certainly seemed as if she were truly half in and half out. It struck her that she'd lived her entire life that way: poised to live but never really living.

She turned and sat on the window seat, facing the door. She thought of her mother's room again, just a few feet away. Was it locked? She swallowed hard. What would happen if she slipped inside . . . just for a moment? Just thinking about it, she was once again gripped by a mixture of muddled emotions—fear, curiosity, sorrow—but none stronger than longing. She felt literally pulled toward the room.

Before she could change her mind, she rose and went to her bedroom door. Cracking it open, she winced at its whining creak. She peered down the dim hallway, first one way, then the other. Seeing no one and hearing nothing, she tiptoed across the hall. In a flash, her hand was on the knob, twisting. The door was locked, and she felt a sudden twinge of despair. She worried that Bill might have heard the clicking of her attempt, and nervously she glanced down the hallway again.

She crept back into her own room, closed the door, and turned out the light. Slipping beneath the covers, she pulled them up to her neck and held them tightly as her eyes became accustomed to the dark. In spite of her fatigue, sleep did not come immediately.

Her mind wandered, as she tried to process everything. She was struck with the realization of how easily she was remembering things she thought had been buried in her mind. It called into question Dr. Roeske's declaration eight years before.

. . . "You've repressed your entire childhood, Jessie."
She'd responded flippantly, "So what?"

"Repression is a form of emotional protection, but it carries a heavy toll," the doctor replied.

"What's the worst that could happen?" Jessie asked.

Roeske tried to change the subject, perhaps weary of her combativeness. But she pressed him, ready to argue. "C'mon. You said you'd play fair."

"It's complicated."

"I can do complicated."

"We need more time," he argued.

"Give me your best textbook explanation, Dr. Roeske. Repression 101." She was taunting him, but he complied anyway.

"In your case, it's the habitual avoidance of painful memories, leading to memory specific amnesia. You've buried the pain, but you've also buried the memory within your subconscious. For the moment it seems to work. Unfortunately, pain refuses to be buried alive. It claws its way to the surface until you find yourself experiencing acute emotional responses with no apparent cognitive source. You must uncover and solve the cognitive—the memories—in order to alleviate the accompanying painful emotions."

"English, please?"

"You asked for complicated."

"Doesn't sound so bad to me."

"Visit a mental institution," he said curtly, "and you'll see a few extreme examples."

"Excuse me?"

"It's called insanity, Jessica. Worst-case scenario, repression can lead to insanity."

"Oh, puhlease," she whispered to herself. . . .

Her memory of that session was laced with regret, and she now wondered if she had wept because she'd been denied the chance to apologize for her poor behavior.

Her mind drifted to her mother's old room. The last time she'd seen it, there were stuffed animals on the bedspread, huddled beneath another four-poster white-laced canopy bed. The rich oak wood flooring was accented with a braided multicolored wool rug and pieces of her mom's childish artwork graced the wall closest to the fireplace.

Beneath the tall windows was another window seat, with interior shutters opening outward toward the expansive backyard, overlooking a rich, dense collection of maples and oaks, which rarely thrived in Colorado. Like Peter Pan's entrance into a fantasy world.

Jessie had asked her father about the room, and as usual he was *not* impressed.

. . . "Mom loves it," Jessie had protested. "It's cool. It's like going back to when she was my age."

"Your mother doesn't understand what your grandmother is trying to do," her dad said, looking away as if he'd said too much.

"Do what?"

Preoccupied with his tools, her dad was silent.

"Trying to do what?" she repeated.

Her dad sighed. "You wouldn't understand."

No kidding, Jessie thought. . . .

Her head pounded and the room swirled. Leaning up on her elbow, she felt dizzy and a little nauseous. She made her way to the private bathroom adjoining the guest room and found an aspirin in her travel case. She filled the crystal glass beside the sink with water and swallowed the bitter-tasting tablet. A strange revulsion swept through her, and she gripped the sides of the sink. Her field of vision went black, and for a moment she considered slipping to the floor slowly instead of fainting but struggled against it. Suddenly she found herself kneeling on the floor anyway, and for a moment she wasn't sure where she was. She took several deep breaths, now grasping the sink legs. Confusion overwhelmed her.

Too much, too soon, she thought faintly. The whole day, including her encounter with Brandon last night, was like overeating and suffering from indigestion. "That's all . . ." she whispered. "I'm emotionally exhausted. The old memories have thrown me for a loop."

But you didn't remember everything, did you, Jess? You've barely grazed the surface. Hardly a nick. If you did remember—truly remember—your life would never be the same. . . .

She shivered. The words seemed to come from outside of her.

Where did they bury your mother?

Jessie pulled herself to her feet, violently pushing the thoughts or words or whatever they were to the back of her mind, and held the edges of the sink with both hands, leaning down. She was making an effort to get back to the bed when another wave of nausea swept through her. She slumped to the bathroom floor again, realizing that nothing she'd eaten tonight was going to be digested.

Fifteen minutes later, she finally made it back, slumping into bed only to encounter an immediate spinning of the room again. She closed her eyes tightly and took deep breaths. *It's the altitude,* she told herself and eventually her mind settled down. She fell asleep just after midnight.

Chapter Twelve

IT WAS FIVE-THIRTY when Andy rose for the day. He showered, threw on a pair of khaki shorts and blue T-shirt, and slipped into his sandals. He'd slept restlessly, glancing at the clock off and on all night.

He stopped at McDonald's, picked up a large coffee, and headed for the mountains. Highway 105 was nearly deserted on a Sunday morning as he headed south. He opened the windows and let the wind blow through his hair.

"Mom, Dad, there's something you need to know."

"What is it, son?"

Andy shook his head and sighed. He'd never really appreciated the expression "stuck between a rock and a hard place" until lately. "What am I supposed to do?" he whispered to the wind, but his vague prayer only seemed to bounce off the morning sky.

Why do I feel so alone?

When he reached Palmer Lake, he considered turning around. It was only seven, and he'd been driving around for an hour. Instead, he continued on Highway 105 to Monument, stopping at a greasy spoon for breakfast. After eggs and hashbrowns, he read the Sunday paper for an hour, sipping coffee refills.

Long about eight-thirty, he decided to go to his old childhood church, just down the street, if for no other reason than for something to do. *Who knows?* he thought. *Maybe I'll see someone I know.*

◆ ◆ ◆ ◆ ◆

Jessie . . .

Jessie opened her eyes. The frilly see-through curtains billowed in the slight breeze, cooling her face. Early dawn was breaking through. Had she slept at all?

Jessie . . .

She held her head up, holding the sheet to her chest, eyes darting about the room. The whistling wind played tricks with her mind. Flat on her back again, she stared up at the underside of the canopy, gripping the covers all the way to her neck and shivering.

Jessie . . .

She closed her eyes. *I'm dreaming . . .*

Where was the voice coming from? Eyes open again, she turned to the door. How could she have forgotten? Her mother's room was across the hallway! She pushed the covers off and swung her feet to the cold floor. Her slippers were still packed away in the car. She sat there for a moment, staring and imagining the door beyond that, straining her ears. . . .

Jessie . . .

"Is it you?" she whispered back.

She thought of her robe, packed away. In her pajamas, she made her way to the door and placed a tentative hand on the knob. She twisted it slowly, then pushed it open, revealing the door across the hall. It was partially open. She squinted her eyes. *It can't be.*

Last night it was closed. Locked. From across the hall, she peered into the room, unable to distinguish anything in the murky darkness.

Jessie . . .

"I'm coming, Mom." She was halfway across the hall when she

heard steps to her left. She turned and was startled to see her grand-mother in a blue robe.

"Just what do you think you're doing?" Grandmother asked.

"I heard a voice."

"Impossible," her grandmother snapped, her face sinister in the morning shadows.

"My mother is in there," Jessie insisted.

"Don't be ridiculous."

A man came up behind her grandmother. It was Bill. Without speaking, he exchanged worried glances with Jessie's grandmother, then headed back down the hallway. What was he going to do?

"Jessie, I've been worried about you. You've been imagining things again."

Again?

Her grandmother extended her hand. "Come with me."

Now frantic, Jessie ignored the outstretched hand and pushed her mother's door fully open. She groped for a light switch and clicked it, but nothing happened. "Mom? I'm here!"

And then Jessie saw her. She was looking out the window to the backyard wearing the beautiful yellow sundress. *I was right all along!* she thought.

"Mom?"

But her mother didn't budge. She was still gazing out the win-dow. Jessie couldn't even see her face, but she began to run into the room, reaching for her mom, but she couldn't make any forward progress, as if she were running on a treadmill. Panic shuddered through her. Desperation filled her lungs. "I'm coming, Mom!"

But her mother didn't hear her. Jessie kept running, running, running, but she couldn't get any closer. Tears of frustration burst from her eyes. Surely, her grandmother was right behind her. And what was Bill doing? Had he gone to make a phone call? Who had he called?

Something grabbed her from behind and she was being pulled backward. The men in white coats had already arrived. "No!" she screamed. Something like a shirt was thrown over her head, and her arms were pulled violently behind her. "Please, no! Please, no! My mother is still alive!" She kept screaming. "Don't you see her? She's wearing the sundress. She needs me!"

◆ ◆ ◆ ◆ ◆

Jessie startled herself awake breathing heavily, blinking away the fading images of the dream. Gradually, her heart rate settled down, and she regained her composure. From the lingering bits and pieces she recognized it as her least favorite dream, the variation where she believed her mother was still alive. She shuddered. She hadn't struggled through that particular dream in a very long time.

When she finally looked around the room, she felt the momentary confusion that comes from waking up in a strange place. Then she remembered driving to Colorado from Kansas yesterday . . . driving to Palmer Lake, and then . . . here.

She sighed, feeling foolish indeed. *What was I thinking?* Whatever she *had* been thinking, she was thinking more clearly now. Surely her grandmother wouldn't assume a relationship based on one short visit.

She sat up, pulling her legs over the bed and touching the hardwood floor with her pinky toe. Cold. *Put one foot in front of the other,* she told herself, testing her weight on both feet. *I'll be leaving here soon.*

She headed for the bathroom. *Talk about overreacting,* she thought, remembering yesterday. Who cared who owned her parents' old house?

The whole confrontation thing was beneath her. *Grandmother can have the house.* Yes, it was a very good thing she was leaving soon. Tomorrow, she'd be on her way to Oregon, and by the time she arrived she would have forgotten this ill-advised trip down memory lane. *Who says repression is so bad?*

In the Sunday morning sunshine, the bathroom fixtures were

winter bright. Everything seemed whiter—the tile floor, the sink, the Jacuzzi tub—in the morning light. A wallpaper border met the ceiling with a strip of colorful red and yellow flowers woven into ivy.

She took the longest shower in memory, shampooing and conditioning her hair and shaving her legs. When she was done, she felt like a steam-cleaned raisin. Jessie reentered her bedroom with a towel wrapped around her body and dressed quickly in baggy jeans, an oversized gray T-shirt, and pink slip-ons.

When she wandered downstairs, the house was still. She crossed the oversized entryway and headed toward the grand room, where kitty-corner to the elegant fireplace, her grandmother's white Steinway glistened in the morning dawn. On the wall beside the fireplace was a larger collection of framed photos.

Off the grand room was another door, which led past an additional stairwell to the upstairs, then on to the kitchen, where Jessie discovered Bill sitting at the table in the sunny alcove. He was reading the newspaper and sipping a cup of coffee.

"G'morning, sunshine," Bill greeted. "Up early, aren't you?" He was wearing a plain T-shirt and black-rimmed glasses were balanced on his nose. His silver hair had a tinge of blue-gray in the morning light. Bill offered her the paper, and she read the headlines while he got up and began tooling around the kitchen. Jessie looked out the window and noticed the gazebo. "That's beautiful, Bill. Did you build it?"

Bill cracked an egg into a white bowl. "You like gazebos?"

"I could *live* in a gazebo," Jessie said with a chuckle.

He regarded her curiously, then resumed his task. "Your grandmother's church is one of those ritual types, complete with a feel-good sermon. Pain free, if you're so inclined."

Jessie hadn't promised anything yet, but if Grandmother's church was as Bill described, no problem. After all, she'd set foot in Darlene's church . . . once.

"Will you be going, too?" Jessie asked as he mixed the eggs.

"I'll be dropping you off," he replied, tossing the eggshells into the garbage beneath the sink. She saw the hesitant, unsure side of Bill again, but his smile quickly returned. Turning back to the paper, Jessie was already dreading his imminent absence.

Her grandmother made an entrance minutes later, and suddenly the temperature in the kitchen seemed to drop a few degrees. Grandmother was dressed in Sunday go-to-meeting style, a white V-neck blouse, an embroidered hip-length cardigan, and an ankle-length rayon skirt.

Bill poured her a cup of coffee, and she chattered about the weather, the garden, her neighbors, her bridge club, her country club, her charity group, and her piano teacher friends, who were hoping to meet Jessie. Obviously, Grandmother's social tentacles were everywhere. She was still talking when Jessie realized she had nothing to wear for church, that is, if she intended to go.

But Grandmother seemed delighted. "I'm sure I have your size." Then she frowned. "Are you comfortable with wearing one of your mother's old skirts?"

Jessie was still considering this when her grandmother added, "I certainly don't think you'd appreciate *my* style."

"I'm sure my . . . mother's skirts might fit . . . if you don't mind. . . ."

"Not at all."

Grandmother returned with a collection of skirts and dresses— solid pleats, crushed velvet, floral patterns—nothing Jessie remembered.

She still has all of Mom's clothing, she thought.

She selected a conservative floral-print skirt with a dark blue background and a white blouse. When Jessie sniffed the collar, she let out a small sigh of relief. Her mother had never worn it.

Her mother's favorite perfume had been Charlie, and in Jessie's experience, the aroma of Charlie lasted forever. In fact, she had an unsent letter from years ago that still emanated the scent.

She went upstairs to dress and apply blush and eyeliner. Staring into the mirror, she wondered again why Bill, who seemed to be so enmeshed in her grandmother's life, didn't choose to attend her church. And he'd seemed almost secretive about it.

Doesn't matter anyway, she reminded herself. *I'll be miles away by tomorrow.*

Chapter Thirteen

AS EXPECTED, Bill played chauffeur, driving them the few miles to church, which was located just south of downtown, on Cascade Avenue. A classically built structure, the edifice had an almost Gothic feel, with elegant maroon brick, Tudor arches, gabled roof, and a magnificent stained-glass depiction of the Last Supper. Bill let them out at the front door, and no mention was made of his return.

Getting into the sanctuary proved difficult, as Grandmother seemed to know everyone, mostly couples in their sixties and seventies, impeccably dressed. She introduced Jessie as if she were traveling royalty. The people shook her hand, some almost too warmly, as though privy to the whole rotten affair—which, of course, they probably were.

Each person seemed to outdo the other in praising his friendship with "Doris, the most generous woman in Colorado Springs," and seemed utterly thrilled to have been singled out for such an introduction. One woman commented on Jessie's resemblance to her mother, a comment that received a quick clearing of Grandmother's throat and an ushering on to the next recipient of her privileged attention. Five minutes of that routine was enough for Jessie. When the opportunity presented itself, she excused herself to the rest room and locked herself in the stall, gathering her composure for the next round.

Eventually they made it to the large sanctuary, which faced an ornate altar. Perhaps a thousand souls sat on hard-back wooden pews with light blue padding. Not enough padding, in her opinion. Once seated, they became the recipients of more than a few casual glances—people who appeared to be looking for someone else, yet allowed their gaze to casually drift in their direction. And Grandmother glowed in the light of human attention.

Jessie glanced at her grandmother and was surprised that she seemed to be silently praying.

The service itself was just as formal as Jessie expected, with a beautiful and complex choir number before the sermon. At one point, Grandmother leaned over, making note of her friends on the choir platform, which seemed to include the entire group. It occurred to Jessie that those who *weren't* her grandmother's friends must have felt they were part of a small disadvantaged number.

As the hour progressed, Jessie thought of Darlene and her never ending invitations to attend church. Afraid to set some kind of precedence, Jessie had steadfastly declined. As a child, she had attended her grandmother's church on a few occasions, suffering through services that were dreadfully boring. Not to mention, she'd missed her friends at the church in nearby Monument. Due to the slim pickings in Palmer Lake, even Andy's family and the Robinettes attended the Monument church.

Pain free, Bill had said when referring to this church. Turned out he was right. The silver-haired minister, in his red-and-white robe, gave a well-crafted sermon on the practice of gratitude. Later, a young woman with straight brown hair performed a technically demanding organ solo, and Grandmother closed her eyes as if in ecstasy, then leaning over at the end, she whispered, "And to think she's part of our church!"

After the service and a few more rounds of introductions, Verona, a friendly Dutch woman who owned a white Cadillac, drove them down Lake Avenue for lunch at the Broadmoor. Grandmother sat up front, while Jessie sat in the backseat.

Halfway to the Broadmoor, Verona meandered onto dangerous ground. "How long has it been, Jessica?"

Oh boy, Jessie thought nervously, anticipating her grandmother's response.

"Verona . . ."

Verona heard the tone in her grandmother's voice and became flustered. "Well, it's wonderful to meet you. Your grandmother has had wonderful things to say." As if she wouldn't have.

Another awkward silence passed as Grandmother looked out the window, a posture that Jessie realized was intended to communicate displeasure.

"I missed the mountains," Jessie offered cheerfully, but it wasn't really true. The growing awkwardness stiffened the three of them into uncomfortable silence. They ate lunch at a ritzy café that was part of the vast Broadmoor resort—patio chairs, umbrella shading, with an overly formal wait staff. Conversation was conducted by Grandmother, who had recovered from Verona's social lapses, and Verona was delighted to have the opportunity to redeem herself.

Later, after Verona had driven them back home, Doris made a point of noting that Verona was a recent widow.

They were still standing in the entryway when Bill emerged from the kitchen with a can of soda in his hand. He tipped his baseball cap.

"Where's your cowboy hat?" Jessie asked.

Bill grinned. "I give it a rest on Sundays."

Grandmother grimaced. "I have to look at that thing enough as it is."

For a moment, the three of them stood in the entryway, looking at each other uneasily, until Jessie realized that they were both wondering what she had decided. She'd promised one day. Was she staying or leaving?

"What are your dinner plans with Betty?" Grandmother asked

casually, but there was something behind her eyes. If Jessie didn't know better, she might have thought it was sorrow, or even regret.

I'm leaving, Jessie reminded herself.

The dinner was at six o'clock, she told them. They wandered through a kind of winding-down conversation, like people do when they are meaning to say good-bye. "You wouldn't get very far," Bill ventured. "Probably have to stay in a hotel in Denver. Seems a waste."

"And yet she'd be that much closer to getting on the road." Grandmother was making a transparent effort to appear flexible.

Jessie avoided Bill's coaxing gaze.

"You never took the gazebo for a spin," Bill reminded her.

Doris rolled her eyes, and the silly gesture looked out of place on such a proper face. She poked Bill in the ribs. "Bill thinks everything is a car. In this house, we don't eat, or walk, or read, or *do* anything. We 'spin it.' Doesn't matter what it is. This morning you may not have realized it, but you didn't eat an omelet, you took his omelet 'for a spin,' and believe me, after eating his cooking, I sometimes do feel as though I'm spinning." Grandmother was uncharacteristically congenial.

Bill twinkled at Doris, then turned back to Jessie, raising his eyebrows as if to say, *See there?*

See what? Jessie wondered.

"Let's take that gazebo for a spin," Jessie said.

"You two go," Doris suggested. It was Bill's turn to roll his eyes, but Jessie was relieved.

They headed through the kitchen alcove and out to the backyard, entering a paradise of color. Her mood brightened when she saw the double porch swing. She felt like a kid again on her way to the park—the closer you got, the more difficult it was to walk calmly. At some point you had to break into a sprint and practically *jump* onto the swing.

"You like?"

"I love."

Bill regarded her curiously again.

"I nearly grew up in a gazebo," Jessie explained. "Our backyard overlooked the park across from the town hall. I could see it from my bedroom window. It tantalized me to no end."

Bill chuckled, and they sat together for a moment, rocking in silence.

"I think this is good-bye," Jessie finally expressed, hoping Bill would understand, yet knowing he would press anyway.

"When do you have to be in Oregon?" Bill asked.

"Two weeks."

"So what's your rush?"

Jessie looked across the yard. There was no pleasure in being begged. "I'm sorry."

"Sorry about what?"

"I can't stay."

"Why?"

She paused a moment but felt emboldened by Bill's frankness. "If I stay, I might say things I'll regret."

"All the more reason."

"No, Bill."

"Your grandmother ain't china glass, honey. Trust me on that one."

"You don't understand. I won't just *say* things. I'll scream." She felt hopelessly adolescent.

"Then let it all hang out. I'll referee." His shoulders hitched. "I've known you all of twenty-four hours, but I've already seen enough of you to know that if Jessie feels like screaming, she probably has a good reason for it."

"I don't want to scream. That's the point." Jessie smiled in frustration. "It's not becoming to a young lady."

"And, of course, we have the risks," Bill added with a matter-of-fact tone.

She sighed. "Like what?"

"The risk of starting a relationship with your grandmother."

Jessie frowned.

"That's what happens after people air their differences, you know. They become friends. Is that what you're afraid of?"

"Not remotely possible."

Bill looked away casually and took another sniff of fresh air.

As long as they had come this far, Jessie ventured further. "Bill, what are you doing here anyway?" She hoped he would understand what she meant, but she'd probably crossed the line.

He didn't even flinch. He took another sniff, removed his hat, and scratched his forehead. "Long story, Jess. Takes several days to tell it." He cleared his throat casually. "Yep, couldn't get that story done by Tuesday. Maybe by Wednesday. But, to tell it right, I'd need till Friday."

"You never quit."

"Done. We'll move you in."

"Excuse me?"

"Sorry, but I distinctly heard a *tone*."

"A tone?" Jessie smiled and leaned back in the swing as the sunlight peeked into the gazebo.

Am I just a glutton for punishment? she wondered. *What could staying possibly accomplish?* And yet something was happening within her, and it had started last night. Her mind was swimming with strange inarticulated questions—a *feeling* of needing to know something. As if she'd been working her way back to this hope-forsaken place, and now she was merely following a script. With this realization, a sense of impending doom nearly overwhelmed her. *This can only end badly,* she thought.

"I'm gonna need to spin one of your Montana breakfasts every morning, or no deal," she finally asserted, and it felt as if she were signing her own death sentence.

"Deal."

Ten minutes later, Bill was carrying in the rest of her luggage. And Grandmother was already talking about tomorrow's luncheon. Jessie went upstairs to take a nap. Lying on her back on the bed, forearm over her eyes, she had just dozed off when her cell phone rang. It was Betty Robinette. Jessie wondered if perhaps there had been a change in plans.

"Would you mind if I invited a guest for dinner?" Betty asked.

"No, of course not," Jessie replied, curious.

"Here, he wants to talk to you."

A man's voice came on the line. "Hi, Jess. This is Andy. Remember me?"

Jessie nearly dropped her cell phone, then composed herself enough to suffer through a strange contortion of small talk with the young boy who'd once been her best friend . . . a lifetime ago.

"It'll be so good to see you," Andy remarked, and then his voice brightened. "Hey, why don't you come early? We can catch up a little."

They agreed to meet at the Rock House. One hour from this moment. She hung up, feeling suddenly nervous. She stepped into her bathroom to check her makeup and run a brush through her hair, then made her way downstairs, telling Bill of her plans.

He seemed delighted. "See? I knew you'd want to stay." He insisted she take "the old Ford," and the way he said it made her wonder if it was a Model T. But when he led her to the garage, she found a pristine silver Mustang, fully loaded, with forest green leather heated seats, sun roof, and an elaborate dash. At the most, it was a mere few years off its prime.

"I'm gonna take this out for a *spin*," she giggled. "And I may not return."

"Atta girl."

She got into the car and peered at Bill through the windshield. He was standing at the doorway, waving—happy as all get out.

The sun was flickering through the pine trees when she backed out and headed down the tree-lined street. Just before Nevada Avenue, she realized she'd forgotten her purse. Since it contained nearly all of her worldly possessions—and her driver's license—she headed back.

Upon arriving she realized Bill—or she via remote—had forgotten to close the overhead garage door. She slipped in the connecting door to the house, remembering she'd left her purse in the kitchen. Worried she might awaken her grandmother, who'd been napping when she'd left, Jessie didn't close the door. Heading down the hallway, she heard voices. Apparently her grandmother was already up.

"Now that she's staying, when are you going to tell her?" Bill's voice.

"She just got here. I'll lose her for sure." Grandmother's voice.

Jessie paused in the hallway. Should she barge in and pretend she hadn't heard? She took another step and stopped. She held her breath, transfixed by the unfolding conversation.

"She has a right to know, Doris."

"Yes, and I'll tell her on my own time."

What are they talking about? Jessie wondered.

"What's on the menu for tonight?" Grandmother asked.

The conversation was over. Jessie backed her way to the garage door, slamming it shut.

"That you, Jessie?" Bill called.

"Forgot my purse," Jessie called back.

A moment of silence, followed by her grandmother's voice. "In here."

They greeted her with smiles, and Jessie grabbed her purse.

"Have a good time," Bill said.

Right, she thought.

✦ ✦ ✦ ✦ ✦

Once she merged onto northbound I-25, she noticed the interstate was rather empty of cars. At this rate, she'd be in Palmer Lake in about thirty minutes. She was so distracted with what she'd overheard, she almost forgot she was meeting Andy.

"She has a right to know" echoed in her mind. Maybe that's why

Bill had been so determined she stay. *They have something to tell me.*

Secrets, Jessie thought. Was it something simple? *"Jessica, I just wanted you to know I bought your mother's house."* No, couldn't be. They were discussing something of deeper import. Jessie gripped the steering wheel.

What are they hiding?

Chapter Fourteen

DORIS WAS STANDING in front of the gazebo when Bill came up behind her, chuckling. "This is about the closest you've ever gotten."

"Doesn't it seem a bit *too* white?" Doris asked, studying Bill's handiwork.

He didn't bite. "Have to admit I didn't quite get it until today."

"Is that right?" Doris replied wryly.

"Jessie took to that swing like Jane in a Tarzan movie."

"Took it for a 'spin,' I gather."

"Took it around the block."

"Mercy," Doris hugged herself, relieved that Jessica had decided to stay. They might actually have a chance to mend their differences. But she was worried, too. Worried that something might go terribly wrong.

Bill interrupted her brooding. "Care to give it a whirl? Seat's still warm. Courtesy of your—"

"I'll pass, thank you."

He was undaunted. "Funny how Jessie loved the white paint. She's definitely not a bare wood type of gal. Kinda like you, huh?

And the swing. Loved the swing. Really, the whole gazebo thing. Who'da thunk it?"

"Very funny." Doris sighed.

"It worked, didn't it?" Bill put his hand on her shoulder.

She felt herself stiffen and hoped he hadn't noticed, but he removed his hand immediately. So he probably had.

Doris sighed again. Earlier, she had asked Bill about his conversation with Jessica, but he'd hedged. He wasn't the type to break a confidence—not that she was asking him to. It was obvious that Jessica had become enamored with Bill, which wasn't a surprise. Nearly all of her old girl friends had a crush on her cowboy handyman.

"She wondered what a local yokel like me was doing in a classy place like this," he'd finally replied, but he was probably stretching it pretty thin, paraphrasing the real question Jessie must have asked.

"Why *do* you stay, Bill?" she now asked, not sure she wanted the truth.

"It's the excitement, Dory. Pure, unmitigated day-in, day-out adventure of what will happen next. Not to mention the paycheck. That's a bit of an attraction, too." He chuckled at his own joke. "Not that I'm overpaid, mind you."

"So you won't tell me?"

"Nope."

They stood there a moment longer, and Doris felt a small sting of jealousy. Jessica was much too eager to visit Betty Robinette. She cringed and headed for the house.

◆ ◆ ◆ ◆ ◆

Jessie pushed the door open. A young man, dressed in jeans and a plaid shirt, rose from his seat, smiling from ear to ear. Jessie was struck first with his height—at least six-two—then with his hair color, a chocolate brown. His skin was tanned and smooth, his eyes clear blue. He bore a much stronger resemblance to his father now but built like a football player. And she wasn't at all prepared for his good looks.

"Andy? Is it really you?"

He laughed and pulled her toward him, giving her a quick hug. She tried not to appear to be holding her breath.

"We grew up!" he exclaimed.

At first she didn't quite know how to respond. It was like opening your eyes under water. Everything suddenly seemed fuzzy again. She caught Betty Robinette's eye behind the counter. Her girls were waiting on several customers. Betty put her hands on her hips and marveled, "Lookee here!"

Embarrassed, Jessie smiled and gave a small wave.

"Can I buy you a cone?" Andy asked.

"Mrs. Robinette doesn't have bubble gum anymore." *Not so nervous I can't crack a joke,* she thought.

Andy gave a mock frown. "Unbelievable. We move away and things go to pieces. Pistachio maybe?"

"You remembered." Pistachio had always been her second choice.

"Sure I remembered. I couldn't imagine anyone eating the stuff."

Jessie grinned. "Yes, I'm afraid pistachio is a refined taste. Like Beethoven and Virginia Woolf."

Andy's fist thumped his chest. "Ooh. You cut me deep, Jess." Then he frowned again. "Who's Virginia Woolf?"

They laughed, ordered their cones, and settled into the corner table—*their* table.

The room was suddenly populated with summer-loving children. Or had she just now noticed them? In a matter of moments the ice-cream line was all the way out the door, reminding Jessie of the crowds that came in waves and that as kids they'd learned how to time it so they wouldn't have to wait in line.

They were forced to raise their voices to communicate above the low roar. But it provided a comfortable sense of anonymity.

◆ ◆ ◆ ◆ ◆

Andy smiled and noticed her blush slightly. "I don't know . where to begin," Jessie said, licking her cone. "How long has it been?"

She seemed less nervous than earlier but still a bit uncomfortable. She'd come nearly undone when he hugged her, and he was afraid that getting older had made a nervous wreck of the most confident girl he'd ever known.

"It's so good to see you again," he said, hoping to put her at ease.

"I'm sorry." She smiled. "It's just so . . ."

"Weird?"

"Yeah, but a cool weird."

Andy agreed, noticing how her eyes seemed to avoid his. "You really look wonderful, Jess."

She smiled demurely, thanking him for the compliment and returning it. "I have to say that I wouldn't have recognized you on the street."

"Nor I, you." Andy chuckled. "But we were only kids, you know."

"Yes . . . of course." She nodded.

"It's not every day I get to thank the woman who was responsible for my orderly academic progression through elementary school."

Jessie bit her lip, meeting his eyes for the first time, and from that moment they fell into a more natural conversation. They compared memories of classmates and talked about old times, doing homework right at this very spot, watching movies at his house while his mother oversaw them with an eagle eye, walking his dog around the lake, fishing in the summertime—rarely catching anything—talking for hours at the gazebo, but most important, riding bikes from one end of Palmer Lake to the other, a trip that lasted all of ten minutes.

He kept studying her, stunned that Jessie had become so attractive. Sure, he'd probably had a grade-school crush on her, but that had been based upon platonic friendship, pure and simple, no matter what his mother might have suspected. And while Jessie hadn't been very cute then, he'd always thought she was as pretty as any other girl in school.

As their conversation continued, he detected little traces, glimpses, of the younger Jessie. While her flaxen blond hair was lighter than he recalled, her face had thinned, revealing high cheekbones. Her lips had changed; they weren't so pudgy anymore but full and mature, and her nose, not model thin, was more endearing because it wasn't so perfect. Little Jessie had indeed become *Jessica*—quite a woman.

As she warmed up to him, her eyes danced with an enthusiastic brightness. She bit her bottom lip often, and it occurred to him that he'd always found that particular habit endearing in other women and now realized where he'd seen it first.

She looked at him with searching eyes that had always seemed to render him transparent, as if she could look through him into his soul, embracing the full meaning of what he said. His thoughts had seemed of paramount importance to her. When she was with you, she was *really* with you.

Her expression turned quizzical because he had opened his mouth to speak and nothing had come out. He'd been staring. . . .

"Do I look that different to you?" she asked.

"No. I mean, sure . . . you look . . . all grown up."

She reached over and playfully touched his arm. "Do you remember . . ." and then she smiled enthusiastically again, as if winding up a memory that had just tickled her. "Do you remember when we watched the *The Wizard of Oz* at your house? And I was too scared to walk home? I only lived next door, for pete's sake!"

For pete's sake? Andy thought, laughing out loud. *There she is again.* "I watched you walk home from my door, and you kept looking back. But, c'mon, I remember those monkeys. They were freaky!"

"I was scared mostly by the witch," Jessie said in a hush, as if she were admitting a deep and dark secret. "But it was the monkeys that pushed me over the edge. Do you remember what happened the next day?"

"Oh no . . ."

"What?" She laughed.

Andy shrugged and winced humorously.

Jessie finished, "I waited for half an hour by the flagpole and you never came out."

"I think I remember. . . ."

"I started walking home alone, and all I could think of was you'd stood me up. I was crushed! And then—"

Andy grinned. "Oh yeah . . . I jumped out from behind Mr. Burgard's bushes—"

"I was so scared and so relieved all at the same time."

"You were relieved?"

"Sure . . . but mostly mad."

"I remember the mad part. I jumped out and said—"

"There you are my little *pretty*!" Jessie squealed. She was laughing again, leaning back in her chair, holding her sides.

Andy could barely contain himself. "I still remember you yelling at me. 'How could you do such a thing? Didn't your mother teach you better manners? Is this how best friends treat each other?' I had never seen you so mad in my life. I mean—I always thought you liked to be scared. That's what I couldn't understand. How many times had we played practical jokes on each other? But this time, there was steam coming out of your ears."

"I wasn't really that mad about the joke," Jessie said, her voice softer now, her eyes meeting his. "It's because when you left me waiting for you at the school I thought you'd forgotten me. I was glad that you hadn't, but I was still mad. And I couldn't admit to you *why* I was mad."

It's really her, Andy thought again suddenly, as if there had been some doubt. He was aware of others in the room, and for a split second he wondered if they were listening, but he didn't really care. "I remember thinking that no matter how bad the school day had been, you would be waiting for me, and even if everything had fallen apart, I knew you'd listen. And understand. And if you didn't, at least you'd pretend to."

Jessie beamed, almost proudly.

"And I remember complaining constantly about school, all the way home, but you never made me feel stupid about it."

"I thought *I* was the one who complained," she said.

"So I forget . . . what happened after you yelled at me?"

Jessie's expression grew animated again. "I was ready to stomp off—all the while, of course, hoping you'd run after me." She narrowed her eyes humorously. "But you *didn't!*"

Andy chuckled. "I remember now. I started melting instead."

"Just like the witch in *The Wizard of Oz*. I mean, I was already walking away when you started yelling, 'I'm melting! I'm melting!'"

They were laughing again, and the memory seemed as clear as the day it happened. "I turned around and watched you slither to the ground, and then you tried to be as flat as paper, and then"—Jessie's eyes danced with the memory—"you started flapping like a pancake, sizzling as if you were on a grill or something, and that was it. I fell apart. I couldn't be mad at you anymore."

Their eyes locked again and they both laughed until they had tears in their eyes. Eventually Andy sighed, catching his breath, and his mouth hurt. Jessie sniffed and wiped her eyes. Andy reached for her arm, and he didn't care how it would be perceived. He just had to touch her, if only briefly.

They talked about unshared memories—junior high, senior high, college, new and old friends, how various current events had affected them . . . each passage of life leading to another until they were nearly caught up. Three hours had passed in no time, and neither had said a word about her parents, yet it seemed to be in the background of their conversation, coloring everything.

Andy finally brought it up and then wished he hadn't. "I'm sorry about what happened. Doesn't seem fair that you moved away just when you really needed a friend."

It was almost a physical reaction—like a turtle retreating within its shell, or an aura of grayness falling over her. She even pulled back a little, and the expression in her eyes was pained, as if he'd actually hit her and she was pretending as hard as she could that it didn't really hurt.

He tried to smooth over the moment. "I didn't mean . . ."

She nodded softly, forcing a smile. Andy felt terrible. Another awkward moment passed.

"I . . . uh . . . need to . . ." Jessie searched the restaurant, seemingly lost for how to excuse herself to the rest room.

He reached for her hand, but she was already getting up.

Chapter Fifteen

"YOU OKAY?" Susan McCormick asked her husband. John had been peeling potatoes over the garbage disposal. Now motionless as a trapped mouse, he stared out the window at their mini aspen grove, which seemed like a forest right in the middle of suburban Denver. He was holding the peeler in his left hand and a half-finished potato in his right.

"Sorry?"

Susan came over and scratched his back. "You're getting old, hon. You were peeling potatoes. Remember?"

John looked down at the potato in his hand. His face remained serious. "Andy called earlier," he said quietly.

Susan was confused. "Oh. So?"

He grabbed the towel and wiped his hands. He turned to face his wife, who gave him another look of impatient curiosity.

"He said he was meeting that . . . Lehman girl, the one we were talking about yesterday."

Susan was surprised. "You're serious? She's in town? Oh my."

"I doubt she's foaming at the mouth, dear," John said as if reading her mind. "Apparently she just graduated from college. According to Betty Robinette, you wouldn't recognize her."

"I imagine not."

John met her eyes with that hesitant look she knew so well and positively despised—that confidential doctor look that said he couldn't automatically tell her everything.

She tried anyway. "What is it, John?"

He tossed the towel onto the ceramic-tiled countertop. "After Andy called, I got to thinking about everything. . . ." His voice trailed off. Once again, he disappeared into his overanalytical brain.

Susan frowned. "I'm going to need a few more smidgens." But John was already heading for his office. Removing her apron, she trailed him to his main-floor office, toward the back of the house. When she reached the room, he was already typing at the computer.

"For mercy's sake, John. What's going on?"

"You remember Olivia, right?"

She paused. "Jessica's mother? Sure. So?"

Her husband clicked away.

"John, please, toss me a bone or something."

He leaned back in his chair. "I read about this a while back. It has only recently become documented."

"What?"

"Just a hunch, dear. . . ." He leaned forward again. More clicking.

"John, please . . ." She put her hands on her hips.

Hello-o? It was useless. When her husband plunged into research, he became oblivious to everything else. Nothing short of a fire could get his attention.

Susan sighed and left the room. Her husband would be back in a few hours. She could only hope.

◆　◆　◆　◆　◆

Jessie stared into the mirror in the ladies' room, her face streaked with tears. It didn't take much to reduce her anymore. Just the mention of her mother's death. *Click. Whirr. Boom. Oh my, look at that poor woman. . . .*

She leaned against the sink. Her eyes were puffing up again, and her mascara, albeit minimal, was streaked. She tried using a paper towel to repair the damage, with mixed results. Andy would think she was a mental case. Poor guy. She tried to smile at the mirror. Pathetic.

What a difference twelve years makes, she thought. *Why do I keep doing these things to myself?* she asked her reflected image, her eyes watering again. She blinked them hard, almost angrily. *Enough!*

When she finally emerged, Andy stood up, looking worried.

Jessie forced a smile. "I haven't been back, you know. . . . It just hits me sometimes. The memories . . ."

"I understand perfectly."

He was terribly gracious, but as sure as the sun rose in the east, she'd already lost him. From now on he would view her differently.

◆ ◆ ◆ ◆ ◆

They walked two blocks up the street to Betty's white bungalow. Betty had left nearly a half hour earlier to begin preparing. The house had a small yard surrounded by a chain-link fence, and a gravel driveway led to a garage behind the house. Betty opened the door for them when they arrived. Andy held it for Jessie.

Stepping into the living room, Jessie was assaulted by the familiar scent—musty, but not unpleasant. Directly ahead was a small dining room and the kitchen beyond that. On her right were a bedroom and a bathroom. Moving slowly with her cane, Betty took them on a little tour and they both commented that the place hadn't changed much. Framed photos and wooden shelves cluttered the walls of the living room, and knickknacks were shoved into every conceivable nook and cranny. Jessie smiled. *Mrs. Robinette always was a pack rat.* An outdated flowery couch stood to the far left, with matching chairs and end tables. The hallway walls were covered with more photos—some framed, a few tacked to corkboard. In some ways, the small house resembled a photographer's studio. In other ways, it resembled a disorganized garage.

With their help, Betty set the table with an array of covered stainless-steel pots and pans, ceramic dishes, and a large salad bowl.

"There we are," she said, eyeing the table. "Would you give the blessing, Andy?"

Jessie bowed her head as Andy gave a formal prayer.

There was seemingly enough food for an army. "Don't want you to go hungry." Betty surveyed the fixings again. Then she frowned. "Oh dear, I forgot the serving spoon for the—"

Jessie rose quickly.

"It's on the counter, sweetie."

They ate and laughed and reminisced, more of the same nostalgic meandering, memories that, this time, included Betty. She seemed ecstatic when Jessie indicated she was staying with her grandmother for a few days, and thankfully no one followed up on the topic. By now Jessie had noticed Andy's bare ring finger, recalling also that Andy had made no mention of a fiancée.

Finally, Betty blurted out, "Are you still engaged, Andy?"

He grinned, reaching for a plate of celery and carrots. "I'm afraid I've been thrown back into the sea, Miss Betty."

Jessie smiled at Betty, trying to pretend utter disinterest in his answer. "The rice is wonderful," Jessie said.

The subjects changed rapid fire, and at one point Betty laughed so hard that she began to cough, and just when she seemed to recover, her cough returned. She nodded while she struggled, napkin to her mouth, a gesture that seemed to imply everything was okay. But it persisted, and then it became worrisome. Andy fetched a cup of water from the kitchen, but Betty only shook her head, giving a final big cough, and then it passed. They all pretended nothing had happened.

Betty clucked. "Andy, you have become quite the handsome young man."

He blushed and then Betty turned to Jessie. "And what do you think of my grown-up Jessica?"

"C'mon, Mrs. Robinette, you're embarrassing us!" Jessie exclaimed, pointing to the bowl on Andy's right, hoping to move the conversation along. "Pass the rice, please."

He only grinned.

"Andy?" Jessie smiled. "The rice?"

"The rice isn't going to save you anymore."

"What?"

"You always were good at changing the subject, weren't you?" he said, chuckling. "Some things don't change." He turned to their hostess. "She hates compliments, you know."

Mrs. Robinette nodded. "That she does."

Andy shook his head humorously. Mrs. Robinette touched Jessie's hand. "Fact of the matter is, sweetie, we all thought—"

"Betty!" Jessie stammered.

Andy laughed. "Ah . . . it's all coming back to me now."

"Yes . . ." Jessie agreed, relieved that the tables had turned. They peered at Mrs. Robinette.

"What?" Mrs. Robinette said with an affected innocent expression.

"It took us this long, but we finally figured it out," Jessie said.

Andy was nodding, playing along.

"Mrs. Robinette . . ." Jessie began.

"Yes, deary." She said the word *deary* with an unconcerned British tone.

"You are a troublemaker."

Betty bit her lip guiltily and they all laughed. Their playful sparring continued and all too soon, dusk was upon them. The evening was coming to a close, but an unspoken realization lingered. None of them wanted it to end.

Mrs. Robinette broached the subject of the Renaissance Festival. "For a while it wasn't much of a family place, but they've cleaned things up quite a bit. I took little Laura last year and she

141

had a wonderful time!" she announced. Betty told Andy about her young friend, and Jessie weighed in with her own first meeting.

Andy seemed intrigued. "Laura lives in my old house?" He looked at Jessie. "I can get off work tomorrow. . . ."

Betty jumped in, "The two of you should go. You'll have a marvelous time!"

"Actually," he said, "I was thinking the four of us should go. It would be fun to meet the girl who lives in my old house."

"I'm afraid I just can't walk like I used to. You three go," Betty urged.

"They have wheelchairs, don't they?" Jessie suggested, turning to Betty.

Betty hedged, but they convinced her, saying, "It simply wouldn't be the same without you." And Betty finally agreed.

"I'll call Laura's mother right now."

Betty made the phone call while Jessie and Andy cleared the table. It was obvious from Betty's end of the conversation that the answer was yes. They encouraged Betty to relax while they washed the larger pans and loaded the dishwasher. Jessie and Andy talked incessantly, falling easily into a long-forgotten pattern, as if nothing had changed. Like rediscovering a dormant part of herself, then accessing it like a computer file and continuing the program where she'd left off. In some ways it felt good; in other ways, it reminded her of living with the constant awareness of her mother's impending death. She found her mind drifting to the old house, feeling guilty because her mother was all alone at home. In the next moment, her spine shivered at the strange illusion.

At one point, during a humorous exchange, Andy and Jessie's eyes had met. "You can't fool me, Jess. I know you!" She'd been surprised, and yet touched, by his somewhat presumptuous remark. *You can't know me.* Nobody knew her anymore, not even the boy who'd grown up in the house next to hers. No matter what Andy thought he remembered, too many things had changed.

Soon it became obvious to them they were nearly overhauling

the entire kitchen in an effort to extend the evening. Andy even found the trace of a leak beneath the sink and went to work fixing it.

In the living room Betty brought out an assortment of old photo albums. After her initial reluctant feelings, Jessie was surprised to find herself enjoying another walk down memory lane through the lens of the town's official photographer.

When they came upon a photo of her father, Jessie cringed. Frank Lehman was leaning against the refrigerator, a stark, almost vacant, look in his eyes.

"That's Dad, all right," Jessie whispered.

"He was working," Mrs. Robinette countered gently.

"He was *always* working."

They found another photo of him in his shop with the same vacant stare. "Didn't he know it's customary to smile for pictures?" Jessie asked, feeling the old bitterness that seemed to bite at her ankles whenever she thought of her father.

"He wasn't himself, Jess. Not those final years."

"How *could* he be? He drank from the moment he got up to the moment he went to bed. Nobody knew but me, because he hid it so well."

Betty sighed softly. "Well, I suspected . . ."

A clang sounded from the kitchen, where Andy was still working under the sink. Jessie continued, "Dad put me in charge, you know. Wasn't just my idea. Sometimes he slept on the couch when he couldn't even bear to be in the same bed with Mom. She cried herself to sleep a lot. I could hear her. And it wasn't just the illness. She was lonely."

Betty nodded slowly, her eyes sympathetic, understanding. "Losing her was the worst possible thing that could have happened to him," she supplied as if she had some kind of information Jessie wasn't privy to. "Grief overwhelmed your dad—wasn't an easy time for any of us."

Jessie felt she might lose her composure. *Drop it,* she thought.

Let her think of him however she wants. But she couldn't. *I was there, too.*

"He abandoned my mother and then he left me. It doesn't get any plainer than that. He took the easiest route possible."

"What do you mean?" Betty seemed genuinely confused. "Do you mean . . . he killed himself? Oh, honey, that wasn't your father. I remember a different man. He wouldn't have . . ." She paused, unable to say the words again. "I can't imagine that he would have . . ."

"Why is that so hard to believe?"

Betty shook her head sadly. "It just doesn't seem—"

"But he did. He *did*. It's not your fault and it's not mine. Just when we needed him the most, he checked out."

Betty's eyes filled with tears, and Jessie felt sorry for being so determined to force her opinion. Betty touched her hand. "Well . . . if he did such a thing, could you forgive him, Jessica?"

No fair, Jessie thought. Forgiving or not forgiving was her prerogative, wasn't it? If she decided *never* to forgive him that didn't make her a terrible person, did it? She looked down at her hands, shaking her head. "Maybe for me, yes. But not for Mom."

Betty had obviously engaged in tremendous personal historical revisionism. She simply didn't, or couldn't, or *refused*, to remember how things had truly been.

Betty appeared to be collecting her thoughts, seemingly unable to conjure something safe to say. She lapsed into more recollections, and slowly her conversation became more religious in tone.

"The church in Monument hasn't changed much. Pastor Tom retired a few years ago, but we have a wonderful new man of God. My, oh my, he can preach the Word."

Betty continued on about church folk Jessie scarcely remembered, and it reminded her of how Darlene, too, had sprinkled her faith into every conversation. Annoying at best, but Jessie had grown accustomed to it. It occurred to her now that the specter of what comes after death must be especially troubling for an older person. Betty's religion was the simplifying filter through which all of life's complicated events could be reduced into manageable bits and pieces. *I wish it was that easy,* Jessie thought.

"I've never stopped missing your mother," Betty sighed, shaking her head. "But I praise God she's with Him now."

Jessie cringed inwardly.

Betty sighed again. "It all happened so quickly. But before I knew it, your mother, your father, and then you . . . *gone,* just like that!"

Like a story without an ending, Jessie thought lamely. Hadn't she tried to end it for years? Mostly, it was memories of the last days she'd tried to bury within the darkest corner of her mind.

They never buried your mother, did they? The same strange thought—out of nowhere again. Jessie hugged herself, shivering.

"Are you okay, honey?" Betty asked.

Jessie forced a smile, taking another sip of iced tea. "I'm fine."

Betty leaned back in her chair, closing her eyes. Her face suddenly seemed serene. "Your mother and I would talk about our Savior for hours. She had such faith. I still remember the day when she found out about you." She nodded proudly. "I was the first one she told. You were their miracle child, you know. Your mother was only twenty-nine, but they'd all but given up."

"So what a cruel joke, then," Jessie replied.

Betty looked confused.

"All she wanted was a child," Jessie said. "I was her entire life. What kind of miracle was that? God pulls the football out like Lucy always did to Charlie Brown. 'Oops! I was just kidding! I only meant to torture you!'"

Betty's expression spelled sorrow again.

"I'm sorry," Jessie said immediately. "I'm so sorry. I didn't mean—"

"You just get it out, sweetie," Betty insisted. "God isn't scared of your anger."

Well, He should be, she thought angrily.

Mrs. Robinette leaned forward, and her eyes took on a curious expression. "Jessie, how could God make it up to you?"

Jessie frowned, then answered petulantly, without thinking. "God isn't in the making-it-up-to-us business, is He?"

"Just humor me." Her eyes were serious.

"I can't answer that," Jessie finally replied.

"Will you think about it?"

"Oh, Mrs. Robinette . . ." Jessie smiled. "It's not even worth thinking about."

"Really?" Betty was suddenly sitting at the edge of the couch, perched like a bird, her eyes intense.

Jessie changed the subject. "Where was my mother buried?"

Betty's eyebrows rose. She cleared her throat. "Let's see . . . I think the urn was placed in a gravesite . . . in Colorado Springs."

Of course, Jessie thought, wondering how she could have forgotten. "You know, I don't even remember the service. It's all so blurry."

"Yes, very quick. Terribly short," Betty said, shaking her head. She looked down at her arthritic fingers, laced together.

Andy came in, wiping his hands on a towel triumphantly. "Finished."

Betty rose stiffly from the couch, a sudden smile lighting her face. "Oh, let me get a photo of the two of you together! A new one for the wall!" In a moment she was back, camera in hand, and in cheerful awkwardness, Andy and Jessie posed for a few pictures.

Afterward Andy turned to Jessie and said, "I know you've already driven past your old house, but I'd like to see mine again. Are you up for a short drive?"

Betty grasped Jessie's arm. "What did Doris *say* about the house?"

"I haven't asked yet," Jessie said.

"So . . . what do you think?" Andy asked again.

Jessie shrugged, then recalled the mysterious key. When she mentioned it, Andy's eyes lit up. "You still have it? Does it work?"

"I didn't try it," she said without revealing that the whole idea of walking through her house actually freaked her out. Especially in the dark.

Andy said, "I'm sure it's been re-keyed by now."

Jessie hadn't considered that. She sighed softly. In spite of the tense discussion with Betty, she felt warm inside just thinking about tomorrow. *Now . . . aren't you glad you stayed?*

"Betty, do you have a flashlight?" Andy asked.

"Well, I'm sure I do," Betty said.

"Andy, what do you have in mind?" Jessie whispered, her heart suddenly racing.

Chapter Sixteen

ANDY WROTE his cell phone number on a business card, and they made arrangements to meet tomorrow at Betty's. When Andy and Jessie kissed her on the cheek, Betty clucked like a chicken. Meanwhile, dusk had turned to night.

Walking to the Rock House, where their cars were parked, Jessie was preoccupied with her conversation with Betty. *We're all growing old,* she thought. *It's not her fault. . . .*

"Up for this?" Andy asked.

She shrugged, giving him a nervous smile.

Andy poked her elbow playfully. "I thought you liked mysteries and being scared and all that."

This is different, she thought.

When they reached his Toyota, he opened the passenger door for her but didn't move aside. "We don't have to do this, Jessie."

"I'm nervous," Jessie admitted. "But curious, too."

"Would your grandmother mind?"

"I don't care," Jessie said softly as she got in. "It wasn't her house."

Settled into his car, Andy pulled away from the curb. The interior smelled of McDonald's and coffee, but the leather seat seemed to hug her. Four blocks later, Andy killed the lights and handed her the flashlight. "Maybe we should have brought two flashlights."

"Why?"

"I'm a little afraid of the dark."

"Huh?"

Andy was grinning at her.

"You're so bad," she whispered.

Together they walked to her old house. Moonlight shimmered off the old roof. Andy's former house next door was fully lit, which made her own seem even darker, almost *too* dark, as if absorbing the light of the entire neighborhood, swallowing it whole.

They walked up the steps, and the porch creaked beneath their weight.

"Oh boy," Andy said. "That doesn't sound good."

"Andy, stop it!" Jessie whispered, slapping his arm playfully. He looked at her expectantly. She sighed and pulled her keys out of her pocket, noticing the ruby-red-slipper key chain. She felt a twitch of embarrassment, wondering if Andy would notice. She'd left the Toto key chain in her purse. It hadn't seemed appropriate to give it to him, and perhaps she wouldn't.

Andy pulled on the scratchy-sounding screen door and propped it open with his foot. Jessie wouldn't have done this alone—not in a month of Sundays. Andy watched as she inserted the key and twisted it. It didn't budge. Andy was right—the lock had been re-keyed.

"It was worth a try," Andy said, letting the screen close shut. They sat down at the edge of the porch, looking out at the silent residential street, some homes brightly lit, others nearly as dark as this one. Jessie felt a little relieved, but Andy was obviously disappointed. *It's the little boy in him,* she thought.

"I remember this," Andy said nostalgically. "Sitting here after school."

"Never at night, though," Jessie added.

Andy chuckled. "No. Never. My mother would have thought

we were kissing or something. I remember Bobby Harrington riding by on his bike on the way to—"

Jessie groaned. "Horrible Harrington!"

Andy began his rendition of Harrington's taunt: "Andy and Jessie, sitting in a tree . . ."

"He was so annoying." Jessie shook her head. "I remember once when you were sick, he offered to walk me home."

"That little sneak . . ."

"Yeah, I said, 'Dry up and blow away,' or something pleasant like that. And then I ran home, but he followed me and kept teasing me, and I couldn't go inside because I didn't want him to see where—" Jessie stopped.

"What?"

"I didn't want him to see where I hid the key!" Jessie exclaimed, staring at her key again.

"There's another key?"

Jessie rose, slapping dust from her jeans. She reached up above the doorframe, into a little carved-out pocket, hidden from eye level. "It can't still be here," she whispered.

But it was. Jessie shook her head. "Surely, it couldn't work."

"Not if your other key didn't work," Andy said.

"Maybe the other key isn't right. Maybe it's from one of my other apartments or something."

Andy opened the screen door again. She slipped the key in and twisted. This time it met with little resistance as she turned the doorknob and the door retreated an inch. Jessie sucked in her breath.

"Well . . . our first mystery is solved," Andy said, peering into the darkness. "No one changed the locks." He looked back at her. "Still up for this?"

"No more jokes, okay?"

"Promise," he agreed.

Jessie followed him into the gloomy darkness. Straight ahead, she recognized the stairway leading to the second floor. On the right was the small family room, to the left, the living room, which led back to the dining room. All were completely empty, void of any furnishings. At the very back, she knew, was the kitchen, accessible through the dining room or the hallway bordering the family room. The entire house had a circular flow, and she remembered her father playfully chasing her around the house when she was little.

Weird, she thought at the sudden memory, remembering what Betty had said earlier, that her father had been "different" once. Round and round they had gone, her father chasing her through the rooms, both of them giggling. Hard to imagine now.

Andy closed the door behind them. "Just in case," he told her. "Someone might wonder."

"I'm wondering myself," Jessie replied softly. They were now entombed in darkness, and it had a strange effect on her. She felt her eyes tearing up at the familiar scent of the house. Maybe nothing had ever changed. Maybe she was picking up where she'd left off. *My mother could be waiting for me just upstairs,* she thought.

"Are you ready?" He was pointing at the stairs.

"Oh, Andy, I don't know—"

"C'mon, scaredy pants." He grabbed her hand, and she allowed herself to be gently led up the stairs, one creaking step at a time. She counted them, just like she used to . . . one, two, three . . . all the way to twelve. When they reached the hallway, Andy paused. "You want to go first?"

"In your dreams."

"Okay, me first."

Slowly, with Mrs. Robinette's flashlight beam shining forward into the inky darkness, they inched down the hallway. When they reached Jessie's old room, Andy pushed open the door and whistled. "You need to see this."

"Andy, so help me . . ."

"I'm serious."

She moved forward and peeked around the doorway. Andy's single beam of light illuminated the wall, revealing the warped and peeling wallpaper of Winnie the Pooh, Christopher Robin, and dancing jars of honey.

She looked at Andy, and he shook his head slightly as though to say, *Unbelievable.* There was no question now. No one had lived in this house, or surely the Winnie the Pooh wallpaper would have been the first to go.

Andy directed the flashlight beam across the floor, and Jessie recognized the wool area rug covering the hardwood floor. "I always envied kids who had carpet," she whispered. "I slept here, but"— she turned and pointed across the hall to her mother's room—"I basically lived over there. Did my homework in a chair while Mom slept or rested. She's—" Jessie took a breath to gather herself— "she . . . was alone all day long as it was." She swallowed hard, glad that Andy couldn't see her in the shadows.

He touched her wrist. "It's okay."

She resisted. "I don't want to cry."

"Should we leave?"

"No," she whispered, looking across the hall again.

By now their eyes were adjusting to the dark. Andy wandered over and looked in the doorway. Jessie took another deep breath and joined him at the threshold, looking into the now empty room.

"I'm glad you aren't alone," Andy whispered softly.

I was their miracle child, she thought, remembering her conversation with Betty. Had Andy ever heard the story? Probably not.

She wandered to the window, touched the blind, and felt the dust on her fingertips. She turned to appraise the dark room again, and for a moment things were clear again. The room was fully furnished: her mother's bed against the wall, nightstands on either side of the bed, the dresser on the opposite wall, the connecting bathroom door next to the dresser. And just as quickly the room was empty again. Jessie felt as if the wind had been knocked out of her.

"I was their miracle child, you know." When she finally whispered the words, it sounded hopelessly childish. Brandon would have laughed. *Snap out of it!*

In the dimness, Andy sat down on the dusty floor, leaning against the wall. He patted the floor next to him. "Talk to me."

She hesitated. She hadn't planned to tell anyone *anything*. His flashlight cast a flattened gleam across the floor. *I know you, Jessie,* he'd said to her earlier.

When she finally wandered over, his outstretched hand guided her down. He made a whistling sound. "I used to wish—" He stopped. "I think it would break my mother's heart if she heard this, but I was always a little jealous of you."

"You're kidding."

"Mom's great, but she's kinda . . . I don't know . . . edgy, maybe. As a kid, I compared her to your mom, and sometimes I would pretend that your mom was mine, too." He sighed into the darkness.

"So we were brother and sister?"

Andy chuckled. "My imagination never got that far."

Jessie leaned her head back against the wall, wondering if Andy had developed some kind of mistaken notion of what her life had been like. Obviously, he was referring to her mother's personality— the way people felt when they were with her. "It's weird, but I can't even remember Mom getting angry. I'm sure she did, but I can't remember it. Maybe I've just forgotten all the bad stuff."

"No," Andy said, "your mom was special. Do you remember the day you fell off the monkey bars? You were only—" he thought a second—"seven or eight, I think."

She did remember it, and her mother must have been in the early stages. Even at that point they were spending most of the day together as if they knew their time together was short. Sometimes, her mother kicked Jessie out of the house in order to spend time with her persistent next-door neighbor who couldn't get enough of the wind in his hair.

"I remember you were staring down at me after I fell." She chuckled. "You looked scared to death."

"The playground monitor came over and told me to run and tell the principal."

"They told me not to move an inch."

"I came out with the principal," Andy continued, "along with a bunch of other teachers. They hustled all the kids inside. You were just lying there, and I started crying because they wouldn't let me stay. I put up a big fuss until they finally gave in."

"I remember hearing the ambulance and I freaked out."

Andy nodded. "You started calling my name and Mrs. Bieber grabbed me and told me to stop crying because you needed me to be strong. So I pulled myself together and said you were going to be okay and that nothing was going to happen to you because I needed someone to ride bikes with. Then you giggled. . . ."

Jessie sighed. "I remember now. It sounded so weird. There I was dying, and all you cared about was a bike-riding partner."

He laughed. "Then your mom showed up. Just like that."

"Someone must have called her."

Andy was silent for a moment. "No, I don't think so, Jess."

"But somebody had to—"

"No one called your mother," Andy repeated. "I was standing there beside the principal when she turned and asked Mrs. Bieber if anyone had called her. Mrs. Bieber only shrugged. She didn't know, either. If anyone would have called your mother, it would have been one of them."

"I never heard that part."

"I never thought about it until later, but I think your mother just knew, Jess. It's like you two were communicating on a deeper level than the rest of us."

Jessie felt the tears come again.

"It's okay, Jess."

"I do remember sometimes we finished each other's sentences, but I always thought that was typical for two people who were together so much."

"It happened all the time. Do you remember that day when we

were grading our math papers in Mr. Thompson's math class?"

Jessie shook her head, then wondered if he'd seen her gesture in the dark.

"You stood up in the middle of class and said, 'I have to go now.' Mr. Thompson nearly flipped his lid, but you left the room anyway. The whole room was stunned. We were all looking at each other, thinking you had lost it for sure."

"Oh yeah," Jessie said, remembering. "I ran home and found Mom sitting on the bed, sobbing. I had never seen her like that before. I mean, Mom *rarely* got depressed."

"No kidding."

"She saw me and tried to stop crying but couldn't. I ran to her and hugged her. She told me she was ruining my life, said she wanted to die soon so I could have a normal life. We must have cried together for hours. She was sad for *me,* and *she* was the one who was dying."

Andy seemed to be struggling with his own emotions. "People like your mom aren't supposed to die young." He blew out a breath with seeming disgust at his own wods. "What a stupid cliché."

Jessie reached over and squeezed his hand. "I've had these dreams for years, you know? She comes to tuck me in at night and I'm too excited to sleep because tomorrow we're going to the park in Monument. The park had everything, remember? Swing sets, slides, acres of grass, tall trees. I always made a few new friends when we went. And Mom was never in a hurry. I'd have to drag *her* away. We'd eat lunch there. We'd toss Frisbees. I remember one time asking her what heaven would be like and she told me, *'One long day in the park, sweetie,'* and that was all I needed to know, because to me, going to the park with Mom was the happiest thing in the world."

She stopped. In the silence, she felt the embarrassing chill of tears running down her cheeks. *Did I really just tell him that?*

Andy was still holding her hand. It was hard to believe that just a few hours ago, they had met each other for the first time in over a decade.

"When they took her away I was a basket case," she continued. "Dad was drinking all the time by then, morning till night. He thought he was hiding it, but I'd smell it on his breath."

Andy squeezed her hand.

"And then one day, he came home and put these pills on the dining room table. I asked him about them. He said Dr. McCormick had prescribed the pills for him. I kept asking questions until he finally admitted they were supposed to cure him."

"Cure him?"

"Sure, and I knew exactly what he was talking about."

"Depression."

"I guess so, but I was thinking of his drinking, too. I remember thinking, *Fat chance.*"

Andy chuckled sadly.

"I was afraid he wouldn't remember to take them. Dad never followed through with that kind of thing. So I reminded him every day."

"Nurse Jessica."

"Much good it did him."

She closed her eyes, and it felt so near again, the days when she came home to find her mother asleep. *This is where it all happened,* Jessie thought. *The best days of my life . . . and the worst days of my life.*

They sat in comfortable silence for a while, until Andy motioned toward the door. "Did you hear that?"

Jessie perked up her ears. This time they both heard it—a creaking noise from downstairs.

Chapter Seventeen

JESSIE STOOD UP and followed Andy to the door. They heard a young girl's trembling voice from the downstairs entryway. "Is that you, Jessie?"

"Laura?"

Jessie grabbed Andy's flashlight and stood at the edge of the landing. Detecting a tiny shadow in the downstairs entryway, she directed the beam to Laura's feet. Wearing a brown robe over her pajamas, Laura squinted in the light, shielding her eyes from the glare.

"Are you okay, honey? Does your mom know you're out?"

"She's working at the club." Laura's eyes grew wide. "Watch out!"

Andy came up behind her. Jessie giggled. "That's not a ghost, sweetie. That's . . ." She turned to Andy. "Who are you?" she asked in a dramatic voice.

Andy grabbed Jessie's flashlight and placed it under his chin, creating a ghoulish mask. "I'm the ghost of Christmas past. . . ."

"Andy!"

Laura giggled. "Cool!" And then she froze. "Wait a minute. Are you Andy from the wall?"

Jessie smiled. "Yep."

"Andy from the wall?" he said curiously.

"You *are* ghosts," Laura said with a hushed, reverential tone. "Can I come up?"

Jessie crouched down and extended her hands. "Be careful, sweetie."

"Cool!" Laura started climbing immediately. "Are we still going to the fair tomorrow?"

"Andy from the wall . . ." Andy repeated and Jessie laughed.

Laura had almost reached them.

Jessie grabbed her hand when she reached the top. "News travels fast."

"Mrs. Robinette called."

"So it's okay with your mom."

"Of course it is," Laura replied. "She doesn't care what I do." Laura released Jessie's hand and ran down the hallway, peeking in all the rooms. "Cool! Cool!"

When Jessie joined her at Jessie's old room, Laura covered her mouth in dismay. "Eeeew! Ick. Winnie the Pooh." She looked up at Jessie. "You didn't actually *want* that on your walls, did you?"

"What's wrong with Winnie the Pooh!" Jessie exclaimed.

"Puh-lease," she said with a roll of the eyes.

Once Laura had finished exploring the rooms, Jessie walked her back next door while Andy waited by the car. Laura was still skipping up and down. If she had a tail, she would have been wagging it. Molly barked at the door but became friendly again when she saw Jessie.

"Tomorrow, right?" Laura said, rubbing Molly's neck.

"Tomorrow." Jessie smiled.

"You won't forget?"

"Impossible."

"But what if you do?"

"It won't happen, sweetie."

"But sometimes Nora, my baby-sitter, forgets stuff."

"I won't, honey."

"It's okay, though, if you do. We could do it another time."

"Do you have a pen?" asked Jessie.

"Sure." Laura ran into her house and came back with a pencil. "Will this work?"

Jessie wrote down her cell phone number on a piece of paper, remembering that Andy had done this earlier for her. She handed it to Laura. "Call me if I forget."

Laura grabbed the piece of paper as if it were a hundred-dollar bill. Her eyes were wide. "Cool! I won't bother you. Promise, promise, promise!"

"Bother me, sweetie."

"Okay," Laura squealed and then she waved furiously.

Andy drove Jessie back to her grandmother's silver Mustang, which was still parked at the ice-cream shop. Jessie reached for the door handle, glancing back at Andy. His eyes were soft blue in the dim light. "You going to be okay?"

"I'm a tank," she whispered back.

"Wanna ride bikes later?"

Jessie laughed, but she almost said, *I have to ask Mom first.* . . .

She got out and watched as Andy waved and drove off. Before getting into the Mustang, she pulled out her cell phone and checked in with her grandmother, who seemed relieved to hear from her. Jessie felt the walls rising within her the moment her grandmother answered the phone.

She got back thirty minutes later and found Bill and her grandmother in the living room. Doris was perusing a coffee table book. Bill had fallen asleep in front of the TV. He woke up and gave her a welcoming smile as Jessie settled into an armchair.

At eleven they said good-night, and Jessie made her way up the squeakless steps. She undressed for bed, feeling the subtle twinges of another headache.

I could set my watch to it, she thought.

She turned out the lights and the memories of the day churned within her. Everything about the day had been like going back in time, which was strangely moving and disturbing. Even the memory of believing in God, and how she had prayed for her mother's healing for years—even *that* had seemed like only yesterday. She'd even discussed religion tonight with Betty as if she still believed God existed. Not in a formless-energy, all-pervasive sense, but in a real, personal sense. As if *anyone* could argue about God's intentions.

But in the end, Andy's buffering influence had gotten her through the day. She recalled her embarrassment at leaving the table, thinking she'd lost him. *I guess I can't lose him that easily,* she thought proudly.

At eleven-thirty her cell phone rang.

"Hello, Laura."

"Uh . . . it's me, Andy."

At first, her heart sank. She suspected Andy had changed his mind about tomorrow, but she tried to keep her tone upbeat. "Is everything okay?"

"I just wanted to tell you—"

"It's okay, Andy, if you need to—"

"What?"

"I'm sorry. You go first."

"Did I call too late?"

"Oh no, of course not."

Andy hesitated, long enough for Jessie to wonder if she'd been too hasty. *Perhaps he's had enough of this basket case.*

"I just wanted to . . . say that . . . I'm really looking forward to tomorrow."

Jessie felt her cheeks warm. They talked for another half hour, which passed so quickly it felt like a minute. Then she got another call. She apologized to Andy and pressed the flash button. When she returned, Andy was curious.

"That was Laura," Jessie offered. "She was calling to make sure I was real."

Andy chuckled. "Funny . . . that's what *I* was doing."

* * * * *

After they hung up, her headache worsened but not nearly as oppressive as last night. At two-thirty she wandered into the bathroom for a glass of water and another aspirin. Back in bed, she stared at the top of her bed for a while, aware of the clicking, popping, and creaking of the old house.

An hour or more seemed to pass and she worried she'd be too tired tomorrow. Then she heard the distant sounds of the TV from downstairs. *Bill must be up. Maybe he has insomnia,* she thought, wondering if she shouldn't join him, since neither seemed to be sleeping tonight. The floor creaked outside her doorway, and she gasped when a thin line of light appeared beneath it. The door slowly squealed open.

Jessie sat up, the panic building, until she looked across the room and realized where she was, and the relief was profound. She lay back down, trying to catch her breath.

Her own body was smaller again, her little hands holding the covers. She touched her hair; it was short again, chin length. The walls were covered with Winnie the Pooh and Christopher Robin. A subtle breeze tickled her window screen. She smelled the aroma of the Russian olives just outside. And Mom was there, standing in the doorway to check on her, as she did every night. She was wearing the yellow sundress, the one from Oregon.

What a nightmare! Jessie thought, thankful for having awakened. She grinned and whispered to the ceiling, *Thank you, Lord, for keeping me safe.* And then she giggled and added, *Even in my dreams!*

Her mother crept into the darkened room, walking on tiptoe.

What if she thinks I'm sleeping? Jessie thought.

"I'm still awake, Mom."

With the hallway light on her back, her mother's facial features were hidden in the shadows, but her blond hair, which fell to her shoulders, glistened with a healthy luster in the light from the hallway. Jessie gazed up at her mother.

Mom leaned over and kissed her cheek. The scent of Charlie mingled with the unmistakable smell of her Mom's own natural scent.

"Oh, Jessie, you're crying. Is everything okay?"

"Everything's great."

"Are you excited about the park tomorrow?"

"I can't wait!"

"I'll fix sandwiches in the morning."

"Tuna fish?"

Her mom wrinkled her nose. "Tuna fish?"

"Please?"

"Tuna fish it is." Her mom laughed. She sat at the edge of the bed and Jessie felt the depression of her mattress.

It is real, she thought. *Mom's really here!*

Mom stroked her arm and brushed the hair out of her eyes. "How did your hair get so blond?"

Jessie giggled. "I had good genes."

"And a little sun." Mom smiled, taking Jessie's hands within her own. "Honey, you're crying again."

"It's nothing."

"Something at school?"

"No."

"Andy?"

"We're cool."

"You're cool, eh?"

She paused. "Do you like him, Mom?"

She nodded. "You have very good taste, sweetie." Her mom leaned over and kissed Jessie on the cheek again. "Sure there's nothing you want to talk about?"

"Would you stay until I fall asleep?"

"I'd be happy to."

"I may not fall asleep for a long, long, long time."

"Then I'll stay till you do."

"You don't mind?"

Mom smiled. "You're my longed-for child. Have I ever told you that?"

Jessie giggled. "Not enough!" Her mother's smile turned sly and she tickled Jessie under the arms, and they both squealed.

"Turn over, sweetie. I'll rub your back."

Jessie panicked. On her stomach, she'd be asleep in minutes. "Can I stay this way?"

"Of course."

"Tell me a story . . . Snow White. I like the way you tell it."

"Hmm. Now that you mentioned it, I thought up a couple new twists."

"Really?"

"Just to keep it interesting."

"But it ends the same way, right?"

Her mom's eyes turned mischievous. "I don't know . . . maybe the prince shouldn't kiss her this time."

"Mom!"

"Okay, okay. A kiss it is. . . ."

The most creative storyteller in the world began to weave her own version of Snow White, with a few unique twists and turns. Jessie savored the story, holding on to consciousness for as long as she could. But she was helpless to fight the scratchiness behind her eyelids and fell asleep long before Snow White awakened to love.

Chapter Eighteen

THE ALARM RANG. Jessie turned to it, confused. Why would it ring in the middle of the night? She reached over and turned off the alarm, then sat straight up in a panic, searching the room. The room had changed again. The walls were eggshell white. Gone was Winnie the Pooh. Her legs reached the end of the bed.

She leaned back, closing the tears behind her eyes. *Hold on,* she thought as the sinking realization continued to set in. She tried replaying the dream over and over again in her mind, as if by sheer will she might slip back into it. Eventually she fell into a dreamless sleep and awakened to the ringing of her cell phone. Fumbling for it, she inadvertently pushed it off the nightstand. It clunked to the floor but continued ringing. Leaning over the bed, she grabbed it, nearly falling out of bed. Half asleep, she pulled herself back up and answered it.

It was Laura. "Wake up, sleepyhead. Did you forget? We're going to the fair! You're dressed, right?"

Jessie covered her eyes with her arm.

"Jessie?" Laura's voice thinned. "Are you there?"

"I'll be right there, sweetie."

◆ ◆ ◆ ◆ ◆

Jessie dressed quickly and rushed down the hall to the stairway. She reached the bottom of the stairs and realized she'd left her cell phone on her nightstand. Dashing back up, she was startled by the sight of a woman standing in the hall in front of Bill's room. The woman waved. "Jessie?"

She looked to be in her midforties and she was wearing jeans and a tan sweatshirt, quite a change from the maid uniform Jessie remembered. "Maria? Is that you?"

Maria's eyes danced. "Howdy, stranger!"

They hugged tightly, and Jessie recognized the odors of Pine-Sol and lemon.

"You haven't changed, Maria."

"Well, *you* have!" Maria laughed, making a measuring gesture in front of her own waist. "You were this high last time I saw you."

Jessie asked about her family, and they chatted for a bit. Jessie tried to pretend she wasn't in a rush as Maria recounted the various escapades of her children, fully grown now, and her husband's home remodeling business. When their catching-up reached a lull, Jessie pointed toward her mother's room. "Does it look the same?"

Maria shrugged. "I really don't know what's in there, since I don't clean it anymore." She thumbed through her arsenal of keys and they rattled in her hands. "I don't even have the key anymore. I suppose Bill dusts it now."

Maria glanced toward Bill's room. "Well, I guess I'd better get back to work. We had some great talks, didn't we?"

Jessie nodded, but she was distracted by the information. Had her mother's room changed? Why was it locked? "Let's talk some more later, okay?" Maria said, moving down the hall, waving good-bye.

After grabbing her phone, Jessie hurried down to the kitchen to say good-bye. Her grandmother wasn't there, but Bill's eyes lit up. "You're kinda late, ain'tcha?"

Jessie made a grimace.

"Taking the Ford?"

"Oh . . . well . . ."

Bill was already up, grabbing the key from the cabinet. "I insist. A dashing young lady such as yourself needs to travel in *style*."

❖ ❖ ❖ ❖ ❖

Jessie pushed the speed limit, reaching Palmer Lake in record time. She parked the car at Betty's house, and Betty met her at the door. "Andy's already here," she said, looking apologetic. "The leak in the sink came back."

Jessie offered to get Laura while Andy finished working on the plumbing, but Betty hesitated. "Be careful. Michelle's a tough cookie, Jessica."

"Who?"

"Laura's mother," Betty said. "I'll let her know you're coming."

How bad can she be? Jessie thought on the drive over. Laura was waiting on the front steps when Jessie pulled up. She popped to her feet like a jack-in-the-box, looking like she was fit to be tied, making a frantic *come here* motion with her hands.

"Mom's inside. She wants to meet you."

Laura held the door open for Jessie. She wrinkled her nose, whispering, "Everyone tells me our house smells like a dog, but I can't smell it anymore."

Laura wasn't kidding. It didn't just smell like a dog, but instead what a dog shouldn't be doing indoors. This definitely wasn't Mrs. McCormick's house anymore. The carpet was stained, the ceiling was cracking, the walls were chipped and flaking, the entire living room was covered in clutter, and the haze of nicotine lingered.

Laura led Jessie to the kitchen toward the back of the house. Her mother was sitting at the kitchen table, cigarette in one hand, coffee cup in the other. She was wearing tight-fitting cut-offs and an unbuttoned flannel shirt over a white T-shirt.

She put the cup down. "About time," she said and then turned to her daughter. "Laura, me 'n Jessie here, we're gonna have an adult convo, okay?"

Laura looked back at Jessie with a worried look. Jessie smiled, trying to reassure her, but she was starting to wonder what she'd gotten herself into. Michelle looked more than a little rough around the edges, with dark circles around her bloodshot eyes and a pasty complexion.

Laura scampered off to the living room, and Michelle took another puff, narrowing her eyes at Jessie. She twisted her mouth to blow smoke in the opposite direction without removing her gaze. She smiled, but her eyes were fierce and taunting, and she wasted no time. "I don't know what your angle is, but I work awfully hard to put bread on this table, more'n twelve hours a day sometimes, and a lot of people come around here making me look bad, like that ice-cream-scooper lady."

Surely Jessie had missed something. "Michelle, I don't mean any harm. . . ." The woman's name felt strange on her lips. Other Michelles she'd known were very proper highbrow types. "I don't . . . have an agenda here."

Michelle raised her eyebrows. "Well, Jessie, everyone has an *agenda*." She said the word with slow deliberation, implying that Jessie had been trying to embarrass her.

Jessie inhaled deeply.

"I know all about you, Jessica Lehman," Michelle said with that same slow, almost mocking deliberation. "I know *all* about your family. I know *all* about your father. And about your mother." She took another puff, blowing it sideways, her eyes fixed upon Jessie. "You and I ain't so different. Your clothes are a little newer, may-be. . . ." She gave Jessie an up-and-down scrutiny that bordered on lewd, then another cynical smile, as though Jessie had been weighed and found wanting.

"We need to get going . . . if we're going," Jessie said softly.

"Got a plane to catch?"

It was then that Jessie noticed a small line of something white on the table. She put two and two together but tried to keep her newfound awareness as surreptitious as possible. *Salt?* she considered. *Maybe sugar? You bet. All in a nice little row. . . .*

"I'm doing some baking." Michelle giggled a husky, obnoxiously taunting giggle, and it was suddenly obvious to Jessie. Based upon Michelle's strange behavior, caffeine and nicotine weren't the only foreign substances in Michelle's bloodstream. The brazen way she flaunted her illicit lifestyle was rather astonishing. Perhaps she was too stoned to comprehend her own behavior. *Maybe she wants to be caught,* Jessie thought. *Maybe she wants Laura to be taken away from her. . . .*

"We need to go. . . ."

"What's your rush?" Michelle asked, crushing her cigarette in one of the dozen or so foil ashtrays lying around the kitchen. She called for her daughter, and Laura came running to the kitchen doorway. "If you run away again, I'll sic Molly on ya."

Laura frowned, setting her chin into a pout. She glanced at Jessie and scampered off in the direction of the front door. Jessie heard the front screen door bang. Michelle chuckled.

"Nice meeting you," Jessie lied. Michelle merely gestured with her cigarette. Jessie pushed her way out the front door. Laura was already in the car, buckled in. Jessie got into the driver's seat and started down the block. At the end of the street, Jessie stepped on the brake and turned to Laura. "You okay?"

Laura shrugged. "Mom's a kick, huh?"

Yeah, Jessie thought, slipping the car back into gear.

They drove straight to Mrs. Robinette's house and parked in the gravel driveway.

Andy and Betty were sitting on the porch. Apparently the sink leak hadn't been too serious.

"Wait here, sweetie," Jessie said to Laura. She slammed the door.

"It's fair time," Andy called, but his smile diminished as Jessie approached them.

"We need to call the police," Jessie said to Betty.

Betty didn't even flinch. Her face settled into a grimace. "I take it you met Michelle?"

"The woman's stoned out of her mind."

Betty shook her head sadly.

Jessie was confused. "But I saw her—"

"Jessie, I'm glad you talked to me first."

"Betty—"

"It's a game," Mrs. Robinette interrupted. "Do you think she cares about meeting her daughter's adult friends?"

"Huh?"

Betty shook her head again. "Michelle *was* an addict. Or she may still be. Coke. Crack. You name it. Guess who turned her in two years ago."

"You?"

"Yep. The court sent Laura to live with Michelle's crackhead sister. Six months later, Michelle comes home and Laura is back with her mother. Claims to be off the coke, but she's furious at this community. Furious with me. Why didn't she just move away? I don't know. Anyway, she starts playing games with us. Makes it look like she's still taking the stuff. I can't tell you how many times somebody has snitched on that woman. They search the house and she just laughs. They put her through a drug test. Three times, Jessie. They never find anything. The last time we called, the police refused to investigate."

Jessie was chagrined.

"Yep," Betty continued. "We fell right into it. We've cried wolf too many times. In fact, that *might* have been real coke you saw, but there's no way the authorities would respond. The police think we have it in for her. And they're right. We're doing everything we can, but nothing works. She's an unfit mother, but she's smart enough to play the system."

"So what do we do?" Jessie asked. "Surely there's something . . ."

"We pray, Jessie."

Same as nothing, she thought, gathering her composure.

They heard the car door click open. Laura peeked out. "Hey guys, we're burning daylight." She giggled.

Andy stood up, but he seemed sobered. "Let's make some *good* memories today."

Chapter Nineteen

TOGETHER, THE FOUR OF THEM drove in Andy's Toyota sedan several miles north to Larkspur, the location of the Renaissance Fair. It wasn't like other fairs with merry-go-rounds, livestock shows, and rutabaga contests. This fair was based entirely upon sixteenth-century life in Elizabethan England. Signs at the front entrance declared: *We accept Master Card and Lady Visa.* The employees wore ruffled outfits of the time, adorned with lace and gold tassels, speaking a language that resembled hip King James lingo. "Welcome, lords and ladies!"

Andy rented a wheelchair for Betty, who after putting up a mild fuss, finally acquiesced; Andy and Jessie took turns pushing. They were surrounded by court jesters, jugglers, fire eaters, knights in shining armor, fair maidens, and countless other characters. Laura was like a kid in a toy store. Jessie wondered if she might explode with joy. They watched several performances, including a sword swallower, short Shakespearean plays, and minstrels playing lutes, flutes, mandolins, and handmade skin drums, but avoided, on Betty's advice, the off-color comedy show Puke and Snot. They visited the craft shops, bartered for pewter, sniffed perfumes and soaps, ate turkey drumsticks, and drank dark coffee.

Andy bought hats for everyone. For Laura, a princess hat; for Mrs. Robinette, a queen's crown; and for Jessie, a Juliet cap—a graceful white veil attached to a rich white velvet and gold-trimmed hat, with a pearl strand on top of the hat and more pearls dangling around her face. Jessie bought Andy a Romeo hat to complete the picture. Mrs. Robinette snapped photos of them, chirping happily.

Midafternoon they signed Laura and Betty up for an hour in the art tent, a do-it-yourself world of watercolor painting and craft making. "What about Jessie?" Laura asked, her eyes pleading. "Isn't she going to play?"

Andy crouched down to her level. "She needs a little rest."

"Okay." Laura shrugged, soon becoming captivated by the artistic possibilities.

Andy and Jessie wandered across the gravel path to an umbrella-sheltered outdoor café table.

"Are you worried about me, Mr. McCormick?" Jessie asked, pulling out her wooden chair.

"No. I was just hoping we would have some time to, you know, to talk."

"You don't *talk* at a fair, silly," Jessie said playfully.

Andy ordered lemonade from an undistressed damsel while Jessie ordered tea. Then he asked, "So when are you leaving?"

"Wednesday."

He seemed to consider this. "Still difficult?"

Jessie paused, her attention momentarily distracted by a juggler. "The memories are difficult," she said. "Not so much the present." She thought for a moment. "In some ways things change; in other ways, they stay the same."

Their beverages arrived and Andy took a drink. Then he gave her an appraising gaze, and she found herself wanting to explain further. That in itself was so strange to her, so different from their past. *What is the difference?* she thought. *Is it the place? Or is it just Andy?*

Andy leaned forward, hands clasped. He looked so absolutely

adorable and silly in the Romeo hat that it was difficult to carry on a serious conversation. He caught the hint and removed the hat, grinning.

"Sometimes I think I've moved on, but then other times . . ." Jessie sighed, giving him a self-deprecating what's-wrong-with-me frown. "Surely this isn't what you wanted to talk about."

Andy rubbed his chin. "When we were kids, we would talk for hours."

"Yeah," she agreed. "Time always went so fast and we'd have to head back home before we knew it."

Andy grinned. "You'd say, 'I've gotta go—Mom's calling.' And I'd say, 'That wasn't your mom—you're hearing things,' because I wanted you to stay longer. But we'd head home anyway. Your mom would be sitting on the porch waiting for you, smiling and sipping iced tea or something."

Jessie looked down at her hands. "You mentioned yesterday how my mom and I had this . . . connection."

"Ye-ah . . . ?"

"Sometimes I didn't really hear her," Jessie admitted quietly. "And sometimes I wondered if she ever *actually* called."

Andy leaned back in his chair, seeming to consider what she'd said.

She shrugged. "I don't know . . . sounds silly." She took a deep breath and blew it out, then fixed him with another gaze. "Remember what you said yesterday about pretending that my mom was your mom?"

Andy frowned humorously. "Now *that's* a deep, dark secret."

"But I felt the same way, you know."

"About my mom?" Andy kidded.

"No, silly," Jessie said. "About your dad."

"Oh yeah, I guess I can see that," he replied. "Dad's pretty cool."

Jessie smiled at the memory. "I always wished that your dad and *my* mom could have gotten together."

"That would have solved *both* of our fantasies." They laughed.

Jessie wanted to say more but knew it would have sounded horribly selfish. Truth was, she'd always longed for a *real* father—a father just as cool as her mother. A father with a real personality, who didn't come across like a shadow on the wall. How on earth had Mom ever fallen for him? Then she remembered their playful racing around the house—such a stark contrast to his later days. *Have I merely forgotten the happy times?*

Andy had that contemplative expression she remembered from his youth, when he was sorting things out but didn't quite know how to say what was on his mind.

"What is it, Andy?"

He shrugged, pursing his lips. "I was talking to Betty this morning. . . ." He looked down, apparently uncomfortable.

"It's *me*, Andy," she said, but words were almost too intimate and she felt a little embarrassed. "You can tell me."

He met her eyes. "Betty mentioned your conversation from last night, while I was working on the sink. . . ."

"I wasn't very nice," Jessie said, wondering if she shouldn't apologize, realizing that Andy would likely have continued on the same religious path from his youth. Of course he was a Christian. Hadn't he been engaged to an evangelist's daughter? Just thinking about it gave her a sinking feeling.

She sighed inwardly. Andy was probably going to try to reconvert her, and she wondered if Betty had put him up to it. The question of religion could divide people in a heartbeat. *This is where things fall apart*, she thought.

She fiddled with the pearls of her Juliet cap, wanting to change the subject. And then realizing how silly *she* must look, she removed her hat.

Andy rustled in his chair. "Let's not go there," he finally said, smiling encouragingly. "We're having too much fun."

Jessie was tempted to let it drop. Push it under the rug. Ignore it. "You want to know where I am, don't you?"

"No. It's personal, and I shouldn't have—"

"I don't believe in religion anymore," Jessie broke in, and she watched his reaction. Perhaps he winced, perhaps not, but he was regarding her curiously, seemingly taken aback by her admission.

"I see . . ."

"My roommate was a Christian. Wasn't easy getting along, but eventually we agreed to disagree."

She continued as if needing him to understand. She told him of her first week at college, how she found Darlene from a newspaper ad, how they'd sometimes argued about Christianity.

Andy listened patiently, but his manner seemed almost regretful.

She forced a humorous smile. "So . . . can we still be friends?"

"That won't ever change." He lowered his gaze again, and another moment passed as he seemed to gather his thoughts. When he looked up, he said, "Jess, I have to watch myself around you. I could start telling you my deepest secrets."

In spite of the honest, almost intimate admission, the moment was awkward. She narrowed her eyes and made a sinister "crazy man" face. "Ve haf vays ef meking you tawk!"

Andy laughed, leaning back in his chair, appraising her carefully. "I've missed you, Jess."

She wasn't sure how to respond. Finally Andy sighed again and it seemed as if he'd been winding up for this moment. For a day at the fair, they'd become hopelessly serious—a stark contrast to the festivities going on around them. The place was filled with people in outrageous costumes. Children were laughing, screaming. And here they were talking about something as serious as heaven and hell.

"I don't believe it either, Jess."

His words hung in the air. At first she was confused, because she hadn't been expecting it. The emotions that followed his admission were mixed. On the one hand, she felt enormously relieved. *We're both on the same side of the fence.* Yet it didn't feel like a celebration. More like a bitter aftertaste to something that had tasted very sweet at first. Or like admitting to a mutual failure. Maybe they had simply grown up? Moved on? Everyone discards Santa Claus, don't they?

Andy's expression was cautious again. "Remember I said I was engaged once?"

She nodded.

"Her name was Elizabeth." He spoke the name with near reverence.

He described his engagement to the daughter of a famous evangelist, then progressed to his experience with Professor Neal, and it crossed her mind that Andy was confessing. The intimacy made her feel uneasy and yet extremely honored. The roles were settling in again from the old days, when he would ask her questions, and she would respond as if she had the answers in her back pocket. She asked a few clarifying questions, but mostly listened intently. When he finished, Andy seemed tired, not so much physically, but emotionally.

"I'm familiar with the arguments," she finally told him. "I took a philosophy course in school, but it only brushed the surface."

"So . . . what do you think?" he asked.

Jessie shrugged. "I never really gave it much thought."

"So . . ."

"What's *my* reason?"

Andy nodded.

She smiled, dramatically delivering a line she remembered from her old philosophy textbook. "'The nature of this world, the nature of our existence, the nature of suffering, is not compatible with the concept of God as articulated in Christianity.'" She'd meant for it to come out mildly humorous, but it fell flat.

"You *have* given this some thought."

"Only because of Darlene."

Andy looked down and he seemed disappointed. She could imagine what he was thinking. He'd just bared his soul and she'd responded flippantly. She wondered if she *wanted* to be as understood as he seemed to want, especially when it came to this part of life. "My mother . . . and everything . . . you know how it was . . ."

"You mean what happened to her?" he asked.

"Well, sure." She was startled by the tone in her own voice, the bitterness that came whenever she thought or talked—which was rare—about her mother's illness.

"That's probably what it's all about for you."

Jessie frowned. "What do you mean?"

"You're . . . ticked."

"Of course I am."

"But that doesn't mean—" Andy hesitated—"that you don't believe, does it?"

Jessie felt her frustration building. "Sure it does."

"You're angry."

"You bet I am!"

"Then who are you angry *with*?"

Jessie felt as if she'd been slugged verbally. "You're just playing with words, Andy. And it's not fair."

Andy shrugged. "But you just indicated that you don't believe because of the suffering in the world."

"That's part of it."

"What's the rest?"

She felt stupid but said it anyway. "A real God would have healed my mother. Okay?"

"Maybe *that's* it, then."

The conversation was starting to feel like the ones she'd had with Darlene.

Andy continued. "You're disappointed."

"The Bible is full of these blatant promises," she argued, "'Ask and you shall receive' and all that. There are dozens just like it."

"I'm sorry, Jess."

"What did you expect from me anyway?"

"What I've always expected. What I depended on . . ." He

licked his lips, as if evaluating her receptiveness. "Honesty," he finally declared. "That's what you always gave me. Even as a kid, I knew you were telling me the truth as best you could, no holds barred."

"So you're saying I'm not being honest now?"

"I'm saying you haven't really given it much thought because you'd rather be angry. You've stopped thinking."

Jessie pursed her lips. "That's not fair, Andy. You don't know me anymore—"

"Yes I do," he interrupted.

"No you don't."

"You may have changed, but you're still—"

Jessie held up her hand like a stop sign. "Please. Stop saying that."

"Don't you remember—"

"I don't *want* to remember anymore—"

"But, Jess—"

"People grow up," Jessie finished. "I don't wear my life on my sleeve anymore."

"Is that how you want to live?"

"Yes," Jessie replied firmly. The tiny crack had exploded into a giant chasm, breaking them apart.

Andy leaned back, as if the conversation was over. A minute passed in silence, and Jessie wondered how something so good had suddenly turned so bad.

Andy met her eyes. "Still friends?"

Jessie smiled, but it felt weak. "Of course." She looked at her watch. They'd been here for an hour. As if on cue, they were interrupted by shouts. Laura was pushing Betty in her wheelchair, and in her lap were their watercolor paintings. Andy caught Jessie's eye again. His face communicated warmth and reassurance.

At least I didn't hope this time, Jessie thought. *I knew we were doomed from the very beginning.*

They attended a few more shows, but the day was obviously

winding down. Betty looked tired, although she pretended otherwise. Only Laura was eager to stay. When they finally headed toward the exit, Betty pointed to a craft shop across the way. "I'd like to get a souvenir."

Andy wheeled her to the shop while Jessie and Laura waited on a bench. "Do we *have* to go?" Laura whined.

Jessie checked the time. Five o'clock. "We've been everywhere, sweetie. And Mrs. Robinette is wiped out."

Laura nodded glumly.

In spite of the earlier tense discussion, Jessie was enjoying the wait, the exuberant buzz of the crowd. More and more people were heading out the exit. Dads were carrying bags of souvenirs. Moms were holding the hands of their children or pushing strollers. The conversation with Andy played in her mind as she waited. Laura sat still, crestfallen, apparently lost in the specter of going home. Jessie felt sorry for her.

Among the exiting people she spotted a blond woman wearing a yellow sundress. Jessie's mind clicked and everything went numb again. Fuzzy. Automatic. Jessie put her hand on Laura's shoulder. "Stay here, sweetie."

"Where are you going?"

Jessie didn't reply as she rushed across the pathway, weaving between couples and families. The closer Jessie got, the farther the woman seemed to diminish into the crowd.

"Wait!" Jessie whispered, but the woman couldn't possibly have heard her.

A man stepped in front of Jessie, and they collided. "Sorry . . ." Angrily he stepped aside, but the woman in the sundress had disappeared.

Jessie stood in the middle of a crowd of people, circling around and around in one spot, her panic building. *Where'd she go?*

And then she spotted her. She took off again, this time in a full sprint, and by the time she reached the woman, she had completely lost her composure, not to mention her grip on reality. She slowed down at the last minute and reached out and touched the woman's shoulder.

"Mom?"

The woman turned and Jessie shrank back in horror, realizing what she'd just done. "I'm sorry, I thought you were someone . . ."

The woman forced a smile, and her little girl looked up at her and said, "Mom, who's that?" The woman, who was no older than Jessie herself, smiled again, but there was a glint of fear in her eyes. She didn't even answer her little girl, instead pushing her forward, saying, "Just keep walking, okay?" Yards away the mother glanced back again, likely worried that the "crazy" woman was still following them.

Jessie just stood there, the entire park swirling around in her mind like a Tilt-a-Whirl. She felt a hand on her own shoulder. It was Andy.

"You okay?" he asked gently.

Jessie hugged herself. "I just . . . I thought I saw . . . someone I knew."

Andy slipped his arm around her. "Too much excitement, huh?"

She nodded. They walked back to the bench, where Laura was fiddling with one of her toys, and Mrs. Robinette was serenely examining a piece of carved wood.

Chapter Twenty

ANDY AND JESSIE helped Mrs. Robinette into her house. She marveled at the "wonderful day" and hugged Jessie, who promised to visit again.

Jessie hurried back to the car to wait with Laura, who seemed to be descending into despair, a startling contrast to her earlier exuberance.

"Can I get you anything?" Andy asked Betty.

Betty took a tentative cane-assisted step. "Just a kiss on the cheek."

Andy complied.

"Now don't keep your lady friend waiting," she clucked.

"Laura doesn't look so good," he commented.

"Today was a good day for her," Mrs. Robinette said. "Outings like these are few and far between."

Jessie got back out of the car and met Andy on the porch. "Laura isn't ready to go home yet."

"Ice cream, maybe?" Andy offered.

"You always could read my mind."

Andy raised his eyebrows humorously. "I thought I wasn't allowed to talk that way."

"Don't make me hit you."

They drove to Betty's shop, where her daughter, Kay, was running things. Laura, whose smile had made a faltering reappearance, ordered mint chocolate chip. Andy watched curiously as Jessie stepped up to the plate.

"Pistachio again?" He asked.

"Not tonight," she said slyly. An immediate throwback to their childhood. "Okay, Mr. Andrew, go for it," she challenged, making a sweeping gesture with her arm.

Andy ordered banana nut for her.

Jessie began laughing.

"Am I right?"

"Not even close. Are you serious? Banana nut?"

After settling on butter pecan, they sat at their old table. Laura was still a bit sullen, so Andy and Jessie attempted to put a positive spin on the end of a glorious day. They reviewed the various events and activities at the fair, and eventually Laura began giggling again.

Andy's cell phone rang and he intended to let it go, until he checked the ID. It was his dad, who rarely called Andy's cell number. Smiling apologetically, he headed outside where the reception was clearer.

"Andy, where are you?" His father sounded worried.

Where am I? "What is it, Dad?"

"Is Jessica still with you?"

Andy looked in through the shop window. Jessie noticed him looking and gave a gentle wave. "I'm not following you. . . ."

"Have you talked about anything?"

"Dad, just say it."

His dad paused. Andy turned toward Elephant Rock, which was visible above the building across the street. Long shadows were already descending upon the mountain-enclosed village, matching the growing shadows of his own mind. His father was obviously troubled about something.

"What is it?" Andy repeated.

When his father finally continued, his tone was grave and his words were measured. "Andy, there's something you need to know. . . ."

◆ ◆ ◆ ◆ ◆

Jessie smiled as Andy entered the shop. He smiled back, almost too brightly. Laura had been chattering about her friends at school, describing their hair colors and styles. *"I want to be a hair stylist when I grow up,"* she had told Jessie. *"They get to wear purple whenever they want."*

Something was troubling Andy. She remembered the way he'd always overcompensated when he was a kid, especially when he was trying to hide something, and he was the worst fibber on the planet.

"Everything okay?" she asked.

Andy didn't respond. "So . . . get enough ice cream?" he asked Laura, who shook her head and took another bite.

"That'll never happen!"

He laughed and Laura giggled. Jessie watched him, wondering what had changed so quickly. Laura took another long, slow bite. Jessie finally caught Andy's eye, and he winked at her.

An hour later, they dropped Laura off, and she trudged mournfully to her house. They heard Molly's muffled barking, and then Laura suddenly appeared in the window, waving. It had an almost desperate quality.

"You okay?" Andy asked, looking over at her.

"Her mother is a witch," Jessie replied.

Andy looked at the house again, pondering the situation. He straightened in his seat and stared through the windshield, lost in thought. "I hope I didn't offend you earlier, Jess."

She leaned back in the leather seat, taking a deep breath, unwilling to belabor the obvious. "I get too worked up sometimes."

Andy put the car into gear.

"Do you remember when we used to ride to the top of the hill?"

"I thought you'd never ask," Jessie whispered.

They drove up in nostalgic silence, his headlights blazing a trail. Reaching the top, Andy parked on the gravel road in front of an apartment complex, facing Elephant Rock to the east. To their right was the majestic southward corridor to Colorado Springs.

Andy cut the engine and they settled into a comfortable stillness. From this vantage point they could see their old haunts: the lake, the gazebo, the town hall, the school and flagpole, and the gift shop.

"Shouldn't even be called a town," Jessie suggested. "It's so tiny."

"It was our whole world."

"A village, and barely that."

They talked some more, nothing controversial, and the minutes passed effortlessly. The town lights grew in proportion to the dimming of the evening. Before long, the dash lights were illuminating a misty green into the interior of his car. Andy turned in his seat, facing her. "Why *did* you come back, Jess?"

She frowned thoughtfully and considered telling him the truth: *I was zipping along on my way to Oregon when a giant hook descended from the sky . . .* but then realized this was the perfect opening. She dug into her purse and pulled out a white box, handing it to him. "This is why—my sum total reason for coming home."

Andy raised his eyebrows but accepted the gift. He brought it to his nose and sniffed.

Jessie laughed. "What were you expecting?"

"Cologne maybe?" Andy chuckled.

"Just open it, silly."

He pried the lid off and removed the Toto key chain, holding it as if it were pure gold. "Hey . . . I *do* remember this."

"I forgot your twelfth birthday, remember?" She opened her purse again and pulled out her own key chain, comparing the two. "I stopped by Finders Keepers a couple days ago. Happened to see it."

He was still examining the key chain. "Doesn't *this* take me back." He whistled. "Do you remember Mrs. Peterson?"

"How could I forget?" Jessie answered. "I honestly think she hated kids."

"It's like we had a time limit or something."

Jessie nodded. "I remember telling her once that I would never steal anything and that she could frisk me if she needed to, but I was going to take my time looking around. Or she could call the cops!"

"You were gutsy," Andy said, grinning. "You actually *said* that?"

"I had a lip."

"Still do."

"Thank you."

Andy was still staring at the key chain. "Well, let's do this right now." He removed his keys from the ignition and, one by one, put each of his keys on the new ring, like an important ritual or ceremony. Then he caught her by surprise. He spoke softly, carefully, as if he were walking on broken glass. "What happened at the fair today?" His gaze was clear and unwavering, and she knew instantly what he meant.

You mean, why am I so messed up? she almost said, tempted to brush it off with another joke.

"I told you about the dreams, remember?" she began. He nodded, encouraging her to continue. "This is going to sound strange." She was staring out the window, emboldened by the top-of-the-world perspective.

"The dreams come almost every night. . . ." She described them, how they had evolved over the years yet in many ways stayed the same. A few varieties on the same theme, with little difference between them. And in the dreams her mother always wore a yellow sundress.

"I freaked out today," she admitted. "I saw a woman in a yellow dress, and everything went crazy." She closed her eyes, feeling ridiculous. Now that she was actually *saying it,* she questioned her own sanity. "I had this counselor once," she continued. "Actually he was a therapist with a bunch of fancy letters behind his name, and all he ever wanted to discuss were the dreams." She chuckled at the memory. "'Dreams are the key to your subconscious,' he once said." She stopped and looked sheepishly over at Andy. "You don't want to hear this. . . ."

"Tell me," Andy replied simply.

Jessie reached up and rubbed her shoulders. "In spite of his stuffy background, he was a neat guy, just a little stuck in the world of Freud." She peered out the window again, down the glorious corridor. The view had a trancelike effect on her, like an inkblot test that reaches into your mind and pulls out the truth. She glanced at Andy again, and he seemed concerned. "You look worried. Am I scaring you?"

He shook his head, but she sensed something else. She let her head drop back against the seat.

"He said I was a repressed soul, that I needed *closure,* and I remember laughing at him. 'Do psychiatrists actually use that word?' And he said, 'Call it what you will, but the story isn't finished for you yet, not if you want to be emotionally healthy.'"

"The story?" Andy said.

"Yeah. I think he'd keyed in to how much I liked to read. I'd told him I'd started *War and Peace* and really hated it but was determined to finish it anyway."

"So . . . what did you think about what he said?"

"I didn't *want* to be emotionally healthy," she replied. "Not if that meant the dreams would stop. I actually cherished them . . . and yet they . . ." She stopped. *And yet they tormented me. . . .*

Andy continued his probing. "So the shrink thought the dreams meant you needed closure?"

Jessie nodded. "He said my subconscious was trying to communicate with me."

"Oh," Andy said with a tone of wonder. "Like a secret message in the back of your mind. . . ."

"Weird, huh?"

"No. Makes sense."

"He said my mother was like a phantom limb."

Andy frowned. "Phantom limb? That's seems a little weird."

"Well . . . he knew the circumstances of how they took my mother away, how I never saw her again." Jessie shivered at how easy it had become to talk about her past with Andy—*things can change in a moment.* In spite of their earlier disagreement, she also marveled at the ease with which they had dropped into their former roles again, like fitting the pieces into a puzzle. But she also remembered the childhood arguments. Things weren't so different after all. Even as youngsters, they'd had a way of challenging each other.

Andy's expression was too serious, and she was struck again with the notion that he knew something he wasn't sharing. He finished for her. "So . . . do you sometimes think your mom didn't actually die?"

She looked him in the eye and pondered his statement. "I sometimes *feel* as if she didn't die, but I never really *think* it."

Andy nodded once and began rubbing the steering wheel with his palm, obviously formulating his next words.

"What?"

He turned in his seat. "It makes perfect sense. You and your mother were very close."

Is that what you really want to say? she wanted to ask but couldn't.

"They took her away and you never saw her again," Andy said.

Jessie squeezed her key ring tightly.

"And you never visited her in the . . . hospital?"

"No. I don't think so." A faint image flashed in her mind. She tried to follow it, but the memory flicked away like a slippery fish.

"You don't remember?"

Jessie shrugged. "I think I just . . . tried to bury it." *Good choice of words,* she thought.

"I think your therapist was right," he submitted. "Your dreams are telling you something."

"Okay, Dr. McCormick. What is your prescription?" Jessie grinned, hoping to lighten the conversation. Poor Andy looked as if he were being led to the gallows. The thought struck her again that their entire conversation had been a kind of setup. "Is this what you *really* wanted to talk about, Andy?"

"Why do you ask?"

She was tempted to throw it back in his face, the comment he'd made at the fair about honesty. But she didn't. "Maybe this is why I came back," she said, letting him off the hook.

"Why?"

"To finish the story somehow."

He gave a subtle shake of the head, seemingly not convinced. But by now their conversation had piqued her curiosity. Never before had she been this open about her mother's death.

"Do you remember what happened after my mother died?" she asked, looking straight ahead.

"Our friendship basically ended."

She frowned. "I don't remember that. . . ."

"You stayed in your room. You didn't come back to school. I knocked on your door and your father would answer, and he could barely speak. He looked like living death itself."

"That's because he was practically dead. Did you come to his funeral?"

"I stood right next to you."

"I threw a big fit before the funeral," Jessie remembered. "The coffin was closed and I demanded they open it."

"Why?"

"Because I wasn't *convinced*."

Andy whistled. "Did they open it?"

"Yep."

"Did you have nightmares?"

"Not one," she whispered. "Seeing him dead was closure for

me. I was convinced he was gone." It struck her what she'd just said, and her entire body broke out in shivers. *But I never saw my mother dead. . . .*

She turned to Andy. "How do you prove someone is dead?"

He looked at her incredulously. "What?"

"What would I do?" she whispered. "How would I start?"

He thought for a moment, and then, sighing, he pulled a piece of paper from the glove compartment, removed a pen, and began scribbling. "I've worked for my dad before," he explained. "I'm not sure this is *proof*, but as far as legal details, this where you start. . . ."

Jessie leaned over to watch him write. Once finished, he handed her the paper.

"A death certificate can be prepared by any number of people," Andy said. "Coroner, attending physician, hospital authority, or funeral director. Then it's supposed to be filed at both the county and state vital records office. You can order a copy of the death certificate, but it takes a while."

She studied his list of three Web sites.

"These should be up to date," Andy said. "I haven't checked in a while."

"Isn't there a social security death index I can access?" she asked.

"The Social Security Administration doesn't provide it directly," he replied. "Various commercial interests assemble an index from the death master file and offer the information for a fee, but depending on your source, it's notoriously incomplete."

She read through the Web sites again. "What's the last one for?"

"My mother is into genealogical research. She uses that site for researching our ancestry—it'll give you access to any public records: birth, marriage, death, census, you name it. That's her user name and password."

"Maybe I should just start there."

Andy shrugged. "Don't forget the cemetery and the funeral home. They have records, too."

She met his gaze, and he smiled back.

"Why don't you just ask your *grandmother* for the death certificate?"

Jessie smiled sheepishly. "I suppose that would make the most sense, wouldn't it?"

Andy gave her a friendly wink. "Are you free for dinner tomorrow?"

"That would be great," she said, staring at his list again. Her mind was elsewhere. She was formulating a few ideas of her own.

Chapter Twenty-One

THE FRONT RANGE was a silhouette against the darkening horizon. Andy's thoughts were accompanied by the hum of the highway and the rush of the wind against his windows. He hadn't even turned on the radio, preferring to drive in the clear blaze of his own anguish, the silence like a black hole, siphoning out the poison of despair.

He was discouraged with their argument over religion, chagrined with his own need to be right, and yet saddened at Jessie's position. What a difference a few years made. When they were kids, it was *she* who had lived on the edge of faith.

At least once a week, like a ritual, they had ridden their bikes to the top of the hill in Palmer Lake. They exerted a lot of energy to make the journey, but the view was worth it, giving them the illusion of worldly dominance. Looking back down toward the southeast, they embraced a view of the Front Range, just as they had tonight.

He remembered one afternoon in particular, when Jessie had been lost in her own thoughts, lost in a grief that would soon swallow her whole. He'd asked her why she was so preoccupied, and she'd turned on him with fire in her eyes.

. . . "Aren't you keeping up with current events?"

"I'm sorry."

Tears had sprung to her eyes. "Nobody believes me. Everyone thinks my mother is going to die." He wanted to embrace the same conviction she had, but it was difficult. "Andy, do *you* believe me?"

Of course he didn't, but if he told her that he did, she would either call him on it or her eyes would flicker with disappointment. You didn't lie to Jessie and get away with it; she had uncanny instincts. Even at the tender age of twelve, Andy had discovered that life rarely delivers what we want.

She was still waiting for him to answer when he decided to fib anyway and let the chips fall where they may. He would say what seemed right—the proper thing, as his mother had always taught him. Just when he was about to open his mouth, it occurred to him that he *did* believe her. He didn't have to lie after all.

"You do?" she asked, her eyes searching his. He nodded with full confidence into the look of marvel in her eyes, and he'd never felt prouder to be her friend. At that moment, they were just two kids believing God for a miracle, both of them utterly convinced it would happen. . . .

Thinking on it now, twelve years later, he was still struck by the feeling of transparency that had always been a part of their every discussion.

Had he really believed? Wasn't it simply the aura of Jessie's relentless faith that had momentarily gripped him? Considering the ultimate result, it didn't matter anymore. No wonder she'd ditched her faith.

In recent years he'd heard his share of testimonies in church regarding answered prayer, and they'd always seemed a little forced, circumstantial, or too simplistic: *"God helped me find my keys"* and that kind of thing. Even people who didn't espouse a particular religious persuasion would speak of miraculously answered prayer, not to mention the New Agers, who had virtually coined the term *creating your own reality*.

He recalled a certain seminary student who had given a testimony about God's answer for financial assistance, only as the story went, God apparently missed the deadline. The young man was forced to quit school because "God didn't come through." He returned home, abandoning his training to become a minister, terribly embittered. One day, about six months later, he discovered some insurance documents in his possessions. They turned out to be more than just routine papers, indicating a cash value policy that could easily be withdrawn to the tune of several thousand dollars—more than enough to cover his expenses. The punch line to his story was he'd received the mysterious documents a few weeks *before* he needed the tuition money, proving God had answered after all but had kept the answer hidden in order to test his faith or perhaps redirect his course of life. Needless to say, his broken faith was restored.

Thinking now of Jessie's fondness for country music, he wondered what she thought of Garth Brooks's song about unanswered prayer. The song told of a chance meeting between a man and the woman he'd once begged God to allow him to marry, only to realize that if his prayer *had* been answered, he would have missed out on his present wife, who was the true answer to his petition.

Tonight he'd seen the same glint in Jessie's eyes, the old determination, the old faith—at least some form of it—and it had broken his heart. In spite of what she might say, she was still thinking, still believing on some level, that her mother wouldn't—or didn't—die. He wondered, in fact, if she might *never* believe it.

But none of that really mattered now. In fact, their discussion regarding the details of her mother's death would soon be insignificant. In spite of everything that had transpired today, in spite of everything they had discussed, he was haunted most by the look in Jessie's eyes when she'd encountered the woman at the fair.

He sighed, wondering how he could possibly tell her the truth.

He'd almost told her tonight, but she'd seemed too vulnerable, and besides, he hadn't been completely sure yet.

His cell phone rang. It was already in the cradle, ready for hands-free operation.

It was his dad. "Are you alone now?"

"I'm five miles away from home."

"Oh . . . are you . . ."

"I mean Castle Rock," Andy finished, realizing his father's confusion. As far as his father was concerned, and as long as his son remained unmarried, home would always be his parents' house.

"Did you tell her?"

"How could I?"

"Well . . . do you think she knows already?"

"I don't know." Andy sighed. "I don't think so." But it seemed like the kind of thing she *would* know. He wondered if Jessie had simply refused to acknowledge it. Could he blame her?

"Maybe she does," Andy continued, wishing the whole thing would just go away.

Jessie had obviously lived a sheltered life for many years. And she'd been estranged from her grandmother, the only other person who would have had access to the truth. Considering everything that had happened between them, it was unlikely her grandmother would have told her, but maybe her grandmother still *intended* to tell her.

"Explain it again," Andy asked, and his father complied, starting from the very beginning.

◆ ◆ ◆ ◆ ◆

Eleven-thirty. The lights in the magnificent house were off when Jessie got back. She'd spent the last couple hours in a restaurant drinking coffee, working through the crazy idea that was formulating in her mind.

She let herself in with the key Bill had given her earlier. She couldn't find the entry light, so she relied on the moonlit shadows to make her way across the entryway to the stairs. Padding up the steps, she heard a squeak and stopped. *You missed one, Bill.*

Another squeak. The sound was coming from below her, from her grandmother's room downstairs, or maybe from the study next to her room, which had been her grandfather's office. She had very few memories of the man who'd died and left her grandmother set for life. She'd once asked her mom how he died, and she replied, *"A stroke, honey." "What's a stroke?"* she asked, and her mother carefully explained it. Just thinking about it hurt Jessie's head.

According to her mother, her grandfather was only fifty when he passed, becoming yet another part of her grandmother's life that she never talked about. It seemed as if Grandmother had forced the entirety of her existence into conformity with her all-important "appearance."

When Jessie reached the end of the hall, she paused before her mother's former room. Impulsively, she tried the door again. Locked.

Once in her own room, Jessie tossed her purse on the bed. After a moment's reflection, she slipped back downstairs again, only this time taking the back way, the set of stairs that led directly to the kitchen. As she went, she formulated an excuse in case her grandmother happened to wander in. *Couldn't sleep, needed milk, wanted to see the place in the moonlight . . .*

She found the kitchen empty and opened the key cabinet. There were five good candidates. She slipped them into her pocket and climbed the back stairs. Glancing back down the hallway toward Bill's room, she pulled out the keys and tried them, one by one, her heart in her throat.

No good.

Disappointed, she returned to her room. Opening her purse, she retrieved a credit card. She went back to the door, intending to slide the card into the wood, but a strip of misplaced wood prevented insertion. Jessie wiggled the doorknob, then cringed at the noise she'd made.

Back downstairs, she replaced the keys. Her nerves calm again, she paused in the alcove looking out the windows to the gazebo—magical in the moonlight. The sight reminded her of the gazebo in the park . . . times she'd slipped outdoors after Mom was asleep and Dad hadn't come home yet. Back when the impossibilities seemed possible.

She hurried upstairs again and to bed with a renewed sense of purpose. She set her alarm for seven o'clock but awakened at three. She stewed in bed for two hours, watching the shadows dance across the wall.

I'm going to finish the story once and for all, she thought.

It was time to explore the depths of what she didn't remember, to look under the bed and face the monsters. It was time to move on with her life, in every aspect. Time to face the truth of her mother's passing.

While so many things had been repressed, she knew somehow she could remember them again. She thought of last night's dream and the utter joy she'd felt, and then the corresponding despair upon awakening. Again and again throughout her life, she'd ridden the roller coaster, up . . . down . . . up . . . down. But no more.

I'll convince myself, she thought, thinking of her father's coffin. *Maybe I can't look into my mother's coffin, but I can do the next best thing. . . .*

Soon she would leave this hope-forsaken place and never return. Her newfound determination reignited the old anger. No wonder she had stayed away for so many years. Nothing would ever change the fact that her mother had died in the company of mentally ill strangers. Why? Because of her grandmother's wicked meddling. Nothing would change the fact that her father had killed himself over grief—amplified by her grandmother's actions. The state would never have stepped in if Grandmother hadn't initiated a lawsuit to gain control. Not only had she bought the old house, but now she locked her daughter's room in her own house as if even the memories belonged to her alone.

Andy had volunteered what to do. Jessie couldn't wait to get started. Go to the library and pull up the death records. After that she planned to visit the cemetery. Somewhere along the line, she intended to get into her mother's room, even if she had to kick the door down. Hopefully things wouldn't come to that.

If all else failed, she would go to the institution itself. But thinking about the place of her mother's death caused flickers of memories to dance at the edge of her mind. Andy had asked her, *"Do you remember visiting your mother?"* And she hadn't. Yet there was *something* . . . bits and pieces. It was like pulling up a rope attached to a three-hundred-pound anchor, inch by painful inch.

I was there, wasn't I? She closed her eyes, focusing on the little that she did remember of the place. Fragmented recollections. She remembered meeting her grandmother and Mrs. Robinette in a room. There were male nurses in a hallway. . . . And then the images faded again, like a wisp of smoke.

Eventually, she slept fitfully and awakened at six-thirty. She showered and dressed, but her eyes were still sunken from lack of sleep. Her arms tingled, and her legs felt weak. She wasn't sure if she had dreamed last night or not.

When she met Bill in the kitchen, her good-morning smile felt pasty on her face. "I'll just have some fruit," she told him. "Maybe some toast, too."

"Should I take it personally?" He chuckled.

They sat in silence a few moments until Grandmother joined them. Bill made several comments about the local news while Grandmother busied herself. The sunshine was muted by mini-blinds.

"Still tired, kiddo?" Bill asked.

Jessie shrugged, forcing another smile. Mentally, she was tracing her route to the library in downtown Colorado Springs, only a few miles away . . . Nevada to I-25 to Bijou and she'd be there.

"Do you have a copy of my mother's death certificate?" she asked suddenly. Grandmother's hand quivered and she set her coffee cup down. "Well, now . . . I'm sure . . ."

Bill smiled curiously. "Now there's a question you don't hear every day."

"I'd have to . . . hunt around . . ." Doris replied faintly, without indicating she was interested in doing so.

Bill stood at the counter pouring another cup of coffee, and her grandmother turned her attention again to the paper, suddenly preoccupied.

That was only my first question, Jessie thought.

Her grandmother cleared her throat. "Would you like to attend our luncheon?"

Not in a year of Sundays, Jessie thought. But she said she would and took a sip of orange juice. She caught Bill's eye, and his expression struck her as strangely empathetic.

"We'll leave at eleven-forty," her grandmother instructed as she slipped out of the room.

Bill was silent as he cleaned up. He didn't whistle and he didn't turn on the radio.

Jessie excused herself, and instead of wandering upstairs, she went through the alcove door and crossed the lawn to the gazebo. She sat in the swing, mulling over her conversation with Andy and the strange way he'd looked at her after the cell phone call at the ice-cream shop.

❖ ❖ ❖ ❖ ❖

Bill dropped Jessie and her grandmother off at the Broadmoor Hotel promptly at 11:45. They walked beneath the royal red awning, and a doorman opened the door to the hotel. He nodded his red hat and said, "Have a delightful visit." Jessie answered, "Thank you, we will," but the doorman was already greeting another older couple.

They walked across the elegant tiled floor to the escalator. At the top was a large hall with decorative furnishings, modern paintings, more marble floors, and elaborate wood molding.

"I wanted you to see Broadmoor East first, before we have lunch," her grandmother explained in her matter-of-fact tone. "They've redecorated the whole place."

Jessie's previous request seemed to have been forgotten. Or perhaps Grandmother had forgiven her indiscretion. They explored the lovely room, then headed out another set of double glass doors, to a small courtyard with a sidewalk circling the lake. Crossing a bridge, they wandered to the opposite side, to Broadmoor West, then entered in through another set of glass doors, following yet another hallway to the left until they reached the restaurant.

There were seven of them for lunch, gathered around a large round table. Each lady was impeccably dressed, leaving Jessie feeling out of place in her mother's navy blue skirt and cream blouse. She was introduced by her grandmother as each lady nodded and smiled, studying her.

After a few minutes of conversation, it became obvious to Jessie the women all had similar backgrounds—degrees in piano performance as well as prestigious husbands. And her grandmother was the ringleader, which wasn't a surprise anymore. They each kowtowed to Doris Crenshaw, hung on every word, and never disagreed with a single opinion she expressed.

They discussed the piano teachers' association, and while only a few of them were still on the board, they still considered themselves the true leadership. They talked about the other members as if stricter membership requirements were desperately needed to filter out the riffraff. They talked about their students as if they were helpless geniuses in need of their enlightenment. And they talked about the symphony as if it were a disgrace to the community.

Jessie drank her lemon-flavored water and watched the clock.

"I was simply appalled," commented one woman, who had said her husband basically ran NORAD, "when she told the entire group that scales aren't for everyone." She was referring to a representative from the Music Teachers National Association, MTNA, who had given a pedagogic seminar to their teachers' group.

"I think she was referring to the less-talented students," one teacher interjected, which was apparently the wrong thing to say. The entire group shook their heads in displeasure, and the poor woman took her censure with courageous humility.

"And to think she is from the MTNA," put in another woman. "We're witnessing a national devaluation on the importance of pianistic technique."

"It's the computer age we live in," Jessie's grandmother added, and the entire bunch leaned forward, as if unwilling to miss a single word. "There's no patience anymore and no discipline. We are depending upon our keyboards, our synthesizers, and our computer programs to fill in the gaps of our undertrained musicality."

"I *sold* my electronic keyboard," another lady admitted, aligning herself with Grandmother. "From now on it's acoustic piano alone, and if that costs me students, so be it."

One woman with two or three chins leaned over as if revealing a dark secret. "And not to mention this class piano thing . . . it's simply ridiculous."

They nodded in unison. They were *private* teachers, after all. If you were willing to sink to that level, you *could* make more money by teaching class piano, but you were committing a sin of biblical proportions. All manner of shoddy technique could slip in when you weren't looking.

At one point, Jessie had had enough. After her lunch of salad greens, Jessie placed her white cloth napkin on the matching tablecloth and excused herself. The moment she entered the exquisite hall, which led back to the glass doors, she felt a load lift from her shoulders. For a brief moment, she even contemplated just walking out of the hotel and hailing a cab.

Wouldn't that embarrass Grandmother? Jessie thought bitterly, but she felt empty in her soul, and she couldn't imagine that her mother would have ever done such a thing, much less thought it. A few minutes later she headed back in and settled down at the table. No one seemed to notice she'd returned. They were discussing a particular teacher's penchant for stealing other teachers' students.

By the end of the meal, the group had reached a consensus that it was up to teachers like them—the enlightened ones—to save America. Otherwise, the Russian pianists would conquer the world.

Chapter Twenty-Two

BILL WAS WAITING for them on the curb. Jessie slipped into the backseat while Bill held the door for her grandmother.

"So. Did you all get your consorting, plotting, and devious undertaking out of the way for another week?" Bill asked.

"Oh, Bill," Doris replied with mild disgust.

When he'd settled into the driver's seat, he twinkled back at Jessie. "Was it as unbearable as I think it *had* to be?"

Her grandmother let a small sigh escape her lips.

"It was bearable," Jessie said, smiling. Bill chuckled and pulled away from the curb. The three of them traveled silently all the way home.

"Do you need to lie down a bit?" Bill asked Jessie after they'd entered the house. Her grandmother was already heading down the hallway.

"Why, does it show?"

"Look a little peaked, that's all."

Jessie headed upstairs, and the sudden fatigue hit her so hard she had to nearly pull herself up by the railing.

"Can I get you anything?" Bill called up from the bottom of the stairwell.

"Nothing. Thanks anyway," she said. Bill nodded and headed back to the kitchen.

From the moment her back hit the mattress, she began to drift away. Normally unable to sleep in what Darlene had always called "the coffin position," Jessie was aware of sinking backward . . . down . . . down . . . and her last thought before falling asleep was to wonder if the only incomplete story was the short story she'd begun the moment she'd taken a wrong turn.

She awakened some time later to the sound of footsteps. Groggy, she leaned up, listening. The sounds seemed to come from across the hallway, her mom's room. She pulled herself over and nearly fell back into the mattress. Pausing a moment at the edge of the bed in order to gain her equilibrium, she wandered across the room, then out into the hallway and discovered the door ajar.

She stood there for a moment, taking it in. *Am I dreaming?* She squinted to focus better. It *was* open. She crept forward, listening carefully. Was someone still in there? It seemed to take forever to cross that short distance. She slowed again, straining her ears.

When she was a foot away, she pushed on the partially open door. It creaked softly and she peeked inside. No one was there, and the air seemed charged with static electricity. The shades were drawn, but filtered light illuminated the bed and she detected the faint aroma of Charlie. Her mother's room at home had always smelled of the lovely fragrance.

Jessie stood in the entryway, taking in every detail. Just as she had remembered. Her mother's grade-school years had been preserved forever. Crossing the threshold, aware of the slippery feel of oak flooring, Jessie recalled overhearing a conversation between her grandmother and her father.

"I did it for her," her grandmother had said. *"Olivia told me that her grade-school years were the happiest of her life. So I re-created it to look just like that. We had plenty of photos from that time. I replaced the rug, the bedspread, the curtains, repainted the walls. Some of the stuffed animals had been thrown away, of course. Finding those was*

more difficult but not impossible. As you can see, stepping in here would have been like going back to the happiest time of her life."

Jessie stood in front of the closet. She reached for the knob. It creaked open and she saw her mother's clothes, a collection of colorful outfits, and then . . . the yellow dress, almost hidden within the variety.

She reached for it and the fabric felt smooth between her fingers. Noticing something beneath the hanging clothes, she knelt and saw a backpack, light blue-green and nylon. The one Andy used to carry for her on the way home from school unless he was carrying his own backpack. *Why would Grandmother keep it?* she wondered.

Jessie unzipped the backpack, the contents startling her. Her old things had never been removed. A spiral notebook. A math book that had never been returned to the school. Pencils and a couple of children's books. A real time capsule. She shoved it back toward the closet wall, then stood up, gathering her wits. Touching the footboard of the bed as she rounded it, she tiptoed to the dresser, noticing the narrow top drawer was slightly ajar. She reached for the white knobs and pulled. Instead of gliding, the drawer rasped on the wood.

She held her breath as she appraised her mother's photo albums inside. Reverently she lifted the top one—blue cloth, no label—and just before she opened it, she saw the next one, right below the first. The Oregon scrapbook.

She removed that one instead, trading it with the first, setting it on the bedspread, then kneeling before it. She traced the cover with her fingers . . . *Oregon Coast* . . . and then the date. She would have been five years old. She opened the first page, suddenly remembering the last time she'd seen it. She had been with her mother on her sick bed, reliving happier moments. In the last months before they took Mom away, she had spent a lot of time with these old scrapbooks.

The first page contained the origins of the trip, a picture of her mom holding what seemed to be three airline tickets, hugging

Jessie's grandmother and mugging for the camera. As always, Grandmother looked stiff. But Mom seemed to ignore that.

Another pose at the Portland Airport. Her mother was smiling in front of the blue rental car, gripping a travel brochure. Little Jessie was holding on to her mother's leg, smiling up at the camera. Next page, pictures of Astoria. Apparently, they had traveled northwest before beginning their coastal drive south. None of this was familiar. An assortment of coastal photographs—Cannon Beach, Tillamook, her mom and dad in swimsuits, and several of Jessie: building a castle, sitting on her dad's shoulders in ankle-deep water.

Jessie's eyes filled with tears. The whole Oregon fantasy made sense now, and she couldn't help but wonder how much of her life had been dominated by things she no longer remembered.

Finally a little close-up of her holding an iridescent butterfly shell and her mother's written narrative beneath the pictures: *Little Jessie holding a favorite "shell." You asked me, "Mommy, is this where butterflies come from? Are they hatched?" I told you that it's no coincidence that butterfly shells look just like butterflies. God's mark is on the smallest details of creation and on the tiniest details of our lives. He puts clues into nature and even into the ordinary routine of our lives, clues that seem to have nothing to do with each other, like shells and butterflies, and yet are connected by a common Creator. You had such a look of wonderment! You just nodded your head and I was so amazed . . . my smart little butterfly girl.*

Jessie closed the album and blinked her eyes. *Hold on* . . . The last line of the Oregon scrapbook read: *You cried when we left. You talked about it for months afterward. I promised you we'd return someday. And you said, "Okay, Mommy, but when?" Soon, my sweet butterfly girl, very soon.*

Instead of looking at another album, Jessie began sorting through the drawers, starting at the top left one. She immediately came upon some old letters wrapped in a rubber band. From the handwriting and the addresses, she realized they'd been written by her mother. Strange. Did her grandmother ask for her daughter's old letters to be returned? Jessie wouldn't put it past her. Then a single envelope at the bottom of the drawer caught her eye. Written in her mother's handwriting, it was addressed simply: *My dearest Jessica*, and just below, in smaller letters, *Please open on your twenty-first birthday.*

It took her a moment to realize what it was. Jessie placed the letter on the mattress and stared at it, a mixture of emotions flooding through her. *When would she have written it?* she wondered. *And why didn't my grandmother tell me?* But the answer to that was obvious. Her grandmother surely had never intended to reveal it.

Jessie began to open it, placing her thumb in the tiny crevice of the corner, but stopped. She was desperate to read it but nervous. Closing her eyes, she squeezed out the tears that seemed so close to the surface. It wasn't the right place or the right time to read this special note from her deceased mother.

She heard distant footsteps. Standing quickly, she slipped the letter into her pocket and considered her next course of action. Her first reaction was to hide in the closet. But no . . . she would finally face the music. She removed the letter and held it in her hands, suddenly emboldened by her growing anger. Waiting, she stood still as a rock.

When Grandmother opened the door, she walked several steps into the room before realizing Jessie was standing there. "Oh, Jessica . . . I didn't expect to find you . . ."

Jessie placed the envelope on the bedspread in front of her grandmother. "You had no right," she whispered.

Grandmother frowned and her head jutted back in confusion. But when she looked down at the letter, recognition crossed her features. "Jessica—"

"When were you going to tell me?"

"I-I . . . forgot," she sputtered.

"This doesn't belong to you," Jessie said, her words measured and careful.

The older woman had the look of someone who'd been

ambushed, and it wasn't until now that Jessie realized her grandmother was holding an envelope of her own. "Jessica, please . . ."

"Why did you buy our house?"

Another look of confusion. "You don't understand—"

"How could I?" Jessie shot back. "You've taken away everything that ever belonged to me. First you stole my mother—"

"Oh no, Jes—" Her grandmother looked horrified. She put her hand to her mouth. "Your mother is . . ." And then she stopped. "Your mother was . . ." She squeezed her eyes tightly shut, her face contorted with the effort. She began speaking before she opened them again. "You left . . . so suddenly, Jessica. I never had time to explain." Her breathing was labored. "I never intended for . . . but . . . I'm so sorry. . . ."

Jessie glimpsed movement from the doorway. Bill had come upstairs and now appeared shaken by what he was encountering. Grandmother turned and noticed him standing there.

"It's too late for 'sorry,' " Jessie replied stonily. "I'm leaving tomorrow. I won't be back."

Her grandmother flinched but didn't reply. Bill opened his palms, a conciliatory gesture. "Jessie . . ."

"Don't . . ." she warned.

Bill stopped and licked his lips as if reconsidering his approach. He turned to her grandmother and their eyes met. An unspoken communication passed between them, and it seemed as if her grandmother said no with her eyes. He nodded slightly.

More secrets, Jessie thought angrily.

She grabbed her mother's letter from the bed and began walking past her grandmother. Bill stepped back to allow her to pass, but when she reached the hallway, he called to her. She turned quickly, preparing another retort, and saw the brown envelope in his hands.

"You were asking about this," he said. He extended the envelope, the one Grandmother had been holding.

Jessie took it from him, avoiding his eyes, and strode to her room. She grabbed her keys off the dresser and stormed down the hallway. At the bottom of the steps she ran outside, and by the time she reached her car, she was shaking. She opened the car door and slipped inside but could barely put the key into the ignition her hands were trembling so. Tears blinded her vision.

That was not how she had ever imagined a confrontation with Grandmother. The poor woman had wilted before her eyes.

When Jessie pulled away from the curb, her tears came in torrents and guilt flooded her soul.

Chapter Twenty-Three

JESSIE OPENED THE BROWN ENVELOPE at the stoplight. It was her mother's death certificate, just as she had suspected—handwritten and faded. What was the point of going to the library now? Here it was—proof of her mother's death.

In the moments before the light turned green, she pondered her next stop. She checked the time. Almost two o'clock. She had three hours before Andy planned to pick her up for dinner.

I'll study this at the library, she decided, glancing at her mother's letter, which rested on the passenger seat. The confrontation with her grandmother still echoed in her ears, including her cryptic half statement: *"Your mother is . . ."* Present tense.

Jessie wasn't the only person living in the past. In their own ways, neither of them had accepted the reality of her mother's death.

Jessie touched the letter, noticing the residual scent of Charlie—something she hadn't noticed before because the entire *room* had smelled of the fragrance. Either the letter had been sprayed with the cologne or it had absorbed the scent of the room. She traced her mom's handwriting with her fingers. Mom had still been alive when she'd written this letter. And, for a moment, Jessie felt as if she were still here. . . .

"My mother is dead," she whispered. But those words never sounded emptier—not empty in the sense of sadness, but empty in the sense that the whole of her being still couldn't say them and truly believe. "My mother is alive," Jessie whispered next, and the statement felt true. *Maybe Brandon was right,* she thought, her spirits sinking. *Maybe I need help.*

She steeled herself again. *No. I'm okay,* she thought, squeezing her eyes shut. *I've come a long way since Friday.*

The traffic light turned green. *I can do this. . . .*

◆ ◆ ◆ ◆ ◆

Doris sat on her garden bench on the stone patio with colorful petunias and daisies all around. She looked out at the gazebo. The backyard was so peaceful and quiet, inhabited by finches and blue jays, surrounded by large, healthy trees. At the edges of her private paradise, the tall cedar fence eliminated all visibility.

In the midst of the city she felt totally protected, separated from any sense of connection to the hustle and bustle of modern life. The yard was like a miniature Garden of Eden and yet, in spite of the calming beauty, in the midst of her well-planned environment, her world was falling apart.

"Hi Mommy, I brought you some flowers," little Olivia had once said when she came home from school. Doris had reprimanded Olivia for picking them, reducing her sweet little girl to tears.

"If only I could have it all back," Doris whispered to the memory.

Her mind was a jumble of emotions. She'd always had the best of intentions, but she'd learned years ago that good motives don't protect you from terrible mistakes.

"You stole my mother," Jessie had said and it was true. Doris had lived with the guilt of that. At times, she thought she had effectively submerged it below everything, buried it so deep within her it

would never haunt her again. But it came up anyway, like the weeds in her garden.

She had to keep culling her garden of regret, but while a few flowers grew to obscure the weeds, the soil of her life's garden was basically corrupt. Staying ahead required exhausting vigilance, pulling them out one by one, but the guilt was never far away. There wasn't enough clamor of life, enough busyness, to cover her pain.

"You stole my mother."

She'd rehearsed it often in her mind, telling herself that she'd made the right decision. Surely, there had been no other decision to make. But the guilt of it all was nearly destroying her. And memories of the past were obviously ruining her granddaughter's life.

She sighed deeply, as if to exhale the pain, but it couldn't be released that easily. Doris held her chest and her breathing was labored again.

Olivia had once said, *"Mom, no matter what happened when I was a child, I forgive you."*

Doris had answered flippantly, *"Livvy, please . . ."*

Olivia had discarded her religious roots and gone radical. She'd become a "born again" Christian. *"I know you were doing the best you could,"* Olivia had said.

Doris had wept later, just as she did now. Sometimes she still stood in her daughter's room and closed her eyes, and little Livvy was back again. Doris clearly remembered the little-girl voice: *"Mom, look what I painted."* Life was still full of possibilities. Redemption was in reach.

But nothing could erase that dreadful Tuesday. The people at the mental health center had called her in the morning. She'd known the moment the phone rang but refused to answer. Maria had been the one to finally pick up the phone.

"Do we have the right number for Olivia Lehman's family?" they'd asked her.

"That's correct," Maria had answered, her voice breaking.

They aren't even sure of our number, Doris remembered thinking later.

♦ ♦ ♦ ♦ ♦

She was still sitting on her bench when Bill strolled out, his eyes worried. "You okay?"

"I need to be alone."

He thumbed toward the house. "I'll be in the kitchen."

She nodded absently. He ambled back in, and her mind wandered off again.

I've lost her, she realized. For the past decade she'd wanted to repair her relationship with Jessica, but in the end, she simply wasn't capable of it. She thought of Bill, realizing how much she depended on him, and she wondered for the life of her what she would do if he ever left. *And yet, how can I blame him?*

If he knew the truth about her, the *whole* truth, life as she knew it would be finished in a heartbeat. And yet . . . would that be so bad?

Bill was at her side again. "Dory, please. Come inside." He put his hand under her elbow, and this time she allowed herself to be led inside.

"I've lost her, Bill."

He put his strong arm about her. "Everything will be fine."

"No, Bill. Nothing has ever been fine."

♦ ♦ ♦ ♦ ♦

Jessie entered the silent world of bookshelves. Students sat in study cubicles; old men sat on couches reading newspapers from far away. At the front desk she asked for a letter opener. She found a row of study cubicles, each containing a computer. Most were occupied, but one was empty. She sat next to a couple of college girls, giggling as they typed.

Removing her mother's letter—it was only one page—Jessie braced herself and began reading. . . .

My dear Jessica,

If you're reading this, then know I'm looking down on you bursting with pride at the wonderful young woman I've always known you would become. . . .

Jessie closed the letter, unable to read any more. She held it in front of her so it wouldn't become spotted with tears. Taking deep breaths, she exhaled slowly.

She buried the letter within her shirt, then picked up the death certificate again, analyzing the details, as if she might actually sear the truth into her mind. The certificate included name, date of birth, social security number, level of education, last known residence, certifying physician, place of death—including the room number—time of death, and cause of death—in this case: dementia—and a plethora of other seemingly insignificant cold facts. Nothing about what a wonderful mother she had been. No space for the details that *really* mattered.

Jessie studied the document for a while longer, noticing that several lines were left blank, including cemetery/crematory and method of disposition. *So much for checking the funeral home,* she thought.

Actually, the whole thing seemed fishy. Why was the death certificate handwritten anyway?

Imagination working overtime, she thought.

She glanced at the computer. *I'm here now,* she thought, connecting to the Internet and typing in the El Paso County Department of Health and Environment Web site from Andy's list. When the site loaded she clicked on Birth and Death Records and read the instructions. It offered hoop-jumping details for obtaining a death certificate, which Jessie didn't need anymore. She wanted simple verification of this one—the one Bill had given her.

She found the number instead and dialed it on her cell phone. After swimming through a series of recorded messages, Jessie remained on the line. Finally a real person answered, "El Paso Vital Records."

Jessie presented her request but was denied. "Only in person," the woman said. "With proof of kinship."

"Can you just verify that you have—"

"Only in person," the woman repeated. "We're across from Memorial Park."

Jessie thanked the woman and hung up.

She navigated to the Web site of the Colorado Department of Public Health and Environment and found the same song and dance. She could obtain a death certificate online, in person, or by mail. The online and mail procedure would take days, or she could make a request in person—in Denver. She dialed the direct number and her request for over-the-phone verification was denied again.

I'm just wasting time, Jessie thought. She went back to the last Web address, then logged on using Susan McCormick's user name and password. After clicking on Search For Your Ancestors, Jessie typed in her mother's name and last known residence. Nearly a hundred matches returned, countless Olivia Lehmans spread out under Census Records; Birth, Marriage, and Death Records; Military Records; Periodicals and Newspapers; and Membership Lists.

Under Birth, Marriage, and Death Records, Jessie clicked on Social Security Death Index and studied the names. Here, there were only five Olivia Lehmans, each listed with birth date, death date, last residence, and social security number. None were her mother.

Jessie leaned back in her chair and sighed, remembering what Andy had said about online death records: notoriously incomplete.

Getting up, she went to the reference desk and asked for help from a blond librarian who looked to be in her fifties.

"Verify a death?" the librarian asked.

Jessie nodded.

The lady thought for a moment, then handed Jessie yet another Web address. "The information is free," she assured her. Jessie thanked her, went back to her cubicle, and typed in the address. This time the site's online blanks asked for extensive information including social security number, date of birth, and date of death. Jessie provided it, then clicked Search. The Web site flickered out for a second, then reappeared: No Records Found.

"Notoriously incomplete," Jessie whispered to herself.

She heard the shuffling of shoes and turned to notice the same friendly librarian standing behind her.

"How's it working?"

"Nothing," Jessie replied. This time, she handed the death certificate to the lady. "I can't seem to verify this information."

The librarian smiled. "You know . . . why don't you just call them?"

"Sorry?"

"The Social Security Administration. They'll verify this over the phone."

Jessie smiled. When the librarian left, Jessie found the number on the Web and did just that. By now, her expectations were zilch. If the county and state wouldn't give her verbal information, why would anyone else?

Eventually, after responding to various recorded menus, Jessie found a living, breathing person. She presented her request as politely as possible, expecting another denial.

"What is the name and social security number?" the woman asked.

Jessie gave it to her gladly. The woman clicked away for a few moments, then returned. "I'm sorry. We have no record of her death."

Jessie was stunned. "Why?"

"Either she's not dead or no one reported it to us."

Jessie thanked her and hung up. She punched in Andy's number. It rang five times before he answered.

"Hey there," Andy greeted, his tone upbeat. "Any luck?"

Jessie described the situation, even mentioning the death certificate Bill had given her.

"I guess there's been a mistake," Andy said. "Like the woman said, nobody reported it to the agency." He paused. "But you *do* have a death certificate, right?"

"Yeah," Jessie whispered.

"So there you have it," he concluded. "Are we still on for tonight?"

"I'm an expensive gal," she joked, but her mind was a million miles away.

"I can dress up," he suggested.

"I'm kidding. . . ."

"See you about five?"

"I'll be waiting," she said.

She hung up the phone and continued pondering the death certificate.

Two and half hours to go before Andy came to pick her up. She studied the death certificate, noting again the blank lines. According to Betty, the urn was buried, probably in the same cemetery where her grandfather's remains were buried. *Why isn't this recorded on the death certificate? Why no mention of cremation?*

Jessie left the library, hopped into her car, and placed the letter and death certificate on the passenger seat. She headed east on Pikes Peak to the Rose Garden Cemetery.

Coming up on Union Boulevard, she realized she was driving adjacent to Memorial Park. Just ahead was the El Paso County Health Department. She debated for a second, then turned right.

Half a block away, she turned left and parked behind the tan building with green trim. She went through the glass doors and started down a long hallway. Halfway down, she opened the door to Vital Health Records. It was a tiny room, with four cubicles behind a protective glass window above a counter. A stout woman rose from her desk and smiled. According to the name tag, her name was Linda.

Jessie made her request.

"Are you kin?"

Jessie displayed her driver's license, and Linda scrutinized it.

"I don't need the death certificate," Jessie told her. "I just want to know if she's in your records."

Linda shrugged and reached for a pen and a piece of paper. "What's the name and social security number?"

Jessie handed her the death certificate. Linda examined it, seemingly confused.

"I'm not sure it's—" Jessie struggled—"legitimate."

Linda went to a desk piled high with papers and began typing at a computer. Jessie held her breath. Linda paused and studied the monitor. She typed again, then waited. Her head shook subtly and she glanced up at Jessie curiously. Getting up from her desk, she handed the certificate back to Jessie. "We *should* have record of this, but we don't."

"You mean . . . no one recorded it?"

Linda shrugged. "I've heard of the doctor. Can't believe he would have missed this."

Jessie thanked her and headed back down the hallway. *This is getting ridiculous,* she thought.

Located in southern Colorado Springs, the Rose Garden Cemetery was surrounded by tall ponderosa pines. Knowing her grandfather was buried here—recalling an image of a large monument—Jessie reasoned this must be where her mother's grave was, as well.

Near the entrance, Jessie stopped to inquire of the location, as if she knew for sure it was there. "Olivia Lehman, please . . ." In spite of her hunch, she was actually startled when the young groundskeeper in jeans and a green button-up shirt handed her a map and gave her directions.

She drove along a winding narrow asphalt road, barely wide enough for two cars to pass. Arriving at the general location, she pulled off the road and set out on foot. The directions weren't easy to follow. She searched the area for nearly fifteen minutes until she finally found the tiny plaque, obscured by grass and dirt. Betty was right—her grandmother had buried the urn. One more detail Jessie had forgotten.

She hunkered down, wiping away the dust, tracing the inscription with her fingers. *Olivia Lehman, beloved daughter, wife, and mother.*

Mother, she thought. *My mother.* Anger was building again. Apparently Olivia, the beloved daughter of her grandmother, namesake of her great-great grandmother, wasn't important enough for a large headstone, or even a larger plaque. She recalled an image of her grandfather's nearly six-foot-tall monument. Olivia had been granted a tiny speck of granite far off the beaten track, as if Doris had been somehow embarrassed by her daughter's death.

Jessie stood up and studied the tombstone. She'd intended to find proof; intended to convince herself. So here she was. Her mother's grave. But the *feeling* of proof was utterly absent.

Her cell phone rang.

"Jessie?"

The voice sounded familiar. "Brandon?"

"Where are you?"

Where am I? "I'm visiting my grandmother."

"I thought you went to Oregon."

"Brandon, what do you want?"

"I lost your number. That's why I haven't called, but Darlene gave it to me. I wanted to see how you're doing."

She sighed. *Of course . . . the post-breakup-are-you-okay call.*

"I'm fine," she whispered defensively, wondering if she should inquire of his well-being, then realizing she didn't care. Here she was, standing at the edge of her mother's grave and her old boyfriend had called just to make sure she hadn't hung herself over him. *Puh-lease,* Jessie thought. "I have to go," she said.

"Why?"

"I'm busy."

"Jessie, I didn't call to say hello, okay?" He stammered awhile longer, until she realized why he had called. "I was wrong about us. . . ."

She let the words swirl in her mind for a moment. Unbelievable. Brandon was trying to patch things up. A first.

"No, Brandon. You weren't wrong."

"Let's give it another . . ." He was still talking when Jessie removed the phone from her ear and stared at it. She considered pressing the Off button with no fanfare, no send-off, but he'd probably think they lost their connection and call again. She put it back to her ear and heard the rest of it. ". . . will I see you in Oregon?"

There was no point in continuing the conversation. No point countering his arguments. She was wasting precious cell battery.

"Bye, Brandon."

"I'm sorry?"

She pressed the button and stared at the phone again. How weird. She'd actually been missing him. It took hearing his voice again to set things straight.

Maybe I never pick the right guys, she thought, smiling to herself. Dismissing the phone call, she dropped the phone back in her shirt pocket, then looked down at her mother's gravestone. She tried imagining the urn it was supposed to contain. Was it gold or silver? Brass? Was it heavy? Rusted? The whole thing was like trying to wrestle into a turtleneck two sizes too small. Nothing fit.

She walked to the car and headed back through the winding cemetery road as shadows of the pine trees flickered on her windshield. The groundskeeper was now eating a sub sandwich. When Jessie inquired of the burial records, he simply handed her a business card. "They handle everything," he informed her and returned to his sandwich.

Back in her car, she grabbed her cell phone and dialed the number on the card.

A woman answered, "Rose Garden Cemetery . . ."

"I have a question about my mother's grave," Jessie began, not sure what she would say next. *Is she really buried there?* Yeah, that would be a good one.

"Concerning maintenance?"

"Uh . . . no. I need . . . more general information."

"I'm afraid our computers are down, but may I call you back?"

Jessie closed her eyes. *This is pointless.* But she finally agreed, giving the woman her mother's name and the site number according to the map the young man had given her.

"May I have a number where I can reach you?"

Jessie gave her cell phone number and hung up.

Her phone rang again. Looked like Brandon wasn't taking no for an answer. She checked the ID, but it wasn't Brandon's at all. "Hello?"

"Jessie?" A girl was crying hysterically.

"Laura?"

Laura's words came out hitched and labored. "Mom kicked me out."

Jessie was stunned. *Who kicks out a ten-year-old?*

"Oh, honey. Where's Mrs. Robinette?"

"She's not home," Laura whimpered into the phone.

"Do you have any friends close by?"

"Noooo."

"I'll be right there, sweetie. Wait for me at the Rock House."

"It's closed."

"How 'bout the gazebo?"

Laura whimpered again and hung up.

Chapter Twenty-four

JESSIE DROVE EIGHTY miles an hour on I-25. Her imagination conjured the worst. Had Laura been beaten? *So help me,* Jessie thought angrily.

She found Laura huddled against the splintered wooden slats of the gazebo, dressed in faded oversized jeans, a white T-shirt, and a pink sweater. When she saw Jessie, she burst into tears. She lurched down the steps, running to Jessie and sinking into her arms. After a long hug, Jessie led her back to the gazebo. Laura began hyperventilating again.

Jessie pulled her closer. "Let it go, sweetie. It's okay . . ."

Laura leaned against Jessie so heavily that she had to brace herself with her left hand against the gazebo. When Laura finally settled down, she began to tell Jessie what happened. Apparently a terrible argument with her mother had resulted in Michelle lifting Laura by her arms and plopping her outside the door. Michelle had screamed, *"Don't come back!"* as she slammed the door.

"Has that ever happened before?" Jessie asked.

Laura shook her head.

Jessie took out her cell phone, but before she could explain,

Laura placed her hand on it, her eyes pleading. "Every time they come, I get into trouble."

"Who?"

"The social workers."

Jessie sighed, placing it back into her pocket. "They don't do anything?"

"You should see my mom," Laura told her. "They *always* believe her."

"What do *you* say?"

"*Whatever Mom tells me,*" Laura replied, shrugging her shoulders. "Do you think I want to live in a foster home where the kids beat you up and the parents stick you in a corner and the rats chew at your ears while you sleep?" She started crying again.

"Foster homes aren't always like that."

"It is for Sally," Laura shot back.

They stood there while Jessie pondered what to do next. She could almost see Laura's future. She had all the marks of a child whose innocence was being robbed one memory at a time. At the moment, the youngster seemed mildly naïve, but eventually she would be broken, and by the time Laura reached middle school, she would have gravitated to friends similar to her mom. She might try drugs by the time she was twelve. By thirteen she'd be smoking. Sex would become old hat by age fourteen. High school, if she made it that far, would be a playground of rebellion against authority. By the time she reached eighteen, her life would be cast into its bitter mold.

"What does Mrs. Robinette say?"

Laura shrugged again. "Sometimes we pray."

Jessie was silent, unsure of what to say.

"Mrs. Robinette takes me to church. She invites my mom, but Mom doesn't go. Mom is really mean to her, but Mrs. Robinette keeps calling anyway. Sometimes Mom drops me off at her house. Calls her my geezer baby-sitter."

Jessie smiled, not surprised that Betty would keep trying.

"Sometimes I wonder if God even hears me," Laura continued. She looked up at Jessie. "Do you pray about stuff?"

Their eyes met and Jessie tried to formulate an answer. Should she be honest or simply say the right thing? And what was the right thing anyway? "Honey, I just don't pray much anymore."

Laura's eyes widened, and Jessie wondered if she had just done a terrible thing.

"Do you go to church?"

Jessie was about to reply when Laura said, "Mrs. Robinette said you used to go with her when you were my age."

"She took me every week," Jessie said. "When my mother couldn't go and my dad stopped going."

Laura hunkered back into Jessie's side. "I talk to God by myself sometimes. Mrs. Robinette says that Jesus is my best friend."

Jessie sighed softly. "What do you pray for, honey?"

"A *real* mom," Laura finally whispered. "Just like the one you had."

"Honey, my mom died."

Laura pulled away, meeting Jessie's eyes. "But you have good memories, don't you? Mrs. Robinette told me about your mom."

Jessie nodded. "Very good memories . . ."

Laura began shaking her head angrily. "I don't *have* any good memories and I wish my mother *would* die."

Jessie squeezed her shoulder. "I don't blame you for how you feel, but—"

"You'd be a good parent, you know," Laura announced suddenly. "You have all the right stuff."

"Honey, that's nice of you," Jessie said, stroking Laura's head. Without thinking, she prayed, *Dear God, please save this little girl. . . .*

But in the next moment, the impossibility of it set in, not to mention the unlikely chance that God even gave a rip.

"You do believe, Jessie—you're just angry," Andy had said.

And I'm still angry, she thought.

"You okay?" Laura said. Her eyes were serious. "You look different."

"I'm fine," Jessie whispered.

"Mrs. Robinette and I have this deal when we're eating ice cream together," Laura said.

"What is that?"

"We don't cry when we're making happy memories. Crying is for afterward."

Jessie wiped her eyes. "Okay." It was almost humorous. After all, Laura had been crying since the moment she'd arrived.

"I'm probably going to cry when you go. So I think we should wait until then."

"Deal," Jessie agreed.

"Deal," Laura repeated. Then she sighed, biting her lip, sinking into Jessie's shoulder again. "When are you leaving?" She whispered so softly that Jessie didn't understand at first.

"Tomorrow."

Laura pulled away again, her eyes frantic. "Why?"

"Sweetie—"

"Stay longer . . ."

"Honey . . ." Jessie paused and then pulled out her cell phone again, displaying it like a badge. "I carry this everywhere, okay?"

Laura nodded, staring at it as if the phone had acquired super powers.

"I'm going to give you a different number for my cell phone. It won't cost you anything, because the charges are automatically reversed."

Laura's eyes widened again.

"I'm your new friend. I can even be your big sister if you like, that is, until you get tired of me. And even if I don't hear from you for months, you can always call me up out of the blue, if you want."

"Anytime? In the middle of the night?"

"That's the *best* time to call," Jessie replied with a little wink.

Laura's face wrinkled. "But I don't want you to go. Andy

doesn't, either. You should marry him and live here."

Jessie shook her head. "I can't marry Andy, sweetie."

"But why?"

"Well . . . for one thing, he hasn't asked," she said, thinking that such an answer should pretty much settle it for a ten-year-old.

"Maybe he will."

"Probably not."

"But you hope so, right?"

"Laura—"

"Oh! I know," Laura squealed, "you could ask *him*!"

Jessie laughed. "Girls don't do that."

Laura looked confused. "That's the silliest thing I've ever heard!"

"He's my friend, that's all." Jessie sighed.

Laura looked a little dejected and then her countenance brightened again. "I know. Let's just run away. You and me. Andy too. I could save you some time, you know. Instant daughter. Skip the diaper-changing stuff. I'm not a bad kid, most of the time. I have bad moods, but I can clean those up in a jiffy. What do you say?" Her thin voice had begun to tremble, and she was looking at Jessie expectantly.

Jessie pulled Laura close. "Hey, kiddo, crying is for later, remember?"

Laura nodded and wiped her eyes.

"Nothing would make me happier, but running would be wrong, sweetie. Just call me, okay?"

She felt Laura's head nod against her chest.

Eventually they settled into a subdued conversation about Laura's friends at school, her favorite movies, TV shows—too many in Jessie's opinion—and her favorite mystery stories. Laura, obviously, had no guidance. It reminded Jessie again of how protective her own mother had been. Her mother had replaced the temptations of Jessie's life with her own unreserved, unhurried presence. Jessie had never missed what she couldn't have desired: an empty, fake world of nonexistent video relationships. The few movies they did watch were carefully screened, and they watched them together; Jessie was still amazed at her mom's ability to apply a spiritual parallel to nearly every Disney story. Every rescuing prince was a symbol of Jesus. Every bad guy was a symbol of the darkness beyond. And every reconciliation or redemption had its place in her mother's view of God's reality.

But Laura, at ten, was already "beyond" Disney. She was watching material that wouldn't have been appropriate for a teenager. Jessie just wanted to rescue her somehow, take her back into her own childhood, a world of pure innocence. But time was running out, and the road ahead was going to be difficult. Only unconditional love would save Laura now. The influence of Betty Robinette was going to have to work miracles.

Before long they were laughing and giggling. Eventually Laura announced, "I think I should try to go home." She grabbed Jessie's arm. "Will you come with me?"

Jessie agreed but worried that her presence would make Michelle angry again. "I'll drop you off, sweetie."

"Okay."

Jessie opened her car door, and Laura jumped in, settling into the seat as if she'd been there a thousand times before. "This is really cool!" Laura said, studying the instruments. "Is this car fast?"

"Fast enough."

Jessie removed a pen and paper from her purse and wrote down the toll-free number. Laura accepted the paper as if it were a huge candy bar.

When they pulled up in front of the house, Laura made no attempt to open the car door. Her little mouth was working and her eyes blinking. "Maybe this wasn't such a good idea."

Jessie patted her leg with assurance and shut off the engine. She dialed Laura's number and Michelle answered on the second ring, but when Jessie identified herself, Michelle swore into the phone. "What do *you* want?"

Jessie looked over at Laura and smiled as if the conversation were pleasant. "Hi, Michelle, just bringing Laura home. Are you available to talk?"

"Drop her off and beat it."

"Good. I'll be right in." Jessie said good-bye just as Michelle began to cuss into the phone again.

Jessie smiled over at Laura, who seemed stunned with the easy conversation. "Things are cool?"

Jessie shrugged. "I'll be right back." She slipped out of the car and walked up the steps to Laura's house. Molly began barking before Jessie got to the door. Michelle was standing at the door, cigarette in hand. "I don't need none of your lectures."

"I didn't plan—"

"Beat it." Michelle's eyes were full of rage and a discussion seemed pointless.

Jessie began to worry about something else. "Are you loaded, Michelle?"

Again, the fury in her eyes flashed. "Do I *look* loaded? Would I be this uptight?" Michelle laughed sarcastically. "Loaded is when you answer the door and say, 'Oh hi, how nice of you to drop by. Feel free to steal anything you want.'" Michelle raised her eyebrows mockingly. "Get it?"

"Just give me a minute."

"Give me my daughter or I'm calling the cops."

Jessie crossed her arms. She glanced down the street, calculating the risk. "Okay, Michelle. Call 'em. I'll wait." Jessie had started to head back down the steps when she heard Michelle unlatch the screen door and kick it open. "You have two minutes, Goldilocks."

The stench was excruciating as she entered the house. Molly was yelping from a back room. Michelle backed into the living room as if she were afraid of Jessie. She crossed her arms defensively, taking another drag on her cigarette.

Jessie was trembling inside but tried to hide it. "I'm not here to blame you, Michelle."

Michelle was making mocking expressions with her eyes as if to say, *Is that right?*

Jessie took a deep breath. "You said you already know about me. So then you must know I lost my mother and my father. What you may not know is that I spent years in foster homes. I've learned the hard way—"

"So we're trailer trash sisters, eh?" Michelle said, squinting with a ghoulish smile.

"No, that's not—"

"You're trying to convince me you ain't some rich kid coming home to collect her inheritance?"

Jessie flinched. Michelle's features had become stony and cold.

"It's easy to forget what we have until it's gone. . . ." Jessie stopped. She wasn't doing very well.

Michelle shook her head with utter contempt. She nearly hissed her words, "If you *ever* come near my daughter again, both you and that ice-cream bunny will regret it."

"I just wanted to—"

"But what you *did* was interfere."

"Michelle, please . . ."

Michelle pointed at the door. "Your two minutes are up."

Jessie was too stunned to move. They stood there a moment appraising each other, then Jessie reached for the door and slipped outside, walking down the steps to the car.

Laura was smiling as she looked out the car window. Jessie felt terrible. How could she let Laura live in an environment like that? Laura pushed open the car door just as the screen door slammed behind them. Michelle was standing at the top of the steps. "Laura, get in here now!"

Laura looked stunned. She turned to Jessie, who had knelt down in front of her. "Didn't go too well, huh?"

Jessie made a sorry face. "Will you be okay, sweetie?"

Laura shrugged, and a look of resignation crossed her features. "She's always this way. I'll be fine." And with that, she headed up the sidewalk. The sense of betrayal nearly tore Jessie apart. *How can I just watch this happen?*

Laura climbed the steps and shuffled past her mother into the house as Michelle gave Jessie another look of contempt.

"I was only trying to help," Jessie said softly, standing up.

Michelle tossed her cigarette butt into a section of weeds, gave Jessie another squint, and retreated into the house, slamming the door behind her.

Chapter Twenty-Five

ANDY SPENT THE MORNING calling new prospects and consoling old customers. He left for home halfway through the day, too distracted to work any longer. Fortunately, his sales quota was beyond acceptable, and he could afford to slack a bit. His boss had even patted him on the back several weeks ago, saying, *"Slow down, McCormick, you're starting to make me look bad."* He spent the afternoon sitting on the couch in his apartment, staring at the empty fireplace.

. . . "Explain it again," he'd asked his father last night, and his father had given a near-textbook description of the nature of dementia.

Dementia wasn't an illness per se, but a description of symptoms that accompany an illness or degenerative brain disorder. Infections, alcoholism, or head trauma could cause dementia symptoms, and there were hundreds of other causes. All rare. Most lethal. And every year, new variations emerged.

According to his father, Olivia Lehman was believed to have a very unusual brain disorder—a form previously unidentified by neurologists. Generally classified in the category of early onset dementia, the unnamed disease apparently mingled the genetic aspects of Huntington's disease with the complications of vascular dementia that involved ministrokes—and sometimes major strokes. It was these strokes that contributed to the unpredictable nature of the disease, affecting areas of the brain that differed from patient to patient.

Olivia's brain disorder was passed genetically; her own father had died of a stroke related to this type of dementia. As with Huntington's disease, there appeared to be a fifty-fifty chance of passing the errant genes to an offspring. If a child or young adult was found to be a carrier, the chances of exhibiting the symptoms of the illness were a hundred percent. It was only a matter of time. But while people with Huntington's disease might live productive lives for decades, the vascular component of Olivia Lehman's debilitating illness and eventual death indicated that her disease was far more fatal.

Finally his father asked him the question he'd been dreading: "Does Jessie exhibit any symptoms of dementia?"

"What, exactly?" he asked.

His father went through the list: confusion, difficulty speaking, memory lapses, poor coordination, headaches, and on occasion, hallucinations.

"Hallucinations?"

"Very rare with dementia but not unknown," his father had replied clinically. "In view of her risk, any mental anomaly must be taken into consideration."

Andy remembered Jessie's altercation with the woman at the fair and her later explanation of it as an outgrowth of the strange dreams she'd been having for years. *"I saw a woman in a yellow dress, and everything went crazy,"* Jessie had said nervously, laughing it off.

His father continued. "People with dementia become 'changed' people. They become easily disoriented. Concentration is very difficult at the later stages. It's just very hard to predict how someone will respond to this condition. In fact, I knew a gentleman with a similar dementia who couldn't remember that his wife had died. A very deluded man indeed."

Andy shuddered. *Going from bad to worse.* "Coming back has been very difficult for Jessie. She barely remembers anything."

His dad wasn't buying it. "So there's something?"

"It's nothing," Andy insisted. "Stress does strange things to our minds. Isn't that what you always say?"

"Nothing changes the fact, Andy. She *must* be tested, and soon. Remember, she has a fifty percent chance of *not* being a carrier."

Fifty percent chance? Andy's spirits were hitting rock bottom. *Not good odds.*

"Tell her the truth, Andy. Tell her what I've just told you. We can arrange the initial blood test here at my clinic if that would help her feel more comfortable, but eventually she'll have to be referred to a neurologist. They've come a long way in a decade."

"No cure?" Andy asked.

"Not for a genetic carrier," his father confirmed, then hesitated. "Andy, I need to speak as a father now, okay?" And then his dad said something he'd rarely said before. "Don't get mixed up with this girl, Andy."

"Dad . . ."

"I'm serious, son. You remember how it was with Olivia. Eventually she lost her coordination completely and became bedridden. Her last days were lived in total confusion with rare moments of lucidity. A few years with Jessie would be a living hell."

Andy felt his ire rising. "She's already been there and back, Dad."

"That's not the point. Her sickness doesn't obligate you."

"I can't just abandon her."

"You just *met* her."

I've known her my entire life, Andy thought but didn't say. His dad wouldn't have understood.

"Dad, this is the girl who took care of her mother for years. She even had to remind her alcoholic father to take his depression pills. Who's looking out for *her*?"

"Just don't marry her."

Andy was flabbergasted. "I never said—"

"I know how you like to help, but . . ." His father's words trailed off. Silence filled the room at that point and the space felt like a closet. When his father spoke again, it was to ask a completely unrelated question about Jessie's father. "Did you say Frank was an alcoholic?" . . .

This morning the whole interrogation had begun again. His mother had called, begging him to reconsider.

"Reconsider what?" Andy asked, initially confused.

"You deserve someone healthy," she said.

"Mom, you're way ahead—"

"You can't save this girl," his mother interrupted.

"We don't know anything for sure, Mom."

"There's nothing you can do."

"I can help her," Andy replied impulsively, and his mother nearly cried. Then his dad got on the line again, obviously pressured by his mom. "Don't be rash, son."

"I have to go to work," Andy finally said, realizing there was nothing he could say to counter their impression. Their memories were dominated by the old Jessie, who must have appeared as quite the curmudgeon at age twelve. They were doing what any protective parents might do—they were looking out for their son. They'd seen the terrible tragedy of Olivia Lehman up close and personal.

But none of that mattered now. Meeting Jessie again had been like finding something he had long forgotten but had been searching for his entire life. His mother would have said, *"Take an aspirin, Andy. It'll pass."* His father would have given him the old advice he'd offered Andy at least three times a year: *"Men can fall in love in a moment. It takes women much longer."* As if that had much to do with anything.

But he shuddered to think what they would say when they discovered Jessie wasn't a Christian anymore. That, of course, would lead to a bigger question. . . .

No, his parents wouldn't understood. *They don't even know the truth about me,* he realized. *How could they understand my heart?*

Does God even know my heart? he thought suddenly, still staring at the fireplace.

For years he'd been praying what seemed like hopelessly desperate prayers—*Help me understand*—but it seemed as if God had turned His back. *"God doesn't answer the prayers of the infidel,"* his mother might have said bitterly.

"What about the prodigal son?" he might ask. According to Scripture, God would be eagerly looking for him to return. *"Come home, son,"* his father would say. But that begged the question, *"What if I can't return?"*

"Then you will die in your sins," his mother would say and then begin crying again. *"Just believe, Andy! Just believe!"*

He'd long ago stopped attending the Wednesday night services at his church. Everyone would stand and sing and clap their hands through nearly forty minutes of exuberant praise and worship. He used to observe his friends and other churchgoers bouncing like jumping beans, singing with their arms outstretched, lost in a spiritual frenzy, and ask himself, *What is wrong with me?*

Why can't *I believe?* Andy asked himself again, pondering a question that had haunted him for years.

At the very minimum, he believed in a God who'd created the world. That much had always seemed obvious. It didn't require scriptural authority. The truth of God's existence was written on the hearts of man. *Isn't that what the apostle Paul said?* Evidence of divine design was everywhere you looked.

But then what? Andy thought for probably the hundredth time. He sighed and leaned his head back, and in spite of his turmoil, a reassuring warmth filled his soul. In a few hours, he'd see Jessie again. *At the very least, I can stop thinking about myself. I can do something right.*

The sense of despair over Jessie kicked in again. There was no way out of this. From his own observations, she was either in need of extensive psychological therapy or the undiagnosed symptoms of dementia had already begun, in which case she would have a few very difficult years to live.

He pondered yesterday's religious discussion and shuddered. If the latter were true, how would she feel about God then?

◆　◆　◆　◆　◆

After waiting a few minutes, Jessie put her car in reverse and slowly backed up, settling in front of her old house. Her phone rang and Jessie nearly jumped. It was Laura. "Why are you still here?"

Jessie looked up at Andy's window. Laura was holding the curtain back with one hand, holding the phone with her other. "I was worried," Jessie replied.

"What're you going to do?"

Jessie shrugged as if Laura could see her. "Visit my old house again."

"Oh . . ." Laura dropped the curtains and disappeared into the room, but her voice continued. "Aren't you scared?"

Jessie looked at the house. "Guess things change, huh?"

"Sometimes," Laura whispered.

"Hey, sweetie, don't make your mom mad by talking to me."

"Mom's passed out on the sofa."

"Oh," Jessie replied. "I'm glad you're okay."

"My bottom is real sore," Laura told her, and then before hanging up, she whispered, "Thanks for the number. I'll never lose it."

Jessie put the cell phone in her pocket, locked the car, and headed up the sidewalk. Out of the corner of her eye, she saw Laura pull back the curtains again and wave. Jessie waved back.

"Please, God, wherever you are," Jessie whispered, "save this precious child."

Why was it so easy to slip back into the old patterns of praying to God as if He would answer? *Wishful thinking,* she thought, but was that so wrong? At the very least, it was the kind of wish that *should* be true: a God whom you could trust.

"Get it out, sweetie. God isn't scared of your anger," Mrs. Robinette had said. *"How could God make it up to you?"*

By saving my mother, Jessie thought suddenly, to which Betty Robinette would have replied, *"But He did, honey. He took her home."*

Jessie looked up at the closed curtain again. "Save that little girl," she whispered once more, and tears filled her eyes, not just over Laura's situation but over the terrible things she'd said to her grandmother. *"I never had time to explain,"* Grandmother had said.

At the door of her old house, Jessie reached up and found the key again. Then she took a deep breath, unlocked the door, and pushed her way in. The old *click* and *whirr* happened again, and she almost expected to see the old couch. Instead, as before, the dungeonlike darkness permeated every corner of the room. Yards of dark fabric covered all the windows.

She closed the door and stood in the entryway for a moment, allowing her eyes to adjust. She remembered her mother's letter in her pocket and decided this would be the place to read it.

Jessie headed upstairs. It was dark, so she counted the steps again, just as she had as a little girl. When she reached her mom's room, she paused in the entryway. The sense of anticipation had completely replaced the fear. She nestled against the corner of the room, on the floor, just a few feet from where she and Andy had sat.

Chuckling to herself, she realized she'd forgotten a flashlight. She leaned her head back against the wall and pulled out her cell phone to check the time on the illuminated face. Just as well. She had to meet Andy in thirty minutes. She dialed his number and he answered on the first ring.

"I might be a little late," she said.

"Oh, you're not here?" he asked. "I'm just pulling up."

"You're early."

"Couldn't wait to see you."

"Oh, that's sweet," she said. "I can't wait to see you, either."

When they hung up, Jessie looked around the room, holding her mother's letter in her hand.

"Your mother is . . ." her grandmother had said.

My mother is what?

A slip of the tongue is all, Jessie thought.

"You left so quickly," her grandmother had said.

By now the room seemed lighter. *Exposure,* she thought. *Look into the dark long enough, and you become accustomed to it. . . .*

Your mother is . . .

Means nothing, Jessie repeated to herself.

And the computer records?

"Nothing," Jessie whispered, realizing again she might have to live forever with the constant unfinished feeling. *I'll have done my best, though,* she thought. *I will have looked under the bed and faced the boogeyman.* She remembered the mathematician whose life was featured in the movie *A Beautiful Mind,* a man who'd learned to function in spite of his ever-present hallucinations.

You grow to accept it. You look into the dark and become accustomed to it.

And if the fear disappears, well . . . I'll settle for that.

Chapter Twenty-Six

THE MAN JESSIE had referred to as Cowboy Bill answered the door, and sure enough, he was wearing a cowboy hat—soiled white and rippled.

"You must be Andrew," Bill welcomed with a grin.

Andy returned the smile, shaking Bill's hand.

Bill stepped aside, opening the door wider. "I was just planting a few flowers around the gazebo." Bill gestured for him to follow. "I'm afraid Doris is a bit . . . under the weather. . . ."

Walking into the entryway was an experience. The ceiling was twenty-five feet high if it was an inch. Jessie was right. This place was incredible. Bill led him through a set of French doors to the left into a sunlit alcove, then through another set of doors leading outside to a brick-covered courtyard. A white gazebo stood in the middle of the yard, reminding him of the one in Palmer Lake. The flowers, exploding from nearly every vacant spot, were reminiscent of Mrs. Browning's garden.

"Jessie will be here shortly," Andy said and then felt presumptuous, as if he knew something Bill didn't.

Bill stopped in front of the gazebo, pointing to a small plot of bare soil near its edge. "Whadd'ya think?"

"Looks to be the only spot left."

Bill laughed as if Andy had told a whopper of joke. He gestured to the gazebo swing. "Care to give it a spin?"

Sitting on the white wooden slats, Andy was surprised with the size of the gazebo, at least fifteen feet across.

Bill leaned against the railing looking out at his garden. "I'm afraid I've enjoyed this thing more'n Doris," he offered. "At least she likes to look at it."

Andy pushed himself gently on the swing.

"Jessie tells me you was engaged to that TV preacher's daughter?"

Andy smiled. He'd probably be telling that story for the rest of his life: The fish that got away . . . her name was Elizabeth and her daddy was . . . and watch their eyes bug out. *"What was he like?"* they would ask. But his whole perspective regarding Elizabeth had changed. He no longer felt he had missed his only hope for happiness. *There are second chances,* he thought and right there, sitting in the middle of the yard, talking to Bill, he realized his dad was right; love had taken but a moment. His poor mother would spend a week or longer recovering in bed.

Andy provided a few interesting details about Elizabeth's father, the behind-the-scenes activity of a TV ministry. Bill listened with fascination. "So ya think he's the real deal?"

Andy chuckled. Elizabeth's father had reminded him of a back-slapping salesman, the kind he hung out with all day, but he couldn't vouch for his integrity.

"He seems sincere," Andy finally replied, and Bill winked as if he got what Andy hadn't said.

"I go to this tiny church over in Widefield," Bill told him. "After I drop Doris off at her 'dress-up church' downtown."

Andy nodded and Bill took it as a cue, describing his pastor as rather feisty and the congregation as a bunch of well-intentioned sinners humbly seeking God. Andy wondered if Jessie knew Bill was a Christian. Yet he was intrigued with this cowboy. His manner put Andy completely at ease, and they were now having a conversation as if they'd been friends for years.

Bill slapped his leg with something apparently hilarious. "We got this guy at our church . . . Buzz, right?"

"Buzz?"

"That's what his wife calls 'im."

"Does he look—"

"Yep. Buzz cut an' all."

Andy laughed and Bill continued. "They tell me this guy used to swear like a sailor. Drink like a fish. And he was rather nasty. But all that changed one day."

Andy felt his eyes glazing over, figuring Bill was about to go into the conversion experience.

"Buzz had himself a near-death experience," Bill went on. "Some kind of heart attack or something."

That's even worse, Andy groaned inwardly. He'd often wondered if near-death experiences, or NDEs, as he'd heard them termed, weren't simply hallucinations. Like the sightings of UFOs.

Cowboy Bill was just getting started. He described Buzz's "testimony," complete with an out-of-body experience, the tunnel thing, the life review, and best of all, the Being of Light.

Or the devil himself, Andy thought humorously, remembering the general cynicism about the nature of NDEs.

"He said he'd never felt more completely loved, more fully known—a total sense of serenity. He said it was like the best drug you can imagine!"

That's a new one, Andy thought, smiling charitably. "A drug?"

Bill shrugged. "He said the words to describe it were basically worthless. He was angry when they resuscitated him. Angry for days, in fact. Said he's been spiritually lonely ever since, but in the meantime, he stopped chewing, stopped drinking, stopped swearing, and started going to church." Bill chuckled. "And he's not a half-bad guy!"

"So . . . what do you think, Bill?" Andy asked.

Bill shrugged and looked down at the floor, then frowned as if he'd seen something that displeased him. He looked out toward the fence for a moment before replying. "I thought about it a bit, you know, and it occurred to me, I don't really know one way or the other, but—" Bill repositioned himself against the railing, pausing again—"I got to thinking, would the real thing be any less?"

"I'm sorry?"

"Well . . . if the near-death thing is fake, or if it's the devil, or whatever, wouldn't whatever *really* happens on the other side be as good, if not better?"

Andy had never thought of it that way.

Bill continued. "Buzz described a personal being who knew everything about him, warts and all, yet smothered him with unconditional love. A personal being who knew the exact moment he was going to visit the other side. He showed up just to tell 'im his time wasn't up!"

"Let me guess. They told him he needed to clean up his act and start loving people." Andy couldn't keep the cynicism from his voice.

"Naw. Actually He didn't tell 'im to *do* anything. But Buzz said he started loving God that day. I guess the 'obey' part came later."

Bill wiped his face with his plaid sleeve. "For the longest time it bothered me, 'cause I don't usually buy that kind of thing. But I saw how Buzz changed and all, and I actually wanted to believe him. And then one day it just occurred to me that I didn't care whether Buzz was right or not. Like I said, I knew that what was waiting for me, for all of us, had to be as good if not better."

Andy thought again of his friends worshiping God, experiencing Him personally. They seemed to know what God was like. Bill was right. God had to be better than the best thing you could imagine. But it certainly didn't prove that Christianity was true.

Bill cleared his throat. "So . . . where ya at with all this?"

Andy sighed. Country-bumpkin Bill couldn't even begin to keep up with the kinds of struggles that crossed Andy's mind. "I have a problem with the historicity."

"You don't think it really happened?"

"I just . . . doubt it," Andy said softly.

Bill seemed to consider this for a moment and then launched off into the typical argument regarding Jesus: "Who do you think He was? A liar, lunatic, or Lord?"

"If it was all made up, or if it's a legend, then you can't use that argument," Andy replied.

"Then what do you do with the apostle Paul?" Bill was still leaning against the railing, and so far his tone was casual, non-threatening—but that often changed when people got serious about discussing religion.

Andy was already planning a conversational exit strategy. "I'm sorry?"

"Seems like Paul had a good head on his shoulders. At one time, he was dead set against the gospel, wasn't he? What convinced him it was true?"

"He had a hallucination."

"But he knew the disciples, right?"

"Sure, but . . ."

"Did they pull the wool over his eyes? And then submit themselves to terrible deaths to prove a lie? If *I* were Paul, considering his background and all, I would have had a few questions to ask. And one would be: 'Hey, boys, where's the empty grave?'"

Andy gave an accommodating smile, and Bill took off on another subject.

◆　◆　◆　◆　◆

Jessie was driving back when her cell phone buzzed.

"I wasn't able to get back with you sooner," the woman from the Rose Garden Cemetery explained. "And I have to apologize," she continued.

"Oh?"

"Well . . . most of my records are up-to-date, but for the life of me, I can't find any record of your mother's interment."

"Interment?"

"Burial," the woman clarified.

Jessie was confused. "She was cremated, wasn't she?"

"Yes, but according to my preliminary records, burial of the urn was scheduled but never completed. I mean, I should have a record of it, but I can't find it."

"I don't get it," Jessie said. "Why might that be?"

"Well . . . I'm sure we just lost the records, but . . ." The woman's voice trailed off. Then she sighed into the phone, "This is so embarrassing."

Jessie tried to make sense of it. "Maybe my grandmother changed her mind?"

When the woman didn't answer, Jessie realized she'd blown it. This was the first time she had mentioned another party. Perhaps the woman was thinking through the implications.

"You're not—" a rustling of papers—"Doris Crenshaw?"

"I'm her granddaughter."

"Oh," the woman replied nervously. "I should probably speak with her, then."

Jessie repeated the question but tried to make it sound hypothetical. "Does that happen often? Somebody changes their mind?"

The woman hesitated. "No . . . not really."

Jessie was trying to grasp the implications. "Can you tell me—" Jessie paused. *This was getting too weird.* ". . . where they cremated the body?" She shivered just saying the words.

The woman hesitated again. "Well, I suppose that's not classified information. Let me see here . . ." Another pause. When she spoke again, she chuckled. "The paper work I have doesn't list that, either. But there are only so many funeral homes in town. Call them all. One of them should have the cremation records."

After hanging up, Jessie pulled over to a convenience store just off Fillmore, found a phone book, and called the funeral homes with the most prominent yellow-page ads. Once again, while all claimed to have meticulous records, none of them had any record of Olivia Lehman.

Maybe I missed one, she thought, getting back into her car. Now only ten minutes from home, Jessie tried to make sense of the whole situation. She'd set out today to find some kind of closure in the details of her mother's death. Instead, she'd found exactly the opposite.

One by one, she went through it all again, determined to find an alternate explanation. First item: No death records existed, except for the death certificate she was carrying around. Probable answer: Somebody failed to record the death certificate, that's all.

Number two: No cemetery records. Answer: Her grandmother changed her mind. Maybe the urn was in her grandmother's bedroom. Maybe her grandmother sprinkled the ashes somewhere. There were a dozen maybes. Any of them could work, not to mention the possibility of errant records. Isn't that what the woman suggested?

Number three: No cremation records. Answer: This one was easy. She hadn't called every funeral home in the book; only the ones with the biggest ads.

Jessie sighed into the silence of the car. What difference did it make anyway? Her mother was dead. Case closed.

Nice try, she thought, unconvinced by her own arguments. It was starting to feel as if she'd found a tiny piece of ice in the ocean, only to discover it was attached to a giant iceberg beneath the black water.

She had no choice now. She *had* to visit the place of her mother's death.

❖ ❖ ❖ ❖ ❖

By now Bill and Andy had settled into a far more benign conversation.

"Do you have family, Bill?" Andy asked.

"A daughter," Bill replied almost absently. "Ain't seen her in thirty years." He shook his head slightly as if trying to rid himself of the memory. "I tried to make contact once she hit her twenties. But she kept hanging up the phone. Returned my letters unopened, as if to make the point as clear as possible." Bill sighed. "She remembers things I don't, so I figure it's only fair. She's got a stepdad. Guess she only wants one dad at a time, although I can't say I ever was much of a father." His last words were spoken as if from a deep well of regret. "She'd be forty by now. I've missed her entire life."

Andy was surprised with how suddenly Bill's manner had changed, and he was sorry he'd asked the question. Yet he couldn't help wondering what Bill had meant by "she remembers things I don't."

Bill must have read his mind. "I was a drunk," he finally said. "Plain and simple. Knockdown, pass-out drunk. And I was a *mean* drunk."

Bill glanced over toward the house, and his face broke into a big grin. Andy followed his gaze. Jessie was just stepping outside and she looked beautiful wearing tan slacks and a colorful shirt, the sleeves rolled to the elbow. "Am I interrupting anything?"

◆ ◆ ◆ ◆ ◆

Doris still hadn't made an appearance by the time they left. Bill, on the other hand, was like a father hen. He walked them to the door and waved good-bye, grinning from ear to ear.

Taking I-25 north, they turned off the Bijou exit, and in minutes, they were parking on the street in front of the restaurant. It had a long green awning and tall windows looking out toward the mountain range.

After the hostess seated them, Jessie made a face. "Laura called me," she said and then proceeded to tell the story. In between the details, the waiter came and took their orders. Andy ordered pasta; Jessie, chicken. "I wanted to put the poor girl in my car and just drive," she told him. "Get her out of there."

"What would Betty do?" Andy asked.

Jessie bit her lip and the saddest look flickered in her eyes. "Pray." She took a sip of tea and pursed her lips regretfully.

"So what do *you* think?" he asked.

Jessie shook her head. "Let me put it this way . . . I'm a good candidate for a millstone around the neck." She looked away, as if embarrassed.

Andy silently recalled Jesus' words about the consequences of offending "one of these little ones."

When their meals arrived, Jessie described her visit to the cemetery and the subsequent phone calls to the cemetery office and the funeral homes.

Weird, Andy thought, *but not unexplainable.*

At some point, she told him about the argument with her grandmother.

"Long time in coming," he said thoughtfully.

She only shrugged, her manner regretful again, and the more she talked, the more distracted she became.

He told her about his visit with Bill and his church attendance. Jessie's eyebrows raised. "He never said anything to me."

As the meal progressed, Andy searched for the right moment. But just exactly how does one broach the subject anyway? *Jessie, I know why you've been hallucinating. I know why you've been so confused lately. You might be dying.*

Over dessert, she invited him to come with her to the institution. Andy had immediate visions of *One Flew Over the Cuckoo's Nest* but accepted her invitation, if only to be there if something went wrong. "Think it's open late?"

She frowned. "I forgot to call and find out."

"Well, let's just stop by," Andy said, thinking that at the very least it would extend their evening, not to mention buy him more time. "So . . . are you still planning to leave tomorrow?"

A shadow crossed her face. "I think I should, don't you?"

"Why don't you move out here?" he suggested. "Finish your master's degree in Colorado?"

She appeared to consider this, meeting his eyes, as if pondering his intentions. "I'd like that," she finally said, nodding thoughtfully.

Andy reached for her hand and she seemed nervous and elated at the same time.

"I'd like to see more of you," he said.

She smiled, blushing. "I'd . . . like that, too." Then she chuckled, as if snapping out of her distraction. "Andy, you're embarrassing me!"

They laughed, but it was a good soul-warming laugh.

"Are you worried about doing this?"

She frowned, confused.

"Going to the hospital?" he added. "We don't have to . . ."

She shook her head. "Oh no. I *do* have to."

"But you're not afraid?"

She paused. "I think I am . . . a little, but . . ." Finally she shrugged. "I can't explain it."

"That's okay," he offered.

They settled into more benign conversation. Andy found himself wondering again if she already knew the truth, but still doubted it. From the quality of their time together, the near intimate discussions, surely she would have mentioned it.

Suddenly she reached over and squeezed *his* hand. "I'm so glad you'll be with me."

He knew she was referring to tonight, but he was thinking about the future. *And I'll stay right with you,* he thought. *No matter what.* He felt his own eyes tear up, but he blinked quickly. She didn't seem to notice, or maybe she was too polite.

After they finished dinner, Jessie gave Bill a quick call to ask for directions. Bill offered her the information without asking any questions, for which Jessie seemed grateful. Then they headed south into the darkness of post-twilight.

Chapter Twenty-Seven

ANDY PARKED at the outer edge of the parking lot, beneath a buzzing, flickering streetlamp. The redbrick three-story building sat on the side of a ridge, surrounded by an assortment of conifer trees. A wire fence circled the perimeter of the roof, and bars covered the windows. In the parking lot, a small island of grass harbored a simple flagpole with a wooden sign and white painted lettering: Colorado State Hospital. Despite the trees, there was little aesthetic value to the appearance. No bright flowers. No lavish design.

Andy said he would go in alone to check it out and see if they could gain admittance. As she waited, Jessie leaned back in her seat and rested her eyes. Light shadows danced on her eyelids from the streetlight like a strobe. Brooks and Dunn were crooning in the background: "There ain't nothing about you that don't do something for me. . . ." The music lent an eerie contrast to the dismal surroundings.

Gently, she allowed her mind to focus on the single strand of memory, slipping into it, like putting her foot into a sock, following it where it led . . . but it led nowhere. What could this visit accomplish? She sighed. *I'm getting closure.*

What have I closed so far? She ticked it off in her mind: The

Social Security Administration had no record of her mother's death. Her grandmother had referred to her mother in the present tense. *Big deal.* And her mother's urn had never been buried. *So?*

She opened her right eye and peered ahead. *Just look at this place. I've got a real bad case of imagination,* she thought. *So tell it to my dreams. If you don't mind, I'd like to try drugs and needles first, before we transition to the straitjacket and the padded walls.*

She was awakened by a gentle rapping on her window. Blinking her eyes, she saw Andy leaning over, smiling.

She opened the door and swung her legs out.

"Sorry, didn't mean to wake you," Andy said, crouching down. "You were smiling with your eyes closed. What's so funny?"

"The smile of insanity," she whispered, opening her eyes ghoulishly and then laughing.

Andy's return chuckle seemed forced. Jessie ignored it and asked, "Can we go in?"

Andy shrugged, "The door's open. I would have asked permission, but no one was at the front desk."

"I think this is all the permission we need," Jessie said, placing the certificate in his hand.

Andy studied it carefully. "Very sloppy. Handwritten. That's rare." He pointed to a line. "Your mother's place of death is given as room 116. That's just plain weird. Normally they just list the institution."

Jessie hesitated for a moment, gathering her wits about her. An unexplainable sense of cold embraced her, and she looked at the building and cringed. "My father hated coming here. He said it was dirty, disorganized, and overcrowded, like a holding cell for the living dead."

"Do you remember anything yet?" Andy asked.

Jessie shrugged. "Little pieces. I remember getting here. I remember meeting with Mrs. Robinette, my grandmother, and my father."

"All three of them?" he asked. "Why?"

"I don't know." She shook her head.

He whistled. "The mystery deepens."

"I'm sure it was nothing. Maybe they just wanted to prepare me or something."

"Tell me again how your mother ended up here?" Andy asked.

"The judge placed her here until a final decision could be made. Grandmother had been fighting to put her in a nursing home for Alzheimer's patients, but Dad and I wanted to keep Mom at home."

Jessie's head was already pounding. As she told the story it seemed so clear, as if it had happened yesterday—a dreary Saturday morning. They had been watching cartoons in the bedroom and the men just walked in, like in the movies, two men in white jackets, along with a sheriff and his deputy, and they carted her mother out. Jessie was screaming bloody murder. Her father tried putting up a fight, but he was nothing against the four of them. Jessie finally escaped the goons and ran outside and by then she was nearly hysterical. She reached the gurney just as they were opening the door to the ambulance.

One of the guys grabbed her, but another pushed him aside, saying, *"Let her say good-bye,"* and that *really* freaked her out. She was thinking *good-bye forever.* When she finally squirmed her way to the top of the gurney, her mother's eyes were afraid, but she forced a smile. *"Are we going to the park, sweetie?"* Then she frowned. *"Why are you so sad?" "I'm scared, Mom." "Just pray, sweetie." "Will I see you again?"* Her mother smiled again. *"Sure."* That was the last thing her mother said before they pushed her into the vehicle.

Andy was silent for a moment, digesting her story. When he glanced back at the institution, he asked, "After you visited this place, did you ever ask what happened?"

"Dad said I totally lost it," she admitted. "I was lying in bed that afternoon, or maybe I was napping or something. It was dark out. Dad came in with soup. I asked him why we hadn't gone to see

Mom and he just stared at me."

"We can still change our mind," Andy offered, bringing her back to the moment at hand.

"No . . . let's finish this."

"Why don't we call Betty? Now that we know she was here with you."

Jessie shook her head. "I'm leery of how she remembers the past. I want to get my own impressions first."

Andy gave her that worried look again. *What is it?* she almost asked.

He let out a long sigh. "So . . . what's the plan?"

"We go in and find room 116," she announced with bright bravado.

"Seriously?" he said, looking at the death certificate again.

"I'm making this up as I go." They stood at the entrance. Two steps from the threshold.

"What if . . . something happens?" Andy asked, and his concern seemed to be growing before her eyes.

"You mean if I weird out?"

"No. I mean . . . if you faint or something."

"Then you catch me. Can you handle that?"

Andy grinned. "I'm all over it."

◆ ◆ ◆ ◆ ◆

Doris lounged on a chair in her master bedroom, looking out over the backyard. The sun had fallen behind the trees at the back fence. In a few minutes, the gazebo lights would illuminate Bill's handiwork. Shadows were longer now, drawn across the lawn, but shadows of the past threatened to bury her in darkness.

Bill kept peeking in, and she kept waving him off. "Want some iced tea?" he said at one point, and she declined.

"Ice cream?"

"No."

"Coffee?"

"No."

"Swift kick?"

"Bill, so help me."

All evening he kept wandering back to her door. Finally he asked her outright, "Do you want to talk, Dory?"

"I want to *think*," she insisted. "Hard to do in this place."

He headed back down the hall.

Doris felt she might sink into the very depression she'd never allowed to defeat her before. She thought of all that needed to be done—her latest needlepoint, endless correspondence, her duties for several organizations . . . *Never ending* . . . The thought of filling up every second of her life had always been so comforting, so important . . . so narcotic.

She leaned forward, intending to head for her husband's study, but couldn't get up. The pointlessness of it all struck her deeply, and she sank back into the chair.

"*I'm leaving tomorrow*," Jessica had said.

"Oh, Jessica," she whispered into the growing darkness. "I'm so sorry."

Bill was back again. Doris sighed.

"You oughta know that Jessie just called to ask for directions. She and Andy are going to the mental health hospital." He said it softly, with an almost grave tone.

"What on earth for?"

Bill shrugged. "Haven't a clue."

Surely she doesn't suspect? Doris thought.

Bill took another step into her room. "Are you okay?"

Downward she descended, into her own private pain, realizing that a lifetime of hope was finished. Perhaps it had never existed. Perhaps hope had only been an illusion. *Jessica will never forgive me.*

Bill was helping her get out of her chair. She felt numb, barely coherent.

"I'm calling the doctor."

"No!" she hissed, and Bill nearly jumped. "I'm sorry," she added softly.

"Then get some rest," Bill said as he helped her to the bed. "Lie down."

"I need to put on my . . ." She couldn't finish her sentence. The words were caught in her throat. She began weeping and allowed herself to fall backward onto her bed.

Bill's voice became a distant whisper and . . .

. . . she remembered putting the phone down, surrounded by an emotional haze. Maria was standing near, her hands on Doris's arm. Floating in slow motion, as if she were moving underwater. Maria, who had heard her side of the phone call, was now crying. Doris finally recovered enough to hug her dear maid, who kept repeating over and over, "I'm so sorry, Mrs. Crenshaw. Is there anything I can do?"

She remembered letting go. Shaking her head. It was like a dream and yet, at the same time, so clear. Finding her keys. Maria offering, "May I drive you?" Shaking her head no. Walking to the car, closing the door behind her. Her next-door neighbor, Mrs. McBride, waving. Waving back, and actually smiling while she did it, because she was so good at this sort of thing. Her daughter was dead, but she was still maintaining appearances. Starting the car, backing out of the driveway, driving down Lake Avenue, turning off the radio because she couldn't bear the additional stimulus, couldn't bear evidence that the world continued to function as normal when, in fact, her world had ceased to be.

Taking Nevada to I-25, driving south. And then suddenly she was there—how she got there is still a big mystery—and loathing for that place exploded from every pore of her body. They had killed her daughter, and if she wasn't careful, she was going to begin screaming the moment she walked in the door. It was going to require every ounce of discipline she owned to stay quiet. Then realizing she had made a mistake by coming here alone, because nothing was going to keep her from falling apart. Absolutely nothing.

Her daughter had just died. The daughter who had called her at age thirty-three to apologize for all the pain of their past. To apologize for everything that had, indeed, been Doris's fault. Her stern upbringing had hindered Livvy. Some might say tortured. But Olivia was unusual. She was nothing like her mother, and she had thrived in spite of it. Now, after all these years, when Doris finally realized what a horrible mother she had been, when it was time to find a small measure of redemption, to mend those fences, and to finally make up for the past, Olivia was dead.

All hope was gone. Any possibility of a genuine relationship was also gone and *that* was all she could think about as she walked up to the receptionist's desk. She was overwhelmed with a wave of pure revulsion with her own selfishness. Her daughter's life had been cut short, her son-in-law was deprived of the woman who had loved him, and her granddaughter was left to flounder, and all Doris could think about was her own redemption. . . .

◆ ◆ ◆ ◆ ◆

Jessie and Andy entered the place as if they belonged there. "Appear confident," Andy had said. "Like you've been here a thousand times."

The receptionist's desk was still empty and the entire waiting area abandoned. But the hallways were occupied with wandering patients wearing white robes . . . frizzy hair, blank looks, awkward movements . . . young, old, emaciated, large . . .

"I remember that," Jessie whispered.

"Which way?" Andy asked, his face pale.

Jessie noticed a small room off the reception area. Another flash of memory. "That's where we talked."

Andy followed her to the door, and she opened it slowly, walking in. She turned slowly around, taking in the walls, the ceiling, the floor.

"So . . . what did they tell you?"

"I still don't remember."

Andy found a small hospital map on the wall and was tracing his fingers over the numbers. "What room was it again?"

Jessie handed him the certificate, and when he'd matched the number to a room, they walked back out into the hallway. Studying the certificate, Andy pointed to the left, to a hallway heading east. Jessie felt her stomach lurch. "Where are you going?"

"It's this way."

Images flooded her. A sense, a feeling again. "No. That can't be right."

"But that's what it says here."

"They got it wrong, then," Jessie replied, confused. "Let me use your phone."

Andy handed it to her, and she punched in Betty's number.

"I'm so sorry to bother you," Jessie said when Betty answered.

"No problem, honey," Betty said.

Jessie explained the situation, and Betty was quiet at first. "Which way did you turn to go to my mother's room from the main entrance?"

Betty didn't hesitate. "Where are you now?"

"The waiting room."

A moment's pause. "Your mother's room was to the right, down the west hallway."

Jessie met Andy's eyes. "Down there," she whispered, pointing.

"That's not what it says here," he said.

"Maybe they moved her," Jessie said into the phone.

"No. Your mother's room never changed," Betty replied. "I wish you had told me what you were doing. I could have saved you the effort. That's no place for either of you."

Jessie sighed. *I do everything the hard way.*

"What happened that day?" Jessie asked, glancing at Andy.

"Simple, honey. They sent us to the wrong room."

"I'm sorry?"

"They gave us the wrong directions. We were all confused, you know. At first we thought your mother had been placed in a temporary room."

"Where was it? I mean, the wrong number?"

"Oh my, well, let me . . ."

"I'm by the receptionist's desk facing a waiting area."

"To the left, honey."

Jessie felt the blood drain from her face. It was coming back to her, small flashes, little glimpses.

"What happened in that room, Mrs. Robinette?"

Betty cleared her throat. "That's where you fainted, honey."

"But it wasn't my mother's room."

"We didn't know that at first."

"Who was it?"

"It was just another woman, honey. But we didn't realize it, and I'm afraid you—"

Another flash. "I went ballistic, didn't I?" Jessie began walking briskly down the hallway. Andy followed behind her. They passed several nurses and patients, who didn't seem to notice them.

"I guess you could say that."

"Why?"

"Because they made a mistake." Mrs. Robinette cleared her throat. "But *we* made the biggest mistake. Oh, honey, we should never have let you . . ." Betty's voice trailed off.

A third of the way down the hallway, Jessie paused in front of the room. She turned around; Andy was just catching up with her. She gestured toward the number and then toward the death certificate he was still holding.

"I went in alone, didn't I?" Jessie said into the cell phone, trying to catch her breath.

"You begged to . . ."

. . . Doris had discovered a madhouse upon walking into the institution that day. The orderlies had been trying to restore order to the front room. Papers and files were strewn about the front desk. The receptionist was trying to field questions and provide assistance to nearly half a dozen people. The chaos nearly unhinged her. Her daughter had just died, and the place was in chaos. Her peace-loving daughter had died in the midst of a cacophonous zoo! The indignity—the cruel mockery!

Doris stormed past the reception desk, but the receptionist must have seen her, because she called out, "Mrs. Crenshaw?" When Doris turned, the woman stepped around the desk and thrust a piece of paper into her hand, mumbling only, "Sorry," before returning to her work. Mutely, Doris looked down at the paper. *Certificate of Death.* Some attending doctor whose name she didn't recognize had signed it. She began to tremble. She walked toward her daughter's room on spongy legs. Why had she come alone? She had to concentrate on the direction—which way? Which hallway? Past the chipped walls, the urine smell, the trash in the hallway, the walls unpainted, cracking, the tile chipped and stained. The indecency!

When she found her daughter's room, the door was closed. She pushed herself forward—*Don't think! Just do it!*—and walked in, covering her mouth with her hands.

There she was, lying there, peaceful, now restful, looking as she once had when Doris watched her sleep as a child. They hadn't had the civility to cover her dead body yet. Doris let out a sob, holding her hand to her mouth again.

Her daughter was at peace, finally. The pain, the confusion, the heartbreak was past. She was home. Selfish thoughts of her own redemption vanished. She slowly lifted the sheet to cover her daughter's still face and then she shrank back in horror, nearly tripping over a tray that had been left beside the bed. . . .

Standing before that door was a watershed moment for Jessie. The memories, long blocked, began to pour back. She said good-bye to Betty, hit the End button on the phone, and pointed to the door.

"This is the room," Andy said.

"No, it's not."

"Yes, it is." He showed her the certificate.

"But that wasn't my mother's room. That was . . ." Jessie shuddered. "They got it wrong."

Slowly Jessie backed up against the wall. The terrible memory played over and over in her mind. She was only twelve. All three of them—her father, her grandmother, and Mrs. Robinette—waited for her outside the door.

Another glimpse. The name Olive on the door. *Olive? We figured the name was a mistake,* she thought. The whole place was inept, after all. Of course it was her mother's room. Someone had spelled it wrong. And then Jessie went inside, alone, and approached the bedside. Her mom's back was turned to the door and she was covered with a white sheet. She tapped the shrouded body on the back, but her mother didn't budge. She ran around the other side of the bed and the woman's eyes were open . . . her face a pasty white . . . her hair also blond. If she hadn't looked so much like her mother it wouldn't have mattered. This woman bore at least a passing resemblance, only about fifty pounds heavier. The woman on the bed opened her eyes wider, flew up to a sitting position, and began screaming.

And then the woman jumped to her feet on the bed and began flailing her arms and jumping up and down and screaming . . . and Jessie didn't make the connection that this woman wasn't her mother. She never had time; it all happened so fast. Jessie collapsed, falling to the speckled tile floor, and apparently her father responded to the screams, and they found her seconds later and carried her away to the car.

◆ ◆ ◆ ◆ ◆

A terrible mistake had been made.

Doris had crept closer again, placing her fingers over her daughter's face, and a gasp escaped her lips. She hadn't been imagining it. She reached for her daughter's hand. It was warm to the touch. She touched Olivia's face. Again, warm. Her own body was racked by shudders. This was impossible! She brought her face to within inches of Olivia's face and once again felt the faint whisper of breath.

She turned and from that angle she saw what she hadn't seen before—hadn't been looking for—the subtle rise and fall of her daughter's chest. How could it have happened? Who would have made such an error? But she knew the answer. As sure as the sun rose in the east, she knew.

Her mind began spinning. *What do I do now?* She should find an orderly. Go to the front desk and complain to high heavens. Call the authorities. But suddenly her soul split in half and a sense of despair overwhelmed her once again. Olivia would only continue to suffer in this horrible place. She was sure to die soon. Until then, her pain would continue.

Doris glanced at the death certificate in her hands. They had declared her daughter dead. As far as they were concerned, Olivia Lehman had passed away.

The suffering would only continue. . . .

This barn couldn't save her daughter.

But *she* could.

The madness must end. If she'd ever done anything for Olivia, she must do it now.

I have the death certificate, she thought. "Dear God, forgive me," she whispered, drawing closer to Olivia. Slowly she lifted the covers again, this time completely covering her daughter's face. The weight of her world was upon her, crushing her, but she had no choice. . . .

Jessie would never have understood. No one would have understood. So no one must know, because if they did, they would forever look at her in abhorrence and wonder how she could have done such a thing.

All of her friends who worshiped the ground she walked on—her piano association friends, her bridge club friends, her country club friends, her church friends, and not to mention her piano students—hundreds of them through the years who counted on her to reflect the standards of excellence—they would all abandon her. If the truth emerged, her legacy would be destroyed, like a tiny crack in a crystal heirloom destroys its worth as soon as it's discovered. Then they would haul her off to jail. Isn't that what happens?

Jessica would gladly dial the number. "Hello, I'd like to report a crime." While they waited for the police, Jessica would spit out, "How could you have done this?" They would encircle her wrists with handcuffs and take her off to jail. Cart her out to the squad car in front of Mrs. McBride's outstretched wave, whose face would melt into puzzlement. "Where are they taking you, Doris? Did you do something wrong?"

"I intended to help her," she would cry.

Mrs. McBride would be on the phone in minutes. Jessica would whisper in her ear what she already knew—indeed, what she had known for years: "The road to hell is paved with good intentions, Grandmother."

◆ ◆ ◆ ◆ ◆

Jessie was leaning against the wall, shaken. Andy looked worried. "Are you okay?"

She nodded and pointed toward the reception area. *Let's go.*

They headed back, taking the other hallway to the west. Once again, Jessie led the way, this time following the instructions Betty had given, to a room next to a broom closet, a room she'd never seen or visited. When they reached it, Jessica pronounced, "This is it. This was my mother's room."

Andy checked the death certificate. "Not according to this," he repeated.

"Well, it is according to Betty." Jessie slumped against the opposite wall, facing the room. So what now? What did it all mean? A woman named Olive. The wrong room on the death certificate. Andy approached her, placing a gentle arm on her shoulder. "Let's go."

Chapter Twenty-Eight

THEY SAT IN HER CAR for an hour. Jessie's mind was a mingling of disconnected thoughts, but one kept breaking through, "Something went wrong here," she whispered, her words coming out slow and deliberate. "*Very* wrong."

"Obviously the place was, and still is, a mess," Andy observed. "They probably didn't file the death certificate properly. Couple that with two blond women, one Olive and another Olivia, and because of their disorganization, they confused the names and the room records."

Jessie shook her head. "No . . . there's more to it." In her mind's eye, she saw the demented woman, larger than her mother, standing up on the bed and screaming.

She took a deep breath and sighed. "I had no idea I'd come to this moment."

Andy seemed exasperated, but Jessie only shook her head again. "The more I find, the more questions I have."

"Questions about what?"

Jessie shrugged. "Isn't it strange? Nothing on public record. My grandmother seems to hold the only certificate. She never buried the urn." She looked at him closely, "And today she referred to my mother . . . as if she were still alive."

Andy's eyes held a look of incredulity, and she wanted to ask, *Why do you keep looking at me like that?*

"Jessie, what're you suggesting?"

The streetlamp was still flickering, and the shadows on the window danced. She remembered the first day at Grandmother's, overhearing the strange conversation between her and Bill. *"When are you going to tell her?"* She related it to Andy, who didn't seem impressed. "It's probably about the house, right?"

"Sounded too important for that," Jessie said. "Andy, something is terribly wrong."

That look was in his eyes again and this time she couldn't help herself. "What aren't you telling me, Andy?" She held his gaze as she said it, but he looked away. "What is *your* explanation for all this?"

He shrugged, still looking out the window. He seemed lost in mental deliberation.

She'd had enough. "You've been wanting to tell me something since the night on the hill."

"Jessie—"

"What about your little speech at the fair about honesty? Can't I expect the same from you?"

A look of resignation.

She made a repeated attempt at humor. "Ve have vays, you know." She playfully punched his shoulder, but he didn't respond in kind. It was then that she realized she was right. He *was* hiding something, and it must be something bad. She bit her lip and braced herself.

He cleared his throat.

"C'mon, Andy," she said.

He finally turned to her. "I know what they were talking about."

"Who?"

"Your grandmother and Bill."

Jessie was confused. *"She has a right to know,"* Bill had said.

"I'll lose her for sure," her grandmother had replied. But how could Andy know?

"How much do you know about your mother's illness?" Andy asked finally.

She frowned. "What do you mean?"

"About how it's . . . transmitted."

Her mind leapt forward like a gazelle. While she wasn't that fast on the uptake, she knew how to put two and two together. *His father must have told him something,* she thought suddenly.

Jessie leaned back in her seat, taking several deep breaths. She felt Andy's hand resting on her shoulder. "You mean it's . . . genetic?"

"There's only a fifty-fifty chance," Andy said, his tone reassuring. "All it means is you have to be tested."

Fifty-fifty, she thought.

He began talking again, but she looked out the windshield, shutting him out. *Fifty-fifty?* Fifty-fifty chance of not only dying, but dying the way her mother had. The years before her would be more like death than life. Her entire body was going numb.

And who will care for me? she thought, staring at the hospital building now obscured in darkness. Would she die in an institution? Or would she be cared for by someone who didn't deserve the burden?

"Let's get through the first part," Andy said, his hand touching her arm.

Let's? As in, let us? Her throat closed up. "This is not your problem," she managed to say.

"I'm making it mine."

She turned to him. "You can't just *do* that. You can't just invade my life."

"Jess . . ."

"I *can't* become a burden."

"Jess, first things first. . . ."

Jessie sighed, still peering into the years, a future she'd seen once before. "And no matter what, I will *never* stay with my grand-mother."

"Jessie," Andy began again, exasperated, "let me say this, okay?"

She shrugged her left shoulder and he removed his hand.

"If you won't let *me* help you, then your grandmother is the best choice, but we're still *way* ahead—"

"I'd rather die in there," Jessie whispered, glancing over at the institution.

"Jess, that doesn't make sense. Can't you just drop your . . ." He stopped.

Jessie came undone. "Drop what? My ego?" She pointed to the institution. "My grandmother is why my mom died there. My grandmother is why I never had the chance to say good-bye to my mother." She was losing control of her emotions, her voice rising, but she couldn't stop. "My mom always said that someday I would know my father as she knew him, but my grandmother denied me that chance. As far as I'm concerned, *she* killed him."

Andy's soft words broke through her frenzy. "Your father's death was probably an accident, Jess."

She glared at him. "What are you talking about?"

He took a deep breath. "My father called me this after-noon. . . ."

Incredulous, she listened as Andy explained.

"Your dad never *told* my dad that he was drinking, Jess—"

"But—"

"His depression pills aren't even prescribed anymore because they were so volatile. When you combine them with alcohol—*lots* of alcohol—it can lead to respiratory failure."

She shuddered. She'd done nearly everything to make sure her dad was taking those pills every day—short of grinding them up and putting them in his soup.

"It wasn't your fault, Jess," Andy assured her, as if reading her mind. "You didn't know any better. Neither did my father."

Jessie should have been relieved, but she felt a sharp pain in her stomach. *She had spent a lifetime blaming her father for abandoning her and her grandmother for driving him to it.* But . . . maybe her father hadn't checked out by his own hand after all.

She felt like an overloaded electrical circuit. Too much, too fast. *I'm dying. My father didn't commit suicide. And something very wrong happened to my mother. . . .*

"Andy," Jessie said abruptly. "I need to get back." *And rearrange everything I've believed for the last dozen years.*

"Are you okay?"

"I'm fine," she replied.

Andy put the car into gear, and they drove into the night. The lights of the city blazed before them and the cool summer night blew in through the partially open window. Neither spoke as they continued what seemed like a long trek back to her grandmother's home. Jessie closed her eyes and tried to stop trembling.

When Andy pulled into the driveway, he shifted into park and gave her another sorry look.

"I'm okay, Andy."

"Can I do—"

"I'm fine," she insisted, getting out of his car. "Thanks for dinner."

"Jess . . ."

"And everything else."

Their eyes met, and he seemed to understand that she needed time to sort things out. Andy nodded regretfully. She shut the door abruptly and headed toward the house. She heard his car pulling out of the driveway and felt she might collapse. Every time he left it felt as if the wind were being removed from her sails. She stood on the porch, watching as his car disappeared around the bend. She might never see him again.

At the restaurant, Andy had intimated a romantic interest in her, but she'd been too distracted to respond. Any other time in her life, it would have seemed like a dream come true. But tonight she'd learned any future between them was doomed. She didn't need a neurological test to reveal her personal destiny. Maybe *that's* what her dreams were all about—a warning from her subconscious. A sign of her impending death.

If she had any courage, any decency, any love for him at all, she must never see him again.

"Good-bye, my old friend," she whispered.

Chapter Twenty-Nine

THE HOUSE WAS QUIET and dark inside, as dark as a house with a white interior and tall windows could get, considering the generous display of moonlight. Jessie stood in the entryway for a moment, letting the silence swirl around her. She wasn't surprised that no one had stayed up to welcome her back, but surely they'd welcome her exit. If she left before daybreak, she could avoid her grandmother but still say good-bye to Bill.

"It wasn't your fault," Andy had said.

No wonder her dad hadn't left a note. The original autopsy report had indicated an overdose, which according to Andy's explanation, would be true. Surely Andy's father would have seen the blood alcohol level and suspected an accident, or maybe he just didn't read the autopsy report. Maybe he took the coroner's word for it and didn't investigate further.

Jessie headed up the steps. When she passed her mom's room, the door was unlocked, and not just cracked but wide open. She stood there for a moment, staring at it. *Are we done with secrets? Is that it?*

She considered going in, then hesitated. If she did so, she might never get to sleep tonight. She pulled the door shut instead, then went to her own room and sank onto the bed, covering her eyes with her arm. *Andy thinks I'm crazy, too,* she realized. No wonder he paid little attention to the accumulating clues. He'd lumped everything into his theory of her mental instability—either that or he thought she was already well on her way to full-blown dementia.

Maybe he had *never* believed her, even as a kid. Maybe he'd always been humoring her, telling her what she wanted to hear, going along for the sake of going along.

Lying on her bed, across from her mom's room, where Mom once laid awake at night, the idea of having the same disease didn't seem so bad—more like an undeserved honor, the ultimate gesture of her lifelong loyalty. *We're together again,* she thought. *We're inseparable, even in death.*

She was descending into deepest gloom. Oregon seemed an eternity away. *I was never supposed to reach paradise,* she thought.

She pondered tomorrow again. It would be an awkward goodbye. Bill would give her his puppy dog eyes, and when that didn't work, he'd throw in a wink or two. She smiled thinking about him. If anything good had come of this trip, it was meeting Cowboy Bill.

"Finish the story," her shrink had once urged, and she cringed. Regardless of how silly it now sounded to her, in spite of the sheer impossibility of it, she wasn't sure she even cared to anymore. Regardless of what she uncovered, she couldn't bring her mother back. If the dreams continued, so be it. They were still the best thing that happened to her, tormenting though they were.

She considered finishing her mother's letter. *Why do I keep putting it off?* she wondered. *Am I afraid of what I'll read? Or do I already* know?

Tomorrow, she thought, repeating the mantra of a lifetime. When her cell phone buzzed from the nightstand, she picked it up, glancing at the ID. Andy.

She pressed the Power key, extinguishing the light and the sound . . . and any hope that might have existed between them.

Persistent images of the institution haunted her, including the newfound memory of that poor crazy woman standing on the bed and going berserk.

Nothing was as persistent as Dr. Roeske's words, echoing in her brain: *"Finish the story."*

What was left to do? Nothing had been accomplished anyway. Only more questions had been raised; no satisfying proof of her mother's death had surfaced. It was a wild goose chase, nothing more.

In spite of herself, she listed what she did know: the absent death records, the lack of cremation records, the unburied urn, the room number mix-up—although Jessie wasn't sure what that meant anyway. And then there was her grandmother's slip of the tongue, which of course, meant absolutely nothing except to someone with pathological wishful thinking.

Andy was right and she was wrong.

And yet *it feels right,* she thought. And as a child her instincts regarding her mother had rarely been wrong.

There was nothing left to do but ask her grandmother a series of disturbing questions, which wasn't going to happen. Besides . . . ask her what? *"Where are you hiding my mother?"* Jessie grimaced into the dark. *I'd be lucky if she even spoke to me tomorrow.*

And then a strange thought shivered down her spine—*the downstairs office. Grandmother's papers. That's ridiculous,* she countered. *What could I possibly find?*

Just finish the story, she thought. *Take it to the end.*

She shook it off as a very bad idea, something akin to breaking and entering. She finally drifted off, then awakened some hours later and wandered to the bathroom for a drink of water.

Back in the room, she sat on the edge of her bed, wide awake. Maybe she had been going about it all wrong. Instead of looking for evidence that her mother was dead, perhaps she should have been looking for evidence that she was still alive. She grimaced. *Maybe I am losing my mind.*

It was 3:10 when she dressed in her jeans and a simple blue

T-shirt, the darkest attire she owned. She checked the hall, wondering if Bill was sleeping well tonight. After another moment of hesitation and a few prickly butterflies, she headed down the hall and made it to the steps.

Downstairs, just off the grand room, she reached the office. The door was closed. *What are the chances the door isn't locked?* she thought, grasping the doorknob of the glass-paned French doors. No chance, she determined.

Wandering back across the room, she slipped into the kitchen and rummaged through the keys hanging just above the high-tech blender. White moonlight scattered across the kitchen, flowing unimpeded through the wispy alcove curtains. Grabbing the entire handful of keys, she also lifted a flashlight from the drawer and headed back. She padded across the living room, relying on the moonlight to keep from stumbling. At the doors, she began testing each key, as quietly as possible, until finally the lock turned. She let out a sigh of relief.

Am I crossing the line? she asked herself. *Most definitely.* Going into her mother's room had been a different situation. In fact, one might even argue she had a right to look through her mother's things. But breaking into her grandmother's office was, at best, a gross violation of trust. Besides, her grandmother's bedroom was just down the hall from this room. Any noise she made would be obvious.

Jessie closed the door behind her and stood motionless for the longest time, wondering where to begin. Tall dark-wood bookshelves graced the walls, and a similar desk anchored the middle of the room. Maybe Bill had crafted them in his woodshop of miracles. The computer seemed out of place in a room so elegantly furnished.

Tall windows looked out to the backyard and the gazebo, which seemed like a white castle in the moon's light. The outside world was still and silent beneath the flickering stars. Using the flashlight to sweep around the room—although the moonlight would have been enough—she saw the filing cabinets, and her heart sank. In what kind of fantasy world would they be unlocked? And if locked, where was the key?

Jessie almost sat down at the desk before realizing all kinds of squeaks could emanate from the old chair, and the whole thing was putting her on edge. *I should leave now.*

She took a deep breath and glanced at the cabinet, wondering: where would *she* keep a key? In her pocket? No . . . too inconvenient. She would hide it someplace in the room, reasoning that locking the doors should be enough protection.

She noticed a slight flicker of motion from beyond the glass doors. She froze, her adrenaline pumping, arms and legs tingling with nerves. Maybe it was an outside tree branch causing the moonlight to flicker. Turning out the flashlight, glancing around the study, she asked herself again, *Where would I put a key?*

In the desk? That would make the most sense. Gingerly pushing the chair aside, she leaned over, held on to the knobs, and pulled slowly. Using the flashlight again, she studied the contents—pencils, pens, staples, erasers, markers, letter opener, batteries—but no key. She carefully pushed the drawer shut, and one by one opened the side drawers. More of the same stuff common to any desk—half a ream of paper, a dictionary, index cards, and an address book. Picking up the address book, she flipped through it but found nothing of interest.

She turned her flashlight over toward the cabinet again, and another flicker of motion beyond the French doors nearly stopped her heart. *Tree branches,* she told herself again. She noticed a potted azalea plant at the top of the cabinet and smiled through the goose bumps. Finally, toward the back of the bottom drawer, her fingers found a small key. She held her breath and inserted it into the file cabinet lock. She turned and expelled her breath as it opened.

Working with only one hand free, her other holding the flashlight, she flipped through the top file drawer, perusing a collection of manila files generically labeled Utilities, Phone, Life Insurance, Home Insurance. One file was labeled Brochures. Jessie continued thumbing through the remaining files: Brokerage Houses, Tax Files, Bank Statements.

Opening the bank file, Jessie examined the statements one by one. In the space of an hour, she read through hundreds of canceled checks: grocery, clothing, subscriptions, club fees, restaurants, charities—many charities—Salvation Army, the Episcopal Soup Kitchens, St. Jude's Hospital, Woodland Park Care Center, Compassion International, Pike's Peak Hospice. Jessie was floored by the sheer volume of her grandmother's benevolent giving. When she finally returned the files, she sat at the edge of the desk. *What am I looking for anyway? Hospital bills?*

She opened the top drawer of the filing cabinet again and removed the brochure file. Mostly vacation advertisements, some medical, and a brochure from the Woodland Park Care Center. Jessie stared at it for a moment, then thumbed through the pages, realizing that it was a home for dementia patients.

The kitchen light flickered on, and Jessie jumped to her feet in a panic, her heart slamming. Quickly she tiptoed to the side of the French doors and pressed herself against the wall. Bill or her grandmother must be up. What time was it? She glanced at the wall clock. 4:20. She knew Bill was an early riser, but *four?*

When she heard a gentle rapping on the door, her worst fears were realized. *Totally, absolutely, busted.*

I'm an idiot, she thought as slowly the door opened. *Please let it be Bill.* And it was. He peeked in through the door and smiled as if she hadn't just been caught doing something very foolish. "Hope I didn't startle you."

By now Jessie had moved from the wall and was standing by the desk. "Hey, Bill." Her voice quavered. She didn't know what else to say.

He chuckled, pointing to a flat little metallic panel in the doorframe. "Next time you need to check for motion detectors."

Jessie cringed. It must be linked to his room somehow. He'd known the whole time, probably from the very moment she'd walked in. "I wasn't stealing anything," she stammered. "I was just . . . looking for something."

Bill shrugged. "I knew you weren't stealing anything. Frankly, if you wanted your grandmother's money, she'd gladly give it to you, and I didn't stop you because, well . . . I didn't want you to know I knew at first. But then it just seemed that maybe we should talk a bit."

He gestured to the chair, and she sat down. Bill pulled a small folding chair from the corner. She closed her eyes and let out a muted breath.

"What are you looking for?" Bill finally asked, his tone gentle.

"Information," Jessie replied, sighing again at how stupid it sounded. She hesitated. There was no way out of this, and since Bill's expression was receptive, unthreatening, she decided to take a risk, lay the whole thing on the table. What choice did she have? She began with the lack of death records and went from there, including the unburied urn and the errors from the mental hospital.

Bill listened politely without comment. When she finished he asked, "What does your friend think?"

After she described Andy's reaction, Bill suggested, "Maybe he's right."

Jessie sighed. *Maybe he is.* She grabbed the brochure from the table and handed it to Bill. He smiled, nodding his head, and handed it back to her as if it were hers. "Your grandmother is a very generous woman, but you probably know that by now. Would it be so strange for her to give money to a nursing home that provides care to people who suffered as your mother did?"

"No," Jessie admitted.

He paused a moment, appraising her. "I couldn't help overhearing your discussion with your grandmother yesterday."

"I said what I had to say, Bill."

"I understand," he replied, shifting in his seat. "But I pretty much know her perspective on the whole thing, which you might have gathered if you'd stuck around a bit."

"She took my mother from me."

"Well . . . not technically."

"That's *exactly* what happened."

Bill cleared his throat. "Sure . . . but that's not what your grandmother *intended* to have happen. The final events were out of her control."

"Doesn't matter."

Bill leaned forward. "Jessie, you were young at the time, and from what I understand your mother was declining at a rapid pace."

She crossed her arms defensively.

"Doesn't a mother have a right to worry about her daughter?" he asked, and his gaze was uncompromising. "Doris was worried sick about you, as well."

"She has a strange way of showing it."

Bill nodded strongly. "Absolutely. You have to look beneath the surface of that woman, Jess, but you'll find a gold mine if you do."

She swallowed.

"Your father was drinking all the time, wasn't he?"

"Yes . . ."

"And you . . . what was happening to you?"

"I was fine."

"That's not what your teachers said."

"It was stressful," she admitted. "My mother . . . was . . . dying."

"The entire burden fell on you, Jess. And that was so wrong. You couldn't handle it."

Jessie flinched. Who did he think he was? "Wasn't my mom's fault."

Bill shook his head. "Of course not. But she was too sick to know what was happening to her."

Jessie felt her eyes tearing up.

"Your grandmother meant to *rescue* you."

"Well, she didn't."

"No," Bill agreed sadly.

Jessie let out another painful breath and waited for Bill to continue, but he fell silent. The darkness was giving way to dawn.

Bill cleared his throat and spoke again, "You know, we haven't had a chance to talk like we thought. I was going to tell you my story, remember?"

"I heard a little bit from Andy last night."

"Well, how 'bout I tell you the rest." Bill stared at the floor, then frowned as if dredging up a painful memory. "I was a full-blown drunk when your grandmother hired me to do a little gardening." He caught her eye as if waiting for it to sink in. "Knock down, fall over drunk. I was fired from that Montana ranch I told you about, and by that time, I was drinking from dawn to dusk and hiding the bottles under my bunk, until someone found my stash. After they sent me packing, I moved here, signed up for one of those temp agencies, and slept in the cab of my truck. Your grandmother liked my work and kept me busy. I can do a little of everything, and she's always doing something new, you know. So it was a good match. But she's no slouch. Eventually she discovered my problem."

"She fired you?"

"Not at first. But she gave me an ultimatum. As long as I was attending AA meetings and staying sober, I'd have a job."

"So . . ."

"I laughed at her," Bill said, shaking his head. "You think I was going to pay any mind to this overbearing dame from Connecticut?"

"No."

"Nope," he agreed, shaking his head. "A year later, I was still on the street, sleeping at the shelter, which seemed like a four-star hotel compared to the cab of my truck. Taking day jobs in order to buy liquor. One day I hit bottom, see. I was at the Red Cross shelter, and I prayed for the first time in years, only it wasn't a very happy prayer. I said, 'If it's all the same to you, God, I'd like to check out tonight.' I took another drink from my little vodka bottle, just to prepare myself and think through the options. I remember chuckling to myself at that moment and adding to the end of my prayer, 'unless you got something else in mind. . . .' "

Jessie glanced out the windows at the lightening sky. "Maybe we should . . ." Jessie began, indicating the living room. Bill took the hint. After relocking the office, they retired to the kitchen. He began fixing a pot of coffee as Jessie sat at the table.

Bill continued. "So . . . I was laying on a cot with a hundred other hard-luck stories around me, and someone from the office walked in and called my name. I could barely walk, but I made my way to the front office, and there she was, your grandmother, Doris Crenshaw. She said, 'Bill, I've been worried about you. What in tarnation happened?' And I just started weeping like a baby. She grabbed my arm. 'Let's go, Bill. I've got some work for you,' but first she fed me a meal. I mean, we went to this restaurant, and I devoured nearly everything in sight. People were looking at us and she didn't care. For the first time I realized that sometimes, just sometimes, your grandmother doesn't give a rat's tail what *anyone* thinks.

"Then she asked me, 'Are you done with the bottle, Bill?' And I said, 'Ma'am, I've been done for years, but I can't quit.' She told me about this research she'd done, a better way of quitting than talking yourself out of alcohol, which never worked for me. First she sent me to this dry-out clinic, then she put me up in a little apartment on good faith. She started feeding me these supplements, minerals, fatty acids, you name it. I'm just a recovering drunk, Jess. But she trusted me. The rest is history. I haven't had a drink in eight years."

"That was a pretty short story, Bill."

"Think I told a fib?"

"Said it would take all week," Jessie said. "I'm thinking I got cheated a bit."

"I can go on. . . ."

Jessie smiled.

"Maybe tomorrow?"

Jessie hesitated, and Bill seemed to read her mind.

"Your grandmother's waited a long time to see you, Jess. I think your welcome is rather assured." He got to his feet. "Almost forgot. I've got something to show you . . . well, actually . . . give you."

He went to the counter, pulled out a drawer, and retrieved an envelope. Back at the table he extended it to her. "I'm not good at this kinda thing, but I've been commissioned to do it, because your grandmother figured you'd be gone when she got up. Maybe I should give it back to her and let her do it herself, but I'm feeling a little selfish. Wanted to see the look on your face."

Jessie accepted the envelope and read the outside address. *El Paso County Clerk.*

Confused, she looked up at Bill. "What is it?"

He shrugged. "Ain't telling."

Jessie opened it and found a deed of trust. She checked the address. The transference had been granted twelve years before.

Bill sniffed. "Yep. I'm thinking that look was worth it all, and now I'm sorry she wasn't here to see it."

"The house belongs to me?" Jessie whispered, unbelieving. "My parents' house belongs to me?"

He chuckled again.

Stunned, Jessie stared at the document. "I don't know what to say."

"What's the matter, Jessie girl?"

She shook her head and placed the deed on the table. "Is this the secret, Bill?" She explained and his smile faded from his face. "I didn't mean to eavesdrop," she added, her tone sheepish.

Bill seemed to struggle for words, then shook his head. The overheard conversation was *not* about the house.

"But I think I know," she submitted.

Bill met her eyes again, and as painful as the moment was, she was glad to have finally put an end to all the secrets.

"I'll have some medical tests, and then I'll know what to do."
He gave her another sympathetic smile.

Jessie stared at the deed of trust again. "Thanks, Bill."

The twinkle was back. "You hungry?"

Chapter Thirty

JESSIE AND BILL settled into a hearty breakfast together. By seven o'clock Grandmother had yet to make an appearance. Eventually Jessie trudged back up the stairs. Having lost several hours of sleep, she was exhausted.

She awakened in the early afternoon to the sound of her mom's favorite piano piece—the same one her mother had once played on their piano in Palmer Lake. The piece wasn't difficult; her mother wasn't the best of pianists. Still, she'd loved to muddle through the song.

Jessie jogged her memory. "Humoresque" . . . by Dvorak. It had a lilting, frivolous spirit to it. The second theme was haunting, almost heartbreaking—in direct contrast to the primary theme.

She rose and made her way down the hall and looked over the balcony toward the grand room. Grandmother was at the piano, playing from the music book.

Jessie settled at the top of the stairs and listened. Eventually she heard the shuffling of music and the beginning of another piece, another favorite of her mother's. Jessie recognized it immediately: "Rustle of Spring" by Christian Sinding.

When Grandmother began the next piece, the exact name

escaping her, Jessie headed downstairs, quietly entering the grand room. Jessie slipped into a chair and closed her eyes.

When the piece was finished, Jessie opened her eyes and saw that her grandmother, a woman of near-perfect posture, was slouching, bracing herself up by both arms on the piano bench. Maybe she was aware that Jessie had come down.

"What was that Brahms piece?" Jessie ventured. "The one you always played . . ."

Her grandmother looked up for a moment as if giving it some thought, then nodded slightly. She launched into a soul-stirring melody of profound seriousness, and Jessie was taken back again to happier times, only this time, right here in Grandmother's home. Often following supper, she and Mom would make requests while her father found something else to do. Brahms's "Rhapsody in G Minor," she now recalled from some dusty corner of her mind.

When the piece was finished, Jessie noticed Bill standing at the kitchen door. He smiled, and Jessie could tell from the look on his face something irreverent was sure to follow. "It ain't country, is it?"

Jessie chuckled. Grandmother was shuffling through her music again.

"Dory, you know any Johnny Cash?"

Her grandmother turned to Jessie, and they actually shared a smile. Then the older woman grimaced as she reached beneath the piano bench, removing a book of none other than a collection of Cash tunes.

Jessie grinned at Bill, who seemed to be in his glory. "She plays a mean 'Ring of Fire,'" he said, teeth gleaming.

"Can't *stand* that one," her grandmother protested, bending the songbook to keep it open, but she played it anyway.

Bill sang along as he went back to work in the kitchen. "I fell into a burning ring of fire; I went down, down, down and the flames went higher."

* * * * *

That afternoon, while resting in her room, Andy called several times before Jessie finally answered.

"Would you just tell me that you're okay?"

"I'm exhausted," she replied.

"Are you packing . . . to go?" he asked.

"No," she replied.

"Can I see you again?"

"Andy, I'm not ready to get involved."

"We're friends, aren't we?"

"Of course, but—"

"Then don't shut me out, Jess. I can . . ." He stopped.

Help me? Jessie finished in her mind. "I don't want . . ." She stopped. "I'm fine," she said.

"May I call you?"

She hesitated. "I better go."

After hanging up, she could smell Bill's dinner from downstairs . . . something with onions or garlic. She closed her eyes, squeezing out the tears, and tried to forget Andy's call.

The sound of the music brought her back to reality. Her grandmother was back at the piano, playing a piece from the Classical Era—Mozart, Haydn, or perhaps early Beethoven.

She pondered what Bill had said in the wee hours today. *"Look beneath the surface of her life."* The irony of that statement, referring to a woman who seemed to *live* on the surface of life. Had Jessie misjudged her grandmother by making the same mistake?

She thought of her father's pills again and struggled with a lingering sense of guilt and regret. *I meant well. I was trying to help.* That is where she and Doris Crenshaw had something in common. *Neither of us meant any harm and yet, in spite of our good intentions, things went very wrong.*

An hour before dinner, she finally opened her mother's letter and read the whole thing, from beginning to end.

Do you remember when we walked all the way to Monument on the trail?

Jessie did. They had started early in the morning at the lake, and her father had picked them up several hours later. Her mom had written of other favorite memories, recounting times together, events shared. Occasionally the letter rambled, but overall the letter revealed her mom at an unusually clear moment, something that had been rare in the last days.

I've asked God to keep you in His love, honey. . . .

There had been a time when she herself prayed the exact same prayer for her mom.

There's nothing I need to say here, because there's nothing we haven't already said to each other. . . .

Mom had always treated her with uncommon respect. As if she saw a little adult hidden away inside of Jessie.

I prayed that He might let me see you grow up, but perhaps that is not to be.

The letter was getting harder to read.

Promise me you'll keep believing, sweetie. No matter what happens, hold on to Jesus.

"Too late," Jessie whispered. "I already broke the promise."

Her mother closed with a P.S. and a smiley face: *Did I ever tell you that you were my longed-for child?*

"Not enough," Jessie whispered.

When she was finished, she held it to her heart and lay back on her bed.

◆ ◆ ◆ ◆ ◆

That night, after getting ready to retire, Jessie shut out the lights and knelt beside her bed for the first time in over a decade. She bowed her head, folded her hands, and tried to say something . . . anything. Instead, her tears flowed freely. "I don't know what to say to you," she finally whispered.

She went to bed frustrated. Years and years of walls had locked everyone and everything out. Opening up to God still seemed impossible, especially with such seething anger just beneath the surface. *"Get it out,"* Mrs. Robinette had told her. *"God isn't afraid. . . ."*

Did she even believe God existed? *Who was I talking to if I don't believe?*

"Find me, God," she finally whispered. "Help me."

◆　◆　◆　◆　◆

The next day, at Grandmother's urging, Jessie called a neurologist. "Don't you worry about the cost," she'd said. "We're going to get to the bottom of this."

Jessie talked to a Dr. Sawyer and explained her situation. The doctor transferred her to the nurse to make an appointment.

"Are you a new patient?" the administrative nurse asked.

"I might be," she replied, explaining her situation.

"That will be a very specialized test," the nurse said. "It might take a while for the results."

"I can wait," Jessie said. *Believe me, I can wait.*

Later that morning, Jessie noticed Bill in the garden, planting geraniums along the gazebo. She stood in the alcove a moment, gazing at Bill's flowers, marveling at how she'd looked right through them at first. In such a hurry to get on with her journey, she'd merely observed the surface of their beauty. But this time she was struck with such a feeling of bliss it nearly took her breath away. *Where did that come from?*

Bill looked up when she wandered out and stopped what he was doing. He wrinkled his brow. "Howdy, Jessie girl."

She offered to help, but he waved her away, so she sat on the wooden steps of the gazebo as Bill went back to digging his holes.

"You've been planting geraniums for a week, Bill," Jessie kidded.

Bill chuckled. "Keep getting sidetracked."

"That's a hot pink," she commented.

"Ain't it, though?" he agreed, standing on his knees. He pointed to the one remaining plant and then raised his eyebrows at her.

"I'm afraid my thumbs aren't so green," she said, kneeling next to the old cowboy.

Bill dug a hole, and Jessie pressed the last plant into the cavity, surrounding it with dirt. He stood up, slapping his leg free of dirt.

He removed his hat and wiped his brow. Gesturing to the gazebo, he said, "Let's chew a bit."

"Did I ever tell you how much I love gazebos?" Jessie joked as she followed Bill underneath the pentagon roof, sitting on a bench across from him. "A time or two," he replied, twinkling. She gazed beyond the fence to the Russian olives in the next yard. The aroma wasn't noticeable, but the chalky green was almost startling in the cluster of forest green trees.

Jessie asked why he hadn't mentioned his church attendance. "So . . . you *do* go?"

Bill grimaced. "I guess I tried to stay in the background. This was your grandmother's time." He shook his head as if his own explanation were feeble.

"Background isn't a good role for you," she said with a smile.

◆ ◆ ◆ ◆ ◆

At noon Jessie attended another club luncheon with her grandmother. Another set of interesting personalities, giving Jessie the same kinds of inquisitive glances, but Doris seemed more subdued this time, less outspoken. Jessie found herself watching her, wondering what had happened to over-confident Grandmother.

That evening Jessie knelt beside her bed again, feeling as if her elbows were sinking into the mattress. Something was eating away at her from the inside, forcing its way up. She took deep, anguished breaths, then said, "Here I am again, God. I still don't know what to say." She was tempted to quit and go to bed.

Instead, she whispered, "I'm very angry with you." The flood-gates seemed to open—her tears, the bitterness, the sense of betrayal. It all came out. For an hour or more, she struggled with the pain, talking to God at times as if He were a monster and at other times as if He was everything she had ever hoped He would be. She fell into bed, exhausted, but an underlying peace lingered as she drifted to sleep.

◆　◆　◆　◆　◆

The next morning over breakfast, her grandmother startled her by grasping her hand and asking her to stay for the summer.

Jessie was taken aback. "I need to get to my job."

Doris shook her head vehemently. "You don't need to work, my dear."

"But I should. I *must*."

Her grandmother closed her eyes and shook her head, a small smile escaping her lips. "Jessica, have you looked around?"

Jessie was confused.

"All that I have will be yours . . . one day."

"I didn't come here for that—"

"I *know* you didn't," Grandmother said.

"It's not right," Jessie countered, in turmoil, overwhelmed with such a gesture. "I don't *deserve*—"

Doris put her finger to her lips, and her eyes glistened. "Please think about it, Jessica. Just for the summer, if you wish. You can always go on to school in the fall."

◆　◆　◆　◆　◆

That afternoon the neurologist visit with Dr. Sawyer, a blond woman with glasses, went as well as could be expected. Jessie suffered through a series of questions designed to determine if she was displaying any troublesome signs. Headaches? Confusion? Memory loss?

Jessie answered as honestly as she could, but the doctor's concern seemed to grow with each answer. "Maybe just . . . stress?" Dr. Sawyer suggested, smiling tentatively. "We'll have a better idea in a few weeks." She ordered the blood test, which was administered in the lab downstairs.

Andy called a few days later while Jessie, Bill, and Grandmother were relaxing in the grand room. Bill was reading a magazine, and Grandmother was doing needlepoint. "I'm coming down tomorrow," he announced. "I need to see you."

"Andy, don't—"

"I have to," he said, and hung up before she could object further. For the next few minutes, she dialed and redialed his cell phone, but he didn't answer. *This is impossible,* she thought, unable to stop the tears.

"You okay, Jess?" Bill asked. Grandmother was also looking at her, obviously worried.

"It's nothing," she replied, wiping her eyes with a tissue.

"Would you like some space?" asked Grandmother.

Jessie shook her head. She couldn't get Andy's call out of her thoughts.

Her father had been a different man before her mother got sick. Betty, too, had fond memories of the man before Mom's horrid illness. *What kind of person would I be to let Andy fall in love with me?* she taunted herself. *I would destroy his life.*

Chapter Thirty-One

ANDY CALLED the next morning to say he'd be there in half an hour. *Doesn't this guy ever work?* Jessie thought, hanging up the phone. She waited for him on the front steps. At 9:55, Andy's Toyota pulled into the driveway, and Jessie felt her heart sink.

Andy got out of the car wearing gray chino slacks and a bright-colored T-shirt and holding a bouquet of roses. Jessie winced. He shut the car door and approached the steps.

"You look great," he said, his blue eyes hesitant.

"Thank you," she replied. *I'm not foaming at the mouth just yet.* "So do you."

"Frankly, I didn't expect to find you here." He grinned and pushed the lavender roses forward. "These are for your grandmother."

Jessie squinted. "Oh, they are, are they?"

"Sorry," he added with a glint in his eyes. "Is she here?"

"You are so bad," Jessie accused.

"Well . . . I suppose I *could* give them to you. You won't tell her, though, will you?"

"She might appreciate them more," she said and felt a sharp pain of regret. She'd intended to make the visit very difficult for him, which now seemed impossible. It hurt too much.

Andy was undaunted. "Well . . . maybe you can both appreciate them." He laid them beside her on the step and sat down. "I missed you."

Jessie picked up the bouquet and breathed in the aroma.

"Guaranteed to open," Andy said, "or my money back."

Jessie placed the flowers on the step. Her emotions were a mess.

"I need your help with something," Andy said cheerfully. "A little romantic advice."

"I'll see if I can reach Dear Abby."

"You see, I've met this girl . . . who seems to like being with me . . . and then she suddenly freezes up and *acts*—" he paused for emphasis—"like she doesn't like me." He turned toward her with a look of mock seriousness. "What am I supposed to think?"

"Maybe you read her wrong."

Andy considered this. Jessie felt terrible, but there was no other way.

"So . . . I'm wrong?"

"Things aren't always as they seem." Jessie answered coldly, but her heart was breaking.

"Should I try talking to her?"

"Andy—"

"I want you to meet my mother," Andy interjected.

"It didn't go too well the first time," Jessie replied without missing a beat, looking out beyond the wrought-iron fence. They heard the squeak of the door behind them and turned to see her grandmother looking down at them. "Oh, good," she said to Andy, "I was afraid you'd left, young man."

"No, ma'am," Andy replied.

"You're staying for lunch, right?" Grandmother asked.

"Oh . . . no . . . I didn't mean—"

"Nonsense," she murmured and disappeared.

Jessie shuddered. *From bad to worse.*

Andy winked at her. "That settles it."

"Settles what?"

"We have to get married."

"Andy—"

"Did you see the way she looked at me?"

"What?"

"I saw a tone."

"You *saw* a tone."

He nodded. "I'm approved of. You're finished."

"Andy, you're just—"

He leaned over, and before she realized what he was doing, he kissed her. Full on the lips.

When she pulled back, he was gazing into her eyes. "I love you, Jessie."

Jessie shook her head and sighed.

◆ ◆ ◆ ◆ ◆

Lunch was a miserable affair. Andy was animated and charming. Bill carried on as if Andy were his son, and it was horrendously annoying. Even Grandmother seemed to enjoy herself at moments.

When Jessie went to the refrigerator for olives, Bill was removing an extra serving spoon from the drawer, and Doris and Andy were engaged in conversation. Bill whispered into her ear, "He's quite a looker, you know." He nudged her with his elbow. "I'd tie that one up."

Tie him up? Jessie nearly groaned.

By the end of the meal, she was a nervous wreck. *Andy has no idea,* she thought, steeling her resolve. *He's running on pure emotion. . . .*

As Bill cleared the table, Jessie said, "I have some shopping to do."

"Oh . . . I was hoping we could walk around the Broadmoor lake," Andy suggested softly.

"That's nice of you, but . . ."

Bill settled back in his chair and appraised her curiously. His twinkles were exasperating. *Put a sock in it,* Jessie thought. Even her grandmother seemed a bit taken aback by her attitude.

She looked away but could feel Andy's eyes on her. "I should be going anyway," Andy finally remarked. He kept trying to make eye contact with her, but other than an occasional glance, she refused to meet his gaze.

When the three conspirators couldn't squeeze out another drop of small talk, Jessie walked Andy to the door. She tried to make it a casual exit, quick and graceful, but Andy lingered at the door. "I'd like to see you again, Jess."

"I can't."

"But why?"

"Trust me," she said, struggling to contain her emotions.

Andy glanced down at the floor. When he looked up his features reflected profound disappointment. She sniffed and wiped her eyes, pretending her show of emotion was less than what it appeared. She'd wanted to be colder, more detached. *What sort of person would I be?* she kept repeating to herself, crossing her arms defensively. *How could I ruin his life?*

"Okay," he finally whispered, his own voice struggling. "But I . . . thought we had something." He gave her a gentle nod and smiled warmly, but his eyes seemed to be twinkling like Bill's. He pulled the door open and closed it behind him.

We did, Jessie thought.

◆ ◆ ◆ ◆ ◆

The next day she called Oregon State University and quit her summer job without changing her college plans. She called Darlene, who answered frantically. "Where have you been?" They spent half an hour catching up, and Darlene listened with fascination, positively thrilled that Jessie was patching things up with her grandmother. "It's touch and go," Jessie told her. "A lot of history to redeem." Jessie wondered if Darlene would take that reply as an invitation to talk religion again, but she didn't. And Jessie realized she wouldn't have minded. Not at all. "Have you ever seen the Springs?" Jessie asked.

Darlene chuckled playfully. "You promised me Oregon."

"We've got mountains here."

"Well, why didn't you say so?"

Darlene arrived the next weekend. When she walked into the house, she nearly gasped as she dropped her bags. Bill wandered in and charmed the socks off her. Jessie gave him a few warning glances, but he only twinkled back. Before Darlene arrived, Jessie had sworn Bill and Grandmother to secrecy regarding Jessie's medical test.

They enjoyed a few days of pure frenzy—shopping, hiking at the Garden of the Gods and Cheyenne Canyon, attending a couple of movies, dining at several restaurants.

"Did you find what you were looking for?" Darlene asked on Sunday night, her last night, over homemade milkshakes—another of Bill's specialties. The question didn't seem as probing, nor as invasive, as it once would have.

"I'm closer," Jessie whispered, and Darlene seemed to understand.

"I'm praying for you," she only replied, and for the first time, Jessie found it reassuring. Jessie reached over and squeezed her hand. "Thank you."

Darlene blinked away tears as she squeezed back.

◆ ◆ ◆ ◆ ◆

The largest portion of the days and weeks that followed was spent helping Bill with chores, despite his cheerful objections. Sometimes she shopped with her grandmother, and afterward they would lunch at the finest places in Colorado Springs, as the woman never lost her determination to impress her granddaughter. But her earlier feistiness had all but disappeared, and Jessie seemed to catch her, more and more, in listless contemplation. She would stare off in the darkness of a windowless restaurant, her features almost despairing, and when she snapped out of it, she'd force a smile and say something like, "Where were we? Caught me daydreaming again." But the grandmother Jessie remembered never daydreamed. Ever.

Young Laura called several times a week, and if it hadn't been so pathetically sad, it would have been comical. "Dana's mother won't let me play with her anymore," she once muttered. "So I'm going to call you more."

"Cool," Jessie replied.

On Sunday Jessie attended her grandmother's church, but in the evening she went with Bill. His church reminded her of the Monument church she'd attended when she was little. They sang worship songs, some of which Jessie recognized because of Darlene's worship CDs, and a few hymns, which had been her mother's favorites.

Each night Jessie knelt and prayed. Sometimes her efforts were feeble; other times, it seemed as if she'd grasped the robe of God himself. But the more she prayed, the more she was drawn back. *Am I just afraid of dying?* she once asked herself. *We're all dying,* she realized, *some at slower paces than others.*

She thought of the Canaanite woman who persisted in pleading with Jesus in spite of Jesus' initial rejection, until He finally declared, "Great is your faith, woman," and it encouraged Jessie to keep fighting through.

She found a Bible in the bookcase, and in the mornings she began reading small sections, starting slowly, worried she might find something that would disturb her, perhaps even infuriate her. So many of the verses were caught up in the days with her mother, and yet one in particular struck her: *You will seek me and find me, when you seek me with all your heart. . . .*

That's where I am, she thought.

In spite of her tentative, sometimes despairing, steps, she found herself gripped at the oddest times by that same feeling of utter joy.

She was reminded of one of Darlene's books, *Surprised by Joy*, written by C. S. Lewis, recalling that Darlene had once proposed the author's experience as an argument for the faith.

At the time it didn't impress Jessie in the least, but now it was almost mystifying, this almost disconnected feeling of pure *happiness*. Here she'd only taken little baby steps, hadn't really made a commitment at all, but it seemed to her as if God had already met her halfway.

Later that week she called Betty Robinette and scheduled a short visit for the afternoon. "I'll take you out to the B&E Filling Station," Jessie offered, and Betty was delighted. Her favorite restaurant.

Jessie then worked up the courage to call Michelle and offer her services as a baby-sitter.

Michelle snorted into the phone, "I'm starting to think you're some kind of child molester."

"Michelle, please."

"Laura's got her own friends, you know. Kids her age."

"I was just thinking maybe I could be like a big sister."

Michelle laughed into the phone. "Well, don't that beat all. You think I can't be a mother?"

"It's just that . . . you work a lot. I'll do it for free . . . for a while," she stammered.

"Stay away from my daughter," Michelle finally said just before hanging up. Jessie was still stewing when Laura called an hour later. *What a mess,* Jessie thought.

"That went reasonably terrible," Laura giggled into the phone. "I can sneak down to the Rock House, you know."

"No, honey. It's not right."

"Okay," Laura replied, her voice dejected. "Then just keep calling my mom."

Yep, that'll work, Jessie thought. "Honey, I'm praying for you."

The phone went silent for a moment. "You are?" Laura finally got out. "But I thought—"

"Things change," Jessie told her.

"Cool!"

During the weeks that followed, Grandmother continued to exhibit unusual behavior. More staring off into space, but most unusual was her drastic curtailing of club activities. "They can muddle without me," she told Bill in Jessie's hearing.

"Yeah, but can you muddle without *them?*"

"Bill, you're like . . ."

"I know, I know," Bill said, winking at Jessie. "I'm like a porcupine in a balloon shop."

A few days later, Bill confided in Jessie. "She never just *sat* alone like this before." He began shaking his head sadly.

Sometimes in the evening, Jessie would look up, only to find her grandmother staring at her affectionately, then glancing away. But that wasn't the worst of it.

"I'm so glad you came home," Grandmother said to Jessie one day, tearing up. "It's meant the world to me."

Her compliment was very touching, but also disconcerting. Her grandmother never complimented anyone. Even Bill was the recipient of a few harrowing moments. One day he pulled Jessie aside and complained, "She told me she's grown accustomed to my cowboy hat."

"We've got one sick woman on our hands," Jessie said, smiling, trying to lighten the moment.

"I'm telling you," Bill said. "It's rather . . ."

"Freaky."

"Yeah, that's it."

Dr. Sawyer called on a Thursday. The results were in. "Let's schedule an appointment so we can discuss it," the doctor suggested, sounding rather upbeat.

Jessie had almost forgotten. In fact, during the last few weeks, she'd begun living as if her potential illness didn't exist. More than that, she'd found herself not *caring* about the results—surrounded by a new peace in the Lord that transcended her worries.

"May I call you back and schedule it later?" Jessie asked.

Dr. Sawyer seemed hesitant, then agreed.

Jessie hung up, knowing she was slipping back into the old patterns of denial.

I'll call in a few days, she rationalized. But in her heart, she already knew the results, didn't she? What did it matter if she waited?

She informed Bill and her grandmother of her decision, glossing over it. "Maybe I just need to prepare myself," she told them. Grandmother's expression was worried but understanding. And that was the end of the discussion. For now.

◆ ◆ ◆ ◆ ◆

In August Doris pulled a few strings and was able to leapfrog Jessie over some of the admissions process, enrolling her in Colorado College, an elite downtown college only a few miles away. She'd first offered Jessie a round-trip ticket to Oregon, but the idea had long since lost its appeal. A lifetime of planning and dreaming had simply fizzled away. For the moment, her life belonged at home. *How odd,* she thought, *that I would think of my grandmother's house as home.*

Eventually life settled into a routine, accompanied by the scent of fall and the subtle promise of Christmas. Grandmother, although less feisty, seemed to have passed the worst of her depression. Michelle eventually succumbed to Jessie's offer, but only because of the attraction of free baby-sitting. Jessie took those opportunities to introduce Laura to an entire collection of Disney animated movies, old and new, and Laura was absolutely enthralled. Jessie elaborated on the moral of each story, as her mother once had, and in time, she planned to talk Laura out of the ghost books. Slowly, she exerted her influence, knowing that only eternity would reveal the results.

And Bill? Well, sometimes it seemed as if Bill was the cog that turned the entire wheel of the household. He shuffled through his daily routine like a hapless clown sometimes. Day after day, his country music grew louder and louder, and Doris didn't seem to notice anymore.

Jessie continued to mourn her decision regarding Andy, sometimes crying herself to sleep. Sometimes she caught herself second-guessing herself, daydreaming of a possible future with him—what might happen if the test results returned negative. Most likely, however, he'd have already moved on. That seemed more likely than any silly fantasy she could concoct.

The dreams of her mother continued, although they became less disturbing. In her prayers she began to thank God for the tragic events of her past and the beauty of the spiritual relationship that was opening like a flower with glorious promise, giving her renewed hope that in time things would improve.

It can only get better, she thought.

Chapter Thirty-Two

ANDY WENT SKIING alone on the first weekend Breckenridge opened. His mother didn't appreciate ski season, because it interfered with their Saturdays, and she didn't so much care for football season, either, because it made her husband unavailable. In fact, anything that came between her and her men was considered a sworn enemy.

Andy had consoled his mom by agreeing to a Saturday night dinner *and* a Sunday lunch. Sometimes he felt he had to negotiate with his own mother.

"I need to talk to you and Dad."

"What is it, Andy?" Mom's tone was suddenly worried.

"Tonight, Mom."

"Toss me a little crumb?"

"Tonight, Mom. I'm sorry."

"Mercy, Andy. You and your father's secrets are going to be the end of me."

He felt bad about scaring his mother. He hadn't intended to, but at least it gave him a deadline to formulate his thoughts. He *had* to go through with it now. In spite of the loneliness of skiing on his own, he had plenty to keep himself occupied, and yet every time he got on the lift, he felt distracted, wishing Jessie were sitting next to him. He'd tried calling a few times since their last meeting, but their conversations had been short and terse—Jessie was obviously shutting him out of her life. As troubling as that was, it wasn't the only thing that had kept him preoccupied these last few months.

"What convinced him it was true?" Bill had asked regarding the apostle Paul, and the question had nagged him. Sure, he'd long been aware that Paul, once known as Saul of Tarsus, had accepted the truth of the resurrection of Jesus of Nazareth long before the Gospels were written. He'd also accepted that there were scores of brilliant men and women, all much smarter than he, all with access to the same information, who had no problem making a stand for Christ. But this time it had taken no more than a simple man like Bill to really shake him up. In fact, it had never occurred to him that someday he might actually doubt the veracity of his own conclusions.

What is my problem? he thought again for what seemed like the thousandth time. He spent the afternoon in the ski lodge at a table with a note pad, scribbling and rescribbling, taking one last stab at trying to figure it all out—as if a few hours of spiritual contemplation were all he needed to figure it out.

Andy arrived at his parents' home at about six. His father, wearing a bright holiday sweater, met him at the door. "Saw your car, Andrew. Have a good day on the slopes?"

Andrew, is it? His father was already in a formal frame of mind.

In the kitchen, his mother barely acknowledged him. She was tossing a salad with Italian olives, baby tomatoes, and green peppers. "Well, did you have a good time on your precious slopes?"

Andy kissed her cheek.

"Well, well, well," she muttered. "Must be pretty serious if you're already buttering me up."

"Oh mercy," Andy repeated his mother's catch phrase, smiling to himself.

They ate in the formal dining room. His father discussed issues dealing with his medical practice—patient challenges, hospital politics, drug issues. His mother shared her own latest challenge: expanding the reading library at church.

"So . . . what's up with you?" Dad finally asked just as Andy had taken his last bite of apple pie.

Andy gave Mom a reassuring smile, but she only narrowed her eyes. He took a deep breath and let it out slowly, then fished a photo from his front pocket and handed it across the table to his mom, who frowned when she received it.

"Who is this?"

His dad gave his mom a puzzled look. "Dear?"

She handed the photo to his dad, who appraised it carefully.

"Does she go to your church?" Mom asked.

"Very attractive," Dad finally added, to his mother's snort of displeasure. Andy suppressed a smile. His father had already committed himself, but then he gave Andy's mother a supportive look, as if to say, *I can take it all back.*

"That is the girl I want to marry," Andy said simply, and he almost added, *if she'll have me.*

His mother paled, and his father nearly fell off his seat. "Andy, how long have you known her?"

"All my life," he replied.

His parents exchanged a worried look, and his mother spoke first. "This is Jessica Lehman, isn't it?"

"Yes. Mrs. Robinette took the picture. Here's another one of us together."

His father grabbed the second photo, squinting. This time his parents huddled together, analyzing what little information a photo could contain. "She seems—"

"Very different," his mother finished, sounding confused.

"Well," Andy shrugged, "she's twenty-four now. Just graduated from college."

"Really?"

"Yes. Degree in finance."

"Oh my," his mother uttered, raising her eyebrows. "She doesn't *look* sick."

Andy had determined not to overstate his case nor look like a romantic dunce, but love has a tendency to make blathering fools of the most composed. "I was born to take care of her," he said, cringing the moment he said it, although he could have gone on and on, ad infinitum.

His father turned to him with a serious look. "So . . . *this* is what you wanted to discuss?"

"Not exactly," Andy said. "Just . . . the first thing. . . ."

Mom was still gazing at the picture. "Is she a Christian, Andy?" As usual his mother had gotten to the crux of the issue.

"I don't know," Andy replied, though he had a pretty good idea that she wasn't.

"Oh, Andy . . ."

When he looked up, his father was clutching his mother's hand. The closeness of their family had sometimes seemed repressive, especially for an only child. After all, here he was a twenty-four-year-old man trying to get his parents' blessing on a course they couldn't possibly approve. Yet he was old enough to see that the rewards of family outweighed the loss of independence.

"Oh, Andy . . ." his mother repeated, shaking her head, and then tears began to streak her face. It seemed such an exaggerated response that Andy's father looked as bewildered as he felt himself. Mom sniffed slightly and Dad leaned back, grabbing a tissue box from a small table. After she removed a tissue and wiped her eyes, she met her son's gaze and said simply, "Then who will bring you Home, Andy? What will become of you?"

Andy shivered and his father looked stunned. It had never occurred to Andy that his mother might already know about his religious struggles. She wasn't one to mince words about such things, but perhaps the collapse of her son's faith was something she couldn't bear to admit even to herself. It also explained her determination to marry him off to "a nice Christian woman." In his mother's world, the wife helped immensely in stabilizing the home, offering spiritual support.

"Andy," his father began, "what *do* you believe?"

Andy hesitated again. He'd been asking himself the same question ever since Elizabeth canceled the engagement, but it was Jessie, in spite of her own struggles, who had finally brought everything to an apex for him.

Andy shared with them the whole story, starting with his own foolish spiritual bravado, then on to his consequent sinking like a drowning man into a sea of unbelief. It took a full hour to thread the story for them, and they appeared more dejected the longer he continued. He purposely painted the events as hopelessly as possible, trying to stack the deck, because if he didn't, when they heard his final conclusions they might not be very pleased. . . .

. . . *Why do I keep coming back to this?* he'd asked himself in the loneliness of a clamoring crowd of skiers catching a breather till their next ski run. He'd barely heard the noise of the room, although on a few occasions, some young woman would catch his eye from across the room and smile flirtatiously. He returned a warm but less than enthusiastic smile, then looked away, thinking only of Jessie.

In spite of the chaos of the ski lodge, he'd wished to be someplace different, where the routine of life couldn't lull him into the old patterns of thinking.

All that afternoon, he felt like the man pounding at the gates of a giant castle, to no avail. Why did God seem so distant? Where was He?

And why am I so unhappy? Andy wondered if he could dig deep enough into his heart to find at least a semblance of an answer.

But the answer was obvious. *I'm lonely.*

And not just lonely for Jess but lonely for God. Lonely for what I had before.

For some reason he had always felt compelled to make sense of life, and while that was biting off more than he—or anyone—could chew, it occurred to him that no matter his ultimate conclusions, no matter how deeply he pondered man's existence, one thing was obvious:

Something went terribly wrong here. The entire scheme of life, all of mankind, seemed to testify to this. His own heart illustrated this innate wrongness—an obvious depravity—in spite of the fact that outwardly he appeared to live a good and clean life. Even mankind's aversion to suffering and pain indicated that humanity wasn't supposed to live in a suffering world. No matter how you sliced the deck, no matter whether you bought the story of a Garden of Eden or not, something had gone terribly wrong on planet earth.

And in turn, those very things seemed to point to—seemed to *demand*—the need for redemption. Yet, from his cursory understanding of the religions and philosophies of the world, only Christianity offered a means. While he couldn't speak for the world, he could speak for himself. He knew his own heart, his own pride and selfishness, and knew without a doubt that he needed redemption. He needed a Savior.

Our hearts are restless until they find rest in thee, Augustine had written, and despite his intellectual struggles, Andy knew firsthand the angst of restlessness. At one point he'd briefly—*very* briefly—dabbled in New Age thought, only to abandon it with a fervor that far outstripped his abandonment of Christianity. The god of other religions seemed so impersonal, weak, insufficient. But why was that so disturbing to him? Did his heart innately *know* God must be different? Did his heart *know* the truth even while his mind struggled to believe it?

It struck him so deeply then, so obviously, that he wondered why he hadn't thought of it before. He *wanted* Christianity to be true. He *wanted* to believe in a God who knew him personally, who loved him more than *His* own life.

Freud was wrong, Andy thought. *Our wishes, our wants, if interpreted correctly, ultimately point to reality. How can we, as human beings, long for something that doesn't exist? How can we long for God if He doesn't exist? And how can we long for redemption from suffering and sin if redemption doesn't exist?*

For Christians, the means of that redemption was the cross—once metaphorically foretold by the serpent on the stake, which the Israelites, if willing, could behold and be saved.

But I still don't understand, Andy thought.

The cross is foolishness to the wise, the apostle Paul had indicated.

Andy shivered. *I need the cross whether I can fully understand it or not.*

In that moment, Andy made a decision. He had *enough* evidence. Bill was right—the highly intellectual Paul would not have been foolish enough to simply accept the word of a few uneducated fishermen. The future writer of the Epistles would have demanded evidence.

So, following his heart, Andy chose to bow before the cross, regardless of doubt, because even his intellect told him that the cross, whether metaphor or myth—or the absolute truth—was what he needed. So there in the chalet, he bowed his head—his intellect—to God, and his prayer of surrender echoed the man of old who said to Jesus, "I do believe; help me overcome my unbelief."

Would God accept such a feeble sacrifice? Would God forgive his strange mingling of belief and doubt? While the answer seemed to be implied within the mercy of the Scriptures, he had no choice anyway. It was the *only* first step he could make, albeit the most faltering step he could imagine.

It was four-fifteen in the ski lodge when Andy rose from the wooden table and headed for home. In the car, he turned on a CD of worship songs that Chris had given him, and the ensuing sense of relief and joy was so profound he found himself humming along—as if finding a long-lost cherished possession. The castle door had finally swung wide. . . .

Until now his parents had been listening in stunned silence. His Mom glanced at Dad, whose eyes flickered, as if trying to ponder the strange story Andy had just shared.

"So . . . you believe, but you still have doubts?" his father finally asked.

"There are so many things I don't understand. I want to believe, *completely* believe. But I'm not there yet, Dad. It's just so . . ." Andy hesitated. He didn't really expect them to understand. How could they when he barely understood himself?

Mom began shaking her head, but the aura of despair had left her. At the very least, she seemed hopeful.

Andy sat and waited, expecting his parents to attempt some kind of religious browbeating. When his father finally spoke it was with a tone of resignation. "Andy, I live in a world of science." He met Andy's eyes and hesitated again.

Andy dropped his gaze to the table. "I'm sorry, Dad. I didn't mean—"

"I make my living by conforming to physical evidence. But there are some things that can't be subjected to *physical* proof. There are certain important things that we must simply believe."

Andy nodded. "And that's what I'm doing."

Mom broke in. "But there *is* evidence, John."

Dad began nodding his head very deliberately. "Yes . . . of course. *Good* evidence. My bookshelves are filled with that evidence. But in the end, our grasp of Christianity is *based* on faith. It's based on our surrender to God, not a perfect grasp of the historical details or the doctrines of Christianity. It's based on our heart and our kneeling before the Lord Jesus on the cross." His father leveled his gaze toward him again. "Is that where you are, son?"

Andy nodded. "Yes, Dad."

His father smiled for the first time. When he reached out his hand, Andy grasped it. "Just don't stop seeking the full truth."

"I won't," Andy promised.

His dad's smile turned to a grin. "I didn't even know you were gone, Andy," he continued, his voice now husky, his grip firm. "But welcome home."

At that point Dad asked if they might pray together, something they'd always done as a family. Together the three of them joined in a humble prayer of thanksgiving, thanking God for His wisdom and asking for renewed strength to follow Him in spite of *any* struggles that they might encounter—be it pride, selfishness, bitterness, or simply the human inability to transcend doubt.

When they were finished, Mom shook her head. "Mercy, Andy. You sure know how to make a scene!"

Andy chuckled sheepishly.

"So when are we going to meet Jessica?" Her eyes were suddenly worried again, and his father looked uncertain. No doubt they were worried about her influence.

"She refuses to see me," Andy replied, and Mom closed her eyes again, sighing with what seemed like profound relief.

Dad seemed relieved, as well. He clapped his hands, rubbing them together. "Now . . . what about finishing that jigsaw puzzle?"

Chapter Thirty-Three

ON THE MORNING of September third, more than three months after her granddaughter first arrived, Doris awakened to the silvery gleam of moonlight through the half-open bedroom blinds. She went to the window intending to close them, to shut out the light, but she felt a pull from within her so powerful she almost gasped. She opened the blinds fully instead, peering up at the bright full moon, as if it might tell her something.

But something else had awakened her tonight, and it wasn't just the moonlight. *I can't continue on this way,* she told herself.

Sitting on the bed, she draped a maroon robe around her shoulders, went to the intercom above her light switch, and buzzed her handyman.

"Doris?" Bill answered sleepily.

"I'm sorry to wake you," she said, "but I need to talk."

Bill initially sounded alarmed, but she assured him she wasn't experiencing any medical problems. "Meet me in the office," she told him, tightening her robe and heading down the hallway.

Bill soon joined her. The back of his hair was sticking up, and he was wearing the robe Doris had purchased for him years ago.

"Are you all right?" he asked, his eyes solemn.

Shivering, Doris sat at her desk and pulled the robe tighter around her thin frame.

Bill offered, "Want some coffee?"

Doris shook her head as Bill sat down at the corner of her desk.

She looked down at her hands, twisting her fingers obsessively until Bill reached over and placed his own hand on hers. "It's okay, Doris, whatever it is."

"No, Bill, it's never been that. Never."

"Doris, everything seems worse in the night. Shouldn't we wait till—"

"I have to tell you now. I can't stand another . . . She gasped and swallowed hard.

He leaned over, taking both of her hands in his. "Dory, what *is* it?"

She closed her eyes, but her vision was filled with a past that only seemed to get darker as the seconds ticked by.

"Dory?"

"I need to tell you what happened the day the hospital called me."

Bill frowned. "You mean when Olivia died?"

She released her hands from his, glanced toward the window momentarily, then met his gaze again. "You may not want to work for me anymore. . . ."

"Oh, Dory, for goodness' sake, what *is* it?"

She breathed deeply, and the panic of revealing the truth after all these years was almost more than she could take. "It's time," she whispered softly.

Exhaling sharply she began, starting with the phone call, the feeling of shock that permeated every moment, every movement, driving alone to the hospital, retrieving the death certificate from the front desk, the cacophony of the surroundings that day, plodding down the hallway, and finding her daughter . . . alive.

She stopped there. As Bill's eyes opened wide, his face paled in the glow of the desk lamp. She took another breath, but in doing so, she felt her face grimace. Breathing was agony. Bill narrowed his eyes. "What happened, Doris?" He leaned forward, his hands flat on the desk.

Another anguished breath, another torturous release. She shuddered and wondered if she could continue, but she did. "Livvy was suffering in that place, Bill. It was my only chance to help her. . . ."

"What do you mean, Doris?" he asked, his tone flat.

Doris placed her hand over Bill's, but she wasn't sure whether the gesture was meant to calm herself or him. She composed herself and continued, "I placed the sheet over Livvy's face . . . and then . . ."

She revealed the secret she'd hidden in her heart for twelve excruciating years. . . .

◆ ◆ ◆ ◆ ◆ ◆

Jessie awakened at three in the morning to the sound of footsteps and faint voices coming from downstairs. She lay awake for a moment, pondering the brightness of her room. *The moon must be full,* she thought, and then she recalled the dream she'd had just before she'd awakened. It came back to her in bits and pieces at first, but eventually she remembered the entire dream.

She and Andy had been riding their bikes to the top of the hill when she'd realized that her mother was calling her home. Andy put up a fuss but agreed to turn around and head back down. "We didn't even make it to the top," he complained.

"We'll come back another day," she said.

When they arrived at her block, she saw her mother in the distance, sitting on the porch sipping iced tea, enjoying the sunny day. But the closer they got, the more concerned Jessie became, until her concern turned to horror. Her mother had *changed*. Her face was pale, her body scary thin, her hair stringy and matted.

Jessie nearly burst into tears, but her mother only laughed. "Oh, honey, don't look at my body. Look at my *soul*. It will never die."

Jessie was nearly inconsolable. "What happened? I was just riding bikes with Andy and then . . ."

"It's still me, sweetie," her mother said, extending her hand, smiling with courageous warmth.

Jessie pushed off the covers and stumbled to the bathroom. Turning on the lights, she stared into the mirror and nearly wept at the fear in her eyes. She swallowed several gulps of water, wiped her face, and turned out the harsh light.

Back in the room, she sat at the window seat with her head bowed, hands on the back of her neck. *Let it go,* she berated herself. *It's over. The past is finished!*

◆　◆　◆　◆　◆

"I had only minutes to decide," Doris told Bill, who was obviously fully awake now. "I did the only thing I could do. . . ." She hesitated again.

"Doris, please . . ." He was still struggling to keep up, but he did his best to comprehend.

"I called the Woodland Park Care Center," Doris admitted. "And I arranged for Livvy's admission."

. . . The Woodland Park Care Center agreed to send a van for Olivia. They didn't ask questions, and Doris didn't volunteer information. Forty-five nervous minutes later, Doris met the Care Center men at the door, then led them back through the frenzied waiting area, to Olivia's room. To avoid arousing the men's suspicion, Doris had already lowered the sheet from Olivia's face.

As they pushed the gurney down the hallway, however, Doris replaced the sheet over her daughter's face. "I don't want anyone leering at her," she explained to the men, who merely shrugged at her strange comment.

When they reached the waiting area, Doris's stomach was in knots. She worried that someone might approach them. After all, the Care Center men certainly didn't appear to be mortuary personnel.

They were passing the desk when one of the busy administrative nurses happened to notice them. Doris was prepared to present the death certificate, but instead of detecting something amiss, the nurse gave Doris a quick but sad smile before turning away.

When they reached the doors, Doris saw a hearse parked out front. *Who's that for?* she thought, realizing that someone else must have died here this morning. Later she would wonder if *that* had caused the mix-up leading to the errant death certificate.

The moment Olivia was in the van, even though she'd just defied a court order by rescuing her daughter, Doris breathed a sigh of relief.

On the way up Ute Pass to Woodland Park, Doris had to make one final decision. What would she tell Jessica and Frank? By now they had already been informed of Olivia's death. She had only a few panicked hours to make up her mind. At this moment, Jessie would be in the throes of anguish, as would Frank. But what would Frank do if he discovered the truth? Would he demand that Olivia be returned to the mental hospital, threatening exposure if Doris didn't comply? Or would he simply seize the opportunity to expose her anyway, just to exact some kind of revenge?

Upon Olivia's arrival, the nurses' diagnosis settled it for her. They informed her that Olivia had only hours to live. *At least she won't die in that other dreadful place,* Doris thought.

She called Maria and made up a story to explain her delay, then waited for her daughter to die. But the unexpected occurred. Olivia rallied, and the nurses were confounded. In the early hours of the next morning, however, Olivia slipped into a coma.

"I'm sure she has only a few hours at the most," the nurse explained, worried for Doris's state of mind.

A day passed, and then another, and Doris was forced to create and carry out a strange farce—a memorial service. Frank, of course, was stunned that she'd "cremated" the body so soon, which created an even greater rift between them. And Jessie never forgave her for denying the right to say good-bye to her own dear mother.

Weeks passed, and Olivia continued to survive. Weeks turned to months. Frank's passing was a terrible weight upon Doris because she suspected that she had been part of the cause. Jessie refused to stay with her, running away so relentlessly the state obtained custody and placed her in the foster care program.

Olivia's coma state lingered. And months . . . became years.

Chapter Thirty-four

SITTING ON THE WINDOW SEAT, Jessie turned and stared out at the quiet street through the sheer curtains. A slight breeze wafted in through the partially open window and a small whisper accompanied the silence. She noticed the clock across the room— 3:35—and shuddered. *Some year I'll get a full night's sleep.* Pulling her legs up to her chest, she wrapped her arms around them and tugged so tightly her back hurt. She closed her eyes and prayed, *Dear Lord, help me finally let it all go.*

When she looked up, she heard the muffled sound of a phone ringing. *Who would call at this time of night?* Her first thought was to assume it was some kind of prank call, or wrong number, or maybe . . . very bad news.

Jessica wondered briefly why Bill or her grandmother didn't answer the phone, but the next emotion was so strong that it struck her like a physical thud against her chest.

Jessie picked up the extension on her nightstand. "Hello?" she asked tentatively.

"This is Tammy Henderson. . . ."

"Um . . . yes?"

"From the Woodland Park Care Center? I called to tell you—"

"Um, I'm not—" Jessica thought she heard a click on the extension.

"Mrs. Crenshaw?" the caller asked.

"No, I'm sorry . . ." Jessica began.

Her grandmother came on the line. "This is Doris Crenshaw. I have it now, Jessica."

"Okay. Sorry. . . ." Jessica mumbled, hanging up. A sudden sensation began prickling its way along her spine. Her heart began to pound within her and she sat up straight, her memory whirling. What had the caller said? *Woodland Park Care Center . . .*

◆　◆　◆　◆　◆

Nurse Tammy Henderson hung up the phone, shaking her head at the strange turn of events. Doris Crenshaw, the woman who had visited her patient religiously for over a decade, was obviously stunned. Who could blame her? Tammy could barely believe it herself. She had stopped by the room to assess the automatic feeding system, only to be struck by the beautiful moonlight glowing through the window. It granted such a peaceful feeling that she had been reluctant to leave.

She had paused at the bed and looked at Olivia's face. So thin, so white, and yet in the subtle light her face had an almost angelic glow, and her breathing seemed serene, even peaceful.

"Where are you, Olivia?" Tammy whispered softly. She stroked Olivia's cheek, then held her hand, squeezing as much assurance as she could into a tiny gesture.

For years, the third-shift nurses had discussed their longtime resident, wondering if she would ever regain consciousness. Curious, Tammy had done her own research on comas and was surprised to discover that people could come back after many years of unconsciousness. In fact, some had awakened after a decade or more. She also learned that for many, the coma state has almost a cocoon effect, locking the patient in time, even to the point of stopping any progress of disease.

"She *might* wake up," Tammy had once suggested to her co-workers. But even she didn't really believe it. Still, Tammy had often whispered a prayer over her dear patient, hoping that she might be the one to greet this woman if she ever did awaken, to be the first to say, "Welcome back!"

"Sleep tight, Olivia," Tammy said, knowing she must leave Olivia and get back to her rounds. Then she froze. *What on earth?* A shadowy movement had crossed Olivia's face, obviously caused by the outside clouds, but it startled her. Either that, or her mind was playing tricks on her.

"Olivia?"

Too many late hours, she told herself, but upon closer examination, she gasped. Her mind wasn't playing tricks after all. Olivia's eyes were open, but not blankly open, as if in response to some kind of muscular aberration.

Olivia's eyes were *following* her. . . .

Tammy gathered her composure, and in spite of the tears in her eyes, and the lump in her throat, she fulfilled her longtime wish. "Welcome back, Olivia!"

◆ ◆ ◆ ◆ ◆

Ashen faced and trembling, Bill and Doris dressed in their respective rooms, then met in the upstairs hallway. It now made sense to Doris why she'd awakened when she did. It hadn't been the moon or the guilt. Over the phone, the nurse had declared the impossible, and Doris had struggled to comprehend both facts: *She's awake?*

And *she's lucid?*

Doris asked that the news be repeated several times. But then the nurse gave her the worst news of all, which seemed like a cruel joke. "In the past hour, Olivia's vital signs have diminished drastically, and she appears to be going downhill very quickly."

"But why now?" Doris had asked.

As they paused at the top of the stairs, Doris struggled with how to approach her granddaughter and tell the amazing yet painful truth.

"Do you want me to wake her?" Bill asked.

"Isn't it time I faced up to this?" Doris replied, and she turned toward Jessie's room.

When she knocked, Jessie was already sitting at the edge of the bed, fully dressed. Her eyes were clear and focused, her hair pulled back, and her face expectant, as if she already knew.

"She's alive, isn't she?" Jessie asked.

Doris nodded, tears brimming in her eyes. "Just barely," she whispered, and the look of despair on Jessie's face broke her heart.

"Is she conscious?"

Again her grandmother nodded. "Yes, but the nurse said she was slipping away fast. We don't have much time."

◆ ◆ ◆ ◆ ◆

Jessie sat in the back of the car, a profound fusion of emotions flowing through her. Even before her grandmother had come to her room, the clues had mingled together in her mind—the phone call, the *knowing*, her grandmother's previous dejection, the dreams—until they had coalesced into one final truth, one that in so many ways, she felt she had always known.

In spite of the swirling questions, the urgency of the moment seemed to inhibit an exchange of information. The time for questions would come soon enough. For now, it didn't even matter how she had come to this point. She wasn't even tempted to believe she was dreaming, because she knew she wasn't. This moment was more real than in her entire life.

The sense of anticipation dominated every other thought, every other emotion. What would she see when she arrived? How would her mother appear? Apparently her mother was lucid, but what did that mean? Could she talk? Could she understand?

Expectancy mingled with a sense of profound impatience. After all these years, would she miss her mother by mere minutes?

"Hurry, Bill," Doris urged, and Bill kicked it up a notch. Once they reached Highway 24 and headed up the winding mountain pass, they had nearly thirty minutes to go.

"Please hurry, Bill," Jessie whispered.

She had the disconnected sensation of observing herself from the outside. She wondered how anyone else might feel to discover that their loved one was still alive, after their world had been reordered and rearranged—after years of coming to grips with the loss and the grief. The shock rolled over her, and in spite of her recent suspicions and a decade of dreams, nothing could have adequately prepared her for the final reality of this moment. Absolutely nothing.

In spite of the sense of urgency, in spite of the gnawing fear that they might not arrive in time, Jessie could not think of her grandmother without realizing she'd been betrayed one more time. One more lie revealed. One more reason to distrust.

The realization was met with little emotion, as if she had no space left to hold this glaring truth—although someday it was sure to return and demand an accounting. She would have to contemplate that later. For now, one thing remained. Only one.

My mother is alive. . . .

For a moment Jessie was tempted to retrieve her cell phone and call Andy. But she resisted. If he was here with her now, he'd have his arms around her. He'd be consoling her. He'd be peering at her eyes, trying to read her emotions, more than eager to help her through this. The thought of that was almost unbearable.

Every ounce of energy was for her mother now. She could scarcely wait!

In Woodland Park, Bill turned onto Highway 67 going north. Several miles later he turned left down a dirt road. *It's beautiful here,* Jessie thought.

Another turn and they were there. This place looked like a peaceful hospice retreat. Not an institution. *Thank heavens.* Jessie sighed with relief. Instead, it looked like an oversized country inn edged by a canopy of pine trees, the sun flickering through the needles on the eastern side. The building was tan clapboard and had a covered porch across the front, trimmed in white. About ten cars were parked in the black-topped lot and a sign over the entrance announced: Woodland Park Care Center.

Bill hurried out of the car and opened Grandmother's door and then her own, almost simultaneously. Doris turned to Jessie, her eyes belying her regret, but Jessie glanced away as Bill ushered them quickly to the building. Whatever Grandmother might wish to say to her, Jessie could not receive it now.

Immediately upon entering, they stepped into an echoing linoleum hallway. Off to their right was an office. Straight ahead the hallway led toward the back of the building. Jessie's senses took in everything, and with everything came a sense of déjà vu. She experienced the same feeling that had followed her throughout her life, starting when she and her mother were so completely tuned in to each other's thoughts and feelings. Her mother's presence was *everywhere* in this place.

Grandmother glanced back at Jessie expectantly before moving down the corridor. *Of course,* Jessie thought. *She's been here before.*

Halfway down the hallway, a brunette nurse met Grandmother, who was still several paces in front of her and Bill. Bill placed his hand on Jessie's arm, his eyes apologetic, a little embarrassed, too, as if by his connection to her grandmother, he had been part of the charade.

The panic that had been building in her heart now threatened to tear her chest to pieces. *Please let it not be too late. . . .*

Grandmother turned toward Jessie, and the nurse, whose name tag said Tammy, warmly offered her hand. "She might only have a few hours," she said, meeting Jessie's gaze, a mixture of curiosity and recognition flickering in her eyes.

She knows who I am, Jessie thought.

Her grandmother was still standing there, her fingers fidgeting, waiting for the go-ahead.

When they continued down the hall, the nurse said, "The doctor's in with her right now."

"Has she . . . said anything?" Doris asked.

Tammy turned, smiling. "No, but her eyes are open and she seems to be looking for something . . . or someone." Again the nurse glanced over at Jessie.

They turned down another hallway, and several nurses were standing in front of the door, whispering excitedly. Jessie's legs began to feel rubbery. Bill slowed up. He took her left arm, "You okay, kiddo?"

Jessie leaned hard on Bill. "Don't let me fall."

"You won't," he assured her. "I've got you."

Doris and the nurse were talking, but the words weren't registering anymore.

Years from now she would look back on this moment, recalling the brink of wonder, and hope, and fantasy just before jumping off into pure reality. In some ways this moment would always feel like a dream to Jessie, in spite of confirming details—although she'd never had a dream of this magnitude before.

Grandmother paused at the door, then turned to Jessie. "Would you like to go in first?"

Jessie hesitated, a leaden mixture of dread and longing squashed her stomach. "I'll be right behind you."

The room had landscape pictures on the walls, a few nameless medical machines in two corners, several carts, and an IV stand. Because the doctor was leaning over the bed, obscuring Jessie's vision, her first glimpse was of the blanket-covered form, which seemed impossibly small. *Too slight to be my mother,* she thought.

Jessie took several steps sideways, and a still profile slowly emerged. The woman's skin held an unnatural yellowish cast, her light gray-blond hair, lifeless on the pillow, thin and scraggly. Her eyes were closed. But the pinched thin face was unmistakable. Hot pain seared Jessica's chest and she pressed her knuckles against her lips to keep from crying out. It was the face from last night's dream. *"Honey, don't look at my body. Look at my soul. . . ."*

Before leaving the room, the doctor whispered something to Grandmother, something about sleeping, then turned to Jessie and smiled encouragingly. Doris reached for her daughter's right hand, kissed it gently, then beheld Olivia's face with something akin to adoration.

Then, tenderly, she replaced the hand on the mattress. Her expression seemed stoic but vulnerable. Softly Tammy slid a chair next to the bed beside Jessie. "I'll leave you alone for a while."

Grandmother nodded. "Let me know if she awakens," she said to Jessie. She gestured toward the door. "I'll be outside with Bill."

Jessie wanted to whisper something back—something reassuring, something comforting—but it would have felt empty on her lips. Her grandmother closed the door behind her, leaving her alone.

Jessica sat down and gently picked up her mother's fragile white hand. She lifted it to her lips and kissed it, just as her grandmother had. The machines hummed and the heart monitor blipped a slight but regular rhythm.

"Mom?" Jessica whispered, at first feeling self-conscious. How strange the words sounded on her lips!

"Mom. . . ?"

Tears began running down her cheeks. Her mother might never awaken. They might have been too late. But for now, she was still alive, and Jessie didn't care how silly, or stupid, or pointless she sounded. She'd waited an entire lifetime to talk to her mother one last time.

"I'm sorry I wasn't here. I'm so sorry. If I had known, I would have been here every day. I would have read you all our favorite stories."

She wiped a hand over her face, contorted now with the anguish welling up within her, filling her chest and lungs, threatening to render her speechless.

"I'm especially sorry that I wasn't here when you awakened. When I think of you looking for me and wondering why I wasn't near. . . ."

Promise me you'll keep believing, sweetie, Mom had written. *No matter what happens, hold on to Jesus.* Sobs overtook Jessie and she covered her mouth with her hand. "I'm sorry I didn't keep my promise. I let go, Mom, but Jesus never did."

She stroked her mother's precious hand. "I wish I could hear your voice one more time. I wish I could tell you how much I love you. I've missed you so much. There's not a day that goes by that I don't think about you or wish I could talk to you or feel your arms around me."

She looked at Mom's face, unchanged, unmoving, and she began to sob again. She pressed her mother's hand against her cheek, oddly comforted by even this closeness. She sat that way quietly for a few moments. *Will she slip away without awakening again?*

Then she thought she heard something, likely voices in the hall. She listened again, hoping the doctor wasn't returning already. Minutes passed and no one came in.

"Once upon a time there lived a young woman named Snow White . . ." Jessie began, and she told the story as her mother once told it, a twist here, a surprise there, a dozen short people, an evil queen, a dashing prince. But in the end she provided her own finale: ". . . and Jesus leaned over her still form and kissed her awake into everlasting life. And when she looked around, it was just like a giant park with swings and monkey bars and picnic tables!"

Jessie smiled through the tears and looked up at the clock. Over an hour had passed.

Please God, let Mom wake up. . . .

◆ ◆ ◆ ◆ ◆

With her face in her hands and her handsome old cowboy beside her, his arms around her shoulders, Doris sat in the waiting room.

"Don't you want to be in there?" Bill asked.

Doris shook her head. "I've had many years. It's Jessie's turn."

"What if she wakes up?"

"Someone will come for me," she replied.

A nurse stopped by and asked if they were hungry.

Doris smiled as warmly as she could but declined.

"Classy joint," Bill commented once the nurse had left. He gave Doris a reassuring smile.

"Oh, Bill . . ." she said painfully. "What have I done?"

"Things are going to be just fine, Dory. You wait and see."

She didn't have the wherewithal to argue, amazed that Bill was still by her side, still looking at the bright side of things. Surely by now he realized she'd deceived him—that her frequent visits to the Care Center had all taken place under the guise of attending yet another club function.

Tammy stopped by several times to keep them apprised of Olivia's condition. So far, no change. The longer they waited for her to awaken, the worse Doris felt. Her emotions rocked between the anticipation of speaking to Livvy and the painful dread of knowing that, in all likelihood, Jessie would never forgive her. Doris knew there was such a thing as a last straw. It wouldn't matter that she'd convinced herself she was *protecting* Jessie from the truth, allowing her granddaughter to get on with her life. Of course, Jessie wouldn't see it that way.

She tried to keep her mind focused. She might have a final chance with her daughter, a true good-bye, one last opportunity to say all the things she'd never said before. She'd been saying them in her mind for years. Having Olivia back for even five minutes wasn't worth the deception perhaps, and it wasn't worth the pain her granddaughter had endured. But it was worth more than her own life. *Please God,* she whispered.

* * * * *

Nurse Tammy came into the room a few hours later. Jessie was still holding her mother's hand, whispering things she'd longed to say for years. A shadow fell over the nurse's face as she evaluated the instruments. She bit her lower lip and glanced at Jessie; the meaning was all too clear. Time was running out.

"Have you tried to rouse her?"

Jessie nodded.

Tammy sighed, shaking her head. "We may have missed our only opportunity."

Not what Jessie wanted to hear, but just having this time was more than she would have imagined. There was something between them, even now—no audible voice, but in that strange way of knowing, that inexplicable bond that had always been between them—the bond that brought her mother to the playground when she'd fallen, the bond that urged Jessie home when her mother was weeping, and the connection that had always called Jessie home when she'd strayed too far.

Perhaps wishful thinking, but her mother's face seemed to relax and become more serene. Jessie felt an unexpected peace wash over her, as well.

"She's slipping away," Tammy quietly announced. "It won't be long now." Jessie silently prepared herself for the actual moment.

When Olivia opened her eyes, Jessie wasn't expecting it. In fact, she had been leaning over in her chair, holding her mother's hand to her face, eyes closed.

It was Tammy who spoke first. "Jessie . . ."

When Jessie looked up, her mother's eyes smiled.

"Mom?"

Olivia nodded slightly.

"Do you know me?"

Another weak nod. Jessie looked up at Tammy, who seemed stunned. "Please get my grandmother," she whispered urgently.

Tammy blinked. "Of course, I'm sorry." And the nurse rushed out the door..

With much effort, Olivia swallowed and her mouth opened, but only jagged breathing emerged. Her mother's lips formed the silent words, "My butterfly girl . . ." and Jessie's heart leapt within her.

Her mother's gaze took in Jessie's now-grown form and her eyes shone. She shook her head from side to side, so subtly it was almost imperceptible. She seemed to be imbued with a sense of awe, and it struck Jessie as impossible to imagine—to go to sleep one day when your daughter is a young girl and wake up the next and she's twenty-four. Then her mother lifted her hand an inch off the bed.

Jessie took her hand in both of her own and began speaking. The words caught in her throat at first, but she forced her way through, not caring whether she was making sense or not. Jessie began to reiterate much of what she had shared earlier, before Mom had awakened. And her mother was nodding slightly.

A few moments passed and Jessie looked over her shoulder and saw Grandmother coming into the room, her face ashen, ravaged with raw grief. When Olivia saw her, she smiled again, extending her hand ever so slightly.

Doris's reluctance disappeared, and she rushed to her daughter's side.

Jessie kissed her mother's hand again and quietly excused herself, over her grandmother's objections.

"Grandmother, this is your time," she said.

Jessie closed the door behind her and leaned back against it. A sense of pure, unmitigated peace washed over her again. When she opened her eyes, Bill was standing by the wall, his posture hesitant, cowboy hat in his hands, his eyes lingering on the floor. *Good ol' Bill, too polite to wear a hat in the nursing home.*

He wasn't ready for her, but his arms opened quickly enough when he realized she was hugging him.

A few minutes later, Grandmother peeked out the door, looking much better than when she'd walked in. She gestured for Jessie, who quickly slipped back into the room. Mom's eyes were still open and she looked at the two of them together—grandmother and grand-daughter—and smiled her widest smile yet.

Soon she fell asleep again. Grandmother was still on one side of the bed holding Mom's hand, Jessie doing the same on the other side. Tammy came in with another nurse and checked the monitor reading. The moment of passing was imminent.

Her mother opened her eyes one last time, and Jessie reached over and stroked her hollow cheek.

When her breathing stopped, the nurse quietly announced, "She's gone."

It was eleven o'clock when they left the room, both exhausted in body and grieved in their hearts. In the hallway, before they began what seemed to be a long walk to the car, Grandmother touched Jessie's arm, her face a mixture of torture and hope, her eyes burning a hole through Jessie's soul. Grandmother looked away, but Jessie reached back and linked her arm through her grandmother's. Their eyes met again, and great understanding passed between them. Although words would one day be spoken, for now, their mutual heartache was more than enough.

Epilogue

THE DEAD OF WINTER. Jessie made her way to the Oregon coast at last, courtesy of a round-trip ticket, a gift from her grandmother. She stood on the rocks as twilight fell—warm coat clutched around her, waves crashing at her feet, the bluster of a cold, moist wind pummeling her—thanking God that she hadn't chosen to continue driving straight west those many months ago. *A lifetime ago,* she thought with a shake of her head.

This will all pass away, she thought, peering into the eternity of the waves, listening to the mournful cry of the sea birds as if they were longing for the day when redemption would touch every living thing.

The sun fell quickly as she sank to the edge of a mossy rock and, mindful of the sea birds, carefully avoided anything that seemed to be more than moss or rock. She thought of Bill and his ragged good-bye at the airport and her grandmother's curt response. "Oh, for pete's sake, Bill. Can't you handle her being gone for one week?"

"You should always say good-bye as if you'll never see them again."

"Oh, for pete's sake."

"I'll be back soon," Jessie encouraged, struggling with her own composure.

"Not soon enough," Bill had replied, blinking away tears.

Jessie could hardly believe how close she now felt to both Bill and her grandmother. Bill had once said, "That's what happens after people air their differences. They become friends." At the time Jessie had decided a relationship with Grandmother was impossible and had said so. But she was so wrong.

After her mother's bittersweet death, a renewed wave of anger had tried to erode the fragile bond between Jessie and her grandmother. The more Jessie thought about all the years she had missed with her mother, the more the bitterness grew. Grandmother should have told the truth, like Jessie's dreams had tried to do for so long. Yes, she understood her grandmother's initial reasoning for the secret, but as time wore on and her mother continued to live, Doris should have put aside her fear of self-incrimination and revealed the facts. Jessie knew she had shared in the guilt—the unopened letters and unreturned phone calls—but her grandmother *could* have found a way to make her listen.

So finally Jessie took Bill's advice and confronted her grandmother. "You should have found me and stood under my window and screamed at the top of your lungs or-or . . . written it in the sky, 'Your mother is alive!' Or something. *Anything!* You should have told me!"

"I know. You're right," her grandmother whispered, head lowered, voice broken. "I'm so terribly sorry."

Her remorse was thorough, so painfully clear, that Jessie chose to forgive her grandmother, and she also watched her grandmother eventually be able to forgive herself. Bill was right. Sometimes strong words *do* lead to strong relationships.

As time passed, Jessie began to feel more rested. Sleeping through the night was effortless, and except for the single dream she'd had a few nights after her mother's passing, the past few months had been virtually dream free. In her final dream, her

mother came to tuck her in again, like old times. Winnie the Pooh
was back and Tigger, too.

In the dream her mother's beautiful silhouette was illuminated
from the hall light, and once again she was the essence of youth and
vitality. *True youth is beyond the grave,* Jessie thought, and her
mother, wearing the same sundress, pulled up the covers. "Are you
ready for tomorrow?"

"I can't wait," Jessie replied, breathing in her mother's gentle
and sweet fragrance.

Mom leaned over and wiggled her nose on Jessie's nose.

"That tickles," Jessie squealed, and then she played dumb.
"So . . . where are we going again?"

"Silly . . ." Her mother tickled her again and Jessie squirmed
happily.

"The park?"

"I can't *wait* to swing on the swings," her mother confided mis-
chievously.

"Is Dad coming?" Jessie asked suddenly, and her mother's nod
surprised her.

"He'll really be there?"

"You'll see."

"Can Andy go along?" She was pushing her luck.

Mom patted her face. "Of course he can."

"I'll ask him."

"You do that, sweetie."

They talked for a long time, but in some ways it felt like only
minutes. In other ways, it seemed as if a lifetime passed—although
it didn't matter because her mother was never in a rush.

When Olivia gave her a final kiss, Jessie grabbed her mother's
neck. Olivia sighed happily, "Oooh, sweetie, you're strong."

Gently Jessie pulled her mother even closer. "Have I ever told
you how much I love you, Mom?" Her mother gave her a knowing
wink. "Not enough, sweetie."

When her mother finally headed for the door, Jessie saw her

father in the shadows and was startled again. She pulled her hand out from beneath the covers and waved. "Good night, Dad." He waved back, and she was sure that he smiled, and she thought she might have seen a twinkle in his eyes. Strange. She'd never seen it before.

◆ ◆ ◆ ◆ ◆

In December Laura's mother was picked up for DUI, and her car was searched. Finally busted, Michelle was arraigned on charges of drug possession, and Laura was handed over to the state for foster care.

Jessie discussed an idea with Bill and her grandmother. They agreed it was worth the risk, although it was understood that Jessie would be forging a very important relationship just at a time when her own future was in question. But Jessie, and indeed all of them, had learned an important truth, that all we have are moments anyway, and we must live them to the fullest . . . with heartfelt courage.

Jessie petitioned the court for immediate temporary custody, and it was granted. A few weeks after that she was approved as a foster parent. At first, the sense of responsibility was overwhelming, but the memory of her mother's example became a source of encouragement. She knew it wouldn't be easy raising Laura, considering her background, but as Andy had once told her, *"Nothing easy is worthwhile anyway."*

In October, Jessie had finally sat down with Dr. Sawyer to hear the results of her blood test. The diagnosis confirmed her worst suspicions . . . she tested positive as a carrier. Her grandmother took it the hardest, and Bill was worried sick, but they had to face the facts—no one really knew how much time she had. After all, her grandfather hadn't exhibited any symptoms until a few months before he suffered a stroke and died at the age of fifty. No one could seem to agree on whether Jessie was already manifesting symptoms. "We'll have to wait and see," the doctor had finally told her.

"It's just a roll of the dice," Bill muttered.

I'll live every day I have to the fullest, Jessie decided when she'd finally recovered from the painful blow. *And I'll live for the Lord . . . like my mother did.*

Her mother's Prince of Peace had become Jessie's Lord of Life. With her newfound joy in God, every scent was sweeter, every sunrise brighter, every taste more delicious. The small things of life remained minute, and the large worries and frustrations were handled with newfound perspective.

◆ ◆ ◆ ◆ ◆

Jessie looked out across the ocean. In spite of the growing cold and the buffeting wind, she was reluctant to leave. When the sunset reached its full glory, with oranges and yellows and reds painted across the sky as if just for her, she thought of the ordeals she'd encountered to get to this point. *I might have missed out,* she thought, shuddering.

When he came up behind her, she accepted the warmth of his sheltering arms and felt the last remnants of loneliness flicker away. He held her tightly, his chin on her shoulder, his warm cheek against hers. She sighed with relief.

"So this is your paradise?"

"It is now," she chuckled, pulling him closer.

"It's fantastic," Andy observed, tipping his chin toward the sunset. "But we have sunsets in Colorado, you know."

"Are you sorry you came?" Jessie asked, smiling.

"Are you kidding?" he said. "I'd follow you to Siberia."

"This isn't Siberia."

"Feels like it. It's pretty cold."

She wrestled his arm playfully but laughed when he nuzzled his nose into her neck.

"Have I told you lately how much I love you?" Andy whispered into her ear.

"Not enough," she replied.

"Isn't *that* the truth?" Andy said, launching in with another tidbit from his overactive mind. "The feeling of every good relationship on earth is that it's not enough. Every joy reminds us—"

Jessie turned and put a finger to his lips. "Enough of that thinking stuff. Just hush and kiss me."

"Ahhh, the kiss," he said as if pondering it. "The *true* meaning of life. The noble pursuit. The symbol of life-giving breath!"

"Andy, so help me—"

But when he did kiss her, it was enough to make her forget his penchant for overanalysis. When they settled back down on the rocks again, his arms warmed her from the descending temperatures, making the sunset all the more glorious.

"Did you just say you'd follow me to Siberia?"

"I knew this was coming."

"Well, if *that's* the case, then you wouldn't mind"—she was fingering her new wedding ring as she said it—"if we declared country music the official music of our household."

"Siberia is sounding better all the time."

"Don't worry, we can take it slow," Jessie assured him. "We'll start with crossover. A little Shania, a little Faith . . . go from there."

Andy made a face. "You mean like boiling a frog? Raising the temperature by little increments so the frog doesn't realize it until it's too late?"

"That's *exactly* what I had in mind." Jessie laughed. "Before we know it, you'll be singing, 'I hear that train a-comin'.'"

"Or praying for the rocks to cover me."

"You won't know what hit you."

"What if I never make the leap?"

She sighed. "Then I'll have no choice but to love you anyway."

"That's awful 'country' of you," Andy replied, and they laughed.

They joined hands and prayed, praising God for the beauty of His creation and thanking Him for each other.

After savoring a final sweeping look at the ocean, they navigated back over the rocks and trudged through the sand, back to their suite at a fine hotel, another wedding gift from Grandmother and Bill.

Bill had been deeply moved when Jessie had asked him to give her away. Her revitalized grandmother had thrown her all into planning the ceremony, albeit a rather modest one, according to Jessie's wishes. As a final gift, Doris and Bill had insisted on keeping Laura with them so Jessie and Andy could spend their honeymoon alone. When the newlyweds returned to Palmer Lake in a few days, they would be moving into Jessie's family home, where, with dear Laura, they would begin a new life, and a new family, together.

Of course, neither knew exactly what their future held or how long they would have together—but who does anyway? They had each other and they had their family, but most importantly they had a faith, new and fragile though it was, like a rosebud in springtime.

No matter what happened, no matter the suffering or disappointment, their ultimate purpose was to travel with hope and courage, and to be ready—whenever the time came—for Jesus to call them home.

About the Author

DAVID LEWIS is the collaborating author of the bestselling novel *Sanctuary*, with his wife. An accomplished keyboard artist and former piano instructor, he is an avid reader of fiction and a student of apologetics. Born in Minnesota and raised in the Midwest, Dave enjoys early-morning jogs and vacations along Oregon's coastline, as well as travels to New England. He and Beverly make their home in the foothills of the Rocky Mountains.

Acknowledgments

Many thanks to David Horton and Julie Klassen for their keen editorial insight. I'm also grateful to Gary and Carol Johnson for believing in this story from its inception, and special appreciation goes to Barbara Lilland. Thanks to Janie and Jonathan for filling our days with laughter and warmth, and to Julie and Ariel for providing the spark that ultimately led to the title.

Most importantly, I wish to thank my dearling, Beverly Lewis, for her love, prayers, and everlasting support. As Vanauken once said (*A Severe Mercy*), "If it's half as good as the half we've known, here's *Hail!* to the rest of the road!"

Spend More Time in Small Town America

THE HALO SHE GLIMPSED AROUND THE SUN was the first sign that this might be it—the place she was longing for. Filled with hope, Alessi Moore pulls into Charity during a snowstorm. Enraptured by the pure, serene beauty of the little town, she just knows something good is coming.

Her almost heavenly impression is quickly dashed by an unforeseen loss. Left with nothing but the clothes on her back, Alessi sets out to discover what lies beneath the surface of this picture-perfect town.

Halos by Kristen Heitzmann

SUTTER'S CROSS IS A QUAINT SOUTHERN town nestled in the evocative Appalachian Mountains, where people live in comfortable homes, have comfortable portfolios, and wear comfortable clothes. They expect their faith to be comfortable as well. Then a remarkable turn of events startles Sutter's Cross out of its complacency.

Elegant and quirky, full of nuance and clarity, W. Dale Cramer's debut novel infuses life and depth to characters both unique and authentic. *Sutter's Cross* illustrates the monumental worthiness of relationships and presents a fresh view of redemption.

Sutter's Cross by W. Dale Cramer

The Leader in Christian Fiction

◆ BETHANYHOUSE